Magic Arrives

Andy Zach

Magic Arrives

First Edition, 2026

This is a work of fiction.
All the characters and events in this book are fictional or portrayed fictitiously, and any resemblance to real people or incidents is purely coincidental. This is a work of parody and not to be taken seriously.

Author: Andy Zach
Cover Illustration and jacket design: Sean Patrick Flanagan
Edited by: Dori Harrell
Formatted by: Rik Hall

Published by: Jule Inc.
2419 W. Madera Ct
Peoria, Illinois 61614
andyzach@andyzach.net

ISBNs:
Hardcover:978-1-959962-05-2
Paperback:978-1-959962-03-8
ebook: 978-1-959962-04-5

LCCN: 2026902933

Published in the United States of America

Dedicated to the author of the first fantasy I read,
Marian Cockrell, author of *Shadow Castle*

Acknowledgments

First I want to acknowledge my illustrator Sean Flanagan, who did another great job on the book cover. His covers get more comments than my books do!

Next, let me mention my children, Tori, Olivia, and Ray. They help me brainstorm ideas and test my writing and make it better.

Along those lines, I applaud my editor Dori Harrell, who aside from providing professional editing and helpful feedback, also encourages me as an author.

Finally, I always have my wife Julie. She patiently listens to me explode with laughter as I read my own jokes to her and then she suggests how the story could be better.

Contents

Prologue

25,000 BC

The galactic black hole began eating another object. The planetoid survived far longer than the average planet or star due to its supernatural density. Forged long ago at an earlier age, the intense radiation from the whirling maelstrom and swirling magnetic fields did not affect it. Not until it spun near the speed of light did the immense tidal forces crack its surface.

Spinning ever faster, each fragment resisted the stupendous forces around the black hole until finally they shattered. Finally this unique element transformed into pure energy. It radiated in all wavelengths of visible light, and beyond, to light never seen before.

The radiation coalesced oddly, through forces unknown to science, into a single beam of energy radiating from the black hole. It swept out like a searchlight from the galactic core and across the light-years—straight toward Earth and its teeming multitudes.

Fortunately, Earth was twenty-five thousand light-years away from this cosmic conflagration. Unfortunately, this happened twenty-five thousand years ago.

Magic arrived on Earth.

Chapter 1 - Tea

Sunday, October 4

I made our pot of tea, English Breakfast. Each morning Jane and I sip the hot beverage in our easy chairs in our living room. We had an early freeze that October, and the chill air gripped the house. We turned the heat down at night and up when we get out of bed. Our elderly Victorian home had an old furnace, and it took over an hour to warm the house.

But tea made everything better. I heard Jane settle into her easy chair. I could tell by the squeak when she rocked back.

In the kitchen, I poured a mug for each of us and added milk. “Jane, are you ready for your tea?”

“You bet,” Jane called. “And can you grab a biscotti for me too?”

“Sure thing. A biscotti sounds good to me too.”

I grabbed two biscotti out of our cupboard and took them and her tea mug to the living room, which stretched an echoing thirty feet. But our two leather easy chairs flanked the crackling fireplace, which Jane had started.

Jane smiled at me as I placed the mug and biscotti on her side table. I took a moment to take in the sincere love shining in her hazel eyes. I barely saw any gray in her blond hair. Forty years of marriage had not diminished our love. I took my biscotti and plunked next to her, enjoying the warmth from the fireplace.

“Thanks,” she said.

“You’re welcome. Thanks for starting the fire. I love not having to rush off to work in the morning, since I retired.” I’d worked as a programmer, trainer, and documenter in my career.

“Me too.”

Jane had been an office manager at a construction firm.

I opened my biscotti, took a crunchy bite coated with chocolate, and reached for my mug. It wasn’t there.

“Grrr!” I wrinkled my face like a gargoyle.

"What's wrong?"

"I left my mug in the kitchen. I hate it when I do that."

"Wouldn't it be nice if it'd come when you call it?"

I laughed. "On little legs. I'd just say, 'Come here, tea mug!'"

We laughed. We laugh together nearly every day. I rose and then stopped. I heard an odd tap-tapping. Almost like our little corgi but even smaller and lighter.

"What's that? Is that a mouse?" We had mice in our house every fall until we trapped them.

"It doesn't sound like one."

From the dining room came my tea mug on four little legs, scampering across the floor. I reached down to pick it up, and it jumped into my hands. The legs disappeared.

"That's different," I said,

"Uh, that's never happened before, not to us or anyone else I've ever heard of."

"It's like my wish for the tea mug got granted."

"Exactly."

"That's convenient." I sipped my tea. "That's good tea."

"Did you rub any magic lamps?"

"No. "

"Did you throw a coin in a wishing well?"

"No. I wonder if we can make any other wishes?" I sipped my tea. "Mmm."

"Mmm," Jane agreed as she took another sip.

"Mmm," the tea mug purred.

Chapter 2 – Pinkie

Sunday, October 4

I hugged my dragon, Pinkie, as we went outside to play. I'd had him since I was a baby. My mom had bought him for me. My older brother, Lamar, went outside with me. My mom, Shannon, had told Lamar that morning, "Lamar, if Shayla wants to go outside, you go with her. Don't let her out of your sight. If you see trouble, both of you get out of there." I knew trouble sometimes happened in our neighborhood.

She'd turned to me. "Shayla, don't go running off without your brother. You listen to him and do what he says. I'll be back at five." Then she'd left for her job at Wal-Store.

Lamar and I walked out on a fine fall day. I watched the robins hop along the ragged grass in an empty lot. We hiked to a neighborhood park a few blocks away from our apartment. Lamar pushed me on the swings and then on the merry-go-round.

"Shayla," he said, "I'm going to play basketball with my friends over there. You stay here till I come back."

I watched him jog to the court next to the park. "Pinkie, what do you think of that? We gotta play by ourselves. What d'ya wanna do? You want me to push you on the merry-go-round? Okay, I'll try."

It wasn't as hard as it looked. I worked it up to speed and then hopped on next to Pinkie. "I'm almost a big girl now. I can push the merry-go-round all by myself. And I started kindergarten this fall."

I spun the merry-go-round again and again till I got tired. "You getting hungry, Pinkie? I am. What do you eat? Bugs? Huh. Whatever. Let me get you some."

I knelt on the grass next to the merry-go-round's sandpit. I loved the smell of the grass. I poked around the dirt and found some ants and pill bugs. I put one of each in my hand and gave it to Pinkie.

"Num num! Tastes good, don't it? D'ya want more? Okay."

I gathered more. Then I heard something like fireworks coming from the basketball court. "What's that, Pinkie?" I picked up my dragon and ran to the court to check on Lamar.

Some big guys had guns. They were chasing the boys off with lots of yelling. "No little kids here! This court is for men, for our gang!"

Lamar ran in my direction.

More young guys came up. "Hey, what d'ya think you're doing? This is our turf. Get out of here." They had guns too.

Someone shot a gun. Then a whole firecracker string of shots rang out. Some guys dropped on both sides. The first group ran into the park, then hid behind the playground equipment and started firing again.

A bullet zipped over my head. "Get down, Pinkie!" I fell on top of him, protecting him. I peeked and saw Lamar running full speed toward me. Then he fell.

"Lamar!" I crawled to him. His blood oozed from his back, warm and sticky. He moaned.

I cried.

The blood spread over Lamar's shirt like spilled tomato juice. He stopped moaning. I made my own wet spot crying over him. The bullets still zipped above us. I could taste my salty tears. Pinkie squeezed between us.

"Oh, Pinkie, I wish you'd gobble up those guys with guns like you did those bugs!" I cried with all my heart to my magic dragon.

Pinkie shook in my hand. He felt like my mom's cell phone when it buzzed. Then he grew out of my hand. My pink dragon ballooned to dog size, then horse size, then elephant size, then bigger. The shooters turned to my giant stuffed dragon, flapping his pink wings in midair. Both gangs shot at him.

Like a cat jumping on a mouse, Pinkie gobbled up a shooter, then the one next to him. Six more gangbangers disappeared into his huge pink mouth before both gangs turned and ran.

"Yay, Pinkie! You chased away those bad guys!" Then I saw Lamar again, quietly bleeding on the ground.

"Oh, Lamar, get up! You've got to take me home!" I lay on his still body, crying into his wet shirt.

* * *

I cried myself to sleep. When I woke, Lamar was cold. The shadows were lengthening. Mom would be home soon.

"Lamar!" I sobbed again. A shadow covered me. Pinkie swooped down. The grass flattened under his big pink feet.

"What's wrong, Shayla?"

"Pinkie, Lamar won't get up. I-I-I think he's dead!"

"You've got to wake him up, like you did with me."

"Good idea, Pinkie." I didn't notice that Pinkie talked way clearer than he used to. I shook Lamar with all my might. "Lamar, get up! You've got to wake up, just like Pinkie. Get better right now!"

"O-o-h," he groaned. He rolled over and looked at me. "What happened, Shayla? Why is my back all wet?"

"There was a fight between two gangs and y-y-you were shot. You're bleeding."

He took off his T-shirt. "Yuck! It's all bloody." Something fell to the ground. "What's this?" He picked it up. "It was in my shirt. It's a bullet! Why do I feel better? I remember getting shot now."

"Lamar, I wished you'd get better so we could go home." I peered at his back. "You're all bloody, but there's no hole in it."

"And the bullet's out." He showed me the bullet, bloody and smushed on one side.

Pinkie landed next to us and burped.

"What's that?" Lamar stared at the huge dragon, his eyes bugging out.

"Pinkie, of course. I wished he'd eat up those bad guys with guns, and he did."

"Let's go home. Pinkie will have to stay outside. He's too big to fit in our apartment. He's too big to fit on the basketball court!"

Lamar was right. Pinkie's butt and tail filled the basketball court, and he stretched across the grass to us.

"Nah. Pinkie, go back to your regular size."

"No problem." Pinkie shrank, and I picked him up.

"Let's go."

Lamar closed his mouth and followed me home. I knew the way. I just wanted Lamar for protection.

Chapter 3 – Fire

Sunday, October 4

"What are your plans for our state if you're elected governor?" the attractive news reporter, Julia Awesome, asked the first candidate.

George Whipplesmith smiled at the camera. "First, I must say I want nothing more than to serve the people of this great state—"

Immediately his pants caught on fire.

"Yowww!" He leapt up screaming.

"Drop and roll!" a firefighter yelled from the audience. When the politician didn't listen, he tackled the burning man and rolled him on the studio floor until the fire was out.

After the hubbub subsided and Mr. Whipplesmith stopped crying, the EMTs took him to the hospital.

"I'm sure we all hope candidate Whipplesmith will suffer no permanent harm," Julia said. "Ms. Eleanor Everest, after this terrible incident, will you be able to answer some questions as the remaining candidate in this debate?"

"Of course, Julia. I express my sincerest condolences to candidate Whipplesmith—"

Her pantyhose and skirt blazed into flames.

"Eiiii!" She rolled on the floor.

Ms. Awesome took a floor mat and wrapped her legs, putting out the fire.

This time the hubbub didn't die out.

Shaking, Ms. Awesome told the viewers, "We'll have to cancel this live event due to fire on the candidates. I return you to our network studio."

* * *

I normally hated it when my parents watched the evening news. It was so depressing, with people lying and accusing each other of terrible things. It didn't help that my parents always got upset, yelling at one political party or another for lying.

But my sixth-grade teacher gave us the assignment to watch

the news and report on what we heard, so I was stuck.

"Wouldn't it be great if everyone's pants caught on fire if they lied?" I asked my parents during a commercial.

"Yes! I'd love that!" my dad said with a laugh.

"People would catch on fire all the time," Mom said with a smile.

I grinned. "That's what I wish for then."

"That's wishful thinking," Dad said. "But it'd be fun. What's on next, Sean?"

I looked at the app on my phone. "The debate between the two candidates for governor, Whipplesmith and Everest."

"I don't know much about either of them. Let's watch it, Phil."

"Sure, Shirley."

I sighed. It'd probably be boring.

Chapter 4 – Spot

Sunday, October 4

I woke up hungry, as I always did. I went to Master and whined, as I always did. He barked, as he always did. I looked at him steadily, as I always did. He whined at me and filled a bowl with food.

"Thanks, Master!" I wagged. He petted me, so I knew he understood.

Thinking back on it, even then his bark seemed different to me, like it had more meaning than just, *Don't bother me*. But that wasn't when things really changed.

Master and I were playing fetch later that day with a ball, when it fell into a pocket in the wall. There were many paper things lined up on the wall on a little shelf above the floor. There were more shelves with more paper things going up to the ceiling. I had never bothered with them before. They were Master's. I could tell by their scent.

I reached in with my paw to get the ball. When it came out, my nail dragged one of these paper things out. I grabbed the ball in my mouth, and my eye fell upon the paper thing. It had a picture of a black-and-white dog just like me! I had never noticed that before.

I also noticed squiggles above the picture and an image of a little master on the cover. I sniffed it. It smelled like Master. The little master didn't look like my master. But somehow this was my master's.

I dropped my ball, even though we were playing, and I picked up the paper thing carefully. I have a soft mouth when I want to. I took it to Master, gave it to him, and then wagged my tail. Maybe he'd figure out I wanted to know more.

He laughed. "So you want me to read my old first-grade reader to you?"

Somehow I understood his bark, although I didn't wonder about this at the time. He was going to tell me about the black-and-white dog on the bundle of paper.

I jumped and wagged vigorously.

"Who can say no to that?" Master smiled at me.

I sat and quivered.

He bent the pile of paper, and it opened like a door. He pointed to the page. "*Spot and the Ball* is the title. You must have seen Spot. That's your name too." He pointed at the black-and-white dog, and I wagged.

"And you're a beagle, like Spot here." He pointed to the black-and-white dog.

I wagged harder.

"And you know what a ball is." Master moved his finger to a flat ball on the page. It didn't smell like a ball, but it looked a little like a ball. I wagged.

"Dick and Jane are looking for a ball." His finger circled the two little masters on the page. Again, there was no smell but his. I knew those were names, but why were they different names than the smell?

"There is Spot looking for the little ball." Master tapped the tail of a little dog. His front part was hidden in a flat green thing.

I watched carefully. What would happen next? I couldn't guess.

"And Spot finds the ball. Where's your ball?"

I knew! I ran and brought it back to him.

"Good boy. Do you like reading? I think you understand me."

I did! I understood his words perfectly. I never had before. The reading seemed to help. "I understand!" I barked.

Master's mouth dropped open. "You understand me!"

"Of course I do," I barked back.

"And I understand you." He wasn't barking, but I understood him.

That was how it started.

Chapter 5 – Paradise

Sunday, October 4

"O-o-o-h," I groaned as I rolled over in my bed. My arthritis hurt the most in the morning. I could feel every bone in my back. But that wasn't the worst.

I knew I had to get up this morning. I had no time for lying about, getting slowly unkinked and limber. I had to go to the airport and fly to see my grandchildren in Cleveland. At least it was warm here in Paradise, Arizona. Not in Ohio.

I might as well get the worst over with. I rolled off the bed onto my feet. Pain stabbed my ankles, knees, and hips. I gasped and slowly straightened.

There. I was standing. My pains subsided to a dull ache from my ankles to my neck. Then I took a step. Ouch. With each step, a spike of pain flared in my joints. But it was less than the first time I'd stood.

Coffee. I had a pot from yesterday. Too bad it wasn't freshly brewed. How nice it'd be to smell brewing coffee as I stepped into the kitchen. Then the smell hit me. And the sound of water trickling.

I looked upon a fresh pot, just finishing its brew cycle on the kitchen counter. Just what I wished for. How'd this happen? My son had a timed coffeepot that'd start in the morning before he woke up. Mine was old, fifty years old, dating from when I was a single woman after college.

As I stared, the smell of the coffee made everything feel better. "Wouldn't it be nice if the smell of coffee cured arthritis?" I talked to myself, as I often did since my husband, Ray, died five years ago.

The more I breathed the scent, the better I felt. "Maybe I'll be completely cured if I drink a cup?" I joked. I poured a cup and added pure cream. Might as well enjoy the fat. I was seventy-seven and I didn't know how much time I had left.

I felt the warm, creamy coffee all the way down. My aches were completely gone. "That's odd. The last time I was pain-free was, what? Think, Angie. Ten, twelve years ago?" Before we'd moved to Paradise, Arizona. My husband had cashed in his IRA and built a complete homestead off the grid next to the old ghost town.

Suddenly ambitious, I whipped up a southwestern omelet. I made buttered toast with honey and gobbled it all down.

After cleaning the kitchen, I wandered past our living room to my bedroom. I looked fondly at my shelves of science fiction and fantasy books flanking our stone fireplace. I had packed all my favorite stories in my rolling suitcase. Still, I'd miss my other books on my trip.

After changing into my comfortable travel clothing, I rolled my heavy bag out the door to our gravel drive. Ugh! I could barely roll the bag on my smooth tiled floor. I couldn't budge it on the gravel. I pivoted it on the corners and walked it toward my car. It slipped from my hands and fell with a crunch.

"Oooh! I wish you had legs and could follow me!"

Obediently the bag sprouted four legs and trotted along behind me.

"This is creepy. I loved the walking luggage in Terry Prattchett's books, but in real life it's weirding me out."

We made it to the car. I opened the back door. "Hop right in." The luggage reared up on its hind legs and climbed onto the seat, just like a good dog.

"Good luggage!" How do you train luggage? I had no clue.

I did not look forward to the three-hour drive to the Tucson airport. But that was the price I paid for living in the beautiful Coronado Forest next to a ghost town. And my arthritis seems to have settled down.

I chuckled to myself. It's been such a weird morning, why not? If luggage could walk, could I—

"I wish this car would fly to the airport!" I pictured the Tucson airport route in my mind. Up from Paradise to Route 20 and then west. I always liked to get the whole trip route in my mind before I started.

Wings sprouted out the car doors of my old Canolla. They were faded mint green, just like the car.

"Whee!" I yelled as I swooped into the air. I hadn't had this much fun since . . . My memory didn't go back that far.

I turned the wheel, and we swooped back and forth. How could I make it climb? On a hunch, I unlocked the adjustable wheel and lifted it. Up the car climbed. I returned the wheel to its normal location and leveled out.

I looked at the instrument panel. We were going over a hundred miles per hour! I'd get to Tucson in an hour. What would happen if I floored the gas pedal? I pushed it down.

The speedometer soon pegged itself at 120. I didn't even articulate my next wish. The speedometer morphed before my eyes, and the top speed showed 240, and climbing. The wind whistled noisily through the leaky windows. The car wasn't designed for two hundred, let alone the three hundred I just passed.

I kept the gas pedal floored. I was curious what the top-end speed would be. The metallic wings beat furiously, like a hummingbird's. The thrum grew louder. I passed 400 and seemed to peak at 450. Huh. Just like a World War II fighter. I was probably the only girl who'd ever built a model collection of every fighter from World War II. My dad had been in the air force then.

At this rate I'd be in Tucson in another fifteen minutes. I watched the horizon and saw Tucson appear, nestled in the mountains.

This was fun! Should I try to fly all the way to Cleveland in my Canolla? Even at my maximum speed, it'd take over three hours. What if I ran into bad weather? What if I got cold?

I got cold feet—literally. I cranked up the heat. That was better. I wondered what my altitude was? An altimeter appeared next to my gas gauge. Seventy-four hundred feet. I could see Tucson and the Sentinel Peak looming over it. I veered the car south toward the airport.

Oops. I'd better land before I reached the airport. I didn't want to freak anyone out with my flying Canolla.

I backed off the gas pedal, and the car slowed. Three hundred, two hundred, one hundred. The car descended as it slowed. The sun rose directly behind me, so I knew I was heading west. I could see the airport directly ahead of me, which meant the road below me must be South Tucson Road.

I coasted about a hundred feet above the road. How did I

get down? Nothing ventured, nothing gained. I braked. The wings stopped me in midair, and I plummeted. The speedometer went to zero and then back to sixty. I pulled the nose of the car up just in time as I landed on the road. My four wheels squeaked as they went from zero to sixty in a second. The wings disappeared into the doors. A guy behind me honked.

"Sorry!" I waved at him.

He shook his fist at me as he zoomed past.

Then I noticed the engine had never started. I was in neutral, coasting at fifty.

"That's one way to save on gas," I said as I started the car. A police siren wailed in the distance.

"Just a little old lady driving her car, officer," I said, practicing in case the officer pulled me over.

I parked in long-term parking and checked myself in my rearview mirror. My blue-gray eyes peered out from my wrinkled face. I had never used much makeup, and I'd given it up completely when my husband didn't care. I didn't think it would help my face much now. But . . . I did look a little younger. Maybe sixty-seven instead of seventy-seven? Or maybe I was on a coffee high.

"Out you go, luggage," I commanded.

My bag scrambled out.

"Legs back in. I don't want anyone to have a heart attack."

It withdrew its legs. But not before it tilted itself upright on its wheels and extended its handle.

"Good luggage!"

Maybe this trip would be easier than I expected.

Chapter 6 – News

Monday, October 5

I listened to the morning news absently as I drove to work at Oakridge National Laboratory. I'd achieved my dream of becoming a nuclear research scientist four years ago when I'd graduated with my PhD in physics, but I still wrestled with traffic each morning—and office meetings. I had one this morning to finalize our project plans for the coming year. I glanced at the clock: 7:55 a.m. I'd barely make it.

The radio station broke for news. "The spate of politicians' and reporters' garments catching on fire has abated. It seems the fires are connected to something they say. No one has given an exact cause, but reporters and politicians are being careful about the words they choose."

"Huh, that's weird." I'd thought these garment fires were caused by some prankster, but the reports had been coming in from all over the globe for the past day. That was a puzzle I'd have to solve in my after-work hours. Today I would be busy researching possible means of improving nuclear fusion. I had an interesting reaction using boron that might be effective.

I couldn't listen any further. I pulled into the parking lot and ran into the building. It would be close. My tablet bounced against my side in my leather purse. I pulled out my security card to unlock the door, looking at my bad picture as I read "Katherine Garcia." Why were my pictures always so ugly? My eyebrows looked as thick as caterpillars under my black bangs, and my expression looked like I was sucking on aspirin. Maybe next time I'd make a duck face.

I trotted down the hall and saw my boss, Herman Scholl, waiting outside the conference room door for me. His face looked grim below his receding hairline. "Get on in, Katie. Everyone's here."

Uh-oh. Was I in some trouble?

My boss's boss, Smita Vuppuluri, and the director of Oakridge Labs, Winston Williams, were in there, and all of my coworkers. We sat down, and my boss began.

"After yesterday's accident, President Lopez directed us to look into these odd fires starting all around the country and the world."

"What accident?" I tended to interrupt people when I had a question. It was probably a fault, but my urgent need to know made me burst out.

"Didn't you hear? Yesterday he gave a speech to the National Board of Teachers and his pants caught on fire. It was on all the news media."

I didn't watch the evening news, nor did I follow social media, but I remained silent rather than confessing ignorance. I'd been reading a romantic fantasy book last night. "I hope he's okay."

"Yes, he's under observation in Bethesda Naval Hospital. His Secret Service agents got the fire out quickly." Herman cleared his throat and continued. "We've identified over one thousand publicly documented incidents of spontaneous combustion in politicians, lawyers, and car dealers in the past twenty-four hours. There is anecdotal evidence for thousands of others. And that's just in the United States. We have another eight hundred cases on video from around the world. Then there are several thousand on social media."

Then Smita Vuppuluri spoke. "We've got to get to the bottom of this. The president has called in us, the National Science Foundation, the FBI, CIA, NSA, and any other organization that can help investigate."

"We've already divided the evidence into eight groups for the eight of you. You are the best researchers we've got. I'm sure you'll get to the bottom of this phenomenon." She handed each of us a thick binder. "This is your paper copy. You'll have the electronic version in your email. Good luck!"

Whew! I hefted the weighty binder and glanced at it as I walked to my desk. Color-coded pages divided the binder into Friendbook posts, news stories, TokTalk links, Z.com posts, and Viewtube links. At the back I found an appendix with printed newspaper articles and the Wokkapedia page, just published yesterday.

Skimming through the paper tome, I saw hundreds of links

and references.

At my desk, I doodled on my memo pad, drawing a fire. That was a result. What preceded it?

I searched through the electronic document in my email, and I saw that in every case someone was talking, always publicly. I drew a picture of a stick figure talking and linked it to the fire with an arrow.

Something must have caused the fire. I made an *X?* and a vertical arrow to the result arrow.

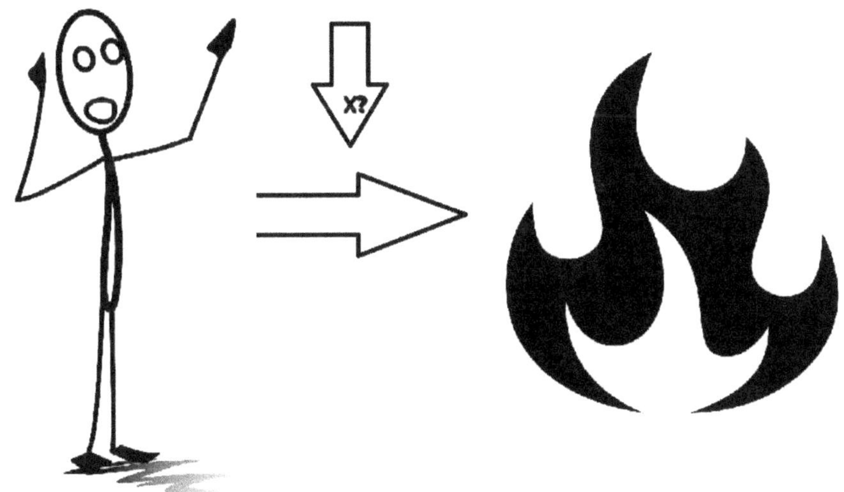

I could start by trying to reproduce the fire. But I had a hunch I needed more on the conditions. Public speaking went on daily worldwide with billions of people. A quick count of my electronic file showed 653 cases. Times our eight researchers, that was roughly fifty-two hundred cases.

I wondered what the time span of the cases was? Glancing at the time stamps, I saw they were already arranged chronologically. The first event occurred at 6:06 p.m. Eastern time. Two politicians in a debate. Both of them had burst into flame after their opening statements.

Curious, I examined their sentences and played the linked video. They spoke normal political palaver but with dire consequences. I winced. Wearing burning pantyhose was no joke. Burning pants couldn't be fun either.

Where was I? Oh, the time span. The last time stamp

seemed to be twenty-four hours later, in Australia. Converting Australian time to Eastern time, it was fourteen after 2:00 a.m. Huh. Did the episodes stop after two?

I called my fellow researchers. They all confirmed their latest episodes had stopped after midnight on the East Coast. The latest episode was 2:21 a.m. EST in India.

I asked for the time stamps of all incidents from my fellow researchers. I plotted the times around the world.

Fascinating. I animated the results. A blaze of fires began in the US, Canada, Mexico, and South America about 9:00 a.m. across all the time zones. Around 9:00 p.m. they began stopping, ending in Alaska and Hawaii. The fires continued in Asia until 2:21 a.m.

I called my boss. “Herman?”

“Hi, Katie. Did you discover the cause already?”

“No. I’m just curious that the episodes ended about twelve hours later in the US. Have any showed up since about two thirty a.m.?”

“Let’s see. That was about seven hours ago. I’ll check with our data collection team and get back to you. They haven’t told me anything since three this morning, when we got the presidential order and the data. What you guys received was the last data they’d collected.”

I spent the rest of the morning collating all the statements before the fires. In each case the politician was spinning the truth. Less diplomatically, they were lying. As far as I could tell, this also applied to the lawyers and car dealers. One of the lawyers burst into flame in a courtroom when she said, “My client is not guilty.” A car dealer creating a video for their used car business turned into a burning-man image when he said, “We have the best cars money can buy.”

So lying caused the incineration of clothing. How? I needed to reproduce the effect. I’d find out the energy source this afternoon.

I mused about how to research this over my lunch outside. Fresh, hot coffee with cream and my homemade peanut butter and raspberry jelly sandwich. I made my own bread, and my mom made the jam from the patch in her yard.

I decided what I needed to do. It’d be uncomfortable, but it was necessary for science.

I pitched my lunch bag into the trash and strode to my car in the parking lot. I drove to a paint supply company and bought several pairs of painter's pants. Coming back, I parked and carried my package toward the chemical sciences lab. I knew they had what I needed. I grabbed it and walked to the testing lab. It was explosion proof, which might be important.

I put on the fireproof pants from the chemical lab and then painter's pants over them. I put safety goggles over my eyes. Bracing myself in the middle of the test room, I held the fire extinguisher. "One and one are three."

Nothing happened.

Hmm. I was afraid this'd happen. Perhaps the lie has to be broadcast. I called my mother.

"Hello, Katie."

"Hi, Mom. I need your help for an experiment."

"How can I help?"

"Just watch and listen."

"What's going to happen?"

"I don't know. That's why it's an experiment." I propped up the phone on a chair and waved at Mom.

"One plus one equals three." My painter's pants burst into flame.

"Eeee! Are you all right, Katie?"

"Sure, Mom." I doused the fire with the extinguisher. "I expected this to happen. I'm wearing protective gear."

"What kind of experiment is this?"

"I'm investigating a phenomenon. Apparently I need an audience for the phenomenon to occur. I'll tell you more when I know more."

I examined the burned remnant carefully. They were completely blackened and charred. I fingered them and tore a hole in the pocket. The fabric was weakened but not completely burned. The inside pocket was unburned. Good. I could use them again.

"Can't you tell me anything?"

"Just a second, Mom." I wrote down my first lie and observations in my notebook, as well as the time and the GPS location.

"Okay, here we go again. I'm telling various lies. I'm trying to figure out why pants catch on fire."

"Uh, I thought that was just a saying."

"It seems to have become real. And here goes the next one." I put my safety goggles back on. "Politicians always tell the truth."

Flame on! Extinguisher on!

"I could have told you that was a lie."

"Right. I'm trying things that I know are lies first. Then I'll test how far I can shade the truth. It seems I need someone to lie to."

My phone rang. "Hi, Herman. What'd you find out from the data team?" Herman was used to my abrupt questions.

"The incidents ended about ten p.m. Eastern time—in the Eastern time zone. If you expand the definition of incidents, they go to about ten fifteen."

"Um, what expanded definition do you use?" I had a bad feeling about this.

"Any kind of supernatural or unnatural or unexplainable event. We've had reports of dragons, flying cars, and walking teacups."

"Dragons? What? Where?"

"In Chicago. It apparently ate several gang members. Then it disappeared."

"So, non-reproducible. Great. Walking teacups?"

"A couple called a news reporter, claiming they could make their teacup walk. The reporter stopped by and filmed it. It was on the evening news in Cleveland."

"Ooo-kay. Get me the address. Please." There. I remembered to be polite.

"I've already sent these additional incidents and a new tranche of data to you and all your associates. What do you have for me?"

"I've been able to reproduce the pants-on-fire incident. Apparently you have to lie to another person while being broadcast."

"Great news! But, er, awkward. I'm in Washington this afternoon and I'll report this to the president. I'm not sure he can do anything about it. See if you can get around this effect."

"Okay. I'll test it and see what I find out."

I didn't have much hope.

* * *

"President Lopez?" I asked diffidently at the door to the Oval Office.

"Ah. Come in, Herman. Tell me all about what the National Laboratory has discovered about these horrible incidents." He leaned back in his chair. He'd restored Truman's old desk to the Oval Office and put Truman's sign there: "The buck stops here." Other than that, his desk was clear.

I turned my gaze to the president's dark, piercing eyes. Their sharpness was in contrast to his pleasant, affable expression and tone. I could tell he was eager for anything I could tell him about the phenomenon. I also knew he wouldn't like what I said.

"We've discovered that lying to another person causes that person's pants to ignite."

"Whoa! That's a problem. I'm surprised there haven't been more incidents."

"We've documented thousands of cases. It seems it requires the lie to be heard by another person. We're researching the limits of the effect now, using our best researcher."

"I wonder if we record a speech and then dub it over a video? Maybe a deepfake?"

I make a note of this. "We'll test that. We're also investigating how we can shade the truth without triggering these fires."

The president shook his head. "Tell the truth? That's out of the question. International diplomacy alone would founder, let alone domestic politics. Everyone knows we slant the truth—neither party is fooling anyone. Politics is like poker—you can't play the game without bluffing."

"We'll run a full set of tests and tell you the limits of this fire problem."

"Good. Accelerate your research. Give your findings to the FBI, CIA, NSA, and any other alphabet agency I might have forgotten. We want to get on top of this and make a nationwide announcement by tomorrow. How about you give me another report at this time tomorrow?"

"Yes, sir. I'll see you tomorrow."

* * *

I glanced at the clock: almost 2:00 a.m. I'd been at these experiments for twelve hours. I'd sent out for a sub sandwich at dinner. My mom had needed to get dinner ready at four, so I'd dragged in some of my coworkers to help, and when they went home, I'd drafted the second-shift janitor, Mike Peete.

"My shift is up at two a.m., Ms. Garcia."

"That's fine, Mike. I'll get the third shift to help. One more test please."

I put on a copper sheath, like a skirt, over my fireproof underwear and attached it to a steel drum. I wondered if it would conduct heat away fast enough.

"I think all politicians are truthful," I lied. I braced myself.

Nothing happened. Why was that?

"Whew. That's something."

"Nothing happened."

"That's what I mean. Why would that happen, er not happen?"

"I don't know, but I've got to go. My son's got a Little League game tomorrow."

"Sure, Mike. Thanks for your help. Tell the third-shift security guy to stop by when you see him."

"Will do. Good night to you."

I sighed. I was tired but satisfied. I'd discovered a lot. Everything was black and white with this phenomenon. Even shading colors from blue to green—I couldn't call aquamarine blue or green without triggering the fire effect. I had to call it "blue green" or "aquamarine" or "turquoise." And it didn't matter if I used another language. If I believed the color was one thing and I said something else, fire burst out on whatever I was wearing.

If no one was listening, no effect. If I recorded my voice on video and showed it, as soon as another person heard it, I went flambé.

I'd burned myself several times. The worst case was when I'd tried aluminum pants. They had melted and splashed on my feet. Ouch.

The temperature generated wasn't constant. It was hot enough to burn whatever I wore—on top. My fireproof underwear protected me . . . mostly.

The third-shift maintenance man entered. "Hello, Ms. Garcia? Mike told me you wanted to see me."

"Hi, er, Cliff." I read "Cliff Edwards" on his security tag. We hadn't met before. "I wonder if you could stop by my lab once an hour for your shift. I'm doing some experiments, and I need an audience for them to work."

"You don't need anything else? Just to have me listen?"

"That's it."

"No problem. See you in an hour. Bye."

I typed up my notes and emailed them to my colleagues and boss. I was stumped. I wondered if the effect would reappear?

"Hi, Ms. Garcia. This is your three am check-in."

"Hi, Cliff. Here we go. One plus one is three." I looked at the lab coat I wore over my underwear. "Nothing happened."

"Was something supposed to happen?"

"I don't know. I'm still learning about what's going on."

"What are you looking for?"

"A reason why people's clothing catches on fire if they lie."

"Liar, liar, pants on fire?"

"Literally. At least until two a.m. That's when the effect stopped."

"Huh. I wonder why?"

"Me too. I'll check every hour until it comes back. Or until I collapse."

I collapsed about eight in the morning as the other researchers came in. I dragged myself home and threw myself into bed.

I often have vivid dreams, and I got a doozy after my crazy night. I was in outer space, watching Earth rotate. My dream was on time lapse apparently, and I saw the sun's terminus sweep across the globe, from the US East Coast to the West. It continued across the Pacific and then on to Asia, then Africa and Europe. The Atlantic Ocean swept by and then the East Coast again.

I woke abruptly. I looked at myself with disgust. I was still wearing my work clothing from yesterday. Had I worn it for twenty-four hours? No, it was one thirty. That was about thirty hours. Yuck. I could smell myself. I didn't even have to sniff my pits.

I threw my clothes into the hamper and myself into the shower. I wondered about the dream. It seemed significant somehow. I'd take a different tack today with my research.

Chapter 7 – Housework

Monday, October 5

I started to make tea again the next morning. Should I try something? Jane and I had talked about the walking and purring teacup, and we agreed it was creepy—but helpful. We hadn't discussed trying anything else, but maybe I should. I was naturally lazy. If the teacups could help make tea, why not?

After filling the teapot with hot tap water, I turned the stove gas on under the kettle. As the water heated, I got the tea ready in the tea sock. I sniffed the tea: Earl Grey, one of our favorites. Now, how could they help in the morning?

"Can you get the water to boil immediately?" I said to the kettle.

The whistle started.

"Can you dump out the hot water and put the tea sock in?" I said to the teapot.

Two arms and legs popped out. It walked on the counter to the sink and poured out the hot water while holding its lid on with a hand. Then it removed its lid and put the tea sock in.

"Great. Now, kettle, pour your water into the teapot." I turned off the gas stove. The whistle died.

The kettle walked on the counter to the teapot and poured in the boiling water.

"Well done. Go back to the stove, kettle." The kettle scuttled to the stove and withdrew its legs and arms. I started the timer. Three minutes.

I sniffed. Yum. Jane had made fresh scones this morning. "Jane, where are the scones?"

"Out here. Come and get them," she called from the living room.

"I'll be there in two minutes! Did you eat yours without tea?"

"I had to taste test them, of course. I still have one left to go with the tea."

"Of course."

The alarm went off. I went to pour the tea and then thought better of it. "Okay, teapot. Take the tea sock out and put it in the bowl."

A ceramic arm lifted the sodden sock out by hand and put it in the bowl to drain.

"Now, tea mugs, line up in front of the teapot." They did, skittering on their spindly legs.

"Pour the tea into each mug, three-quarters full, teapot." It slowly stood on its two legs and leaned over each mug, holding the lid on with one hand.

"Creamer, put one ounce of milk in each mug." The creamer stalked to the mugs and creamed them.

"Tea mugs, follow me. And don't spill anything!"

The mugs climbed down from the counter, as nimbly as mice, and scampered behind me.

"I see you have company this morning. I wondered who you were talking to," Jane said.

"Just the tea things. Jane's mug, go to Jane."

Jane reached down, and the cup leapt into her hands.

"Jake's cup, go to his side table," Jane said.

Hand over hand, it climbed the table and settled on the coaster, next to the dish with the scone. The hands and legs disappeared.

"Is that butter?" I pointed at a bowl of yellow cream.

"No, it's clotted cream."

"I didn't know we had any."

"I got some yesterday at the ethnic market."

"Thanks. I love it on scones."

"We ought to tell someone about our magical tea mugs."

"I called the news about them. They came and filmed it. But I think we should call them again."

"And the kettle. And teapot. And creamer."

"I didn't know about those."

"That's who I was talking to this morning."

"If you're going crazy, then I guess I am too. I wonder if we can get our vacuum to clean for us?"

"That'd be like one of those robotic vacuums."

"Or a sorcerer's apprentice." Jane finished her tea with a gulp. "I'm eager to try it."

Jane tugged out our vacuum, a top-of-the-line upright, and plugged it in. "Okay, vacuum. I want you to vacuum the dining room and living room."

A hand came out of the handle and turned the vacuum on. The hand merged back in, and two beady eyes popped out. It began moving methodically around the dining room.

"Good work! Oh, you've got to move the chairs and vacuum under the table too."

The hand reappeared, moved each chair, and vacuumed under the table.

"Don't forget to put the chairs back."

Obediently it did so.

"Great. Now, on to the living room."

I watched from the dining room, impressed, as the vacuum obeyed Jane's commands. What unpleasant household tasks did I have? The lawn. Did I really want a magical lawnmower running around our yard? Did I want to mow outside in ninety-degree heat? Our fall freeze had been followed by a hot day. Why not try? What was the worst that could happen? I couldn't think of anything worse than mowing in the heat.

"Honey, I'm going to mow the lawn."

"In this heat?"

"I'm going to see if the mower can self-mow like the vacuum."

"Oho! Why not?"

I pushed the mower out of the garage and filled the gas tank. I was about to pull the cord when I remembered the teakettle.

"Okay, mower, start yourself."

An arm came out of the base and pulled the cord. It started, and the arm disappeared.

Wow, this really was magic. The mower had never started with one pull before. "Mow the whole lawn. Don't miss any of the grass."

Two oil-colored eyes popped out of the front of the motor. It took off, about as fast as I could walk. Maybe it remembered the right speed? It followed the edge of the backyard. It went around the garden once, and then again to get the little strip of grass next to the garden. That always annoyed me, having to take two passes to get that strip.

Thinking ahead, I opened the gate to the front yard. "After you're done in the back, go to the front yard and mow the grass there." I swear I saw the motor look at me and nod.

I went inside, poured myself more tea, and snatched another scone. I was bigger than Jane, so I could eat three. I sat on our enclosed, air-conditioned porch and watched the mower work. This was fun! I swallowed a bite of scone. And delicious.

Jane joined me. She had a cup of tea and another scone as well. Good! Now I could eat a fourth.

"All done already, Jane?"

"Yes. The self-operating vacuum is like magic! It moved all the furniture and cleaned underneath it. When it was done, it turned itself off. I worked up an appetite putting it away." She bit into her scone.

"I'm proud of your industry. Not many wives—or husbands—are smiling after housework."

"Thank you. I see you're just about done with the backyard?" Jane pointed outside.

"Oh?" I glanced out the window.

It was just leaving the backyard for the front.

"Yeah. It's hard work, but someone has to do it."

"Even if it isn't you?" Jane smiled, and her dimples showed.

"Yeah. You're cute as the day I saw you in English class." I leaned over and kissed her.

After we fooled around for a bit, I heard the mower in the front. "I'd better go check on the yard."

"Here. Take a cup of tea." She poured me a fresh cup.

"Thanks."

The front lawn was neatly mowed, but I couldn't see the mower from the porch. I stepped off the porch and looked down the side of our house and saw the mower clipping the strip of grass between our neighbor's drive and our house. I watch in horror as it also mowed a foot of daylilies in the flowerbed next to the grass.

"No! Stop!"

It stopped. Half the daylilies were gone, cut to the ground. But the grass was well mowed.

I didn't take any chances. I pushed it to the garage on my own power.

I went inside. “Jane, I’ve got good news and bad news.”

“Give me the good news first.”

“The lawnmower mowed all the grass neatly.”

“So what’s the bad news?”

“It also mowed your daylilies neatly.”

“Arggh! Don’t ever let it loose again!”

“Some more good news: Only half the daylilies got mowed.”

“Grrr. Which half?”

“The half next to the grass.”

“So that’s half my gold ones and half my red ones. I should have put a border around them.”

“No use crying over spilt milk—or mowed daylilies.”

“I think we should report this to the TV news—or some scientists. Nothing happened with the radio station.”

“Or magicians. But I don’t know any.”

“Me neither. Or scientists. But I do know the TV station is right down the street. Let’s go there.”

“I reported this to the other station last time. Let’s try this one.”

Chapter 8 – Lake Michigan

Sunday, October 4

Mommy came in.

"Mommy!" I threw my arms around her neck.

She lifted me up. "Shayla! Mmm, I love you too." She stopped kissing me. "Is that the washing machine I hear? Lamar, did you start a load of laundry?"

"Uh, yeah. My shirt got dirty today. I threw in all the dirty laundry."

"Oh no!" She ran to the washer. "My underclothes are in there!"

"So? They'll all get clean."

"No, they'll get stained. But thanks for helping." She rubbed his head and hugged him. She opened the washer and looked inside. Picking up her panty, she scrutinized it. "Eh, not too bad." She dropped it back into the washer. "Was this the shirt you got dirty?" She held it up.

"Yeah."

"There's still a stain on the back. What'd you get on it?"

"Blood!" I said.

Lamar gave me a look.

"What?"

"Uh, yeah, I got blood on it."

"How'd that happen? Oh, here's a hole. Did you get hurt?"

"No," Lamar said.

"Yes," I said.

"Wait a second. Something's goin' on. Tell me the whole story."

"We went to the park," I began.

"And I played basketball," Lamar interrupted.

"And I was feeding Pinkie bugs when I heard some poppin', like fireworks."

"A gang chased us off the courts," Lamar jumped in.

"And I ran to Lamar and he fell down." I continued the story.

"And I got bloody when I fell."

"He was bleeding all over when I got there."

"I passed out for a while." Lamar kept looking at me.

"And then Pinkie ate all the bad guys."

"What?!" Mommy shouted. "Are you making things up again, Shayla?"

"No, honest truth, Mommy. I wisht he'd gobble them up like bugs. They were shooting back and forth."

"Lamar, was there shooting?"

"Yeah, Mom."

"You know I told you to get Shayla outta there ASAP."

"I was! I was running as fast as I could!"

"And you got *shot?"*

"Yeah, I guess."

"And here's the bullet!" I pulled the bullet out of my pink heart-shaped purse.

Mommy's mouth stayed open as she took it from me. "Lemme see your back, Lamar."

He pulled off his shirt. His back showed clean, brown skin, like always. Frowning, Mommy lined up his shirt on his back. "Where'd you bleed from?"

"Right from the back here." He pointed to the spot.

"There's no wound. But your shirt is still stained, and that is a bullet."

"Oh, I just wisht him better so he could take me home, Mommy."

"C'mon, Shayla, be serious."

"Uh, Mom?"

"Yes, Lamar?"

"When I woke up, I felt the bullet against my skin."

"You expect me to believe that?"

"Maybe you'll believe Pinkie. He was there." I held him up to Mommy.

"Now, Shayla, I know he's your pretend friend, but he's not real, honey."

"He is so! I wisht him alive! He gobbled up those gangbangers."

"Be serious, Shayla."

"I'll show you." I stomped to our porch, carrying Pinkie. The porch looked down on the street below. I opened the sliding door.

"Whatcha doin'?" Mommy followed me.

"I'll wake up Pinkie and you'll see." I put him on the porch.

"Why on the porch?"

"He needs room to grow. Okay, Pinkie, wake up! Talk to Mommy!" My stuffed animal just sat there.

"Shayla, ya gotta keep straight what is real and what is pretend."

Maybe he needed a hug. That's what I did last time. I picked him up and said, "Wake up Pinkie! Mommy needs to see you."

He began vibrating against my chest.

"Yay, Pinkie!"

"What—" Mommy stopped as Pinkie grew to the size of a horse on our porch. He leapt into the air, and his pink wings buzzed like a bee. He grew to an elephant's size and then a whale. The wind whooshed around us and into the house.

"What." Mommy's mouth fell open again.

"Good, Pinkie! Now tell Mommy what happened at the park today."

"Mommy, Shayla woke me up and helped me grow. Then . . ."

* * *

Mommy's mouth opened and closed while Pinkie told her what had happened today. When she heard how Lamar was shot and then alive again, she cried and hugged Lamar hard and then me.

"Oof! Mommy! Not so hard! You're hurting me!" I poked her and pushed her away.

"Sorry, Shayla. I couldn't help myself. This day could have been so terrible, and you saved yourself and Lamar."

"Nah, Pinkie did."

"You woke up Pinkie and Lamar."

"Yeah, but that was just wishin'."

Mommy took a deep breath while the air from Pinkie's wings rushed past us. "Ah, the air smells so good!"

"That's why I like flying."

"Hey, Pinkie! Can you give us a ride?"

"Sure."

"What?" Mommy looked at me and then at Pinkie.

Lamar grinned. "Great idea, Shayla!"

"Hop on." Pinkie hovered next to the balcony and stretched his head down to the railing. Lamar got on first, then Mommy, and then me.

"Where are we gonna go?" Mommy asked.

"Let's go to the lakefront park!" Lamar said.

We'd gone there before for a picnic.

"Can you fly that far, Pinkie?" Mommy asked.

"I've seen the lake from here. It's not that far."

"What about people seeing us? Can you hide in the clouds?" Mommy looked down at the traffic below.

"Of course. It's night too."

"Let's go, Pinkie!" I bounced on his soft, fluffy neck. It was softer than my bed.

With a few powerful strokes, Pinkie had us in the dark, damp, cloud overhead.

"Pinkie, I can't see anything!"

"It's always clear on top, Shayla."

In a minute or two, we were through the cloud. I gasped. I saw millions of stars overhead. The city lights were blocked by the clouds, and we skimmed them like a fluffy blanket. The starlight made Pinkie's fur look dusty rose.

It took a minute for me to feel how cold it was. I snuggled back against Mommy's warm body.

"Ya cold, honey? Me too. Lamar, gimme a hug."

"It's like a Brown family sandwich!" Lamar laughed.

"Are you getting cold? Let me turn up my heat."

"What—" Mommy jumped against my back.

Pinkie's fur warmed up like a heating pad.

"That really feels good, Pinkie. Thanks!"

"You're welcome, Mommy Brown. There's the lake."

The Chicago skyscrapers poked through the cloud like fingers. There were holes in the cloud, like Lamar's shirt. We saw a big hole where the lake met the beach. We swooped down to land.

Pinkie put his head down, and we slid off him like a furry slide. The sand was still warm from the day.

"Thank you, Pinkie. That was one smooth ride. You have a better ride than a pink Cadillac!"

"Thank you, Mommy Brown. It's easy for me to fly."

Lamar ran to the lake and back. "Wow, Mom! It's so cool to be on the beach at night! Too bad we didn't bring along a picnic."

"Hey, maybe Pinkie can go and get us a picnic. What do you think, Pinkie?"

"Maybe. I'm afraid I won't be able to find all your food and picnic stuff. Why don't you just wish it here?"

"Doh! I didn't think of that." I crossed my arms and closed my eyes. "I wish our picnic basket was here!" I pictured it on our refrigerator, where we kept it. I opened my eyes. There it sat, at my feet.

"Great, Shayla!" Lamar leapt on the basket. It was empty.

"Oh, you forgot the food, Shayla!" Lamar looked back at me.

"I didn't think of that."

"I don't store it full of food, honey." Mommy smiled at me. "Why don't you get a loaf of bread and some baloney and cheese from the refrigerator? And some mustard."

"Okay." I closed my eyes again. "I wish for our bread. And baloney. And cheese. And mustard." I opened my eyes and there they were, packed in the picnic basket.

"I'll make some sandwiches for the three of us," Mommy said.

"What about Pinkie?"

Mommy looked startled. She looked at Pinkie, looming over us with his shiny black eyes. "Do you want a sandwich, Pinkie?"

"I'd love a baloney and cheese sandwich. No mustard, please. It makes me burp."

"Okay, one sandwich, no mustard for Mr. Pinkie. I guess you're part of the family." Mommy handed him his sandwich.

He opened his huge mouth like a garage door, with a furry red tongue like our living room carpet. Mommy tossed it in, and he gulped it down.

"Yummy! Can I really be part of the family? Pinkie Brown?"

"Of course! I officially adopt you as our family dragon, Pinkie Brown!" Mommy patted his nose, like the side of a stuffed pink refrigerator.

We all munched on the sandwiches. In the fresh air by the lake, they tasted so good. Mommy made another one for Pinkie.

"Oh, we forgot drinks. Shayla, get a gallon of milk from the fridge and our cups from the cupboard."

"Right away, Mommy." I pictured them clearly. I'd gotten the milk and cups a lot of times, helping set the table. I didn't even close my eyes.

Pop! The jug of milk appeared on the sand. Pop, pop, pop! Our cups arrived around it.

"Thanks, Shayla. You're such a helpful girl!"

"I always pretended and wished before, but today it all started working."

"Today's a day I'll remember forever," Lamar said.

"Me too, Lamar." Mommy sighed.

Chapter 9 – Report

Monday, October 5

"Listen to this, Dad!"

"What, Sean?"

I pointed to an article on my tablet. "The government is investigating all the pants fires. It's not just in the US—it's around the world."

"Let me read that." Dad took the tablet from me and read the article aloud, frowning.

"'No one knows why people's pants literally started catching on fire every time they told the slightest fib'—Well, we do, don't we, Sean?"

I grinned. "We sure do, Dad."

"'—but it's made for very exciting television and maybe not-so-exciting consequences for the person involved. Across all networks, television ratings are up for live news shows. Nine of the top-ten viral videos are of newscasters or politicians bursting into flame.'" Dad paused. "So I guess we've done something good."

He continued. "'Needless to say, local fire departments have been busy. Major businesses have taken to employing small groups of firefighters to follow behind certain people, usually public relations managers or lawyers, and spray them down with fire extinguishers several times per day.

"'None of this was more prevalent than in Washington, where firefighters are kept busy around the clock following every politician everywhere. The fire affliction crossed all parties and affiliations. Politicians' pants were constantly bursting into flame.'"

My dad laughed. "Ha! This'll make voting easier because you'll always know who was being truthful and who wasn't."

"Are there any politicians who haven't been burned yet?" I asked.

"Uh, none that I've heard of. Look, the issue's gotten to President Lopez. He's unleashed hundreds of analysts and scientific researchers on the problem. They're really serious about this. Maybe we should tell them about our wish, Sean."

"Won't we get into trouble?"

"For what? Just wishing people would tell the truth? It's not our fault everyone is in the habit of lying. Let's see. This is a national article." Dad did a quick search and found the closest news outlet to our home. "Here. Our local TV station is on Peachtree Street. Come with me and we can tell them how the fires got started."

"Have fun, guys!" Mom hugged us.

We went to the car.

Walking into the station, I was surprised by how small it was. The studio looked a lot bigger on TV. "How can I help you?" the receptionist asked with a big smile.

"Haven't I seen you on the news?" Dad asked.

"Yes, I do some reporting. I also am a receptionist, and I answer the phone. I'm an intern at the station—Shelley Clark is my name. What can I do for you?"

"We've got a big breaking news story—" Dad began.

"It's about the fires all around the country!" I put in.

Without missing a beat, Dad continued, "—and around the world. We know exactly how and why the problem started."

Shelley pounded wildly on her tablet. "This is great! This might be my big break into the news! Tell me all about it."

So Dad and I gave her all the details.

"That is so cool! Let me get our news head, Fred O'Connell." She ran out the door. A few minutes later she came back with a balding, middle-aged guy with glasses.

I recognized him from the local news and weather.

"Hi, Fred O'Connell. What can I do for you?" He smiled.

"We've got the cause of the burning-pants problem," Dad began.

"We were there when it happened the first time," I put in.

"We were watching the news, the debate between the governor candidates."

"And we all wished their pants would catch on fire when they lied."

"Because we were so tired of the BS they were saying," Dad finished up.

"Um, how is that possible?" Fred's eyebrows climbed toward his receding hairline.

"We don't know," Dad admitted.

"It just happened, just as we wished."

"Assume you did cause this—didn't you know millions and billions of people lie every day?"

"Uh, I didn't think of that," I said.

"We just wanted politicians to tell the truth," Dad said.

"Do you have any proof?" Fred frowned.

"Uh, no? Can you think of anything, Dad?"

"Er, no. Nothing except unwishing it. And I guess I prefer to hold politicians' feet to the fire to make them tell the truth."

"I'm with you there, Dad."

"I'm sorry, but I don't see any way I can report this as a news story. I need some proof. If you think of something, let me know. Goodbye." He turned and left.

We looked at each other.

"Well, we tried. Thanks for your help, Shelley." Dad and I turned to go.

"Wait! I've got an idea." Shelley called us back.

"What?" Dad asked.

"There's a researcher who sent us an email looking for pants-on-fire stories. She's with the federal government. How about I reply to her with your story?"

"Sure!" I had a bit of hope.

"Lemme find the email." She scrolled on her computer. "Here it is. Katie Garcia of the Oakridge National Labs. 'Please send me any news stories you have pertaining to the mysterious pants and skirt fires.' I'll reply with your report. It seems to fit." She looked up at us. "Now tell me your story again in as much detail as you can."

We repeated everything in as much detail as we could remember. Shelley took our names and addresses and sent it off.

"Thanks so much! This might be my big break." She gave us a big smile.

"I hope so!" I said as we left. She was pretty good looking, with sandy hair and a round face and figure.

* * *

Monday, October 5

I hated my job as a garbage collector in Beijing. It wasn't just picking up the stinking, rotting food, vomit, and feces that people threw away, and dumping it, as I was now doing by the incinerator. No, that was the easy part. Then I had to pick through it, looking for paper, phones, and computers that could be cleaned and scanned for intelligence. That was what I had to do next.

I shoveled the crap into the hopper. If I saw any legible paper or electronics, I picked them out and put them in the intelligence bin. Ah. There was an old calendar. Woo! It was a girly one. I eyed it before tossing it into the bin. This still wasn't the worst part of my job.

The tempting girl hurt me more than she pleased me. I knew I could never get a girl like that. They were all stuck up, and I had no money for a dowry anyway. Plus, all my money went to my parents for their apartment. I also had to feed them. In return, I got to sleep on the floor. This wasn't what I wanted, but I could see no way out. But that still wasn't the worst part.

"Liu Fu! Lucky Destroyer! Ha! Why haven't you finished yet, you ugly, stinking excuse for a man?"

That was my boss, Gao Jin Hua. He was the worst part of my job. He tugged the calendar from the bin and glanced through, leering appreciatively.

I longed to wallop him, but I'd be fired and imprisoned. My parents would likely die or starve to death.

"Why are you staring at me when you're running behind? Work faster!"

I shoveled as fast as I could, making a dent in the pile of offal.

"Wait!" With his gloved hand, Jin Hua dug something out of the last shovelful in the hopper. He held a cell phone, inside a bag of garbage that had split.

"Look at this!" He shoved the phone into my face. It reeked and the screen was cracked, but I knew the party wanted all discarded phones, to search them for illegal activities.

"I didn't see it." I bowed my head.

"But I did! I've got a new job for you! Open each bag of crap and look through it. Po Ping, come here and shovel behind us."

Another worker came running.

"Start!" He pointed at a bag of garbage.

I pulled it open. The stink doubled. I flattened the garbage and went on to the next bag.

"Faster!"

Garbage. Feces. Paper. I dumped that in the hopper. Broken junk. Nothing electron—what was this? A gorgeous brass dragon rested in my hand. I rubbed it clean with my glove. Wow. Why would someone throw this out?

"Why are you resting? Throw it away and move faster!" Jin Hua screamed in my face.

"Look at this. It's worth some–"

"Take off your gloves! You're not moving fast enough!" He knocked the dragon from my hand. It clanged on the floor, getting filthy again.

I bent and picked it up.

He took his baton and hit me on the head with it. "Drop the junk!" Bang. "Take off your gloves!" Bang. That one split my scalp. "Move faster!" Bang. I saw my blood splatter on the floor. "Or I swear I'll fire you right now!" Bang.

My hand went numb as he hit it as I shielded my head. I snapped. I rose from my crouched position with a twist and hit him with all my strength. I meant to hit him in the jaw, but I hit him on the side of his face. His blood splattered as he dropped to the floor.

There was a bloody divot where the head of the dragon had hit him in the temple.

Po Ping stopped shoveling and stared. He ran to Jian Hua's side and put his hand on his neck.

"He's dead! I've got to tell the big boss." He ran off at a sprint to the office.

Now I was dead. I ran to my garbage truck. Maybe I could get out in time.

Six feet from the door, a guard with a machine gun stopped me.

I put my hands up, trembling. I still held my dragon. Other guards came and surrounded me. The TV monitors stopped playing Communist anthems, and the big boss, Chen Jia Wei, appeared. His voice boomed over the loudspeaker.

"Liu Fu! There is only one sentence for you—death! Guards, march him toward the hopper."

Hopper? Are they going to incinerate me?

We got there, seemingly instantaneously.

"Push him in."

Roughly, I fell into the pit of stench with a squish.

"Now dump the rest of the garbage on him."

I could hear the front-end loader moving the pile of garbage over the floor. Then WHOMP! A ton landed on me.

I no longer cared about the stench. I just tried to breathe. I wriggled in the offal and made an air pocket. The humid fetid black air was life giving. I still clutched my brass dragon. I had no hope. I'd given up all for the stupid brass dragon. I'd die. My parents would die.

But . . . what if? What if the dragon were magic? "O gorgeous brass dragon, hear me and save me from this garbage!" burst out of my mouth without thinking.

The dragon glowed red hot, burning my hand. Then it grew and wriggled like a worm. It crawled under me and lifted me up on its now broad, brass back. I started to slip off, with the garbage flowing around me. As I scrabbled with my nails, a saddle formed out of brass. I pulled myself in and found stirrups for my feet.

Then we burst out. The dragon flowed easily out of the pit, with its claws digging deep into its metal sides. My saddle was on a hump on the dragon's back and went up and down as we sinuously flowed across the floor.

All the guards stared open mouthed. Then my dragon gobbled them up. Those not eaten began shooting, but the bullets only bounced off the brass scales.

Silence fell. Then I heard screaming. The big boss was on the giant monitor, yelling in horror. I knew what to do next.

"Go to the big boss's office. That's Chen Jia Wei, in the headquarters building." That was the first time I'd called him by his name. Gao had always beaten us if we used his name.

We zoomed over the ground. The dragon was bigger than any I had seen at New Year's and incredibly strong. Chain-link fences parted. Cars and trucks were crushed.

I need a name for the dragon. Liu Fu's dragon? Why not?

“I name you Liu Fu Long!”

Long stopped, turned to me, and nodded in acknowledgment. Then we raced onward.

I wondered how we’d climb to the top floor of the headquarters. I shouldn’t have. Long raced up the side of the building, his claws smashing windows and digging into concrete. I slipped backward off the vertical saddle. A brass back grew to support me. Armrests appeared for me to grip. I could look down and see the dragon stretched ten stories to the ground.

The roof held a beautiful garden. Chen Jia Wei huddled in the center. He began shooting at us with his gun.

“Don’t kill him, but hold him in your mouth.”

Long’s teeth captured Chen. He grabbed the brass pillars holding him in and grimaced in terror.

“Chen Jia Wei, who is your boss?”

“Bei. Bei Wei. He’s the head of the CCP in Beijing.”

“Good. Lead us to him and you’ll live.”

With Long at my side, I could be the head of the Communist party in Beijing. I’d get a mansion, and my parents could live there and get all the best medical care.

But why stop there? I grinned, as I couldn’t think of a single reason to settle for only the head of Beijing.

Chapter 10 – Viewtube

Monday, October 5

"Good morning, Master!" I barked as I jumped up on his bed. It was light outside, and I'd just heard him move in his bed. That meant he was awake. I knew I wasn't supposed to wake him up, but once he was awake, he didn't mind. I licked his face once.

"Ooh." He groaned and then he stretched. "You know you're not supposed to be on the bed." Master looked at me, but he wasn't angry.

"C'mon, Master. I know you don't mind."

"You know, this is pretty darn cool that we can understand each other. I've always wanted to understand your barks and have you understand what I wanted."

"I kind of did," I put in a little yelp.

"Yeah, but now you know exactly. Jump on the floor!"

I jumped. I knew Master was in a playful mood. I was always ready to play.

"Back up!"

Back on the bed I hopped, and wagged my tail. "This is fun."

"Race you to the kitchen!" We raced down the hall. My nails skittered on the slick floor, but I was winning! Then I had to turn. I skidded right past the kitchen, while Master stepped in behind me.

"I won!" He laughed.

"Let's do it again!" I barked.

"How about we get some breakfast? I've got to get ready for work."

I'd forgotten about breakfast! I was always ready for food. "Yes!" I barked and ran to my bowl. I picked it up and carried it to Master and then dropped it.

"Very good! Now just wait while I get your food."

I was so impatient for the food. "I'm hungry!"

"I know." Master loaded the food into my bowl. "Enjoy." He set it on the floor.

Yummy! My tail wagged my joy.

I took a drink and went outside to go potty.

When I came back through the dog door, Master said, "Spot, do you want to go to work with me?"

"Yes!" I barked.

"Follow me to the car."

I followed him to the garage and hopped into the car. I loved watching out the windows while Master drove. It was even better if he opened the window so I could stick my head out. Say . . . I wondered if I could open it. Master always pushed something on the door to open it. I pushed around with my paw until the window rolled down. Yay!

"So you learned how to open the window?" Master said.

"Yes," I barked, but I was confused. It seemed to be a question, but he already knew the answer. Maybe he'd explain.

"Hmm . . . I wonder if you could drive a car?"

Another question, but he wasn't asking me. I barked anyway. "Yes! I'd love to." How hard could it be?

We stopped and jumped out of the car. "This is my HossFit gym, Peoria Power," he said.

I ran around outside wagging my tail and smelling all the scents—Master's and lots of other people.

"I thought I'd show you what we do and you can help me make a Viewtube video."

"What's Viewtube? What's a video?" I barked.

"It'll be easier to show you than tell you." We entered the building.

It smelled interesting. A lot of male human sweat, and some female too. Master placed his phone on something like three sticks and then lifted metal things. He talked, but not to me, so I didn't pay attention.

"Hey, Spot! Bring me those weights over there." He pointed to some smaller metal things. They were covered with rubber and were easy to pick up. I brought one to him in my mouth.

"Good boy! Go get the other one."

I did so, and he started moving with them in his hand and talking again. Maybe he liked talking like I did barking?

He finished talking and plucked his phone from the three sticks. He poked at it for a while. "Spot! Come here. Take a look at this."

He showed me a little picture of him on the phone. He touched it and it started moving and talking, just like he'd done before.

"Cool," I yipped. "But why?"

"Everyone around the world can see and hear me talk about my business. You know how you like to exercise, don't you?"

"You bet!"

"So do people. Now I have an idea for you to make a video as well. I have some customers, but not enough. They pay me money. That's where your dog food comes from—and your ball."

"Oh no!" I yipped and whined.

"Oh yes. Without money, no food for either of us—or toys."

"What do you want me to do?" I wagged my tail a little, hoping I could help.

"Help me make this video." Master put his camera on a tripod.

Master's girlfriend came up. She had light-colored fur on her head. I could tell by his smell he was interested in her. I liked her because of the scent of her sweat. She gave me treats sometimes.

"Why don't you breed with her?" I barked.

"Wha— Did he just talk? Did he say what I thought he said?" she said.

"Oh no! You shut up!" Master yelled at me.

I whined. I didn't know why.

"Are you talking to your dog now, Josh?" she asked him. "I know dogs can't talk. Did you pull a ventriloquist joke on me?" She frowned and seemed angry.

"Yes!" I barked. Then I remembered I was supposed to be quiet. I whined to apologize.

"He's talking! I understand him. Or is that you?"

"No!" Master barked at me. "Not you, Bella. I'm trying to get Spot to quiet down."

"I know that's you, Josh. Your dog sounds like you. Why would you pull that trick on me? I like you okay, but we're not that good of friends that you can get away with this." She smelled angry.

"Uh, he's really smart." Master seemed uncertain to me.

"We're not talking about the dog. We're talking about you

and me. If you can't give me a good explanation or apology, we're through."

"Uh—" Master looked stunned. He smelled afraid.

I whined in sympathy.

His girlfriend kept looking at him, and she smelled even angrier. "Okay. Bye." She left the building.

"What am I going to do with you, Spot?" He knelt and petted me.

I wagged furiously. "I love that! So you're not mad at me?"

"Nah. I didn't know where I stood with her. Obviously she didn't care enough to hear an explanation. Well, we might as well go for broke."

"What do you mean?" I barked.

"Okay, Spot. Here are three dog food bowls."

"Food? This is getting interesting!" I spun around and jumped.

"Look carefully at the words on each. I'll only tell you once."

I sat and watched him.

He pointed to the letters on the side of the bowl. "This bowl says 'Food.' Say that back to me so I know you understand."

"Food," I barked.

"Good. This bowl says 'Good.' That looks like 'food' but is different. Say 'Good.'"

"Good." I wagged my tail.

"And this bowl says 'Wood.' That comes from trees. You like to pee on them. Say 'Wood.'"

"Wood." My tongue hung out in laughter as I yipped. This was getting funny.

"All right. Stay here." Master crossed the floor, while another gym member watched him from the rowing machine.

Master opened my dog food bag and put a scoop in one of the bowls. I could smell it, and I drooled.

He put the bowls down, covered them with dishes, and then came to my side. "Now, Spot, one of these bowls had your food in it, but you don't know which one. Right?"

"Right," I barked.

"Listen carefully. You'll only get the food if you follow my instructions. Can you see and read all the words on the bowls?"

I looked at the bowls on the ground. I could read them, but

each was covered. I couldn't see inside.

"Yes," I barked.

"Go to the bowl that says 'Wood' and fetch what's inside back to me."

I raced to that bowl and knocked off the plate. I grabbed the stick and raced back to him and dropped it in his hand.

"Good boy! What do you think of that, Bill?"

"Pretty smart of him," the man on the rowing machine said. "How long did it take you to train him?"

"No time at all. He's really reading the signs."

"C'mon. Dogs can't read."

"I'll prove it. You switch the signs around however you wish. Then you pick which one he goes to."

"Okay, you're on." Bill jogged to the bowls. He rearranged them and switched the signs around. Then he came back.

"Which one do you want him to go to?"

"Go to the 'Good' bowl, Spot." He looked at me.

I looked at Master.

"Go, Spot," he said.

I raced there and knocked off the plate. The "Good" bowl was empty.

"Bring back the plate," Bill said.

I grabbed it and brought it to Bill's hand. "Good boy. Do you want your food?"

"Yes!" I wagged.

"Go to the 'Wood' bowl and eat what's in it."

I ran back. The "Wood" bowl had the food! Yum! I ran back to Master and sat.

"I can't believe it." Bill shook his head. "You know, Josh, this kind of creeps me out. How smart is he?"

"I don't really know. But I'm going to post this on my Viewtube channel. Maybe he'll drum up some business."

"Don't forget us loyal members when you get famous. Will we still get the founding-member discounts?"

"Of course, Bill. Don't worry. All I need is about double the members I have now and I'll make a decent income. Do you think this video will help?"

"Oh yeah. People love smart dog videos."

"I'll put it on my HossFit channel right away then."

Chapter 11 – Cleveland

Monday, October 5

I woke up in a strange bed. Ah, Jeff and Megan's home. I felt excited. Today was the day I would start my flying taxi service. Lying in bed, I went back over the previous evening's events.

Sunday, October 4

I arrived at Cleveland Hopkins Airport. It was gray outside and sleeting. Goody. Normal October weather. But I still felt fit and arthritis-free, even after a boring flight.

I worked my way down to baggage claim, dreading wrestling my huge bag off the carousel. After a few minutes, it came around. I tugged at it, but it didn't budge. I walked beside it, around the carousel, feeling like an idiot.

"Okay," I whispered to the bag. "When I tug, you jump off, land on your feet, and make them disappear."

I looked around. No one was watching me. I gave a mighty tug, and the bag jumped off the carousel and landed nimbly on its legs, which promptly vanished.

"Well done," I praised. Then I felt like an idiot again. *Talking to luggage? Where's your mind going, Angie? Well, it worked*, I argued back at myself.

My son, Jeff, came up and hugged me. "Hi, Mom!"

He was built tall and lean, a lot like Ray, his dad. My mind pictured a sudden nostalgic memory of Ray.

"You're looking great, Mom!"

"Thanks, son. You too. How are Megan and the kids?"

"They're great. They're sorry they couldn't make it. Violet and Oliver have marching-band practice tonight at school."

He rolled my luggage as we walked toward the car. "Whew! That's heavy. Whatcha got in there? Bricks? How'd you get it off the carousel?"

"I got a little help. Those are books weighing it down, not bricks."

"You should have waited for me."

"You know I don't like to wait."

With a heave and a grunt, Jeff hoisted the luggage into the back seat of his sedan.

"It'll be easier to get out of the back seat than the trunk." Jeff slid in next to me.

The trip across Cleveland was long and boring due to rush-hour traffic and the sloppy weather. We chatted, catching up on what had happened since Christmas, when Jeff and his family had traveled to Paradise.

We finally arrived. I scooted out and headed to get my luggage.

"Let me help you, Mom."

"Let me show you something. Up!"

The luggage jumped up off the seat and landed on the drive.

"Ta-da!" I smiled at Jeff.

"What is that?" He stared from the luggage to me.

"That is how I wrangled my luggage to the car and the airport without you. And that's not all." I bent and touched my toes and then did a deep squat. "No arthritis anymore."

"How did you get rid of that? And what's up with your luggage? Do you have some little motors that bring those legs in and out?"

"That's all just wishing. Ever since this morning, my wishes have come true."

"I don't believe this. Let's go into the house. I've gotta hear the whole story."

I entered their home and smelled freshly brewed coffee.

"Mmmm. I love you, Megan."

Megan smiled as she brought us a tray of cookies. "I know you like your coffee. It's decaf, so it won't keep you awake."

"How do you keep your slim figure when you bake all the time?"

"I guess I just have a high metabolism."

"I hate you," I said with a smile as I ate her cookies.

"Mom, tell Megan and me the whole story about the luggage and the arthritis. Listen to this. I think she's pranking us."

We sat at the dining table, and I told them the whole story of my trip, including my flying car.

Jeff shook his head. "I believe your story even less the

second time. Are you taking new meds?"

"Too bad you had to leave your car in Phoenix. I'd have loved to see that." Megan's brown eyes shone in her pixie-like face, with a pointy chin and light-brown hair.

"Hmm. Maybe it'll work with your car." I rubbed my chin. *I'll have to trim the hair on my mole again.*

"No way," Megan said.

"Let's give it a try. You'll never believe me any other way." I rose and headed for their garage.

"You're right, Mom. I'm not believing any of your story," Jeff opened the door for me. "This I've gotta see."

"Keys?" I turned to Jeff.

He took them off the hook by the door and dropped them in my hand.

As I adjusted the driver's seat of their minivan, Megan slipped in next to me and Jeff sat in the back seat. *I just did this very thing this morning*, I reassured myself. *Just do the same stuff.* I started the car and backed out.

"Where are the wings?" Megan teased.

"You don't want them crashing into the garage, do you?"

"No. Few things are worse than magical wings crashing into your garage." I could hear Jeff's sarcasm. Where did he get that from?

"Let me get up to speed." I headed for the freeway.

"You need to be up to speed?" Jeff asked.

"Of course. This ramp should do nicely." I zoomed up the ramp to I-90. It was ideal. I couldn't be seen by cars or people in their homes.

What did I wish for this morning? Oh. "I wish this car would fly to the airport!" Navy-blue metallic wings sprouted from the doors. I noted I now had four wings with four doors.

They began flapping, like two gigantic bluebirds. With four wheels. Jeff and Megan gasped. That felt good. "Believe me now?"

"How can you fly this thing? It's just a minivan," Jeff said.

"I got an hour of practice with my car this morning."

We soared over I-90. I veered southwest toward Hopkins Airport.

"Watch this." I wished the instrument panel into an aircraft panel.

"I saw it change!" Megan said.

"I can see we're flying, but I don't know how. Minivans aren't exactly aerodynamic."

"Neither are bumblebees, Jeff."

Our speed hit two hundred and kept climbing. Blue blurs and a deep drone were all we could see of our wings. We sounded like a giant dragonfly.

Jeff leaned in between me and Megan from the back seat. "All right. I guess seeing is believing. This is really cool, Mom, but I'm a little nervous. What if we run out of gas?"

I glanced at the gas gauge. We had less than a quarter tank. "It doesn't matter. I flew from Paradise to Phoenix and didn't use any gas."

"That seems to violate the laws of physics," Jeff said.

"Ya think? Maybe because it's magic!" I began singing, "It's magic! You know! Never believe it's not so!" That got a chuckle out of Megan.

"Isn't that one of the old songs from the seventies? I love learning about pop history from you, Mom."

"I listened to that when I was in my twenties."

Megan looked up from her phone. "That's from 1974."

"Yup. I was twenty-eight then."

"This is fantastic, Mom! I wonder what else you can do with magic? Say, what if we hired out our car as an Urber?"

Megan burst out laughing.

"So tell me about this Urber business. Isn't that just a taxi?" I glanced at Jeff and then said to the car, "Go on autopilot back to their home."

"It's not exactly a taxi. Each driver runs his or her business with their own car. You'd use this app on your phone." Jeff showed me his Urber app on his cell phone.

"That'd be fun, with a flying car. We could even advertise it as eco-sensitive and carbon-free. Megan, would you mind if I used your car?"

"Sure. I don't need it during the day. But, Mom, how would you explain a flying car to people?"

"I'd be like Mary Poppins. I wouldn't explain anything."

"Okay, Mom. I sent you the link to sign up for Urber."

Megan looked at me.

"I'll get on it when I get home. I don't want to be on my phone while I'm driving—or flying." I kept my phone in the cupholder when driving.

"I wonder if this magic is related to all of the fires breaking out on politicians?" Jeff said.

"Could be. I wouldn't be the only one wishing for some politicians to catch on fire."

Chapter 12 – Sagittarius

Tuesday, October 6

I felt clean and full of energy. I struggled not to speed to work until I hit the traffic. While I waited in line behind a semi, I reviewed my wacky dream. The Earth rotated daily. Could that be the cause of the variability in the fire effect?

When at my desk, I downloaded the latest data and correlated the phenomenon with the time of day worldwide. I finished entering the starting time and ending time of the effects at each location around the world. I displayed it on a world map and ran the data in a time sequence.

I flashed a red dot when the fire effect showed up. I flashed a green dot when it ceased. I saw a line of red dots begin on the East Coast of the US at about one in the afternoon. It swept across the US, up the coast of Canada, and into Alaska. Then Hawaii, Samoa, Tahiti, New Zealand, and Australia flashed red. Meanwhile, green dots appeared on the East Coast and slowly spread westward.

Japan, China, Southeast Asia, and India turned red as the green line marched across North America. The red line marched across Europe and Africa and then paused before it hit the east of Brazil and then back across America.

"Well, that looks like a global phenomenon coming from outer space. Now, where's it coming from?"

I located the center of the phenomenon as the effect went around the world. Then I called Misty Alcorn, a specialist in astrophysics. We'd met as undergraduates at Case Western Reserve University. We'd hit it off immediately and finished our senior year rooming together off campus in an apartment on Murray Hill. She'd majored in astronomy, and I in physics.

"Hi, Misty."

"Hi, Katie. Let me put you on video. I haven't heard from you since spring."

"Yeah, I've been busy. Oh wow, you cut your hair. It's so curly!" Misty's auburn hair made a reddish halo about her head.

Her blue eyes looked into my brown ones.

"I got it permed when I cut it. Just a different look."

"How's life as a young astronomer?"

"Oh, it's looking up. What's new with you?"

"I got an emergency assignment from the president to look into this pants-on-fire phenomenon."

"I've been following that on social media. Some of the clips are pretty funny. Did you see the one about the weather reporter whose skirt blew up when she said, 'I'm sure it'll be sunny tomorrow'?"

"Uh, no. I try to stay off social media. It's too distracting."

"When you're waiting for a computer to compare telescope photos at three a.m., that keeps you from going crazy. Speaking of crazy, tell me about your assignment."

"I have to find out what's causing it and how to prevent the fires. It's completely disrupted all levels of the government."

"Huh. I didn't know that. You could never tell from here in Arizona."

"The cause is when you broadcast any lie, your pants—or pantyhose or skirts—catch on fire."

Misty laughed. "That explains the various influencers who videoed themselves catching on fire. I thought it was just a stupid prank."

"This is where you come in, Misty. It's a worldwide effect, and it seems to follow the rotation of Earth."

"What do you mean?"

"The effect comes and goes depending upon the orientation of Earth. One-half of the globe is affected at a time."

"Ah, I get it. You think this is an extraterrestrial effect."

"It's my working theory. I've got a database of the effects and their timing worldwide. It peaks at a certain point and affects the whole hemisphere of Earth at that time."

"I'd love to look at your data."

"I figured you would. You always were a data nerd. That's why I called you. Is your email still spacecadet2001@cwru.edu?"

"Yes. Do you still have your CWRU email?"

"Yeah, but I don't use it. I have a .gov one. I'll send you a link to my online folder. Can you identify the potential extraterrestrial sources for this phenomenon?"

"I sure can, at least some of them. We've got a whole galaxy out there. I'll start with the closest sources."

"I'd be happy with a general direction."

"Okay. I've got your email. And now I've got your database. This'll take some time. I've got some work here at the observatory."

"You're at the Kitt Peak Observatory in Arizona, right?"

"Yeah. You caught me before I went to sleep. I've got the night-shift work. I'll take a look at your database after I get up this evening."

"Sounds good."

After we hung up, I perused the data that had come in overnight. There were a lot of new data points, especially in Asia and Africa. Politicians in the Americas and Europe were still the focus of fire departments everywhere.

Major businesses had taken to employing small groups of firefighters to follow behind certain employees and spray them down with fire extinguishers. Public relations, customer service, and executives got the most attention. Most people had adapted to this fire hazard and learned to live with it.

However, some political leaders still scoffed and sniffed at the idea they'd catch on fire—until they did.

"It's not like I haven't documented this to the president and the news media." I shook my head.

Washington, DC, was still the epicenter of self-conflagration. Small groups of firefighters were kept busy around the clock every time the House or Senate met. Certain politicians hired personal firefighters when they traveled. They especially needed them when campaigning for office.

The party or affiliation didn't matter, for politicians' pants or skirts were constantly bursting into flame.

I smiled as I read about a voters' group that documented political immolations. They used this to compile voting guides for each party. *So something good is coming out of this.*

I also had hundreds of emails asking me to look into other phenomena. There were too many to read. I quickly skimmed the subjects. A pink dragon sighting in Chicago? *No. Just no.* Flying cars? *Where do these people come from?*

Now here was something. A family in Toledo claimed to have started the whole pants-on-fire epidemic.

"This'll be good." I smirked as I read the email.

"Huh. They just wished for it? That's so simple that it's frightening. I hope that's *not* true. How *could* it be true, when it looks like the phenomenon comes from outer space? I'd better contact them and get the straight story. Reporter Shelley Clarke, WNWO, TV 24 in Toledo." I called the number.

"Hello? WNWO TV 24, how can I help you?"

"I'd like to speak with Reporter Shelley Clarke."

"That's me."

"Please tell me all about this family who 'wished' politicians' pants would catch on fire if they lied."

"Yes. Feeling guilty, a father and a son came to me and told me they had wished this just before the governor candidates' debate two days ago."

"I find that hard to believe. I'd like to talk to them directly."

"I have to protect my sources' anonymity."

"I'm running an investigation on this phenomenon at the direction of President Lopez. I need to talk to them."

"Oh, I'll check with them and see if they want to talk to you. Give me five minutes and I'll call you back at this number."

"Okay."

How could this be? Why would someone claim anything so bizarre? I puzzled over these questions, when my phone rang.

"Hello?"

"Katie Garcia?"

"Yes."

"I'm Phil Kennedy, the father of Sean Kennedy. I'm married to Shirley. We were watching the news Sunday when we all wished that politicians' pants would catch on fire if they lied. Then it happened."

"Did you do some incantation or invoke some demon?"

"No, it was just a silly wish."

"I hate to do this, but I'll have to come to Toledo and conduct some experiments. Where can we meet?"

"You can come to our house. What time will you meet us?"

"I can get there tonight. Any time tomorrow. What's your address?"

He gave it to me, and I called and booked my flight.

I barely slept. If it was just a mistake, a lucky coincidence, then I just wasted a flight and a few thousand dollars of the government's money. But if it really matched up? What then? What could I do? I didn't know my next step.

And how would either prove or disprove this theory? I fell asleep thinking about possible experiments.

* * *

Wednesday, October 7

My alarm woke me to catch the 6:00 a.m. flight from Oakridge to Toledo. I hopped onto the commuter plane, and we left right on time. I fell asleep immediately, since I'd barely slept. I didn't wake up when we landed in Charlotte for a stopover.

I awoke before we landed in Detroit, feeling inexplicably positive. Somehow I felt I'd get to the bottom of this mystery.

I took my carry-on luggage from the bin and rented a car. I turned on the GPS app and added in the Kennedys' address in Southwyck, a suburb of Toledo.

"Fifty-six miles? Not bad. Fifty-four minutes? I bet I can beat that." I set off to do just that. Once on I-275, I opened it up.

I pulled into the Kennedys' driveway forty-five minutes later. "Good job, Katie!" I felt smug and even more positive about how this would turn out.

I knocked on the front door, and a broad-shouldered man of about forty answered. He smiled, and his brown eyes crinkled. "You must be Katie Garcia. You got here faster than I expected. I'm Phil Kennedy. C'mon in."

I pulled my travel bag in with me. I seated myself on the sofa, while Phil sat on an easy chair. "I got here as quickly as I could. I left first thing this morning from Oakridge. If your explanation can be proven, then my project is complete."

"Huh. I'm not sure how you can prove this. It just happened."

"Yeah, that's what I've been thinking about since I read Shelley's email. That's why I brought this."

I opened my travel bag and took out my fireproof

underwear and a pack of cheap skirts I'd bought at a discount store. "Here are the tools of my trade—at least for this project."

"Uh, clothing?"

"Clothing is essential for testing bursting into flames. Do you have a fireproof area around your house or yard?"

"Sure. We can put you in or next to the firepit in the backyard. That's all stone and brick."

"Great. Let me get dressed."

"I'll call Sean." Phil went downstairs while I went to the bathroom to change.

I went out the back door to the yard, wearing my long insulated underwear under my pink polyester skirt. They clashed. The things I did for science. I sighed.

Phil smirked when he saw me, while Sean, a slender middle schooler, gaped at me. Phil covered his mouth and cleared his throat.

I ignored their reactions. "Okay, here's what we'll do. First, I'll test to make sure the phenomenon happens as usual. I'll read some political speeches that led to fiery outbursts."

I read from my phone. "'As your candidate for Congress, I promise to undo all the policies of my predecessor, who was a miserable failure.'" Naturally, my skirt blazed into flame and melted into a gooey black mess on my underwear. At least it didn't clash anymore.

"You okay?" Sean asked as he eyed the smoking ruins dripping down my gray insulation.

"Yeah. I'm used to this by now. That was a success. We've verified the phenomenon still is in effect. Now, on to experiment two."

I pulled out another skirt, a purple-and-green plaid. I saw why they had been on sale as I pulled the cheap fabric over my underwear.

"What's the next experiment?" Phil asked.

"Just wish that this doesn't happen to me. Even when I lie, wish that my skirt doesn't catch on fire. You and Sean were the two wishing, right?"

"Right. Sean, why don't you do the wish, like you did the first time?"

"Uh, okay. Let me think about what I said." He frowned.

"Wouldn't it be great if Katie's pants *didn't* catch on fire if she lied?"

Phil furrowed his brows. "Yes! I'd love that!"

Sean smiled. "That's what I wish for then."

I scrolled to the next political speech. "'I guarantee my economic policies will lead to an economic turnaround—'" I didn't even finish the sentence before my green-and-purple plaid flamed up.

It quickly burned itself out, leaving a greasy black stain on my underwear.

"Huh. I'm sorry, Ms. Garcia. I thought this'd work."

I sighed, looking at my scuzzy underwear. "Me too. This was the only experiment I thought of that could verify that it was your wish that did this."

"Hmm." Phil rubbed his chin. "We didn't quite replicate our wish." He turned and ran into the house.

"What's different, Sean?"

"All I can think of is—"

"Ta-da! Here she is! Our last wisher, Shirley Kennedy!" A slender woman in jeans and a blouse followed Phil.

"Okay, someone tell me what's going on. Why is our visitor standing in the backyard wearing dirty underwear?"

"It's simple, Mrs. Kennedy—"

"Call me Shirley."

"Surely. We tried to undo your wish about setting pants on fire for just me. Phil and Sean wished it wouldn't happen to me—but it did. Now I'm down to my last skirt, and we want to replicate the original wish—of which you were a part. An essential part, it seems."

"Okay. So we just wish like we did the other night?" She put her hands on her hips.

"Yup. Right after I pull this on." A red-and-green monstrosity went over my hips. It was too small and fit like a miniskirt.

"Let's try this again. Sean?" Phil looked at his son.

"Wouldn't it be great if Katie's pants *didn't* catch on fire if she lied?" He spoke like he was reading a script.

"Yes! I'd love that!" Phil looked his wife.

"Katie wouldn't catch on fire then." Shirley looked at me

expectantly.

"Next speech." I focused on my phone. "'I promise the fine citizens of this city that the tax increase will be used to improve your schools and police force.'"

The skirt remained on my hips in all its ugliness.

I continued to read the speech. "'And furthermore, if elected mayor, I'll root out corruption and inefficiency.'"

Phil grinned. "And there'll be a chicken in every pot."

His pants burst into flame.

I quickly put them out with my portable fire extinguisher. I never conducted pants-on-fire experiments without it.

"Whew! Thanks, Katie. I'd better put another pair of pants on." He ran into the house in his heart-covered boxer shorts.

"You're looking a little thread*bare*," Shirley called after him, grinning at his retreating derriere.

"Surely I bared my soul for science!" Phil called from the door.

"Is that what you call it?" Shirley laughed.

I chuckled.

"Wow," Sean said. "This was the first time I saw the pants-on-fire effect in person. I see why you wear that underwear, Ms. Garcia."

"Call me Katie. Ms. Garcia is my mother. I'm only thirty." I sat down on the patio furniture and typed on my tablet.

"What are you typing?" Sean asked.

"My observations and conclusions. We needed all three of you to undo the wish all three of you had made. It worked on me but not on Phil, so this wasn't just a coincidence. Now, I'd like all three of you to wish this away worldwide."

"I don't think that'll work," Shirley said.

"Why not?" I looked at her, puzzled.

"I don't want to undo the effect. I want everyone to tell the truth. I think Phil does too."

"I want what too?" Phil asked as he came back wearing blue jeans.

"You want everyone to tell the truth."

"Yeah, I do. At least our politicians."

"And I don't know if I could truthfully wish this away either," Sean said. "I *like* seeing liars burst into flame."

“Even me?” Phil asked his son.

“Well, no, of course not, Dad. But you weren’t really lying—you were just quoting a political promise.”

“Like I was,” I said. “I didn’t really believe what I was saying, but the fact I said it to other people activated this wish of yours. Let me get all this down.” I resumed typing.

“Are we going to get into trouble for starting this?”

“I don’t think so. People won’t believe me or you. No one can be prosecuted for wishing. But you bring up a good question—what should I say to my boss? We found the cause of the problem but can’t undo it. Let me think about how to put lipstick on this pig.”

I paused quietly. Everyone looked at me. “Okay. This phenomenon, once activated, cannot easily be undone. I burned myself trying to undo it. Only a second combined effort by you three removed the effect on one person. No one would expect you to do this on each person around the world.” I typed that up. “That’s what I’ll report.”

Phil smiled. “I’ll wish you don’t get into trouble.”

“Nor us,” Shirley added.

“Me too,” Sean said.

I finished typing. “Sounds like we’re locked in for success, based on your earlier wish.”

My phone rang. It showed Misty Alcorn. “Hi, Katie. Boy oh boy, that dataset you sent me was fascinating.”

“So what’s the bottom line? Do you have any results?”

“Do I have results for you! Your worldwide effect comes from Sagittarius.”

“Any particular star or nebula?” I knew a cloud of gas was within that constellation.

“Yes. I can trace it on a direct path to the galactic core, to the black hole there.”

“So what does that mean?”

“This worldwide effect probably comes from the middle of the galaxy, possibly some emanation from the accretion disk of the black hole.”

“Was there any kind of flare-up from the black hole?”

“We can’t really see it in normal light. We can detect gravitational waves and radio waves, as well as infrared.

Nothing showed up on infrared, radio, or gravitational."

"How would we prove this is the source?"

"We have to detect some radiation from there that started last Monday. I'm checking through the data from observatories and satellites around the world. I even checked the gravimetric sensor in Antarctica, but nothing so far."

"Thanks, Misty, for trying. But this doesn't really prove anything."

"Other than an extraterrestrial source from the direction of Sagittarius."

"Or an unrelated coincidence."

"I'm sure it's not."

"Prove it, Misty."

"You're on."

Chapter 13 - Writing

Tuesday, October 6

"Now what?" Jane looked at me expectantly as we left the news station.

"I think I'll write the book I've always wanted to write."

"Science fiction, if I remember correctly?"

"No, it ought to be fantasy."

"How is that connected to us being treated like two senile coots by the news station?"

"This way I'll get the news out about our magical powers without being called a kook."

"That might work. But you don't have any experience writing fiction."

"Huh. I wrote executive reports as a project manager. That's half fiction. And I've read hundreds of sci-fi and fantasy novels. I've always wanted to write a novel."

She laughed. "I love you, you nut. But why don't you write sci-fi, since that's your favorite?" We piled into our car.

"I don't see how I can write sci-fi about all this bizarre magical stuff that's happened to us. It's got to be based on science. I know you read a lot of fantasy, and I've read some. It seems it'd be easier to write if I didn't have to worry about any rules."

"I have some good ideas for your book. And so does the news. Haven't you read about all the people with their pants catching on fire?"

"I avoid the news. It's too depressing. How were their pants catching on fire?"

"They were lying. Listen to this story." Jane picked up her phone and began reading. "'Mayor Beauregard had told his security detail, "Please don't send the personal fire brigade again," before his latest speech.

"'"Are you sure, sir?" His security guard said. He looked worried. "They come highly recommended."

"'"I'm positive!" the mayor snapped. He straightened his

lapels and combed his flowing hair. "I can handle myself."' That's quite a story, wouldn't you say? At the news conference, Mayor Beauregard had just said 'There is no need to worry about inflation' when his trousers burst into flames. His aide doused him with a pitcher of ice water, and he was out a pair of trousers."

I smiled. "Exciting. I like just desserts."

"Don't you see, Jake? This is just like our walking teacups."

"Um, no. How are they connected?"

"Obviously someone wished this to happen."

"I don't see how you got there, but I can imagine someone wishing that on politicians."

"Oh, it's more than politicians. Lawyers, newscasters PR reps, and news commentators have also been set ablaze."

"Maybe I need to read some news. No sense in writing fantasy if it's already fact."

"Or you can extend the news stories into the realm of fantasy."

"I like how you think! If I exaggerate things enough, they'll become funny. Funny fantasy is my favorite!"

Back at home, I researched weird things in the news. There were a lot of them. Someone claimed to have seen a flying pink dragon in Chicago. A guy on Viewtube said his dog talked to him and could read. A minivan was seen in Cleveland with four flapping wings. Then there were hundreds of people bursting into flame. And that was just in the US.

Worldwide, China said dragons had appeared and were ravaging the country. Ireland was overrun with leprechauns, while fairies romped in England. Djinns appeared in the Middle East. It seemed almost too much to write about.

But even worse was, I wasn't sure how I could exaggerate the news any more than it already was. I wrote all the things I had read about, trying to brainstorm. Then I went one step beyond. What if politicians told the truth? No one would believe that was real. How would diplomacy happen? "I've got it! Eureka!"

"What are you yelling about?" Jane asked as she brought a cup of coffee into my office.

Our Victorian home had a corner tower. The first floor had

a round room for a reading nook, with bookshelves and a dark-green velvet bench following the curved wall. The second floor held my office, with my computer and a desk. The three tower windows looked out at our oak tree and the street.

I'd toyed with the idea of remodeling our porch roof into a second-story balcony from our bedroom. We could then have a walkway to the tree and build a treehouse. Maybe someday.

"Are you going to answer me? Why were you yelling?"

"Oh, I was woolgathering, thinking about making a tree house. I have the fantasy theme for my novel: a world where politicians tell the truth."

"Wow, that'd be fantasy all right. I like it. I can hardly wait to read it."

"I can hardly wait to write it." I kissed her. "Thanks for the coffee."

"When can I bother you again?" Jane said with a smile.

"Anytime, of course."

"How about after the cinnamon rolls are done? It'll be an hour."

"I'm sure I'll be hungry by then. I should have the first chapter done."

"Ready. Set. Go!" Jane ran out of the room.

Chapter 14 – Caught

Monday, October 5

"Mom! Could Lamar and I go to the beach with Pinkie? Do you wanna come?" I said to Mom after supper.

"No, honey, I'm too tired from work. We were missing some stockers, and I had to pick and place a lot of merchandise. Those dog food bags are heavy! You two go and have fun." Mom looked outside. The sun set earlier each day. "It looks dark enough. You should be able to hide. Take off from the roof. That's safer than climbing out the window."

"Will do! C'mon, Pinkie!" I grabbed my stuffed dragon. He stayed asleep until I woke him up.

"I'll race you up the stairs, Shayla!"

"No way! I'll take the elevator."

"I'll beat you!" Lamar ran into the stairwell.

I punched the button. "Hurry up, you stupid elevator." Finally it arrived, and I punched the top floor. I hit the Close Door button over and over to make it close faster.

When the door opened again, Lamar appeared, panting and grinning. "I beat you!" he crowed.

"You beat the elevator. It's so slow."

"Yeah, it's old. Mom grew up here, and she says it's the same as when she was a kid."

"Wow. That's old."

We walked onto the roof. I felt its warmth from the day, but the breeze made my cheeks cold. I was glad I wore my jacket. I put Pinkie on the gravel. "Wake up, Pinkie!"

He grew to the size of a small dog and looked at me. "I need a hug to grow more."

"Sure, Pinkie!" I squeezed him hard. "I like hugs too."

"They help me grow, especially your hugs, Shayla." He grew to the size of a horse. He lowered his long neck so we could climb on his back.

"Hey, Pinkie, does my hug help you grow?" Lamar leaned forward and squeezed his neck.

Pinkie grew to the size of a rhino. I saw one in the zoo once.

"Thanks, Lamar! Yes, the more hugs, the better!" He flapped his wings, and we rose in a swirling cloud of dust and gravel.

"I love takeoffs the best!" I yelled.

"I love landings. It feels like an elevator dropping," Lamar said.

"And I love flying above the clouds, looking at the moon and stars," Pinkie said. "Where to, children?"

"The beach!" we said together.

* * *

I looked up from the TV and saw a pink dragon take off from the apartment building across the street.

"What in the world?" I jumped up and opened the sliding door to our balcony. It circled above the building and then began climbing. I pulled my phone from my pocket and took a video of it. I tracked it until it disappeared into a cloud.

"I can't believe this." I replayed the video. The pink dragon flapped from the building to the cloud. It seemed to have two figures on its neck. "Oh wow. Hey, Maria! Come here!"

My roommate, Maria Chen, walked into the room, chewing a taco. She swallowed. "These fish tacos are to die for!"

"Tell me what you think of this video." I showed her my phone.

"Huh. Hey, is that the building across the street? Are they filming a movie over there, or are you prankin' me?"

"Neither. I happened to see a dragon across the street and took this video."

"C'mon. I know you're prankin'. How'd you do it?"

"This is my phone. I stuck it up to the window and pressed the Record button one minute ago."

"Send the video to my computer. I'll prove it's a fake."

I walked into Maria's room behind her. "I know what I saw."

"Yeah yeah, tell me all about it. I'll catch you red-handed, McQueen." Maria turned on her computer and opened her email. "Okay, here's your email and your video. Let's play it and look for editing."

The video played on the thirty-two-inch curved monitor in

slow motion.

"Looks pretty good, McQueen. I've got to give you credit for a good job. Pretty good for an education major."

"So you believe me?"

"Nah. It's probably a deepfake you did by AI. Let's take this still of the pink dragon and do a reverse image search on it." Her hands flew over the keyboard.

"What's a 'deepfake'?"

"It's a well-edited video that's hard to prove it's fake. They're usually generated by AI, artificial intelligence."

"How could I have done that?"

"There are dozens of sites that'll take your input data and make any kind of video you want. Ah, what do we have here?" A page of pink dragon images came up on her screen.

"Which of these look like your dragon?"

"Um, this one, I'm pretty sure."

"Let's see—yep, ninety-eight percent match on your image! Very good. You can buy this stuffed animal for thirty dollars. So I'd say you bought this stuffed animal, took a picture of it and a video of the apartment across the street, and put them together using an AI site."

"I don't even know how to do that! I'm not a geek like you!"

"That's why it's such a good fake. I'd never guess you could do that, Heather."

She used my first name, which meant she was really serious. I glanced out the window. "If you're so sure of yourself, look outside and explain how *that's* a deepfake."

Maria gaped out the window. Across the street a pink dragon landed on the roof of the apartment. Two little kids jumped off, and then the dragon disappeared. One kid ran down the stairs into the apartment.

"Let's go! We've got to investigate this!"

"But I've got homework to grade." Maria dragged me out the door.

The air chilled me with the breeze. "I'm cold. Let me go back and get my jacket."

"Toughen up, McQueen. We'll be in the apartment in a minute."

"You're jaywalking!"

"It's okay as long as you don't get caught. How long have you lived in Chicago?"

We went into the building and to the elevator. "You know that. I'm going on my fourth year here at Xavier."

"Yeah, sometimes I forget you're a corn-fed farm girl."

"Hey. Those are fighting words!" I flexed a big bicep at her, looming over her in the elevator.

"You're only fun if I can get you mad at me. We're on the top floor. Let's see what we find on the roof. Hurry!" Maria sprinted to the stairs.

I followed her.

In the stairwell we found a kid running up the stairs with a picnic basket. "Hey! You! Are you goin' to the roof?"

"Uh, yeah. Do you have some problem with that?"

"No, we've never been there before. We'll follow you." I smiled at the kid. He looked about twelve and wore a hoodie. Maria and I often played good cop, bad cop. She had the mouth, and I had the bulk. It worked on the streets of Chicago.

We tromped up the stairs. With a floor to go, the kid took off the last flight and burst through the door. "Shayla! We've got company!"

We came out right behind him. We saw a little girl in pigtails, maybe five, holding a pink stuffed dragon. It looked exactly like what Maria had found on the internet.

"Hi, kid. I like that dragon. Where'd you get it?" Maria advanced on the girl.

"My mommy gave it to me for my birthday! You stay away or I'll—"

"Or you'll what?"

I shook my head. Maria had all the tact of a cobra.

"I'll have Pinkie eat you!" She squeezed the dragon, and it popped out of her arms like it was alive. Then it grew to elephant size. Then dragon size.

"E-e-e-e-e!" Maria screamed, spun around, and fell, still scrambling backward across the roof.

"We're sorry, kid! We saw your dragon from across the street and couldn't believe our eyes. Now we believe it! Don't let it hurt us." I picked Maria up off the ground and faced the dragon.

Its head loomed four feet above us, with its mouth open, ready to bite us. Its warm breath smelled sweet, like a candy shop.

"How do I know you won't hurt me?" She sounded as skeptical as Maria.

"Hey, Shayla, just have Pinkie eat them, like those gang members. No muss, no fuss." The boy seemed eager.

"Nah, that wouldn't be right. That woman scared me. Now she's scared."

"You got that right, kid." Maria stared up at the gaping maw over us, like a pink awning.

"C'mon, Shayla. Don't hurt us. Your dragon scared us—now we're even. We'll leave you and go home." I knelt next to Maria on the graveled roof. "Please."

"Okay. Do you promise to leave us alone and not tell anyone? Cross your hearts and hope to die?" Shayla said.

"Stick a needle in your eye?" Lamar added.

"Cross our hearts and hope to die, stick a needle in our eye." We held our hands over our hearts.

"I don't think we can trust them, Shayla," Lamar said.

"Pinkie, can you make them keep their word?"

The dragon straightened up. "I can't, but you can Shayla. You're the magician."

"All right. I wish you can't tell *anyone* about me or Lamar or Pinkie, and you can't ever hurt us. EVER!"

I felt weird and tingly all over my body.

"Ew," Maria said. "That's like going down a steep roller coaster."

"That's my little magician!" The dragon (Pinkie?) said. He clapped his forelegs together, shrank, and hugged Shayla.

"Let's test them, Shayla," Lamar said. "What did you see on the roof tonight?"

"Uh, we saw y . . . y . . . y . . . uh." I struggled.

"And the dr . . . dr . . . dr . . . thing," Maria finished.

"What's our name?" Shayla had her hands on her hips.

"L . . ., er, sh . . . uh, I can't say," I said.

"I never saw you before," Maria said.

"I think we're good here Shayla." Lamar looked at Shayla.

"Go home. And don't be so nosy." Shayla pointed to the staircase.

The dragon grew to full size. Shayla and Lamar climbed onto its back, and it took off.

We watched it go into the clouds. Just before it entered the cloud, it vanished.

Maria looked at me. "I'm going to quit drinking and smoking pot."

"I'm going to start."

Chapter 15 – Wishes

Wednesday, October 7

I followed the news closely, and I read all I could about Katie Garcia, including her report on a Washington, DC, news site. It was just as she said. They'd found the cause of the fires but no easy method to stop them. The report said, "The fires are an unintentional side effect of a family and some unknown radiation from outer space."

She wasn't on Friendbook or Why (y.com). I couldn't find anything else about her. I found her on LinkedUp, but she hadn't updated her page for four years, ever since she started at Oakridge National Labs.

I sighed. She was good looking and smart. I knew I wanted to see her again. I didn't care she was eighteen years older. But how?

Clueless, I turned to my homework. History was my least favorite subject. I had to write a paper about Watergate, due tomorrow. I knew the basic facts, but I didn't want to write the paper. But if I didn't turn it in, I'd blow my chance for an A.

How could I write this in the least painful way possible? If Katie were here, I could do it. Hey, I could wish her here! But that'd be too aggressive and wreck her day and probably ruin her experiment. She wouldn't like that at all.

But I could experiment with wishes and report that to her. She'd given us her card with her Oakridge email address. I'd make wishes and tell her the results.

"Here goes! I wish I'd want to do the history report and that I'll get an A on it." Saying it out loud seemed important. I jotted down the wish and the results on my phone. I actually *did* want to write the paper now, just to prove the wish worked.

I started typing on my laptop.

* * *

Thursday, October 8

"Wow, good job, Sean! You got an A on your history report." Mom looked through the papers I brought home from school.

"Good job, son." Dad smiled at me from his recliner.

"Thanks, Mom and Dad." I sat down on the living room couch. I felt guilty getting the results through wishing. I hadn't only gotten an A in history, but I had perfect records in math, science, and English as well. All done with wishing.

"What's the matter, son? You look concerned."

I had to tell them. "Um, I had some help."

"What? Did a friend help you?" Mom asked.

"Uh, no. I wished for an A."

"Did you do the work?" Dad asked.

"Yeah, I typed it up yesterday. It seemed really easy. But I feel guilty about using wishes."

"What exactly did you wish?" Mom asked.

"That I'd want to write the paper. And that I'd get an A."

"But you did the research and the writing yourself?" Dad said.

"Yes."

"That sounds fine to me. You used the wish to motivate yourself." Mom patted me.

"You did all the work. I don't see a problem." Dad crossed his arms and shrugged.

"It's not only history. I've gotten only perfect scores in math, science, and English since last week."

"You wished for A's in those subjects too?" Dad said.

"Yeah. Perfect scores. I wanted to make you proud."

"We're already proud of you, son. You already had A's in science and math and a B in English," Mom said.

"I'm on my way to straight A's."

"But you're doing all the work," Dad said.

"It still feels like cheating."

"You're not looking up the answers on the tests, are you?" Mom looked at me.

"No, I just know them."

"With or without reading the book or hearing the teacher?" Dad raised his eyebrows.

"Um, I don't know. Everything just makes sense. The answer seems obvious."

"I guess I want to know—are the answers just popping into your head, or are you recalling them? If you're remembering things you read or heard, then I see no problem. If the answers are just appearing from nowhere, then I don't know what to think. That's magic."

"Like pants catching on fire," I said. "I can't think of any case of me knowing an answer I hadn't heard of before. I'll look for that."

"Thanks for telling us, Sean." Mom put her hand on my shoulder. "I'm proud that you shared your worry with us."

"I was just feeling kind of fake. You were praising me, and I didn't feel I deserved it."

"Ah. Imposter syndrome." My mom nodded.

"What's that?"

"Artists, authors, and other professionals get that feeling. That they're not real, they're faking their career."

"That fits. I don't feel really smart. I'm imitating it."

"But, son, you really are smart," my dad said.

"And you've always been." Mom hugged me.

"We've always known it. You're just maximizing your potential. It might even be a placebo effect."

"What? I don't know that term either." I frowned at Dad.

"It's when you believe something will work, a pill or a technique, and it does. The result isn't connected to the pill or technique but the belief. It's a real effect, real enough that doctors will use it on patients."

"Huh. Maybe I'm too hard on myself."

Dad nodded. "That fits. I'm hard on myself and Mom is hard on herself. It makes sense you'd have the same tendency."

"Okay. Thanks a lot. I feel better. I'll just keep on what I'm doing, wishing my way to perfection."

"Why'd you start doing that, anyway?" Mom tilted her head at me.

"Well, I wanted to document the effects of wishing for Katie Garcia. I kind of like her."

"Of course! I should have known there was a girl behind this!" Dad threw his arms in the air.

"Phil! She's a grown woman, not a girl! Sean, she's way older than you."

"A man's gotta have a dream." I grinned at her.

Mom threw her hands in the air.

Later, I typed up the results of my grade wishing and sent it to Katie. Maybe she'd email me back.

Chapter 16 – Viral

Tuesday, October 6

I woke up before Master and went out my doggy door to pee. A raccoon had been in our yard, and I peed on its scat. After scruffing the grass, I trotted back inside and jumped on my master's bed. He didn't mind when I did that in the morning. I curled up next to him.

He moaned. "Is it six a.m. already?" He turned on his phone and groaned again. "I'd better get moving. Wait. What's this?" He peered at his glowing phone. "One thousand nine hundred and eighty-three notices from Viewtube? What's going on?"

I knew that was a big number, much bigger than three or even ten. I couldn't understand why Master cared about big numbers. But that was why he was the master and I was the dog. He fed me, played with me, and petted me. What more could I want?

"Spot! Those are comments on our video! We've got over a hundred thousand views! We're famous!"

Master smelled excited. "That's great!" I barked. "What does 'famous' mean?"

"That means a lot of people know us and like us."

"Oh," I whined. "So does that mean we'll get food and toys?"

"You bet! Let's see how this has monetized." He poked his forepaw at the phone. "So somewhere around five hundred dollars so far. That's enough dog food for a year."

"Wow!" I barked.

"Not so loud. But it might be more. We don't know how many views we'll end up with. It's just been over twelve hours now. Let's have breakfast."

I had my morning dog food, which filled the hole in my stomach. Master's food smelled better—bacon. I whined until he gave me a piece. Then I licked his plate.

"You know, for the world's smartest dog, you still act like a dog." Master looked down at me.

"I *am* a dog," I barked proudly.

“Crap, we’re already over a hundred and fifty thousand views. Let’s get to the HossFit gym and see if it brought in any real customers.”

“Right.” I wagged as I followed him to the car.

A line of people waiting to get in greeted us when we got there at seven.

“Sorry to keep you waiting, folks!” Master opened the door.

“Is that Spot? Ooh, could I pet him?”

“Sure.”

A female ran up to me and rubbed my ears. She was a new customer. I hadn’t smelled her before.

“She’s new,” I barked to Master.

“A lot of you are new here. Let’s get you registered.” A line formed at Master’s office.

“Yeah, I saw your video with your dog. I wanted to get into shape. You’re right in town, so I thought I’d check you out,” a man said as he swiped his credit card.

“Me too,” said the woman who’d petted me. “I brought my boyfriend along. He didn’t believe me or the video.”

“I’ll join too if your dog does something smart.” He crossed his arms over his chest and looked aggressively at me and my master.

“Sure. Spot, go out and bring the sign with ‘Food’ on it from yesterday.”

I gripped it in my teeth and dropped it at the desk.

“That was probably luck. Bring a sign without the word ‘Food’ on it.”

“Spot, go get another sign.”

I got the “Good” sign and dropped it at the man’s feet.

“Hmm. So you can fetch signs. But can you read them?” He laughed.

“Food!” I barked at the first one, and I made sure he understood me.

“Good!” I pawed the other one and looked at the man.

His mouth hung open. “Squee! He *talks*!”

His girlfriend squealed. All the people in the office were talking at once.

“I guess I have to sign up. I understood his barks. That’s a new one for me.”

"I knew you'd believe it if you saw the dog, Chet."

"You're right, Thelma. I'll get my money back."

"How?"

"I'll bet with Leroy and Fred about this dog. They love to bet and will fall for it."

The new members signed up, and Master began training them in basic HossFit exercises.

New people entered all day, and they never failed to pet me. I showed off my talking and reading to them. We closed up at seven that night, and I jumped into the car.

"Let's go and celebrate, Spot. Do you want a hamburger, chicken sandwich, or fish fillet?"

We pulled up to the food building. "You mean to eat with you?" I yipped doubtfully.

"Yeah. You've brought in almost half a million views on Viewtube, and we have fifty new members. We're in the money, Spot! You can have whatever you want."

I sniffed the great smells coming from the food place. "Let me have the fish!" My bark rang loudly in the car, but Josh just laughed.

"One fish fillet for you and a double Quarter Pounder with cheese for me."

"Cheese for me too!"

"Okay."

The next day another line of people blocked the door, even longer than the day before.

"Whoa, I'm going to have to hire someone to sign up the new people." Master looked at me.

I waited for him.

"Or I could train you. Just watch me and repeat what I say."

We went into the office and motioned for the members-to-be to gather round. "Okay, I'm training my new employee here, Spot."

Everyone laughed.

"Say hi, Spot."

"Hi," I barked.

Heads snapped toward me. "Did he say hi?"

"He sure did."

"I think you're just imagining it."

"Not all of us."

"Yes, Spot makes himself understood when he barks. Now, pay here by passing your credit card through the reader. Repeat that, Spot."

It didn't make much sense to me, but I yipped, "Pass your credit card through the reader."

People gasped. But Master said, "Good boy, Spot."

"After you've paid, put your name and email address down on this list, and indicate which session you'll join. We close at seven p.m. Repeat that, Spot."

That made a little more sense. People were saying when they wanted to get sweaty. I repeated it. I had no trouble remembering the words, even if I didn't understand them all.

"Your dog is even more amazing in person, Josh," one guy said.

"You should call this 'Spot's HossFit gym.' That's what my friend called it. I didn't believe her, but Spot is fantastic." A young female spoke.

I wagged my tail because of their attention.

Master looked at me. "You like that, Spot? Maybe I'll do that. There's no sense in fighting the rising tide."

"What?" I whined at Josh.

"The rising tide. A flood of water. You can't fight it. You just swim with the current."

I understood swimming with the current. I had swum in a river while Master canoed. "I got it!" My yip came out as almost a howl.

Everyone laughed. Master left to teach his classes, and I registered people for the rest of the day.

On our way home that night, Master said, "Whew! What a day! You got a hundred and five people registered. You're a good employee!"

"Is that like a good boy?" I barked.

"Just like it. Do you want a fish fillet again?"

"Let me have that hamburger with cheese." I couldn't keep the excitement out of my yip.

"You got it. I'll have two chicken sandwiches. I'm hungry."

While we gobbled our food in the parking lot, Master looked at his phone. "Huh. This gal sent me a video of you registering people. Let's watch it."

There I was, in front of a line of people, barking at them. The words didn't come through, but the people understood me. The girl who took the video translated my barks while she giggled.

"That was pretty good, wasn't it, Spot?"

"You bet!"

"She permitted me to upload it to my video channel. Here goes. Our last video is at a million and a half views. I wonder what this'll get?"

The next morning Master said he had a voice message from Jimmy Fellon.

"Who's that?" I barked.

"You'll find out. We're going on his nighttime TV show."

Chapter 17 - Flight 216

Tuesday, October 6

"Hey, Jeff! Want me to drive you to work today?"

"Do you mean fly?" His brown eyes looked into my hazel ones under his raised eyebrows.

"Of course. It's the quickest way."

"Why not? I assume you'll pick me up too."

"Right."

"You're really getting into this flying, aren't you?" Jeff put on his coat.

"Yup. I registered as an Urber driver last night." I followed him out the door to the garage.

"I'd love to be in the car as you take off with your first customer."

"I'm telling them this is a carbon-free flying taxi. If they ask me how it's powered, I'll say 'magic.' That'll put their fears to rest."

"So you're all ready with a line of BS?"

"I've been slinging it since 1946."

We filed into Jeff and Megan's car and drove to the freeway. I took off again, using the ramp, but since it was rush hour, someone was behind me. They honked as the car flapped into the air. I honked back.

"The geese are flying south for the winter," I commented.

"You realize everyone will see you flying. You'll get reported."

"Yup. I'm counting on it. Free advertising."

"You're remarkably nonchalant."

"At my age, what are they going to do? Arrest me for a flying car?"

"Maybe."

"You have some of your dad's negativism."

"I call it realism."

"So did he."

We arrived at Rockwell Automation in Mayfield Heights

without incident, and I landed on Allen Bradley Road without anyone seeing me and dropped him off.

"Thanks, Mom!" He kissed my cheek. "Have a nice flight home!" He went to work, looking at his phone.

Flying back to Jeff and Megan's home in Bratenahl took less than five minutes. I managed to land on their street without anyone seeing me. I dove down until I was skimming the street at sixty miles per hour and then slammed on the brakes and stopped in front of their house. I was tickled I could land in such a short distance.

"Yoo-hoo! Megan! Whatcha got planned for the day?"

"First, I have to take the kids to school."

"I'll take them. They go to Gilmour Academy, don't they?"

"Yup. On Cedar Road. I'll get you the address." Megan gave me the address from her cell phone. "Thanks so much, Mom. This'll save me over an hour. The traffic is terrible in the morning!"

"No problem. I'll fly above it. They'll love flying. Maybe we can go shopping after I'm back."

"Sounds good! Oliver and Violet are eating in the kitchen." I followed her into the kitchen.

Oliver was finishing off his eggs and Pop-Tarts. Violet had bacon and eggs.

"Hi, kids. I'll be flying you to school today."

"Woo-hoo! I'm sorry I missed the trip last night," Oliver said.

"Don't talk with your mouth full," I said automatically, but my words had no heat.

"Sorry, G'ma," he said with his mouth full.

"Chew. Now swallow. Now talk." I ruffled his hair. When he stood, I had to reach up, like I did with Ray. I glanced at Violet. She was watching with amused interest.

"I wish he listened to me like he does to you, Mom." Megan shook her head.

"Could I fly the car?"

"No!" Megan said.

"Maybe," I said.

"I should learn to fly first. I'm older." Violet looked smug.

"You at least have your driver's license. Oliver, no flying

until you learn to drive."

"Can you teach me?"

"You're only fourteen!"

"Lots of kids on Viewtube drive at fourteen."

"They're on farms in the wilderness. You're in a city with hundreds of thousands of people. Why am I arguing? No!" Megan pounded the table for emphasis.

Oliver's head slumped, like his dog died. Violet still looked smug.

"Okay, get in the car. I'll tell you about how I learned to fly."

"Lemme grab my backpack!" He raced upstairs to his room.

"Could I sit in the front seat with you, Grandma?"

"Sure, Violet."

We settled in the car, with Oliver leaning over between the front seats, watching me.

"Huh. It looks just like our car normally does."

"Right. We drive out of the garage and down the street to the freeway," I said.

"Then what?"

"Watch what happens." When on the freeway ramp, I glanced sideways and saw Violet watched as intently as Oliver. "I wish this car would fly." I'd been saying that to myself, but I thought I'd give the kids the full treatment.

Obediently the wings popped out of the door and flapped us upward. The dashboard transformed into a plane's instrument panel.

"Wow!" my grandkids said together.

"That's what I said the first time it happened."

"When was that, Grandma?" Violet asked.

"On my way to Phoenix from Paradise. I dreaded the long trip. Now be quiet. I have to find Cedar Road up here." I swerved south until I saw it. Long and straight, it stretched eastward past I-271.

"There we go. Now help me find your school. I don't know what it looks like from above."

"I don't either," Oliver said.

"I've driven there down Cedar with Mom. It's the first left turn after Som Center Road."

"Thanks, Violet. Som Center's that long north-south street

just past I-271, right?"

"Yup." Violet looked happy to help me.

"Man, I didn't realize how hard it'd be to find your way around up in the air." I turned and saw Oliver shaking his head.

"Yeah, it was hard for me too, and I had driven to Phoenix many times. I just pointed my car east and hoped I'd find the airport."

"At least that's a big target."

"Yes. Now I have to land. Don't bug me and make sure your seat belts are buckled."

"How fast are we going?" Oliver asked.

"About two hundred." I swerved left to land on the road off Cedar Hills.

"How fast do we land?" Violet sounded concerned.

"About fifty miles per hour. Like this." I slammed on the brakes as I skimmed the road. Thump! The tires squeaked as they went from still to fifty.

"Wow, Grandma! You laid a patch of rubber," Oliver said.

"I guess I did."

"Won't you get in trouble for going fifty in a school district?" Violet said.

"Uh, you're right. I probably shouldn't land here. But Som Center and Cedar were packed with traffic. Anyway, we're legal now. Here we are, kids!" I pulled up to the high school.

"Thanks, G'ma!" Oliver yelled as he bounded out of the car.

"Yes, thanks, Grandma. That was really something. You'll pick us up?"

"Yes, I'll be here at three."

"We'll be ready. I love you!" Violet hugged and kissed me.

Glowing all over, I drove sedately out of the school district. I took to the air on the I-271 on-ramp.

I landed on the off-ramp from the I-90 freeway and then drove to my kids' home on Haskel Drive.

"I'm back, Megan!" I said as I walked in.

"Hi, Mom! I got everything done—let's go shopping."

After a nice morning shopping with Megan, including a tasty lunch, I took the plunge. I marked myself available for Urber rides. In less than a minute, I got a request to take someone from a hotel downtown to the airport.

"Huh. They could just take the train to the airport," I said to myself. "See you, Megan! I'm off on my new business!"

"Good luck with your business!"

I flew downtown, landing on the I-90 off-ramp at East Ninth Street. Freeway ramps were ideal for takeoffs and landings. I drove to Superior and turned right until I got to the Hyatt Regency. A well-dressed man in a sharp suit stood on the sidewalk, looking at his phone. Beside him rolled a suitcase.

I pulled up to the curb and parked. "Are you Martin Willoughby?"

He glanced up from his phone. "Yes. Are you with 'Flight 216—Enchanting Rides'?"

"You bet."

"Your car doesn't even have a sign on it!"

"Oh, right. I probably should get one of those magnetic signs. It's not my car anyway. It's my son and daughter-in-law's."

"What kind of fly-by-night outfit is this? No, don't tell me. Just get me to the airport as quickly as you can."

"Sure." I opened the back door for him. "Be sure to buckle up."

He snorted and looked at his phone.

I plopped his suitcase into the trunk. It was way lighter than mine.

"And off we go," I said as I slid in. "When's your flight?"

"One forty-five."

"We've got half an hour. Easy peasy." I saw him raise his eyebrows in my rearview mirror.

"You seem confident. It doesn't seem possible to me."

"It's ten miles or so. We'll be there in five minutes, tops."

"You're going to go a hundred and twenty on I-71?" His eyebrows rose again.

"Not exactly. You buckled up?"

He clicked his seat belt. "Yes."

I accelerated onto the West Shoreway Drive. "Fly, my pretty," I whispered.

Four wings sprouted out and blurred us into the air.

"Whoa! What's going on?"

"Welcome to my company, Flight 216—Enchanting Rides.

We'll fly you to your destination with a carbon-free flight in record time."

"We'll get up to a hundred and twenty?" Martin said as he peered out the window at the ground.

"Nah, we'll peak at two-fifty. I gotta land and drive you around to your gate, so that'll take some time."

"I've never heard of any technology like this! Have you thought of franchising?"

"No, but that's a good idea. Maybe I'll try it."

"You've got a gold mine here. Can I invest in your company?"

"Why not?" I shrugged. Who was I to turn down money?

"I've only got a thousand cash on me. How many shares would that buy?"

"A thousand. I incorporated at a dollar a share. It's a corporation sole, by the way."

"So you're not listed anywhere?"

"No."

"Even better. That means I can get in on the ground floor."

"More like the hundredth story. We're a thousand feet high, but there's the airport."

"Where will you land?"

"On that exit ramp there." I pointed ahead. "Hold on." I braked and we dropped. I eased off and we landed.

"Wow. That was way more fun than I expected to have. I was sure I'd miss my flight. That's why you got the job. You were the first Urber driver to respond."

"Which gate do you want?" I drove around the airport road.

"Seventy-two A, American. I'll give you my thousand cash for stock in your company, but I need a receipt from you."

"Sure." I had a receipt book to track my cash exchanges. I wrote, "Stock certificate for 1000 shares of Flight 216—Enchanted Rides, Angela Hamilton, CEO, CFO" in the description.

"Here you go, Martin. Thank you for your investment. I suppose I'll have to pay you some dividends."

"I wouldn't mind. Or you can list your stock on an exchange."

"Regardless, I'll give you an update on how I invest your

money and how I'm doing. Do you have a card?"

"Electronic. Here, scan this QR code."

I did, and my phone beeped. His website came up. "Okay. I'll report to you monthly about our profits."

"I've got to run. Thanks for the enchanted ride, Ms. Hamilton!" Martin took off at a rapid walk.

Well, that was more profitable than I'd thought. I supposed the thousand dollars was investment and not profit, but that would lead to more profit. I headed for the takeoff ramp.

I had fun flying people around that week, but I felt I needed my own car. I rented one, another minivan. I read the rental agreement carefully. It had no prohibition against magical enhancements, nor flying.

I also added some magnetic signs with "Flight 216—Enchanted Rides" on them, to the doors. Megan watched me in their driveway.

"Okay, Megan, let's see how this one flies. Watch me as I take off."

Inside I whispered, "You can fly now, minivan." I pictured Megan's van's transformation. The van's doors sprouted wings, which flapped as I backed into the street. They were white blurs rather than blue ones. Instead of speeding up, I said, "Fly up. You can do it."

The van flew straight up. I circled the neighborhood and landed, straight down on the driveway.

Megan raced to the door. "Wow, Mom! When you went straight up, you could read the sign on each wing, from underneath! How did you do that?"

"Do what?"

"Fly straight up."

"Oh, I just wished for it, like I did for my flying car."

"Could you enchant our car again? I'd like to try flying."

"I guess you're old enough." I laughed. "And I've certainly got enough customers. I always feel bad about turning customers away when I stop flying. You can keep the money you make. I don't need any more."

Megan installed her app and used my account. I entered her as another driver in our business.

Then we took off for customers.

* * *

"Guess what?" I said when I picked up Jeff to fly him home from work.

"What?"

"Flight 216 has doubled today."

"Wow, how'd you do that, Mom?"

"Megan started flying."

"Whoa! I thought she was nervous about flying."

"She's used to it now. I think she finally believes in the magic."

"So what'd you make today?"

"I cleared about five hundred, and she got six hundred. She got more money on shorter trips. Also, I picked up the kids from school. Plus, watch this."

We were alone on the long drive to Cedar Road. "Up, White Swan." We flew straight up.

"Okay, that's really cool. So you didn't need to go fifty miles per hour after all."

"Nope. I feel like a dummy for not realizing it sooner."

"The rules of magic aren't the same as science."

"What rules?"

* * *

Friday, October 9

My first ride on Friday was to take someone from the airport to the federal building downtown. A gray-haired man in a suit entered. His name on the reservation showed Walter Borthwick.

"This is Flight 216 Urber rides?"

"Yes, sir, Mr. Borthwick."

"I understand you fly your passengers around town. Is that correct?"

"Watch." I drove to the freeway ramp and took off.

"O-o-o-h. So you really can fly. Do you ever run into power lines or radio towers?"

"I'd have to be pretty stupid to do that. There's a lot of space to go around them."

"You'd be surprised at the number of rookie pilots who crash into them."

"Not really. I know how stupid young guys can be. Anyway, this car is a lot more maneuverable than a plane."

"Oh? How so?"

"We can stop more quickly. There's the federal building over there." I pointed ahead of us. "Let's land in the parking lot of the Rock and Roll Hall of Fame." I aimed straight down, and then I slammed on the brakes.

We went from two hundred miles per hour to zero in less than a block. I glided down in a tight circle and then landed vertically in a parking spot.

"See? A perfect VTOL landing."

Walter panted and wiped his forehead with a handkerchief. "Let's just get to the federal building on the ground."

I drove through downtown and we made it there in five minutes. "Here we are, Mr. Borthwick." I parked next to the curb.

"Indeed." He paid online with his app and went around to the driver's door.

"Please get out, Ms. Hamilton." He opened the door.

"Why? Is there some problem?"

He showed me a badge that said FAA. "Yes. I'm from the FAA, and I'm arresting you for flying without a license."

Chapter 18 - Measurement

Friday, October 9

Nothing. That was what I had. No data from any electromagnetic spectrum. No gravity wave from any detector on Earth.

I gritted my teeth in frustration as I drove to work in Oak Ridge. Maybe I'd get some good news in an email this morning. My phone call with Misty last night had not been good news.

"Hi, Katie."

"Hi, Misty. I've been eager to find out what you've detected. What's the good news?"

"Nothing."

"Um, what?"

"No detected emanations from the galactic core since the first day of the fires, October 4."

"Not even gravity waves?"

"That's where I concentrated my work. I checked with every gravitational-wave observatory on Earth. Nothing."

I didn't remember how I said goodbye to Misty. I'd just slunk off to bed last night.

I didn't feel any better this morning, other than a vague hope for my email to give me something. So I wormed through the lines of traffic and parked at the lab.

I had a report to write, but I procrastinated and read my email instead. Most were reports of fires and odd occurrences around the world.

"Wait. There seem to be more occurrences." I charted the incident accounts. They were increasing daily. I re-charted my graph of the globe turning and the incidents waxing and waning. The events waned more slowly. They waxed faster each day.

Whatever was hitting Earth kept increasing.

Then I came to Sean Kennedy's email.

I remembered the slender, earnest adolescent. I read his letter. He'd been experimenting with his wishing and . . . school grades? He'd maxed out his grades and now learned at an astonishing rate. He had doubts about the propriety of these wishes, but his parents assured him he was doing the work.

How could an alien energy make wishes come true? Was it like a magic genie? Or was it just . . . magic? My logical, scientific self rebelled at the thought.

I knew what I had to do. I whipped out my status report on the phenomenon for my boss in less than an hour and booked a flight back to Detroit and on to Toledo. Then I drove home to pack.

On the way, I called the Kennedys.

"Hello?" Shirley answered.

"Hi, Shirley. This is Katie Garcia. Do you mind if I come over again and investigate Sean's latest use of wishes?"

"Of course not. Is he in any kind of trouble?"

"Not from me. But he and your family are my best source for documenting how this interstellar power works. I know for sure you three are using it effectively."

"Interstellar power? Why do you say that?"

"There's strong evidence this phenomenon is coming from outer space."

"Wow. That's something. What time will you get here?"

"Probably by four this afternoon."

"Okay. See you then!"

* * *

I pulled into Kennedys' driveway that evening. Traffic had been bad coming out of Detroit, and I didn't get there until suppertime. I thought of my excuses for being late and interrupting their meal.

"Hi, Katie! You're just in time for supper. I set a place for you." Shirley Kennedy greeted me at the door.

"Sorry I'm late. Traffic was terrible coming out of Detroit."

"This time works out fine. Here's your plate."

I smelled scrumptious roast meat. I saw the chicken on the table, along with baked potatoes and corn. I sat at my place. "I didn't realize I'd gotten so hungry. This is delicious! Thank you, Shirley. Thanks for welcoming me back."

"Our pleasure, Katie," Phil Kennedy said. "Your last visit

was so interesting. Sean was motivated to try wishing for good grades."

"Yes, I got his email. That's why I'm here." I looked at Sean. "After supper, I'd like to test your wishing skills, see what works, and see if I can detect any energy around you as you wish."

Sean's eyes widened. "That sounds great!"

"Do you mind if we watch?" Shirley asked.

"Of course not. Maybe you'll catch something I miss."

After supper and a homemade chocolate cake with coffee, we sat in their living room. I retrieved my instruments and a textbook from my duffel bag.

"Wow, what are all those devices?"

"That's my radiometer. It measures EM, electromagnetic radiation. This is my Geiger counter for nuclear radiation detection. And this is my electromagnetic field detector."

"What do you need all of those for?"

"I want to see if any radiation comes into you or out of you as you wish."

"Into or out of? Where's this radiation coming from?"

"Something is coming from outer space. We just don't know what it is. The news reports from around Earth show the phenomenon waxes and wanes as it rotates."

"Neat. That's fun to think I'm channeling outer-space energy!"

"If we can prove that, my job is done. Here's one of my textbooks on quantum mechanics."

"Uh, how is that going to help?" Sean looked dubious.

"Just read the first chapter, and then I'll give you questions from the back. Try to solve them. If you can't, then just wish, and we'll try again."

"You really believe in going for the jugular with your experiments, don't you?" Phil smiled wryly.

"That seems a rather mixed metaphor. What do you mean?"

"You ran your pants-on-fire experiments on yourself. Now you're using the most esoteric aspects of physics to test Sean's grade wishing."

"Oh. Right. The experiment has to be falsifiable. So I have to do this twice, once before wishing and once after." I looked at Sean, who was poring over the chapter rapidly. "How's it going?"

"I'm reading it quickly because I wished for speed reading. But it doesn't make any difference if I go quickly or slowly. It doesn't make sense. Are quanta real?"

"What do the experiments show? I know chapter 1 has the basic experiments on light quanta."

"Well yes, the experiments show light comes in these little quanta packages. But it is also a wave. So what is it *really*?"

"Heh. That's the question, even to this day. Are you ready for your questions?"

"I'm already confused. You might as well give it to me."

I read from the textbook.

1.8. Exercise problems

1.1. The actual postulate made by N. Bohr in his original 1913 paper was not directly Eq. (8), but rather the assumption that at quantum leaps between adjacent electron orbits with $n \gg 1$, the hydrogen atom either emits or absorbs the energy $\Delta E = \hbar\omega$, where ω is its classical radiation frequency – according to classical electrodynamics, equal to the angular velocity of the electron's rotation.[61] Prove that this postulate, complemented with the natural requirement that $L = 0$ at $n = 0$, is equivalent to Eq. (8).

"Um, what?" Sean looked at me blankly.

"Right. So you have no idea how to approach this question?"

"I don't even understand what they're asking!"

"Right. Just for my curiosity, do you know calculus?"

"No. I've heard of it and that it's difficult."

"Yes and no. It is difficult compared to arithmetic or linear algebra but much simpler than quantum mechanics, which uses it as a tool."

I smiled. "So the first part of our experiment is successful. You cannot solve this problem, even with your recent learning."

"That's successful? I've never felt so stupid!" Sean put his head in his hands.

"But we've just proven that if after wishing you can solve this problem, then you're using this outside force."

Sean's face brightened. "I get it! Let's go! I wish—"

"Wait! Let me set up my instruments." I busied myself adjusting for background radiation and electric fields in the house. "All right. I'm ready. Wish away."

"I wish I could answer this question 1.1!"

"Well? How do you feel?"

"No different. But I need to write something down before I forget it." Sean grabbed a pad of paper and a pen and wrote quickly.

Looking at his answer, I could see it was a clear and succinct response to the question. My instruments never wavered.

"Wow, you did it, Sean! This is a very good answer. Can you explain it?"

He looked at the sheet of paper. "No. It's all gobbledygook to me, like the chapter. I just had to write it."

"Ah. You just wished for the answer, not the understanding. Now wish for the understanding."

"All right. I wish I understood this answer!"

I checked my instruments again. Nothing. Sean stared at his answer.

"Oooh, now I get it. Everything falls into place from Equation (8),

Essential Graduate Physics QM: Quantum Mechanics

$L = m_e vr$ of an electron moving with velocity v on a circular orbit of radius r about the hydrogen's nucleus (the proton, assumed to be at rest because of its much higher mass), is quantized as

$$L = \hbar n, \qquad (1.8)$$

Angular momentum quantization

where $\hbar$ is again the same Planck's constant (4), and n is an integer. (In Bohr's theory, n could not be equal to zero, though in genuine quantum mechanics, it can.)

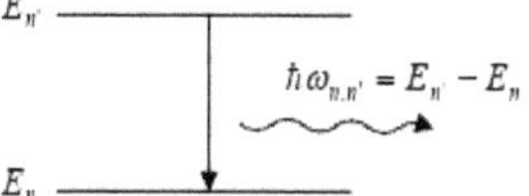

Fig. 1.3. The electromagnetic radiation of a system as a result of the transition between its quantized energy levels.

You can work backward from there to the original assumptions."

"Right. Cool." I was anything but cool, staggered by his sudden understanding. I checked his understanding. "What are *L*, *h*, and *n*?"

"*L* is the angular momentum of the electron, *h* is Planck's constant, and *n* is the integer of the quanta."

"Right again." I sighed. "Your wishing is working, but I can't measure anything!" I clenched my hands in frustration.

"Why don't you wish for an instrument to measure it?" Sean looked at me.

"Uh. I don't know if that'll work."

"You just proved that wishing does work."

"Right." I took a deep breath. I knew it worked, but I didn't believe it. "I need help. Sean, I've never wished before. Will you wish with me?" I held out my hands, and he grasped them with his long, skinny fingers. His palms were sweaty. I wondered why. Somehow, that relaxed me. The whole situation was silly.

Chuckling, I looked at my Geiger counter, my least useful tool. "I wish I had an instrument that measured the strength of this unknown force."

The Geiger counter blurred, like I was squinting my eyes, and changed.

Multiple dials replaced single frequency dial. A rectangular dial read "MU Sensor Intensity." It showed a logarithmic scale from a millionth of an "MU" (whatever that was) to ten million MUs. The needle quivered in the middle, at around 1 MU.

The next dial showed "Background MU Intensity." It had the same calibration, and its needle also showed "1 MU."

The next two dials were circular. The first read "MU Direction, Polar Axis." That showed a needle in the upper left quadrant. The next read, "MU Direction, Equatorial Plane." It showed north, south, east, and west, and pointed southeast. It seemed detachable, so I took the case and held it flat in my hand. It pointed directly at Sean.

I didn't realize how long I'd been staring at the instrument in my hands.

"Are you okay, Katie?" Shirley asked.

I didn't remember letting go of Sean's hands and picking up the case, as I'd been concentrating so hard.

"I guess so. This instrument is measuring *something*. I just don't know what 'MU' means."

“I wish we understood what MU means!” Sean said confidently.

It was obvious. We all said together, “Magic units.”

I half laughed. “The only thing this detector lacks is a paper roll to record the dials’ measurements.”

A roll of paper appeared on the side, rather like a seismograph, showing the readouts of the four dials.

“What about a USB port to record it electronically?” Sean said.

“Why not?” I wished for that, and it appeared above the paper roll, complete with a USB dongle. Printed on its side was “1 Terabyte.” I noted that each time I wished, the directional dial swung from Sean to me.

“Okay, Sean. Are you up for another question?”

“Why not? It doesn’t hurt to learn new things.” He grinned at me.

“Here’s question 1.2: Generalize the Bohr theory for a hydrogen-like atom-slash-ion with a nucleus with the electric charge Q = Ze, to the relativistic case.”

“Uh, sorry. I don’t understand where to start with that one.”

“I’m not surprised. You haven’t learned relativity yet, have you?”

“Nope. I just know Einstein invented it.”

“Wish away. I’m recording.” I watched my dials eagerly.

“I wish I understood this question and can answer it.”

The dials twitched. The MU units on the directional sensor I pointed at Sean went from one to ten and back down.

“I get it now! Wow, relativity’s pretty weird. Here’s your answer.” He jotted it down quickly.

I looked it over. Good answer.

“I’m going to have to get to a hotel room and process all this.”

“Why don’t you stay here? We’ve got an extra room,” Phil said.

“Why thanks. If you could lead me there, I’ve got some thinking to do.”

“We all do.”

* * *

Ah, alone time. The Kennedys were wonderful people, but I still felt drained. I reviewed the graphs of Sean's wishes. There was definitely a surge of MUs from him. I couldn't bring myself to call it "magic." Then the MUs dropped to a background level.

Background level. I compared it to what the direct sensor showed. The direct sensor never showed zero MUs. I tested everything in my room, including the floor and the ceiling. The ceiling had .01 MUs, the floor .005. That made sense if the radiation was coming from outer space. Finally I tested myself—.5 MUs. Huh. I'd only wished once, but I had over a hundred times the MUs in the ceiling.

I went back to the living room, carrying my detector. Phil and Shirley were reading books, and Sean was on a laptop.

"More experiments?" Phil looked up from his book.

"More measurements. I'm looking for a pattern." I checked the ceiling and the floor. They were the same as my room.

I checked Phil—.7 MU. Maybe he wished more than me. Shirley was at .75. Then Sean—2.1

"Whoa! Sean, you have twice as many MUs as anyone or anything else."

"I'm not even wishing. I'm just watching some anime."

"The background MUs are about .4. You have five times as much. It must accumulate in you as you wish."

I thought some more. "It must accumulate in you even if you don't wish. Every object I tested in my room had some MUs in it."

"So what does all this mean?" Sean looked at me.

"I don't know—yet. But I'll find out. I'll go back to my room to think some more and plan my next steps. Thank you all. This has been a breakthrough in this project. Good night!"

I spun to go but stopped and turned back. "Sean, which anime were you watching?"

"An old one, *Princess Mononoke.*" He seemed almost embarrassed by its age.

"Ah, that's a good one. I watched it as a kid. It's *that* old." I laughed and went to bed.

* * *

The next morning the first thing I did was check my MU

charts. As I expected, the background MUs dropped off overnight. But I noted something odd. The pattern didn't match the drop-offs I'd been seeing daily for the past week and a half. The drop-off was even shorter than I'd seen before. The MUs never reached zero; they bottomed out at .4. The same as my MU level.

I reached for the USB dongle to transfer the data to my computer, but stopped. Why not wish? I pointed the sensor at my belly—.4 MU.

"I wish for this MU detector to have a Bluetooth adapter for data transfer."

The face of the detector flickered. A blue light appeared with the Bluetooth symbol. I fired up my laptop and added it to my devices. It showed as "MU Detector." I connected, and it showed up like a disk drive. There were four files of data in standard database format. I copied them over and compared it with my previous data.

I glanced at the printout. My MU level had spiked to 2.1 and then dropped back—to .5.

"So each wish accumulates more MUs." I thought of this happening worldwide to billions of people. Most people weren't wishing, but millions were. The more they had their wishes granted, the more they'd wish. I shivered with a sudden chill.

This energy was being absorbed by people all over the world.

I completed my comparison of the new data to the old. The MU effect extended longer and longer: twelve hours at first, then twelve and a half, thirteen, and today fourteen.

I checked my emails for the latest incidents. Another flying car incident from Cleveland showed up. The FAA had arrested the lady for flying without a license. That was where I'd go next.

I dressed and packed. What next? My stomach growled. Breakfast, of course. I could smell bacon frying. I booked a flight to Chicago. I had to investigate this pink dragon. Then I had breakfast.

Chapter 19 - Advertising

Monday, October 12

"Whew! That's it." I turned from the keyboard, stood, and stretched.

"What's it?" Jane asked from our bedroom.

I was in my office tower room, staring at my computer screen. "I'm done with my first draft of my novel."

"Congratulations! I'm glad to hear it, Jake. I've felt like a widow this past week."

"Aw, let me hug you and let you know you're not a widow."

"Mmm." Jane nestled against my chest. Then she looked up at me. "What are you going to call it?"

"*Sorcerer's Apprentice* is my working title."

"Meh. Won't you get sued for that? That's already a movie title."

"You can't copyright titles. Yeah, I feel the title can be better, but I can't think of anything."

"How long will it take to edit it?"

"I don't know. I've never edited anything before. It took me a week to write. Let's shoot for a week to edit. How about I read it to you? It's only about fifty thousand words." I held out my laptop.

"I'm game. Go for it."

* * *

"'The end,'" I finished, some hours and several oatmeal cookies and cups of tea later.

"Not bad," Jane said. "You can use some more description in spots."

"Yeah. I made notes in my file as I read it. I also marked all the mistakes I made. Was it funny?"

"Parts of it. Other parts just made me roll my eyes."

"Not everyone has the same sense of humor. Ironically, just about everything I wrote about has been mentioned in the news."

"Even the flying car? The stuffed dragon?"

"Yup. Each has been cited by two or more sources. I've got a video of the dragon."

"Whoa. Let me see that."

I turned the laptop toward her and played it. I had links to all my sources in my planning document.

"Wow. That looked real."

"I think it is. The poster just wrote, 'Real or fake? You decide.' It's all over the internet."

"Are you using magic to write your book?" Jane looked concerned.

"No. I never thought of that."

"How about for editing?"

"I don't think so. I have an editing program to find my grammatical errors. I wouldn't trust magic to write my story correctly."

"You're self-publishing this book, right?"

"Oh yeah. There's no way I'd wait years to get an agent and a publisher."

"How long have you been sitting here in your office?"

"Too long."

"Why don't you go out and walk to the lakefront? It does you no good to write a best-selling novel and die of a heart attack. I'd miss you too. It's a beautiful fall day. I'll rake some leaves. That'll be my exercise."

"Great idea!" I kissed her and went out.

The maple and oak trees were turning gold and red. The air smelled of autumn.

I bounded along, my long legs eating up the blocks to the lake. Our street ran north and south in Lakewood. It dead-ended at Lake Erie.

I came to a light at Clifton Avenue. Heavy traffic clogged the road as the evening rush hour began. Two blocks to go. I heard a rapid tapping behind me, like someone running in hard shoes. I turned around and saw a bipedal dinosaur. It seemed to be made out of plastic.

"Whoa! You look like an oviraptor."

It clacked its hard beak, turned, and showed me its tail. Neatly written there, in molded plastic, was "Oviraptor 5 feet."

"Huh. Are you a plastic dinosaur animated by magic?"

It clacked its beak and looked behind it. A swarm of dinosaurs came up the street, two as big as elephants. A tyrannosaurus rex loomed over one. Beside it, equal in bulk if not height, came a triceratops. Barely visible behind the neck shield rode a little kid.

I held my breath as the pack of velociraptors and the bigger dinosaurs crowded around me at the light. One misstep and I'd be squished.

The kid looked down at me from the eight-foot-high back of the plastic creature. "Hey, mister! Why are you waiting here?"

"The light is red. I suppose you'll stop traffic."

"Just wish the light green, mister." The light flashed from red to green. There was no yellow at all in the other direction. Several cars squealed to a stop, while others raced through.

"Thanks. Are these dinos safe to walk with?" I trotted next to the horned dinosaur.

"Yeah, no problem. They just do what I tell them. I hope someone will try to attack me, but most people just run away."

"You wished them to this size and to be alive?"

"Yup. When I saw the video of the flying dragon, I thought it'd be cool to play with life-size dinosaurs."

"I'm going to the lake. My name's Jake. What's yours?"

"Svi."

"Short for what?"

"Sviatoslav. Yeah. I don't like it."

"Do kids give you trouble about it at school?"

"No, it's just too long to print out every day. I'm in second grade."

"Do your parents know you're out here?"

"Yeah. I told them I was playing with my dinosaurs." When we got to Lake Avenue, Svi turned his pack.

"Where are you going?"

"To the park. They like to play in the lake."

"I'll go with you. You've given me some good ideas for my book."

"Wow. You write books, Mr. Jake?"

"This one's my first. It's all about magic in the world."

"That's great. I'll want to read it. I love using magic. It's so easy."

"So where do you store your dinosaurs at home?"

"Oh, I shrink them down and put them in this bag." He pointed to a cloth bag he sat upon.

I walked with Svi and the dinos to the park. It was a warm, sunny day, maybe the last of the autumn. The breeze ruffled the lake into white caps. Svi's dinos raced to the lake and splashed in. Svi threw a stick.

"Fetch, Rex!"

Rex popped out of the water. Five-foot-long jaws snapped, and the stick disappeared.

"Oops. I need a bigger stick." Svi picked up another, threw it, and it grew to six feet long in the air. Rex grabbed it from the air, then trotted over to Svi and dropped the log with a thump in front of him.

"Good boy, Rex!" He touched the log. It shrank back to a stick, and he threw it. Rex raced after it.

I watched for a while. "Hey, Svi! I'm going home for dinner. I'll see you another day. I live on Lincoln. How about you?"

"Quail Court."

"Do you come here every day?"

"Every day I don't have school. Today's a day off, Columbus Day."

"Oh yeah, I forgot. I guess I won't see you until Saturday."

"Yeah, I usually leave in the morning on Saturday."

"I'll see you then. I'll read some of my book to you if you want."

"Sounds great, Mr. Jake. I never met an author before."

"I never met a kid with a pack of dinosaurs before. This'll be fun to write about."

* * *

Back at home, with some of Jane's homemade Reuben sandwich inside of me, I wrote a chapter about Svi. I called him "Fry," short for "small fry," from the character's real name, Freeman. "Ha! 'Real name' in my book." I chuckled as I wrote.

Afterward I went over all the changes I'd noted and Jane had suggested. I finished them off just before supper.

I wandered down the stairs to the kitchen. "What's for supper, honey?"

"Weiner schnitzel."

"My favorite!"

"You say that about everything I make, including the Reuben sandwich you had for lunch."

"That's right. Everything you make is my favorite."

"So why don't you gain weight like I do?"

"High metabolism, baby. You keep me revved up." I hugged her.

"Hmmph!" She snorted, but she snuggled against me.

After supper, I read Jane my revisions.

"Much better. I really liked the chapters about the boy and his dinosaurs. Fry."

"Based upon real life. I met a boy Svi today, playing with his plastic dinosaurs. Fully animated and life size."

I contacted my editor, Sally Wagner, and emailed my manuscript to her.

"What should I do while I wait for Sally to edit my book? It'll take her a month." Jane and I sat before the fireplace after supper, sipping coffee and eating Jane's Linzer torte. Despite the warm day, the temperature was dropping to near freezing tonight.

"Do you have your blurb written?"

"Nope. That's a good idea." I pulled up my laptop and jotted a quick two-hundred-word summary. I read it to Jane. "How's that?"

"Meh. Sounds farfetched."

"Hmm. The blurb is the most important selling tool, after the title and the cover. I wish I could write good ad copy!"

"That's it! I wish for that too."

"Huh?" I said stupidly, mouth agape.

"You big dummy. Use magic for writing ad copy."

"Okay." I looked at what I had written. Obvious crap. I rewrote it and it felt much better. "Try this out."

"Wow. That's much better!"

"Thanks. I wish it were perfect for selling my book." Before my eyes, the copy on my laptop rearranged itself. "Amazing. Listen to this." I read Jane the latest version.

"That makes me want to buy the book."

"Me too, and I wrote it. I'll send this to my editor and see what she thinks."

"Too bad you can't start selling now."

"You know, I can. I'll put my second draft online and put it up for presale on Amazin'. I'll put the release date out until a month and a half after the editing is done, and it can go up for presale."

"Okay. How about your title?"

"*Sorcerer's Apprentice*? Yeah, that's meh too."

"I wish it was a perfect title too!"

"Oh! Me too!" Before my eyes, the title changed. "*Magic Arrives*? Is that really better?"

"Yes. *Sorcerer's Apprentice* is a cliché, but *Magic Arrives* is intriguing. Unusual. Arrives where? What sort of magic?" She paused. "This is exciting. Your first book. I'm married to an author!"

"An unknown author." I smiled at Jane.

"But not for long."

Chapter 20 - Business

Saturday, October 10

"Hey, Shayla! Listen to this," Lamar said one Saturday morning.

I was playing with Pinkie and my doll Cindy. She rode Pinkie and beat up the bad guys. I used Lamar's plastic model pteranodon as my evil dragon. He said I could play with it if I was careful.

"What's up?"

"Listen to this." Lamar read from our tablet: "'In Cleveland, Ohio, a new Urber company has great success using flying cars. Their cars fly from point to point around town, avoiding all traffic. The company, Flight 216, claims the cars are carbon-free. When asked about the technology, owner-operator Angela Hamilton avoided the question and said, "It's magic."'"

"That sounds like Pinkie!"

"Yeah, I think so too. That gives me an idea. How about we sell rides on Pinkie?"

"Oooh, good idea, Lamar. What should we charge? A buck a ride?"

"Nah. Ten dollars a ride."

"Can people afford that? I don't think we have that much money."

"We'll go down to downtown Chicago with Pinkie and sell rides at the lakefront park. There are always a bunch of tourists with money down there."

"But then our secret will be out!"

"No one will know us or where we live. We can use aliases! I'll be Jack Sparrow."

"What's an alias?"

"It's a name you use to hide your real name."

"I'll be Cindy then, like my doll."

"You can make us invisible like you did the other night?"

"Sure. Easy peasy."

"I'll tell Mom. Oh, make a sign too."

"You make it. I'm just learning to write now."

"Right." He wrote something in a black Magic Marker on a big sheet of paper.

"D-r-a-g-o-n. Dragon!" I laughed as I sounded out the big word.

"It says 'Dragon Rides Ten Dollars Per Person.'" He ran to Mommy's room.

She paid bills or something in there. I heard him say, "Mom, Shayla and I are riding Pinkie to Grant Park."

"You've got to stay invisible," Mommy said.

"We will," he promised.

"Okay. Come back for lunch."

"Okay! Let's go, Shayla!"

"Don't forget the picnic basket!" Mom called.

"Oh right. Help me pack, Shayla. You fill the thermos with milk. I'll make some peanut butter and jam sandwiches."

"Don't forget the cookies!" I grabbed two chocolate chip cookies from the cookie jar. Mom had made them last night.

Lamar carried the picnic basket upstairs. I took Pinkie.

We climbed the stairs to the roof, and I squeezed Pinkie. "Pinkie, I wish you were big and invisible to everyone but us! And make us invisible too." That was what I'd said the other night, to hide from the big girls across the street who'd spied on us.

Pinkie grew to horse size. He lowered his head and said, "Hop on! It's a beautiful day for flying."

We climbed on and took off.

"Grant Park, Pinkie. We're going to try something new," Lamar said.

"Goody! I love new things. You know, I'm less than a month old."

"I guess you are. How can you talk?" I wondered.

"I don't know. It must have been part of your wish when you made me alive."

"Oh yeah. I just expected you to be able to talk. I've been talking to you for years and you talked back, in my pretending."

"That's cool," Lamar said. "Pinkie, we'd like you to give rides to anyone we meet in Grant Park."

"You aren't hiding me?"

"No, we're hiding using aliases. That's a pretend name you

use. I'm Cindy."

"And I'm Jack Sparrow."

"I guess I'll be . . . Lord Pink!" Pinkie roared.

"Lord Pink!" I laughed and Lamar did too.

We landed invisibly at Grant Park. A lot of people walked there. We went behind the Bean gate and turned visible.

Lamar held up his sign and yelled, "Dragon Rides!"

No one noticed us. "The sign is too small."

"That's easy to fix." I picked it up and said, "I wish you were the size of a billboard!"

Boom! A huge billboard appeared next to us.

"It's blocking my view of the Bean," Pinkie complained.

"Up on stilts!" I said. Up it went, fifty feet into the air.

"Now you look too small, Lord Pink. Shayla, make him bigger."

"I wish you were the size of an elephant! A whale!"

Pinkie grew to eye level with the sign. He looked around and smiled, showing his pink furry mouth.

Now everyone was looking at us.

"Step right up, everyone! Get your dragon rides for ten bucks!" Lamar shouted.

"Do you take credit cards?" a man asked.

"Nope. Cash only."

"I've got to get to a money machine," the man muttered as he left.

We set about fifteen people on Pinkie. He molded his back fins into seats, complete with buckles and a staircase up his neck. I called him "Lord Pink" out loud. Lamar and I settled on last. I sat in front, and Lamar held me.

We flew around downtown Chicago.

"There's the Sears Building, the John Hancock Center, Navy Pier, and the Shedd Aquarium," Lamar called out.

"How do you know so much, Lam—er, Jack Sparrow."

"It's my business to know, Cindy." He leaned forward and whispered, "I went on a school field trip to these places."

We banked around Willis Tower to fly back to the Bean. Several people screamed.

"Have no fear! Lord Pink never loses a passenger," Lamar said.

Then a lady fell off, screaming. She hadn't buckled her seat belt.

"Don't worry—I'll get her," Pinkie assured me.

"Lord Pink to the rescue!" Lamar shouted.

We dove straight down. More people screamed and another one fell off. Deftly, Pinkie nabbed the lady in his flannel mouth. Then he turned around and caught the falling kid in his cheek. He arched his neck around as he climbed and spat them onto his back.

"Just hold on. We'll land soon." Pinkie smiled at them.

We landed at Grant Park by our billboard. The crowd cheered as the riders slid off, some crying with relief.

"I wish our billboard were a big video showing our flight!"

The billboard began showing the flight around Chicago, including people falling off and being rescued. A huge crowd gathered to watch

"Who's up for the next ride?" Lamar called into the crowd. "Only twenty dollars per person!"

Twenty more people climbed on, and then Lamar and I took off again.

I lost track of how many rides we did that morning. Course, I could only count to twelve, just enough to tell time. Then my phone beeped with a message.

"It's Mom, La—er, Jack Sparrow! It's time to go home."

"Okay, Cindy." He turned to the passengers behind him. "Last trip!"

We coasted back to the park. I wished the billboard back into a sheet of paper.

"Goodbye, everyone!" Lamar and I waved with Pinkie, and we disappeared.

Back at home, we raced down the steps from the roof.

"Mommy! Guess what?" I shouted as we came into the apartment.

"What, darling?" Mommy looked up from her tablet.

"We sold rides on Pinkie! But we hid his name as 'Lord Pink.' I was Cindy, and Lamar was Jack Sparrow."

"What? You're not making sense, girl. You were supposed to stay invisible."

"We were, Mom. Once we got there we used aliases so no

one could track us."

"That's pretty risky. What if someone recognized you?"

"Look at all the money we got." Lamar took out a roll of tens from one pocket and a bigger roll of twenties from another pocket.

"Whoa! How many do you have? Give me those." Mom took the roll of twenties and started counting.

"Sixty-two, three, and four. That's twelve hundred and eighty dollars! That's more than I make in a week!"

"And I got another forty-seven tens. That's four hundred and seventy. Oh, and I've got these." Lamar pulled out some bills from his back pocket. "Four, five, six hundred-dollar bills."

"Show me the Benjamins, Lamar." She took the bills. "Hmmm. You've given me something to think about. For one morning's work, you made over two thousand dollars. That's over a hundred thousand per year if you did that once a week."

"It was fun, Mommy! We wouldn't mind doing this every week," I said.

"Per week? Heck, how about daily?" Lamar grinned.

Mommy punched her calculator app. "Daily is almost half a million a year."

"Whee! We could buy a house!" I squealed.

"I could get a new car," Mommy said. "And quit my job."

"We're rich!" Lamar started dancing around.

"Let me think, Lamar. If we're going to do this, I want to be with you."

"You'll need an alias, Mommy."

"Ha! I guess I'll be She-Ra. She was my favorite as a kid."

* * *

Grrr! I was going crazy. I knew a magical dragon lived next door, but I couldn't tell anyone. The geas the little girl had laid on me kept me from talking or writing about it. Not even with Heather. But I tried again.

"Hey, McQueen."

"What?" She looked up from the couch where she was grading papers. Boring. But it fit her personality. I didn't know why I liked her so much.

"Ya know that thing that happened?" I tensed, but I didn't

feel any hindrance to my speech.

"What thing?" She looked blank. A big square face with brown-blond hair and no expression.

"That thing that happened to us where you said you'd take up alcohol and pot smoking."

She laughed. "Oh yeah. I was just joking. Those things don't appeal to me. What's the point of getting drunk or stoned?"

"I don't care. I just keep thinking about that thing. I want to tell the world."

"Oh, but you can't."

"Yeah. Don't you feel confined all the time?"

"Nah. I don't think about it unless I read some of the magical stuff in the paper. I respect their privacy. Why talk about it?"

"Grrrr. I'm about ready to explode!" I grimaced and gritted my teeth.

"Why don't you publish my video on that social media video site, TokTalk, or something."

"I didn't think I could. D'ya still have it on your phone? Heck, I downloaded it to my computer. Let's see what happens if I watch it."

"Nothing. I watch it every so often. It's still amazing."

"Hmm. I guess we're commanded not to *talk* about it. But publishing this video isn't talking at all."

"You know, no one will believe it, just like you didn't," Heather said.

"Maybe. Here goes the upload. It's on TokTalk. Now on to Viewtube. "

"Why do you bother?"

"I just gotta tell someone. I feel better already." McQueen watched me make a post.

"'Real or fake? You decide.' I like that." Heather nodded.

"Me too. Now we can talk about our video."

"My video." She sniffed. "You were busy internet cruising. I was looking out the window."

"Yeah, yeah, I'll give you half the money."

"You get paid for this?"

"I've monetized my accounts. I get a grand total of twenty bucks a month. Don't spend it all in one place."

“What if she gets mad and comes over and has her dragon eat us?”

“We can deny it all. We can say someone else took the video.”

“What if she lays another geas on us? Worse than before?”

“Don’t be so negative. They probably won’t even notice.” Maria turned back to her computer screen. “Look at all these comments. And I’ve got a ton of emails about this.” She read them aloud. “Congrats from Viewtube for getting a million subscribers. Congrats from TokTalk for making the top-ten videos. And—” She stopped.

“What?”

“One from the federal government. Oakridge Tennessee National Labs.” She read more. “It’s a researcher, Katie Garcia. She’s coming over tomorrow to investigate us and the building across the street.”

“She seems to think it’s real. She’s investigating this magic stuff for the feds. I have a bad feeling about this.”

* * *

“I’ve been thinking, kids. About selling rides this Saturday.” Mommy sat with us as we ate breakfast before school.

I was in to kindergarten and Lamar was in sixth grade.

“What about, Mom?” Lamar asked.

“What if we had two dragons?”

“But, Mommy, we only have Pinkie.” I picked up my best friend and showed him to Mommy.

“Right, Shayla. What if you magic Lamar’s pteranodon?”

“Oooh. I guess I can. But it’s Lamar’s model. Lamar, I think you need to wish it big and alive.”

“I don’t know anything about this magic stuff. It’s all just magic to me.”

“I think you need to wish with me.”

“How about I wish too?” Mommy said.

“Adults can do magic? I thought you had to be little, like Shayla, to believe.” Lamar stared at Mommy.

“Look at this story.” Mommy showed her phone to Lamar.

“‘Woman Arrested in Cleveland for Flying Urber Service. “It’s Magic,” she says,’” Lamar read. “Huh. She looks old.”

"Everyone with gray hair looks old to you, Lamar."

"Of course. What's your point?"

"She's old and she's using magic."

"Okay. I'll try it with you, Mom."

"Tonight when you're home from school. After supper we'll go up on the roof and try it."

* * *

I came home that evening beat, from running a high school class for my internship, but happy it was Friday. Maria greeted me by jumping up and hugging me around my neck.

"What are you doing, Maria?" I brushed her off like an overly enthusiastic terrier.

"Heather McQueen . . ." She grinned like a maniac.

That got my attention. "Why are you using my first name?"

"Our video of 'that thing' has over ten million hits! It's all over the internet!"

"Won't we get in trouble with that family?"

"No way! It's not our fault. Other people shared it. We never said a word, except to ask a question."

Chapter 21 - Wishes

Saturday, October 10

I watched Katie's cute backside go out the door and into her car. Then she drove away.

I sighed. My wish had been granted. She'd come back and noticed me. And then she'd pointed out how much older she was than me. Would she wait for me? Could I wish to grow up faster?

That didn't seem smart. Being twelve in an eighteen- or twenty-year-old body seemed destined to fail. Was I ready to move out and earn a living? I knew I wasn't.

"Sean, what are you thinking?" Mom asked me.

"Oh nothing."

"I noticed you watching Katie."

"Oh, that. Yeah. I like her. She's cute."

"You realize the age difference, right?"

"Of course, Mom. I'm not a dummy."

"I know. But our heart and our head don't always work together."

I sighed. "That's for sure."

Mom stopped bugging me. I went outside to think. How could I get Katie to like me in six or ten years, when I was old enough? I couldn't think of any wishes that would solve my age-gap problem. I just had to grow up.

I sighed again. I'd at least be the best friend I could to her while I waited. I'd help her with this magic business. So what was the latest on the news? I went inside and logged on to our computer.

"Say, do you want to go out for ice cream?" Mom asked me. "Today's the last day Ice Cream Joy is open."

"That sounds good!"

Ice Cream Joy was an old-fashioned ice cream store, serving hard and soft varieties from a walk-up window. It had been in Toledo since my parents were kids.

"Two scoops of butter pecan please. What do you want Sean? Chocolate dip?"

"You bet!" Soft-serve ice cream dipped in liquid chocolate was my favorite.

The worker handed us our desserts, and we saw a scruffy little kid gazing at us. His big brown eyes stared at my cone. "That's mine." Then he was holding my cone.

I stared dumbly at my empty hand and then yelled, "Stop!"

"Give that back!" Mom said.

He turned and yelled, "I'm not here—I'm home!" And then he disappeared.

* * *

"Mmm," I hummed as I ate the chocolate outside of the ice cream. I'd never had this kind of cone before.

"Dak, where did you get that ice cream?" Mom asked.

"Duh. From the ice cream store."

"Gimme a bite." She leaned over and bit off the top of my cone. "Next time get me one too."

Mom never questioned how I got the things, like when our big-screen TV appeared. Stealing stuff had become as easy as wishing. Then I found out I could wish myself home when in trouble. We'd never had it so good.

I felt proud too. Mom cashed the government check each month, and I helped by stealing whatever we needed. I had to use my brain to figure out how to grab and carry whatever we needed—sometimes a big bag or a shopping cart.

For some reason, I couldn't magic the shopping cart away when I wished myself away. Maybe I needed to carry it? I had to carry stuff to it and then push it home. No one questioned a little kid pushing a shopping cart. I was ten, but I looked younger, 'cause I was little for my age.

* * *

"What was that?" Mom asked.

"I guess he was a magical ice cream snatcher."

"Crap. If we've got magical thieves, we're in big trouble."

Mom must have been pretty upset. She never used "crap," let alone real swearing, like I heard at school.

"Let's get you a replacement cone."

I began eating at an outdoor table while Mom finished her

ice cream. She frowned. “Can we wish him back?”

“It’s worth a try.”

“Let’s do it together. Say, ‘I wish that thief was back.’” She put her hands on her hips. “One, two, three . . .”

“I wish that thief was back.”

The scruffy little kid came back. He had chocolate all over his face.

Mom shook her finger at him. “You should be ashamed of yourself, stealing like that!”

“Huh? Everyone steals.” He looked puzzled rather than ashamed.

“I don’t!”

“Then you’re stupid.”

“Where’s your mother and father?”

“I don’t have a dad, only a mom, and she’s at home. She liked that ice cream cone too.”

“Well, take me to her. I want to give her a piece of my mind.”

“Gotta go home.” He disappeared again.

“Do you think we could wish ourselves to their home?” Mom looked at me as she clenched her fists.

“Um, I don’t see how. We’ve got to have some idea of where we’re going. And what are we going to do when we get there? Citizen’s arrest for stealing an ice cream cone? Be real, Mom.”

“Uh, I just want to yell at his mother.”

“I assume she’s a thief too. Do you think she’ll change if you yell at her?”

“Probably not. Let’s go home.”

* * *

Whew! That was a new one. I had never been snatched from home before. I got away again, but they could have gotten me good. If the cops started using magic, I’d be in real trouble.

“Hey, Dak! Why donchu go get me another ice cream? That was good, but it was just one bite.”

“Sure, Mom.”

Chapter 22 - Dog Show

Friday, October 9–11

Master put a vest on me. He showed me what it said: "Spot, the talking service dog. Don't pet, but talk to him."

I was already reading at a third-grade level. I was so proud. Master was buying me steaks. He said I earned them.

"We are flying to New York today. We record tomorrow," Master said.

"Huh. How? We don't have any wings," I barked quizzically.

"We'll use an airplane." He showed me a video of an airplane on his tablet. It had wings like a bird, but it didn't flap.

"Okay. That'll be different!" I yipped

* * *

The airplane flight was long and boring, except for the smells. There were a lot of people and smells, and food was out all the time. Some nice ladies kept giving me crunchy treats. She called them "pretzels." I had a comfortable seat to ride in, next to Master.

A lady came by. "What kind of service dog are you?"

"A talking service dog," I barked in answer.

"Wow. That's wild. I heard you bark, but I understood it."

"Yeah, that was pretty wild for me too," Master said. "It's one more of those magical effects, like pants catching on fire,"

"But what can you actually *do*?" she asked again.

"Anything you ask me to do," I yipped confidently.

"Can you pick up this napkin?" She dropped it on the floor, next to her food cart.

I picked it up and handed it to her, wagging my tail.

"That's good enough for me! I'd like to have you pick up in my house."

I wagged harder and looked at Master. "Could I?" I whined.

"No. We've got to go on TV."

"You're going on TV?" The lady looked back at us.

"Yeah, Jimmy Fellon's show. That's why we're going to New York."

“Wow, could I have your autograph?”

“Sure.” Master signed her paper. “Here. I’ll sign for Spot too. He can’t write yet.” Master traced outside my paw.

“I bet this’ll be worth something after you’re on TV!”

“Who knows?” Master shrugged.

She pushed her cart farther down the aisle.

We got off the airplane and into a car. Master told me it was a taxi. It smelled like dozens of different humans, all huddled together.

“Rockefeller Center,” Master said.

* * *

We walked into the big building and then a room called “the green room.” I knew green was a color I couldn’t see, so I didn’t care.

We met a bunch of people, so I was pretty excited. I noted the smell of the man called Jimmy Fellon, since it was his show.

“Okay, so show me what he can do,” Jimmy said.

“Get me a cue card,” Master said.

“Ha! Does he need cue cards?”

“No, he has a good memory. Read it, Spot.”

“Welcome to *The Show Late Tonight*, starring Jimmy Fellon,” I barked.

Jimmy’s mouth hung open, like he was panting. Was he going to start drooling? I watched with my mouth open, drooling in sympathy.

“That’s amazing! Could I set up something with the orchestra, where they have cards and he goes from instrument to instrument?”

“Sure. That’d be fun.”

“What’d be fun?” I yipped.

“Having you run from instrument to instrument based on the cards.”

“I can hardly wait!” I barked.

* * *

It turned out the orchestra made a lot of noise using different noisemakers—what they called “instruments.” They pulled out their cards.

"Go to the drums!" Jimmy said.

I ran wildly through them until I found the "drums" card. "Here they are!" I barked. The drummer made some big noise.

"Now the saxophone!" Jimmy yelled.

I frantically ran back through the men until I found the saxophone. "I found it!"

Everyone laughed, and the musician made some noise through his saxophone.

"Oh, this'll be good!" Jimmy said.

"We aim to please."

"You said he reads at a sixth-grade level?"

"No, about third grade. I took him through my old school books."

"You still have them?"

"Yeah, I'm a kind of sentimental pack rat."

"Well, just make sure he does the same thing when we record this evening."

"It should be a piece of cake."

"Cake?" I barked. "Where?" I looked around and sniffed.

"That's enough rehearsal. I want you fresh and spontaneous for tonight. Be back at five p.m. for makeup."

"What's makeup?" I yipped.

"That's coloring people put on their faces," Master explained.

"Can I eat it?"

"No, it's not food."

* * *

Later that day we did the whole orchestra-chase thing again. It was just as much fun the second time. Jimmy had the drummer and the saxophone switch cards. They didn't fool me. I still went to the right card.

This time a big audience yelled and laughed and clapped. That got me even more excited.

We came back to sit in some nice chairs.

"I got a gift for you Spot," Jimmy said.

"What?" I yipped with interest.

"A fourth-grade reader! Can you read it for me?" He showed it to me.

"*McGruffy's Fourth Grade Reader*," I barked.

"I understood that perfectly. Man, I wish his barks and growls were in English so the people in the audience could understand him," Jimmy said.

"Yeah, I've thought of that too. I guess telepathy just isn't good enough," Master said.

"Say, why don't we wish together right now?"

"Live? On national TV?"

"Why not? It is a comedy show, after all. At least we won't catch on fire. I hope."

"I'm game. Let's wish. 'Spot can talk English out loud.'"

Jimmy nodded. "One, two, three . . ."

"Spot can talk English out loud!" we said together.

"Did it work?" I asked. My bark felt funny, like it was catching in my throat.

"Yes!" they yelled, and the crowd went crazy.

I tried barking, but I kept saying, "Wow! Wow-wee! Whoo-hoo!" while I jumped in circles around the stage.

After the crowd died down, Jimmy asked me, "How do you like talking aloud?"

"I like barking better. Talking English feels like there's a piece of rabbit stuck in my throat. I don't know whether to swallow or throw up."

For some reason, that made the audience laugh. Then Jimmy made me read the *McGruffy Reader* again. The crowd made noise at that too.

"It's been great having you, Josh and Spot! Will you come on again?"

"Sure!" Master said.

"Of course!" I yelled. If I yelled, English felt more like barking.

* * *

I placed my chair at Forty-Second and Broadway to maximize my traffic. It was awkward maneuvering the manual chair, but I found I got more money with it than with my electric chair. Faith nuzzled my hand, alerting me that someone stood behind me. I backed up anyway and bumped them.

"Oops! Sorry. I didn't see you." Sometimes if I bumped into

someone, they gave me something.

"Oh my, I'm sorry. I wasn't looking where I was going." The lady had a pleasant soprano voice.

"I was just placing my chair against the building for the day. This is my only source of income." I put my plastic bucket and hand-lettered sign down. The sign said, "Please help the blind."

"Here. Let me give you something." The lady put a bill in my bucket.

What bill is it? I asked my dog telepathically.

A ten spot, she answered.

I made a lot more money once I discovered I could talk with Faith and she understood me.

"Thank you so much! God bless you," I said to the lady.

"It's the least I can do after bumping you," she said. "Nice shades, by the way!" She left.

Empty her wallet into my bucket, I wished. I heard some bills rustle in. This was another scam I'd discovered accidentally over the past couple of weeks. I was actually making a decent wage. The perfect crime.

My new fluorescent-blue sunglasses were comfortable—I'd bought them with yesterday's takings. This day was starting well too.

Faith peered into the bucket. *Two twenties and a ten.*

Faith was great at reading the bills, but not so good at addition. She was good with single digits to ten but had trouble with six plus seven.

I tapped my cane in front of me. It clicked against the sidewalk and banged against the bucket. I could hear the rush of many people going by. I could feel the air of their passing bodies. I sniffed. I could smell the scent of sweat, cologne, and perfume.

Good traffic, but not many donations. Maybe I had too much money in the bucket. I put my hand in my pocket and wished the twenty into it. I rolled it into a cylinder and took out my hand.

Someone threw in some change. "Thank you!" I said to the air. They didn't stop to be robbed. A bill landed softly. I barely heard it. "Thanks!" They didn't stop either.

A one, Faith sent to me.

I growled to myself. *What else can I do to make more money?*

A bunch of people passed me. On impulse, *I wish all their cash was in my bucket.* I heard a satisfying rustle. I felt Faith move to peer in.

Wow. There's a twenty, another twenty, a hundred, a fifty, a bunch of ones, a bunch of fives and tens.

I smiled. I wished the twenties, the fifty, and the hundred into my pocket and rolled them up. Faith and I could count the total later today. I knew this day would be a good one. I heard another crowd coming.

Chapter 23 - Competition

Friday, October 9

“Am I going to jail?” I asked the FAA official, Walter Borthwick.

“No, you don’t seem dangerous. Just stay inside your home until arraignment, and no more flying.” He paused. “I will have to impound your flying car.”

“I can’t have that. It’s a rental.”

“Where’d you rent it?”

“Avi’s. The car rental place with the bird logo.”

“Huh. I didn’t know they had flying cars.”

“You don’t have to worry about impounding it. I’ll send it home. Go home, car!” I yelled. The parked car unfolded its wings and took off.

“That looks even weirder from the outside than from the inside. Also, that’s an unlicensed UAV, unmanned aerial vehicle. Let’s get you arraigned and you can go home.”

He marched me inside the blocky government building. An idea popped into my brain. “I have to use the restroom.”

Borthwick nodded. “Okay. I’ll wait outside.”

In the bathroom, I fished a tissue from my purse. I held it in my hand and wished. “Become a valid FAA flying license.”

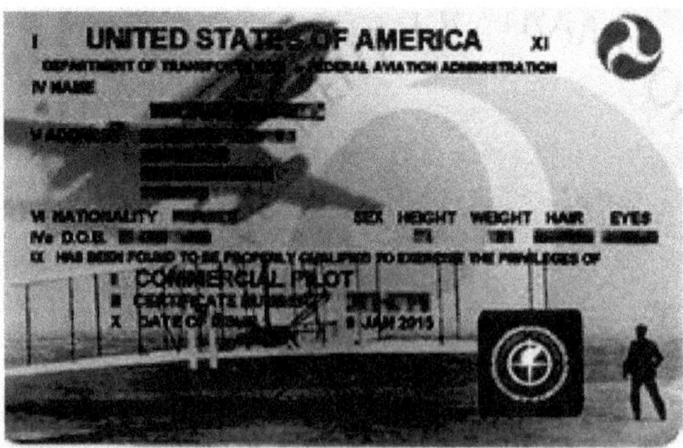

The tissue turned into a plastic license, complete with a seal and signature. I peered at it. Angela L Hamilton, 5’ 2” 115 pounds. Commercial License, Issued October 9, 2027. Oops. That was today’s date. I wished it to become October 5, 2027.

That was when I'd started my Urber business. I put it back in my purse and left with a big smile.

"Hi, Walter! Good news!"

His features turned from confused to suspicious. "What 'good news'?"

"Look what I found in my purse!" I handed him my license.

He studied it carefully. "This looks genuine. I'm going to have to check this out. Come with me."

We went into his office. He started his computer and looked up my license. "Unbelievable."

"What?"

"It all checks out. Your license was issued October 5."

"That's when I started my Urber business."

"The license number matches our records, and the hologram and signature are valid." He frowned. "I don't believe it. This is too convenient. This must be a forgery." He sounded like he was trying to convince himself.

"I just forgot about it until now. I'm not used to getting arrested. And I'm elderly. My memory's not as good as it was twenty years ago."

"How are you getting home?"

"I'll just call my car back. C'mere, car!"

"I can't believe that'll work."

"You don't believe. That is why you fail." I gave him my best Jedi-master look.

Borthwick laughed. "That's a pretty good impression!" Then he did a double take as my car thrummed down like a giant hummingbird into the parking spot in front of the building.

"See you, Ms. Hamilton! It's been a unique experience. Let me know if you renew your license. I'd like to personally test you!"

I rolled down my window and flashed my dimples at him. "You just did that!"

Back in my car, circling over downtown Cleveland, I checked my phone for any people looking for rides. Yup. I had one right downtown, from the casino. I parked in front, and a guy slid in. He had a close-cut beard, a man bun, and a ponytail.

"Where to?"

"Take me to the airport."

"You got it." I did a neat vertical takeoff and then made a beeline to I-71 and the airport.

This guy didn't prepay. "Will this be cash or charge?"

"Cash on delivery. Look at my winnings." He showed me a roll of bills—twenties and hundreds. "How fast can this thing go?"

"I've gotten up to four hundred miles per hour, but it's pretty noisy."

"Cool. Could it fly all the way to Pittsburgh at that speed?"

"Sure, but our ears would be numb."

"I don't care. Let's go."

"Nah. I'm not licensed to do business in Pittsburgh. There's a whole other layer of bureaucratic nonsense to do regional flights."

He grinned at me. "You don't get a choice." He held a chrome pistol to my head. *A .45*, I thought.

"Oh. It's probably not a good idea to shoot your pilot when we're a thousand feet high and going two hundred miles per hour." I put on a pretty good nonchalant act, if I do say so myself.

"I'm a gambler. I'll bet you don't want to die."

"You'd win that bet." I spun the wheel, and we did a series of barrel rolls over the airport. He banged his head against the window, but he was still holding on to his gun.

"Unlock yourself, seat belt." I did another barrel roll, and he rattled around the back seat like a roulette ball in a wheel. This time he was knocked out and let go of the gun.

"Into the glove box, gun." The box opened, and the gun zoomed in. I consulted my tablet on the dash. "Where's the nearest police station?" It flashed "Brook Park Police Department Law Enforcement, 17401 Holland Rd, Brook Park, OH (216) 433-1239."

"Call them." It did. I was glad Jeff had installed a computer screen in my car.

"Hi. I'm bringing in a carjacker to you."

"When? How? What happened?"

I told them about the attempted hijacking and knocking him out by a barrel roll. "He's in the back of my car. I'll be landing in a minute."

"What?"

"It's a flying car. Just look out your window." I landed neatly in a parking space.

Several officers came out. They pulled the comatose bum from the car and carried him into the station. They opened the glove box and carefully retrieved his pistol, using latex gloves.

"Did you touch this pistol, ma'am?" A polite, clean-cut young man questioned me while I stood watching.

"No. I put it in there without touching it."

"How?"

"I opened the door and it flew in while I maneuvered." *Pretty cool, Angie. You told the truth.*

"Fancy flying. Okay, let's get your statement." He led me into the station.

We finished in an hour. "Don't leave town, Mrs. Hamilton. You may have to testify when his case comes up in court.

"All right, Officer."

I grabbed a burger at a fast-food place and then picked up another customer.

* * *

While I was picking up a fare downtown, I was surprised to see a flying school bus soar past the Terminal Tower. I flew closer to it and saw it was black-and-white checked and had a sign, "Checkered Flag Airline." He seemed to be headed for Progressive Field, where the Guardians had a game.

I picked up my passenger, Bill Fredrico, and took off to his home in Brooklyn. The checkered bus zoomed by and almost hit me. I heard an amplified voice, like from a loudspeaker, "Be cursed with caramel!" and my car was coated in caramel. My wings couldn't flap, and we plummeted.

Crap. How did I remove hundreds of pounds of caramel from my car while falling to the ground? Meanwhile, Bill, a middle-aged man with a pot belly and a baseball cap, was screaming like a girl.

Let's see: Calm my passenger and stop our fall. First our fall. "Be gone, caramel." Nothing happened. I couldn't even see out the brown windshield. "Get off my windshield, stupid candy!"

That helped. A glob of caramel the size of a basketball hovered next to my hood. I could see clearly now—I was about five hundred feet from the ground and falling quickly, in a spin. "Get off my wings!"

Nothing happened. "Get off my right wing, stupid caramel!" A beachball-size glob formed, and my right wing flapped. We were two hundred feet from the ground and spinning in the opposite direction now, like a maple-leaf seed. We might survive now.

"Get off my left wing, caramel!" Another candy beachball and we slowed, just fifty feet from the pavement. Brook Park Road, I thought.

I didn't like how the balls of candy were hovering and quivering next to the car, like they wanted to recoat it. I also didn't like how my passenger was hoarsely screaming, "Let me out! Let me out of here!"

"Yes, sir. We're just a mile from your home. You're in luck. Today's free candy day! Every passenger gets as much caramel as they want. Caramel, you're wrapped in bite-size pieces in the back seat." I looked at the windshield glob, two feet away.

It burst into hundreds of pieces of candy. Wax paper appeared and wrapped each piece. My window unrolled itself, and they streamed into the car and covered my passenger.

"What am I supposed to do with these?" he said, with a rasp in his voice.

"Eat as many as you want." I disposed of the other caramel blobs into pieces as well, flying them into my trunk.

We landed in front of his house, but we didn't roll; we squished. I hopped out to investigate, but the door and side windows were covered in caramel too, as well as the tires.

I spoke itemized counter curses on the doors, fenders, headlights and taillights, undercarriage, and tires and wrapped up the whole mess. My magical wax paper seemed to stop it from recoating the car.

"I really thought we were goners there," he panted. "I've never been so glad to be home."

"Normally I'd charge you for the trip, but since we ran into some bad caramel weather, this is gratis. Enjoy your caramel treats." I handed him a bagful.

He eyed it dubiously. “I don’t think I could eat it, but this solves my issue of buying Halloween candy. Thanks for saving my life. I think I’ll have a drink now.” He trundled into his house.

“That was a really dangerous stunt they pulled. I think I’ll have to take some legal action,” I said as I flew home.

“Who are the best lawyers in Cleveland for business damages?” I asked my phone. It gave me a list of law firms. “Sprong, Blodgett, and Whifflehammer” led the list. Five-star rating. I gave them a call and made an appointment for tomorrow morning.

My phone beeped with a text. “Please pick me up at the airport at 10 am tomorrow—Katie Garcia.”

Chapter 24 - Magic

Saturday, October 10

I picked up a rental car from O'Hare Airport and trudged through Chicago traffic. The steady drizzle made it worse. Eventually I came to the apartment of Maria Chen. After parking, I took a sensor scan of the building. It showed just a normal 3–4 MU background reading. I scanned the building across the street. The values ranged from 5–15 MUs, peaking at the roof, right where the pink dragon had been videoed.

Well. It looked like the trip wasn't a waste. I composed my thoughts and questions as I took a slow elevator to the seventh floor.

A tall, square-faced blonde answered the door. "May I help you?" She tilted her head.

"Hello. I'm Katie Garcia from Oakridge Labs. I'm investigating the strange phenomena around the world, by the directive of President Lopez. I texted Maria Chen that I'd be here this morning to discuss her video. Is she here?

"Well yes. But she's indisposed and not available right now."

"May I come in? I'll ask you some questions while I wait for her."

"Okay." She let me in.

I glanced around the apartment and saw the window that looked at the apartment across the street. I walked over there. "Is this where the video was taken?"

"Yes."

"You saw Maria take the video?"

"I took it. She uploaded it."

"I see. What do you think?" I scanned the building from this angle. The MUs read 10–15.

"Think of what?"

"Your video of the pink dragon."

"I really couldn't say."

"That's lame. Why not?"

"Uh . . . magic. That's it . . . magic."

"That's what I'm here to find out. Did you go across the street?"

"Uh, I can't say."

"Oh? Is magic stopping you?"

She nodded frantically.

A short dark-haired woman came down the hall. She wore a determined frown. "Are you Katie Garcia?"

"Yes."

"I was afraid of that, so I hid. But I have to stand with my friend Heather. Let me begin by saying, I can't tell you anything."

"Because of magic."

"Right."

"Did you go across the street?"

"Erg." She seemed to have something in her throat. "I can't tell you."

"I see. Did you upload the video?"

"Yes." She sighed with relief, seemingly happy to have a question she could answer.

"Do you think it's a real dragon?" I tried a direct approach.

"Ach. I can't say," she rasped.

"Then why did you upload it?"

"So everyone could see it. I wanted the world to know." That all burst out of her like a balloon popping.

"Now we know, at least the dragon part. Let's all go across the street together and see what else we find out." I turned to go, but they stood there. "What? You can't leave your apartment?"

"I'm afraid," Heather said.

"Afraid of what?"

"She's afraid something worse will happen to us."

"Ah. So whoever made the dragon magicked you to keep it quiet. And you're afraid they'll do worse."

They nodded vigorously.

"I can't let anyone risk their lives because of my research. I'll go myself." I left.

On the way down I wondered, *How do I protect myself from magic?* The natural answer came to me. *By magic.* I wished aloud, "No magic will affect me today." I didn't know if it would work. I checked my MU level—15, higher than ever before.

At least I felt better about this.

At the other apartment building, I checked each floor for MU level: 5 at the ground, then 6–11 at the sixth floor. Then 10 on the next two floors and 15 on the roof. I went back to the sixth floor and checked each apartment: 6a was 12, 6b was 15, and 6c was 13. I knocked on 6b's door.

"Who's there?" I heard a young man's voice.

"Katie Garcia. Could you answer some questions for me?"

The door cracked. A young brown face peered out from under door chains. "I ain't s'posed to let anyone in while our mom is gone."

"Okay. I'll wait. When will your mom be back?"

"Mebbe two? She works half days on Saturdays."

"Okay, I'll come back then."

* * *

I came back at two after surveying the magic around the neighborhood. The dragon building was definitely the hot spot, although the local playground was surprisingly high as well.

A lady with short black hair and a scowl answered the door. "Are you the woman bothering my children?"

"Uh, no. I just wanted to ask some questions about a dragon on the roof. I'm Katie Garcia from Oakridge National Labs."

"Why would there be a dragon on our roof? Dragons don't exist."

"I've got this video from the internet." I showed her on my tablet.

"Mmm. What's that to you anyway?"

"I'm part of a presidential investigation into all these strange happenings around the world." I showed her my Oakridge employee badge.

"You mean President Lopez?"

"Yes. He's my boss."

"I like him. Okay, c'mon in. I'll hear you out. I'm Shannon Brown." She shook my hand.

I sat on the couch and took my MU detector out of my

backpack.

"What's that?" The bright-eyed young man I'd seen at the door pointed at the machine.

"It's an MU detector. It measures the amount of this mysterious power that causes all these weird things, like pants catching on fire—and dragons."

"Huh. I didn't know anything was behind all that stuff."

"It seems to be building up all around the world—especially in your apartment." I held my voice steady as I read an amazing 50 MU level in the apartment. And 75 in the young man. And 60 from Shannon.

"Lamar, go get your sister—she should be here. That's my son, Lamar."

"Shayla!" Lamar ran down the hall.

A pigtailed girl dressed in pink ran into the room, carrying a stuffed pink dragon. *The* dragon.

I gulped. The dragon read 100 MUs. The girl was 200.

"Well. That seems to be the dragon I saw in the video."

"Ya got a video of Pinkie?" Shayla asked.

"Yes." I showed her.

"Huh. That was from those girls across the street, I bet," Lamar said.

"Lamar, didn't we make them swear to not tell about us?"

"Yeah. I guess this video doesn't count."

"That's what I guess too. It's all over the internet," I said.

"Oh no! We're trying to not draw attention to our private lives!" Shannon said

"Right. We're disguised when we go to Grant Park and give rides."

"You give rides in Grant Park?" I asked.

"Yeah. We made a lotta money," Lamar said.

"I was hoping we'd make enough to get out of this apartment and buy a house somewhere," Shannon said. "And I could quit my job."

"We didn't go today 'cause it's raining." Shayla's pigtails bobbed as she nodded.

"I was going to have you fly Pinkie for me, but it's not a fit day to be out, even for dragons." I shook my head.

"Oh, Pinkie wouldn't mind. He stays warm all the time.

Want me to show you?"

"Yes, but what about videos?"

"Oh that. After we ran into the girls, we had Pinkie turn invisible when we flew." Lamar waved off my concern.

"Okay. If you don't mind, I'd like to see him fly."

"Yay! Mom, could we go and show Mrs. Garcia?" Lamar looked at his mom.

"All right. Dress warmly. I don't want you getting sick and missing school. You'll keep us secret, right, Mrs. Garcia?"

"Just call me Katie. Of course, Mrs. Brown. I will not include your names or your address in any of my reports or research."

"You can call me Shannon, Katie."

I looked into her eyes and realized we were probably close to the same age. Despite our differences, I thought we might become friends.

"Thanks, Shannon. Show me the way to the roof, kids."

Yelling, Lamar ran up the stairs with an umbrella, while Shayla, Pinkie, and I took the elevator.

We huddled on the roof under Lamar's umbrella.

"Now what?" I asked.

"Watch this." Shayla hugged her dragon, and it grew and grew. It towered over us, the size of an elephant—or dragon.

"Hi, Shayla! You brought a friend!" The mouth hung open, like a pink cave.

"Hi, Pinkie. This is Ms. Gar—er, Katie."

"Hi, Pinkie. Let me measure you." The dragon showed 200 MUs, equal to Shayla's. Shayla was up to 300.

"Wow."

"Hop on and I'll give you a ride."

"It's raining, Pinkie!"

"Make Lamar's umbrella big enough for me and I'll keep you dry."

"Good idea! Umbrella, get big!" The umbrella grew to beach size, and Pinkie took it from Lamar. It continued to grow to the size of a pavilion. Pinkie held it up in one pink hand over our heads.

"Hop on now!"

"Don't forget to be invisible, Pinkie!" Shayla waved her

finger at the car-size head in front of us.

"I won't, Shayla."

We climbed on Pinkie's neck. Each of us sat between two pink spikes rising from his back. They took me on a tour of Chicago: the skyscrapers, river, lake, and beachfront. The gray, steady drizzle contrasted with the pink dragon we flew.

Saying little, I noted a steady warmth that came from the dragon, like a heating pad, as well as a sweet smell I couldn't place. Maybe cotton candy?

We landed and returned to the apartment, Pinkie transformed back into a plush toy.

"Thank you, Shannon, for sharing your apartment, your secrets, your children, and your dragon with me. This will keep me thinking for days."

"Aren't you going to stay for supper? I've got cornbread and chili cookin'."

"Sounds great."

The simple meal hit the spot. I relaxed after the brain-numbing revelations of the afternoon.

I offered to pay.

"No way!" Shannon said. "Pinkie paid for our meal this evening from the rides last week. And also, it's more blessed to give than to receive. You don't want to take away my blessing, do you?" She smiled.

I'd heard that saying, but I'd never seen anyone apply it like that.

"Now, you can stay the night, if you want. I'll sleep with the kids, and you can have my bed."

"I'd love to stay, but I've got a flight to Cleveland tonight."

"Whew! They keep you busy, don't they?"

"You don't know the half of it. I have to compose a report on my findings, and everything has political meanings."

"Ugh. I hate politics."

"Me too." I hugged her. "I'm glad to meet you and become a friend. I'll try to come back and see you."

"Bye!" the kids called.

"Bye!" Shannon waved at the door.

"Bye!" Pinkie said, flying above their heads.

Chapter 25 – Sales

Tuesday, October 13

The next morning after breakfast I went back to my office. I had sent my book in to my editor, but I felt I should be doing something. Anyway, I liked looking at the trees from my window as they changed color.

I wondered if I had any presales? After poking around online for a while, I found the right report. “Wow! Ten presales already!”

“What’d you say, honey?” Jane called up the stairs.

“Ten presales already!” I yelled.

“That’s great!” She climbed the stairs. “Let’s go out to eat to celebrate.”

“And spend all the money I made?”

“Why not? What else will we use it for?”

“I like how you think!”

At lunchtime we walked to a local Greek restaurant. I had souvlaki, and Jane had a lamb kebab. Delicious. When we returned home, I checked my presales again.

“One hundred and one!”

“You sold even more?”

“Presold. But yeah. Another ninety-one came in since this morning.”

“I’m too full to celebrate again.”

“Me too. Wanna go to a movie?”

“Why not? What’s playing?”

“*Zombie Turkeys: The Unkillable* just came out.”

“Isn’t that based upon the book?”

“Yeah.”

“I liked the book, but they usually ruin it in a movie.”

“The author, Andy Zach, approved it.”

“Okay. Let’s give it a try. We can always walk out.”

* * *

“The movie was better than I’d expected, but I still liked the book better,” Jane said as we walked out of the theater.

"Yeah, they missed some of the humor, and they dropped out the scene with Obama and Raul Emmanuel."

"It wouldn't be a movie if they didn't cut out stuff. Look at *Lord of the Rings*." She shook her head.

"The movie visualized a lot of it well, but they added too much stuff."

Back at home, I fired up my old desktop computer. It was my son's old gaming computer and still pretty fast, even ten years later. I was eager to see if I sold any more books. The sales page came up. "That can't be right." I cleaned my bifocals. The page updated as I watched. I had over ten thousand presales. I was number one in Amazin' fantasy sales.

I also had hundreds of new emails. Was I getting spammed? Publisher, publisher, publisher—all wanting to publish and promote my book under their label. They all sounded the same, so I guessed it was a kind of spam.

I created a spreadsheet to track them. A column for the offer, the advantages, and the cost. I made a response email after I had entered the 149 offers, asking for the detailed contract and stating I wished control of my book and all copyrights. That should thin them out.

The other emails were mostly my usual junk and bills. There was an offer to make my book into a screenplay. Cool. It was from the same gal who had written the screenplay for *Zombie Turkeys*. I replied, saying I wanted the same contract as Andy Zach. I also copied him on the email, andyzach@andyzach.net. I had that memorized, since I was on his newsletter mailing list.

Jane stopped by my office. "Are you writing your next book?"

"Not yet. I'm toting up the presales for my first one. We're over ten thousand."

"Whoa. How much money is that?"

"Lessee. I get $4.95 for each book. My current sales are"—I flicked over to the tab—"fifteen thousand four hundred and ninety-one. My current revenue is $76,680.45." I magnified the window so it filled the screen.

"Wow. That's more than we make in a year."

"Yep. Now the next question is—" I stopped. The gaudy

profit disappeared and turned to zero. Then it went to $4.95 as another book was sold.

"What happened?"

"I don't know. Our revenue disappeared. Our sales are still recorded. Hmm. This isn't good."

"We lost the money before we ever had it."

"Let's see if I can get it back." I opened a service request with Amazin', the online publishing company.

"It disappeared like magic." Jane shook her head.

"You may be right. How can we ever find the culprit?"

* * *

I was grumpy. A cold, freezing drizzle covered New York. Who wanted to beg in that? Or steal? I was averaging a couple thousand a day, and I hated to lose that. Sure, I could play on people's sympathies and more would stop, but when you were boosting the cash from their wallets, the key was traffic.

Idly I browsed the internet looking for high-traffic sites. My text-to-voice reader said, "The highest traffic sites on the internet."

Rank	Website	Visits Per Month (billions)
1	giggle.com	175
2	viewtube.com	113
3	friendbook.com	18.1
4	yoctogram.com	7.36
5	z.com	7.35
6	Amazin.com	4.23

Huh. Amazin.com was the highest-traffic e-commerce site. Everything else was just social media. Four billion visits per month was over a hundred million per day. If only I could lift some of that money as it flowed in and out. Maybe I could.

I pulled up my bank account. I used PayAll.com to bank online. I used a local bank for small deposits and to transfer most of my cash to my PayAll account.

How much could I steal from Amazin' without them catching me? They had millions of transactions each day. What if I just stole a penny from each? What if it was less than half a penny? Would they notice?

Only one way to find out. For safety, I created a new PayAll account under one of my phony names, "Andy Zach," and gave it a PO box address. Then I wished with all my might, just like I did when I'd wished Faith could read the bills.

Andy Zach was one of my favorite authors. I had all his audiobooks.

"I wish I would get point-forty-nine cents of every transaction from Amazin' from today deposited in my new PayAll account." I had to be specific. I'd learned this the hard way. When I began stealing using magic, the wallets and purses were torn from the people and ended up in my collection basket. That caused an uproar, and I had to return them.

I refreshed my screen on my new PayAll account. The reader said: "PayAll Wallet $481.63."

That was pretty good for a minute. I waited another minute and refreshed. It was over a thousand dollars.

At this rate, I'd make over half a million dollars a day. How would I spend it?

I could get a nice car and a driver. I could get a mansion.

But what did I really want? Power. I wanted it so no one could order me around anyone.

Since there weren't any openings for dictators in the US or New York, I decided to run for NYC mayor. I filed my application online. "Darrell Duncan, candidate for NYC Mayor. Party: Independent."

Chapter 26 – Publicity

Tuesday, October 13

"Okay, kids. We need a family conference. What are we going to do about all this publicity? We're in all the news and social media. Even if we're disguised, people can find us. If the government found its way to our apartment, so can thieves. We can't stay here." I looked at my kids, sitting around our kitchen table.

"Uh, can we move to a different apartment?" Lamar's brown eyes stared at mine. He looked just like his father, God rest his soul.

"We could, but it won't help. People still know who we are. You've lived here all your lives, and I lived here all my life until my mom died. Then I got her apartment. Plus, there's that magic detector Katie had that found our apartment."

"Easy! I just hide us behind a magic shield!" Shayla waved her hand like she was tracing out a windshield.

"That would work, but they still know our apartment building from that video. I think we have to move, like Lamar said. I told you I wanted to buy a house. A few more of these days giving rides and I'll have enough for a down payment."

Shayla jumped up. "Wow! With our own yard? Could we have a swing set? And a merry-go-round?"

"Cool! Could I have a basketball hoop? I could practice until I got good!"

"One step at a time. If we get the same money as last time, we'll need to sell Pinkie rides at Grant Park ten more times for a down payment."

"How about if we use Terry?"

"That's your pteranodon, right? Yeah, that'll reduce it to five times. We could get done this coming week!"

"What if we used Rainbow for rides?" Shayla lifted her flying unicorn with the rainbow tail and mane.

"Sure! Why not? I'll ride her. You get Pinkie, Shayla, and Lamar can ride Terry."

"How about we increase our prices? Say fifty dollars?"

"I feel bad about that. A lot of people won't be able to afford it. I know I missed a lot because we didn't have enough money. And although it's better for you kids now, I know you haven't gotten as much as a lot of other kids. I feel for other families like ours."

"Fifty dollars ain't nothing." Lamar dismissed the thought with a wave of his hand. "That's what those tours cost—on a bus. Tourists are rich. Poor folk ain't in Grant Park buying stuff—they're selling stuff."

"Hmm. I think you're right, Lamar. Okay, let's try fifty dollars a ride this Saturday. If it doesn't work, we can always drop our prices."

"Great! I'll get to work writing up the new price signs. Shayla, you can make them big at Grant Park, like you did before." Lamar ordered Shayla confidently.

"Easy!"

"I'd better practice riding Rainbow."

"You're right, Mom. I've got to get used to riding Terry. Let's go to the beach on them right now!"

"Whee! I'll make us all invisible. Let's go up to the roof!" Shayla ran to the door, carrying Pinkie.

"Hold on, Shayla. Aren't you forgetting something?" I smiled at her.

"I know! The picnic basket!" Lamar reached up and pulled it down.

"I got some fried chicken in the fridge we can pack. And coleslaw. Do you want me to make corn muffins too?"

"Yeah!" the kids chorused.

The kids packed the basket and made lemonade while I mixed up a batch of corn muffins. I used my mom's recipe. They smelled heavenly coming out of the oven. I had a happy memory of my mom baking them for me. Now I was the mom.

"Anyone want a muffin for the trip?"

"Me!"

"Me!"

"Here you go. Let's go up to the roof. Lamar, you carry the basket, and I'll take the thermos. Shayla, you take Pinkie and Rainbow."

Coming out on the roof, Shayla said, "Stop!"

"What?" I looked at her, puzzled.

"Lemme make us invisible." She spun in a circle. "We're invisible, except to ourselves. Pinkie, it's time to grow." She put him down, and he grew to horse size."

"Let me try, Shayla." I took Rainbow from her. I'd bought the stuffed unicorn for her when she was going through her horse-crazy stage, watching cartoons. "Okay, Rainbow, grow to flying-horse size!" I put it down as it trembled. Soon it was looking me in the eye with its black eyes. It nuzzled me gently, shaking its rainbow mane.

"Now I guess I have to do mine." Lamar stared at his pteranodon. "I can't!" He dropped the plastic dinosaur on the ground and covered his face, dropping to his knees.

"What the matter, Lamar?" Shayla patted her brother's head.

"I just can't. I can't do magic like you can, Shayla." His body shook as he tried to hold back tears.

"Here." Shayla picked up the little dinosaur and handed it to him. "I'll help you." She put her little hands around his big ones. "Just wish."

Lamar steadied himself. "I wish you were big enough to fly." He stared at the toy.

"See? Nothing."

"Ya gotta wish *hard*. With all your might. That's what I did when that gang started shooting and I wished Pinkie grew big."

"Huh. I didn't know that. Lemme try again." He collected himself. "I wish Terry was big enough to fly—right now!" Lamar ended with a shout. He suddenly dropped his dinosaur. "Yow. What's going on?"

"It's growing!"

Terry grew to a full-size pteranodon with a thirty-foot wingspan. It cocked its head and looked at Lamar.

"Climb on, Lamar! Do I have to tell you everything?" Shayla giggled.

I laughed too and climbed on Rainbow. Then we flew away.

* * *

In the apartment below, the MU meter jumped. The

background MUs went from 20 to 40. Then the meter sent the data to Katie's laptop, under her seat as she flew to Cleveland.

Chapter 27 – Detective

Tuesday, October 13

So how can I get to see Katie again? She's off chasing down magical leads. I can't bug her with emails. I've got to help her with her magic research in some way.

What about catching the kid who'd stolen stuff using magic? I shook my head. It was just an ice cream cone. So what?

But what if they were stealing other stuff too? I could be a teen detective (I was almost thirteen) like the Hardy Boys or Nancy Drew. They were an old series of books my dad and my mom had around the house. Any time I'd nag them about getting me a phone, they'd say, "Read a book." I loved reading, so it wasn't a problem at home, where I could use the family computer. But I was sure I was the only kid at school without a phone.

Anyway, the Hardy Boys and Nancy Drew always solved their cases, which I thought was pretty unrealistic. But they were well written, and it was fun reading about old times when my parents were kids. Maybe those books were from when my grandparents were kids. They were pretty old-fashioned.

Why couldn't I solve this case? I could use magic! The Hardy Boys didn't have that. Feeling smug, I planned how I'd go about catching them.

The little kid could flee home when he wanted. Could I wish to go along with him? Of course I could.

What then? I'd confront the mom. Yuck. I didn't want to do that. I wanted to be a detective and find out what they were doing, not arrest them. I'd leave that to the police when I got the evidence on them.

How would I do that? Maybe I could plant a voice recorder in their house. Where could I get a voice recorder? Of course, Mom's and Dad's phones had recording apps, but I couldn't take them.

I looked up recorders on the internet. Woof! Most of them cost more money than I had on hand. I couldn't touch my college fund. Ah. There was a budget recorder for only fifty dollars, the Sunny 123.

The Sunny 123 was a bit bulkier than my main pick and its audio quality wasn't as good, but it had a similar layout and navigation system. It did best in quiet settings with minimal background noise.

That should work. I could get it at our local Wal-Store. I dug out my savings from my underwear drawer. I had mowed lawns, raked leaves, and shoveled snow in our neighborhood all year to get spending money. When I had turned twelve, rather than giving me an increase in allowance, my dad took me door to door around our neighborhood to see who wanted chores done. I was surprised by how friendly most people were.

I had been saving most of it for college, but I took out money for spending and for giving at church.

I put the money in my wallet and rode my bike to the store. I barely had enough money after paying the sales tax. No ice cream this week for me. But I did have a leaf-raking job tomorrow after school. I could treat myself then.

After I was home, I read the directions and tested it. I spoke at various volume levels in my bedroom, and it captured okay. I decided to take it to Jefferson Middle School for a test.

The next day at school, I recorded all the lectures in my classes and the kids at my lunchroom table. That would give me a wide variety of sound conditions.

That evening at home I listened to the various classes. They all sounded clear enough. The lunchroom recording was a mess though. I could hear myself speak, but no one else. The background noise was too loud.

Okay. How did I get this into their house? Where did I put it? I didn't know. I decided to scout them out. I biked over to the Ice Cream Joy store—which apparently the owners had changed their mind about closing—and looked for that kid. He was just an average third or fourth grader. I spotted him after an hour or so. I walked up to him. "Hi. I've got a question for you."

"You! You're trouble. You wished me back here."

"After you stole our ice cream. But that's all forgiven. Where do you live?"

"I ain't tellin' you nothin'." He closed his eyes and

disappeared.

I closed my eyes and imagined myself outside his front door. A puff of warm, humid air hit my face. I found myself in an non-air-conditioned hall of an apartment building. Apartment 323. I put my ear to the door.

"Whatcha doin' back already?" I heard a low, gravelly woman's voice.

"I saw that kid again. The one who wished me back from the ice cream shop and his mom yelled at me for stealin' their cone." That was the voice of the little kid.

"I'm your mom, and I'll yell at you if you don't get me a cone right now!"

"Okay, okay." Then I heard a pop. Then the TV grew loud.

I looked at the blank door. Green metal with brass 323 numbers on it. It'd be nice if I had X-ray vision like Superman.

Why not? I wished for it. The door and the wall turned translucent. I see could an overweight woman sitting in a chair watching TV. It looked like a rerun of *Scooby-Doo*.

Where could I put the recorder where it wouldn't be seen? In the chair cushion? It'd be muffled. In the ceiling light fixture? They'd be able to see it.

I saw the kid pop into the room holding two ice cream cones.

"Gimme that, Dak," the woman said.

"Here's yours, Mom." He handed her a chocolate cone. Then he bit into his own.

"Mmmm. Good."

"Yum."

After she finished, she said, "Vacuum this place, Dak. It's a pigsty."

"Sure." An old upright vacuum started and began marching around the room. When it reached the woman's chair, she picked up her feet and it vacuumed under them.

Wow. I never thought of using magic with our vacuum. Why not? Then I noticed how the vacuum didn't go under her chair.

The mom seemed to be behind all Dak's stealing. I turned on the recorder and wished it under the chair. It'd record for a day. I'd pick it up tomorrow and see what evidence I'd found.

I wished myself home, right into my room. This teleportation was handy! I was feeling like a real detective—and a magician.

An idea formed, and I ran into our kitchen, where Mom was making a salad. "Hey, Mom, watch this!"

"What, Sean?"

I pulled our vacuum out of the closet. "Vacuum the house! Just like I always do."

It plugged itself in and began vacuuming, following my usual pattern.

"Oh my! I never thought of wishing for that! Maybe I can wish all the dust away?"

"Why not?"

She looked at the curio cabinet in the living room. "Be dust-free!" The dust vanished.

"I love this! Let's try something else. Be clean, glass." The glass doors of the cabinet turned perfectly clear.

"I never knew housework could be so much fun! Front window, be clean! Oh, I forgot—screen, be clean too." Our dingy screen window became like new.

When Dad came home, Mom said, "Notice anything?"

Dad scanned the kitchen, dining room, and living room. He sniffed. "New air freshener? It smells fresher."

Mom laughed. "Men! At least you're on the right track. I cleaned the whole house better than ever before—with magic. Sean showed me how. Show him, Sean."

I wished the vacuum to clean again.

"I wonder if I can use magic at work?" Dad stroked his chin.

"How would it help you manage projects?"

"You'd be surprised."

When everyone had gone to bed, I wished my recorder back into my room. I listened to it quietly, using my earbuds. Most of it was pretty boring, just TV playing. I fast-forwarded past those parts. Then I heard the mother on her phone.

"Tom? It's Yolanda. I got the TV sets you wanted. Yeah, five of them, seventy-five-inch. . . . I want seventy-five cents on the dollar. . . . I don't care about your problems. I got goods you can sell. . . . We're starving in this stinking apartment. I need at least sixty cents on the dollar. . . . Okay. Fifty cents on the dollar and you pick them up tonight. They're taking up space in my living room. It's already so crowded that the mice are round shouldered. They retail for $1199, so that's $2,995 you owe me for the five of them. I see the cash before you get the TVs. . . . Okay, it's a deal." The TV started up again.

Wow. Apparently she'd gotten her son to steal her some TVs. I thought about it, and he'd have no trouble teleporting them into their living room.

I fast-forwarded past the television shows and heard a noise. "Dak. Whatcha you got for me?"

"I got us some roast beef sandwiches."

"Mmm, good. We're selling the TVs tonight. They'll be out of our hair. I'm trying to think of what to buy with the cash."

"I'd like the latest *Tickman* movie. And Choco-bomb cereal."

"You can just steal the cereal and the movie the next time you go to Wal-Store."

"Oh yeah. How about a car so I don't have to take the bus to school?"

"Cars are hard to steal. They can be tracked by the plates and the VIN numbers. But do we really need them? I'd rather get new furniture."

"You want me to steal them, like the TV? I don't think I can pick them up."

"Nah. I want someone to take the old stuff away. And move in the new furniture."

"Huh. Where do they take the old furniture, anyway?"

"Thrift store? Who knows? Ya wanna come with me to the store?"

"Sure!"

"Can you magic us to the store?"

"Uh, no. I don't know where it is."

"Oh. How about to Wal-Store? Couch Factory is just across the street."

"Easy!"

I heard two pops as the air rushed in where their bodies had been. I scanned through an hour or more of silence, and then I heard them again.

"Mmph. These tacos are good, Dak."

“Mmph. They were easy to steal too.”

“Tom’ll be here in an hour with the money for the TVs. Then we can go back to Couch Factory and pay for the furniture.”

Nothing else happened except for the TV playing. Then Tom came in.

“Hi, Yolanda. This is Larry. He’ll help me move the TVs.”

“Where’s the money?”

“Oh. Here’s the check.”

“I wasn’t born yesterday. I want cash.”

“Ya can’t blame a guy for trying. One, two, three . . .” He counted to twenty-nine and then said, “You got five bucks change?”

“Yeah. A five for a hundred.”

“We’re square now. Once I sell these online, I’ll be back for more.”

“Good.”

The recording ended. Great! Now I had evidence against them. I wondered if I could catch the fence? I ran out of my room.

“Mom! Could I borrow your phone for a picture?”

“Sure.” She handed it to me.

I teleported to the apartment hall. I glanced through the door. All the TVs were gone. I looked out the window. A guy was loading a TV into a panel van. I popped to the ground and caught it on video. Then I zoomed in on the license plate: FNC2SL2.

“Hey, you!” someone yelled at me. I looked up and saw a big guy running toward me. “Why you videoing my van? Gimme that phone!”

He was almost here. “Bye!” I teleported home.

I sent the video to my email and then wiped it from Mom’s phone. I didn’t want to get her in trouble.

I downloaded my audio file and edited it. Then I sent it to the police. I also put it on a thumb drive and took it downtown to their headquarters. I felt like a real detective.

Chapter 28 - All In

Tuesday, October 13

A bunch of new people came into the gym. Master said it was because we did that trip and I started talking. I liked selling to them. They petted me and always said, "Say something, Spot!"

"Join Josh's HossFit!" That's what Master told me to say. Most did.

Master was busy all that day on his computer. He had me show people around the gym. I liked that, and they did too.

That evening we went to a restaurant. I had my service vest on.

"What kind of service dog is that?" asked the woman who greeted us.

"I'm a talking service dog!" I wagged my tail.

"Hey, Spot, sit right here." Master pulled out a chair for me. I hopped onto it and sat down. It was really easy to obey him now that I understood everything he said.

Master sat across from me. "I'm treating you because you've made a lot of money for me."

"Great! So what good is money again?" Money was one of the many new things I had learned that didn't make sense to me.

"If people like what you make or what you do, they give you money to do it more. It's like a treat."

"Oh, I love treats! Can we eat this money?"

"I took some of the money and I bought this meal with it."

"That's good. So we'll have plenty of treats, right?"

"You bet. One of my treats is getting some people to help me. I've hired one of my friends to run the gym. I also hired a student to help with data entry. Then I won't have to stay at the computer all day."

"Great! Will you have more time to play?"

"You bet. I'll teach you many new tricks, you old dog."

Our food came. Master cut mine into bite-sized pieces I could eat off the plate. There was a lot of food. Yummy! Money tasted good.

* * *

I smiled as my bank accounts passed a million bucks. This was a lot better than begging on the street.

I got another idea as I reviewed Amazin' bestseller lists. I went on Amazin' and wished the revenue from each bestseller to transfer to my bank account. Then I transferred it to my PayAll account and closed it and opened another account from another bank. Onto the next bestseller list. I had hundreds of bank accounts.

"Read my current account total, Faith."

You have $2,700,473. Her soft, telepathic voice was music to my inner ear. Who needed a reading program when your dog could read your computer and talk?

"You're a really good girl, Faith."

Thank you, Master.

Now I'd start my mayoral campaign, as an independent. I'd go full media. I was a cinch to win, if I wished it so.

* * *

Yummy! Master gave me another treat. I'd stopped the car perfectly! He was teaching me how to drive. He'd gotten special dog-friendly controls and put them next to his car's steering wheel. There was a tennis ball on top of a stick. The car would turn whichever way I moved the ball! If I pushed it forward, the car went forward faster and faster. If I pulled backward, we slowed down. And the ball was fun to chew too. I got it nice and juicy. I wagged my tail in the middle of the car, next to Master.

"Wow, Spot, you're really drooling. You're just like a dog."

"Thanks, Master!" I wagged my tail harder. Master was teaching me in a big open area. He called it a "parking lot." There were no other cars here. Master said it used to be a shopping mall.

Master was picky. I had to stop exactly in the right place every time I saw a stop sign. Then I had to look for cars and people. Then I had to go again. I couldn't go too fast or too slow. There was a funny dial on the dash with a needle that showed my speed.

Master was patient. Every time I made a mistake, I had to try it again. Every time I got it just right, he gave me a piece of steak. "Nothing but the best for you, Spot!"

I practiced starting and stopping, turning left and turning right. I learned to do everything perfectly—except I couldn't back up. I couldn't figure out how to use either the mirror or the rearview cameras.

"I'm sorry, Master. I just have to turn around to see what I'm doing."

"You're not the only one. Some people are like that too. Only we can keep our arm on the wheel and our foot on the gas and the brake. You can't do that. Hmm. Say! Suppose I put another set of controls on the back of the seat, say right here?" Master pointed to a spot behind me. He stuck his fist up like a tennis ball. I grabbed it in my mouth and pushed it.

"That's it, Spot! That's what I'll do. I'll get another set of these controls and hook it up to the back of the seat. Do you want to drive home through real traffic?"

I barked "Yes!" That felt good. I could still bark, but I had to think about it. Otherwise the human word would come out.

"All right. I'll be your backup. I'll give you instructions as you go."

"Great!"

"Head for the exit over there." He pointed across the lot.

I followed the road lines in the parking lot. That was one of my first lessons. I got to the stop sign at the exit. There were a *lot* of cars going by very fast.

"Wait for a break in the traffic."

I swiveled my head back and forth.

"Just look to your left. When that traffic stops, then look to the right. If both are clear, go."

"Yes, Master." The traffic stopped from the left. I looked right. No traffic. I pushed forward, and we zoomed into the road.

"Turn left!" Master yelled.

I pushed the ball left. The wheels squealed. I straightened out the car.

"Pick a lane, left or right. You're in the middle."

I went into the right lane There was just a dotted line

separating the two.

The car in front of me slowed down, so I slowed too. Then he sped up, and I sped up. This was fun! I wagged my tail.

"Did you see the traffic light back there?"

"No?"

"That's why the car slowed down. When the top light is on, you have to stop. When the bottom light is on, you can go."

"Okay. Driving is complicated! But it's fun."

"Now, turn right at the next light."

I looked at the road ahead. Something was hanging from a wire across the road. It had three circles on it. The top one glowed.

"Slow down to make your turn."

I remembered I had to slow to make a turn in the parking lot. I slowed down and turned.

A car honked behind me.

"You did well. Don't pay attention to the man behind you. He thought you were too slow. I'll give you a steak when we get home."

I drooled a whole puddle.

Chapter 29 – Lawsuit

Tuesday, October 13

I was up bright and early on Tuesday. Not only did I have my business, but I had a 9:00 a.m. meeting with Sprong, Blodgett, and Whifflehammer, lawyers in downtown Cleveland. I hadn't dealt with lawyers since my husband's death, and never with such a letter salad as this law firm.

I flew my car to E. Nine Street and saw the street was totally parked up. Undaunted, I landed on the roof and took the elevator down to the law office.

The secretary was so sharply dressed that her clothing could have skinned a fish.

"I have an appointment to see Sprong, Blodgett, and Whifflehammer," I said. "I'm Ms. Angela Hamilton."

She smiled pleasantly. "Mr. Sprong will meet you shortly. Please be seated. Would you like a cup of coffee?"

I'd been drooling for coffee ever since the smell hit me as I entered. "Yes, please. Mmm. It smells freshly brewed."

"Yes, I just brewed it this morning. Jamaican Blue Mountain." She poured me a cup from a silver pot. "Cream?"

"Yes, please." A silver creamer guided its contents to their destination.

I had savored about half the cup in a luxurious overstuffed leather chair when a balding, portly man entered. "Ms. Hamilton?"

"Yes. Mr. Sprong?"

"Yes, Willifred Aldous Sprong. Please call me Will."

"I will, Will." I grinned.

He smiled faintly back. He'd probably heard that joke a million times. "Please follow me to our client room."

Wood-paneled walls, the scent of leather, and a mirror-bright mahogany finish on a conference table greeted me. Two men stood behind the table. A tall, middle-aged man with hollow cheeks and a jutting chin held out his hand to me.

"Michelangelo Sylvester Blodgett, at your service. Please

call me Mike."

"Certainly, Mike." I shook his hand.

Next to him, a trim, elderly man with thin white hair and piercing blue eyes smiled at me. "Welcome, Ms. Hamilton, to our firm. We're highly interested in your case. I'm Ricardo Philemon Whifflehammer, but I prefer Rick."

"Rick it is, then. Please, all of you, call me Angie." We sat around the table.

Rick began. "We investigated Checkered Airlines after you reported the incident. They are certainly expanding quickly, hiring many drivers. They have six buses running in three shifts throughout Cuyahoga County. They're looking to expand outside the county. We've not found any signs of nefarious activity yet. However, the owner, Hugo Lamacek, left Pittsburgh under mysterious circumstances after his taxi business there failed."

"So how can we win the case? Isn't it just a case of my word against theirs?"

"Quite right, Angie. But we have unique resources." Will pulled a fancy video camera from a case next to the table. It had both a dish-like antenna and a metal wrist strap.

"What's that?"

"Something I invented," Mike said quietly. "We were stuck on a case, and I wished to record the crime after it happened. My video camera turned into this."

"What does it do?" I stared at the device, trying to figure it out.

"It renders a video recording of the memory of the person who saw the crime."

"How does it work?"

"Through magic." Will smiled. "As you well know, as the proprietor of a flying-car business, magic is loose in the world. To our knowledge, we're the first law firm to employ it in court."

Rick continued. "Through judicious use of magical research and investigation, we haven't lost a case since MA."

"What's MA?"

"Magic Arrival. We use it as shorthand among ourselves and our clients."

"So you're going to record their caramel attack with this

camera, from my memory?"

"Indeed yes. With your permission, I'll attach the wristband and record you recounting the attack by Checkered Airlines." Will affably held the wrist strap out to me.

"Why not? There's no pain or side effects, are there?"

"No. Our clients do find their memories clearer and more vivid as they are talking," Mike said.

"Are you ready to begin, Angie?" Will had mounted the camera on a tripod on the table, pointing at me.

"I'm curious to see how this works."

"You'll be able to see it in living color." Rick pushed a button on a remote control device, and a screen descended from the ceiling. "The camera will project what your eyes saw throughout the incident on this screen."

"Wow. That's like . . . magic."

"Indeed."

"Okay, let's begin. I'm eager to see this."

I began recounting the caramel attack. The screen showed the front window of my car. My hands gripped the wheel. I saw the flying bus almost hit me. I saw the car's wings coated with caramel out the left and right windows. I heard the screaming of my passenger.

I paused my story. "I didn't know you picked up audio too."

"Oh yes. It's very useful. We'll contact your passenger and get him to testify in court." Will smiled predatorily. "I hadn't realized he was so vociferous. Was he injured at all?"

"No. No harm done."

"Pity. We can still add emotional trauma to our lawsuit. Please continue."

I recounted removing the caramel curse from my windshield and wings. I relived the plummet to the ground. It looked worse on the screen than I remembered. The caramel wrapped itself into bite-size pieces and zoomed through the side windows. I saw my squishy four-caramel landing in front of my passenger's house and me removing the sticky stuff from the rest of the car. My passenger looked more distraught than I remembered, even with a bag of candy.

"Then he said, 'I think I'll have a drink now.' And he went into his house. That's it."

"Excellent. Thank you so much for recounting this traumatic event in such detail. We have many things for which we can sue Checkered Airlines." Rick's eyes positively twinkled. He looked like a jolly old elf. A skinny Santa Claus.

Will stood, and we followed him out the door. "We'll let you know of the court date, Angie."

"What about payment?"

"We will take our fees out of the defendant's resources." Rick handed me another cup of coffee with the firm's name on the side: "Sprong, Blodgett, and Whifflehammer: Not just words, but results."

"Nice slogan." I sipped the creamy goodness.

"Yes. We got it through magical brainstorming. You may keep the cup as a souvenir. "

"Thanks, Rick. Thanks to all of you. I really feel like you're friends helping me out, not just lawyers."

Rick smiled. "We like getting on a first-name basis with our clients. Our names have been a burden to us, so we like to relieve our clients of that burden."

"Thanks again!" I waved at them as the door closed.

I took the elevator to the roof. My phone beeped.

"Please pick me up at the airport at 10 a.m.," the text from Katie Garcia read.

* * *

A trim brunette slung her carry-on luggage into the back seat and sat next to me in my car. She took out a device from another bag she carried. It had dials and lights over the front. She took a microphone-like object and pointed it at me.

"Is this a stick up?" I asked.

She snorted. "No. This is my MU detector."

"What's an 'MU'?"

"Magic unit. I'm measuring magic in you and your car. Your company is Flight 216, the flying-car company, so I assume it's magical."

"You bet. Watch this." I wished the car into flying mode.

"Whoa. You and your car were at 175, then you surged to 300, and now you're at 250!" Katie said as we took off.

"Cool. Is that good?"

"It's the highest magical reading I've seen since Chicago."

"Was that another flying-car company?"

"Not exactly. It was a flying dragon."

"Now that's magical. This car is made by Croissant Motors, a minivan. Very ordinary."

"Except for four wings flapping at"—Katie whipped out her cell phone and took a picture of the wings—"fifty beats per second. That's like a hummingbird."

"I always wanted a pet hummingbird. You're going to the Sheer Town Hotel, right?"

"Yes. I'm here in Cleveland as an expert witness for a trial, and I've been hired to do some investigation. Plus, I wanted to check out your magic."

"That's a lot to cram into a visit. You won't have time for sightseeing, I guess."

"This trip is it. It's a nice-looking city. Lots of trees."

"Cleveland's called the Forest City. Here, I'll detour over Lakewood."

"That's impressive tree cover. The lake looks pretty."

"It's one of our best features. We'll cut across it to downtown."

We skimmed over the water to downtown. I circled the Terminal Tower and swooped to the Sheer Town Hotel, dropping neatly into an open parking spot.

"Thanks for the ride and the tour."

"This trial, would that be this coming Friday?"

"Yes, how did you know?"

"That's my trial. I'm suing Checkered Airlines."

"Ah, that's the magical company I'm investigating."

"Good luck!"

"You too. I'll see you Friday, I guess."

* * *

I picked up the notarized letter from Sprong, Blodgett, and Whifflehammer. I couldn't ignore this snail mail. I had to sign for it since it came in my name, Hugo Lamacek.

I skimmed it quickly. It was a lawsuit from Flight 216, our chief rival for the Cleveland magical flying market. They were severely undercutting my company's rates and eating into my profit margins.

I'd planned on low costs and high-profit margins from the beginning. I'd bought old school buses and repainted them. I found and trained mages and paid them well, once they showed they could make my buses fly. Then I crammed them with paying customers.

That was why I'd targeted Flight 216 for a magical attack. How had they survived the caramel curse? My mage Owen Gooseberry was certain their chief mage had been in that car. His video showed the car plummeting to the ground. She'd only had seconds to survive. I sighed. It didn't matter. Angela Hamilton had lived to sue me.

I frowned. How in the world did they plan to win this lawsuit? All the attacks were magical, from hundreds of feet away. There was no evidence my company, Checkered Airlines, was involved. Nor could there be. All my magic vanished afterward.

I called my lawyer, Bart Scut, of Scut, Scat, and Scoot. It was time to begin lawfare. If I couldn't eliminate Flight 216 magically, I'd sue them into oblivion.

I permitted myself a full grin. After acquiring Flight 216, I could see my path to full monopoly. First Cleveland, then the Midwest, then the whole United States.

Chapter 30 - Expert

Tuesday, October 13

After settling into my hotel room, I ordered a rental car and planned to go to Checkered Airlines headquarters incognito. I didn't want to go in a rival flying car, like Ms. Hamilton's.

I dressed in jeans and a T-shirt, trying to look like a college student. I put my pageboy cut into a ponytail and added a hair extension. Sprong, Blodgett, and Whifflehammer had contacted me to track Checkered Airlines' magic and see if I could trace it to some of the magical results that caused the lawsuit.

As they had requested, I first dropped by their law office. A well-dressed secretary introduced me to Mr. Sprong. I felt uncomfortable in college casual facing him in his dark-navy suit.

"Ms. Garcia, welcome to Sprong, Blodgett, and Whifflehammer. Willifred Sprong at your service. Please call me Will." A stout, balding man pumped my hand vigorously.

"And you can call me Katie. I was surprised to be engaged by you coincidentally, as I was coming to Cleveland anyway." I followed him into a luxurious conference room.

"Yes. That's the way we operate. We use magic to fight magical crime. When we were engaged for this case, we immediately sought the optimal magical experts to assist us. Your name was first on the list."

I took a wild guess. "Did you do a magical search on the internet?"

"Yes! You're the first one to guess how we operate. Please keep it to yourself. We don't want to help our opposition."

"Naturally."

"Now, are you legally permitted to have a side job while working for the government?"

"I checked that when I received your request. As long as I don't share any secret information with you, I'm not forbidden."

"What is not forbidden is allowed."

"Exactly my thought. What precisely do you want me to

find?"

"We'd like you to connect the magic used against Ms. Hamilton with Checkered Airlines. Ms. Hamilton is certain they were the cause, but that won't hold up in court."

"I have a magical detection device, but I wasn't here when the incident happened." I brought out my MU meter from my backpack.

"We captured Ms. Hamilton's memory magically. Please observe."

Will played a video on the wall screen in the conference room.

"Whoa, that was pretty intense. A caramel-coated car. Had I been in there, I might have screamed too. But Ms. Hamilton's an unflappable character. I met her at the airport. She flew me downtown."

"Now, if you had been in that car, could you have proven the magical caramel came from that flying bus?"

"Sure." I turned on the meter and pointed it at Will. "You have 55 MUs in you. Were you to use magic, I could show it flowed from you to the item in question with this device."

"Excellent! Could you record that flow?"

"Yes, I could. Every measurement from the MU reader is recorded on my laptop and uploaded to online storage."

"Wonderful! And you could print out these measurements and explain them so a jury can understand?"

"Yes. I explain my work to my mom all the time. She's as smart as I am but without the training. However, I wasn't there to record it."

"No problem. A Mr. Bill Fredrico was there. He was the one screaming in the video. He's agreed to testify in the trial. And he gave me these." Will handed me a plastic bag full of wrapped caramels.

"These came from the car?"

"Right off the windshield and into the back seat. We've tracked them from Ms. Hamilton's and Mr. Fredrico's memories. Can your machine track where they came from?"

"No . . ." I pointed the sensor at the bag. It read 133 MUs. Those were magical caramels all right. "But maybe it can. I wish to know the source of this magic in these caramels to show on the screen of the detector!" A new screen appeared next to the MU detector. It said "Owen Gooseberry."

"Owen Gooseberry? Who is he? I wonder if he works for Checkered Airlines?"

"That seems like it would be easy to find out." Will raised his eyebrows at me.

I smiled at him. "Not so ironically, that's my next stop."

"I think this is the start of a beautiful friendship." He stood and led me to the reception area.

"You're another *Casablanca* fan?" I said curiously.

"Indeed. Since I was a kid. I watched it with my parents."

I laughed. "That's how I first saw it too. They had an old DVD."

"We had a VCR. I guess I'm showing my age."

"No harm. I should return with the evidence this afternoon."

"Great! I'll be here until six." We shook hands, and I went down to my car.

I settled in my rental car, somewhat comforted that it did not fly and wouldn't attract the attention of the caramel guys from Checkered Airlines. I had settled on my college-girl dress, thinking of disguising myself somewhat. I hadn't been on any national media, so no one knew my face, but my picture was on the Oakridge employee page—what if someone leaked it?

I played with my MU detector and my laptop. The MU readings were recorded in the spreadsheet. Now I had a new column, "MU Source." Huh. Who knew magic could program a spreadsheet?

My detector was always on. I scanned down the sources, Owen Gooseberry, my first reading, then Willifred Sprong, Ricardo Blodgett, then Michelangelo Whifflehammer. Wow. Working with magical lawyers was not on my bingo card today.

I looked at my MU reader. It looked like a wireless microphone. It connected by Bluetooth to my MU reader and my laptop. How was I going to carry this about Checkered Airlines and explain it? I got an idea.

"I wish you were merged with my phone!" I held the two devices in my hand. In a blink they were one device. It looked like a big, thick phone.

"This looks clunky." Then I realized it unfolded into a wide, beautiful screen with a phone on one side and all the readings of the MU detector on the other.

"Nice." I looked at my spreadsheet. A new name had appeared under the MU source column: Katie Garcia.

"Hmmm. It'd be nice to store each person's magic, to preserve a sample." I imagined a series of batteries hanging off the side of the MU detector. "Make it so, magic." They appeared. Only, they didn't look like batteries but glass cylinders, all empty except one. It had a glittering blue fluid in it. A glowing label read, "Katie Garcia sample."

"Oka-a-a-ay." I sighed. I guess I finally accepted this new energy was magic. Now how was I going to tell my boss?

But that was tonight's worry. First I had to get samples of Owen Gooseberry at Checkered Airlines.

I planned to go as a college student seeking employment. *What could go wrong with that?* I asked myself optimistically. But my gut was uneasy.

I found Checkered Airlines in an industrial section off West 117th. An old brick building had several buses parked in the fenced-in parking lot. As I drove in, one took off, flapping six wings like some giant insect.

Quickly I pointed my phone detector at the bus. MU Source: Tiffany Meriweather.

I walked into the office. There I saw an organization chart with pictures of the employees. One had a star, "Employee of the Month." His name: Owen Gooseberry. I raised an eyebrow and turned to the receptionist.

"Hi!" I chirped. "I'm Kayla Vargas. I just graduated from Case Western Reserve. I'd like to work for your company."

The dark-haired woman smiled. "Hi, I'm Fawn Goodspell. We're glad you're here. We're growing so fast that we're always hiring. What sort of work can you do?"

"I kind of hoped to try one of those flying buses."

"Can you make it fly?"

"Uh, I don't know. Don't you just magic them?"

"Yes, but the magic comes from the driver."

"Oh." I wasn't acting. I had no idea if I could make a bus fly by magic.

"Let's test you. Here's a model school bus. Let's see if you can make it fly." Fawn put a plastic model bus on the desk.

"Okay. Fly around the room, bus!" I commanded.

Yellow plastic wings sprouted out of the sides, and the little bus flitted around like a dragonfly.

"Whoa! That's pretty good. You get to the next stage of the interview."

"What's that?"

"A personal interview with Mr. Lamacek."

"Oh, he's the owner, isn't he?"

"Yes. Please follow me."

We entered the corner office. A burly dark-haired man looked up from his desk. He was good looking in a kind of raw, rough way, with a hawk nose and strong chin.

"Mr. Lamacek, this is Ms. Kayla Vargas. She passed the first test to be a pilot mage."

"Great! Fly your bus in here, Ms. Vargas."

"Bus, fly to my voice!" I commanded as firmly as I could. I could hear the drone of its wings start and grow louder, and the bus came into the room.

"Land it on the desk."

"Land here, bus." I pointed with my finger. Then I felt silly. Buses didn't have eyes. Nevertheless, it landed where I pointed.

"Well done. Are you ready to try with a real bus?"

"Um, I'd like to practice first."

"Right. That's why I'll go with you. I'll help you if anything goes wrong." He smiled. "We don't waste any time here at Checkered Airlines."

"Okay. Let's do this."

We walked out the back into the fenced parking lot. I saw an old school bus from the fifties, with four flat tires.

"We haven't refurbished this one yet. Get in and make it fly."

"O-o-kay." I climbed in.

Lamacek sat in the seat across from me. "Go ahead."

"Bus, fly!" I actually felt a strain in my gut, like I was lifting something heavy. Wings came out and slowly flapped. We stayed on the ground.

"Great. You'll find it easier if you start the engine."

"Oh." I pushed the starter. The wings flapped harder, swirling dust around us.

"Up!" I urged. And up we went.

"Good, good, well done, Kayla. Head for the lakefront."

I turned the wheel, and we did a doughnut a hundred feet in the air. "The sun is over there, so north is here." I floored the gas pedal. The engine roared.

"There's the lake."

"Go over it and circle around the Terminal Tower. Good speed, by the way."

"How does the engine help magic? That doesn't make sense to me."

"Two things. First, your mind knows the engine needs to run for you to go. That affects your confidence or belief. Second, the magic somehow takes energy from the engine and applies it to the wings. Don't ask me any more than that."

We circled the tower, and Lamacek said, "Okay, head back. You've got the job. You're one of the best natural mages I've seen."

"Thanks. But I don't know what I'm doing."

"It's not so much knowing as it is believing that something can be done."

"Ah. I have seen magic work before."

"Most people have by now."

We landed and went back to Lamacek's office.

"I just need you to sign this contract." He handed me a detailed contract, covered in fine print. I skimmed it. Liability. I was liable for accidents I caused. They were liable for any equipment failure. Innovation: Any inventions I created became property of Checkered Airlines. Compensation: $120,000 per year, paid monthly. Benefits: Health insurance, dental insurance. $1,000 deductible. Termination of contract: Checkered Airlines could terminate my employment at any time if they were dissatisfied with me. *That doesn't sound good.* I reread the clause more carefully. No mention of me terminating the contract. I reread the whole contract. Lamacek frowned and twiddled his thumbs. No mention of renewal or expiration of the contract. I chuckled. This was essentially open-ended bonded servitude.

I looked at Lamacek and pursed my lips. "I'm essentially a pilot for you, but I'm not paid a pilot's salary. I'll need at least $200,000." I thought that would put him off.

He raised his eyebrows and nodded. "You're right." He crossed off the $120,000, wrote $200,000, and then initialed *HL*. "Just initial it and sign it."

I almost wanted to do it, just to see what would happen. But no, that'd kill my expert witness work coming up. "Nah. I can't right now. Maybe later." I handed him the contract back.

His eyes opened wide. "You really . . . *must*."

I felt an overwhelming urge to sign it. That . . . wasn't natural. I grabbed the contract back and put the pen on the line. Just before signing it, I whispered. "All outside magic stops at my skin."

"What'd you say? You said something."

"Nothing. Keep your contract. I've got better things to do." I walked out and slammed the door. That felt good.

Back in the car, I reviewed my magical readings. Fawn Goodspell, the secretary: 100 MUs toward me.

"Huh. I wonder what that was for? I wish I could see her purpose." A new column appeared. "MU Purpose." Next to Fawn's name was "Charm, encourage to join."

Quickly I scrolled down the list of magical sources. Vernon Harford, 150 MU Bus Magic; Owen Gooseberry, 250 MU Bus Magic. There was the magic I was looking for. These were readings of the buses I'd walked past to the training bus. Then I saw Katie Garcia—350 MU Bus Magic. The MU meter wasn't fooled by my fake name. Then Hugo Lamacek, 400 MU Encouragement. Again, Hugo Lamacek, 450 MU. Compulsion to sign. Katie Garcia—450 MU, Magic barrier.

"That's a ton of information I need to process. And I have to write a report about all this. I can prove magic is real now."

* * *

I hardly noticed my drive back to Sprong, Blodgett, and Whifflehammer. I analyzed all this information and planned what I'd write in my report.

In their conference room, I relayed my findings to the three lawyers and gave them samples of everyone's magic.

"Wonderful." Will took my samples and my readouts and put them into an evidence folder.

Mike sat rubbing his chin next to him. "Too bad we don't have copies of your machine. We could gather evidence from each of Angie's cars if they get attacked again."

"That's a good idea. You don't happen to have a radiometer or Geiger counter hanging around here?"

"I have an electrometer in my lab." Mike left the room abruptly.

I looked at Rick. "I've never heard of a lawyer or law firm having a lab or an electrometer. I was joking."

Rick smiled. "Mike's our dreamer. He wanted to be a research physicist, but he became a lawyer because it was a family tradition. He compromised by getting a physics degree and inventing and exploring on his own, like our magical memory recorder."

Mike reentered, carrying the electrometer. "Will this do?"

"I think so." I put it on the table next to my MU meter. I put my hands on it. "Become exactly like my MU meter, now!"

The device grew hot enough that I had to jerk my hands away. It melted and morphed into a duplicate of my MU meter, complete with the cell phone connected by Bluetooth.

"Wow! That's great! I'll try this with other devices I have in my lab. Thanks, Katie." He shook my hand, his long fingers wrapping completely around it.

"It's good to have more measurements of this phenomenon. Please send me your measurements. They'll be recorded on the phone."

"Mike, once you get three of them, I'll take those over to Angie and get them installed in all her cars," Will said.

Rick smiled and rubbed his hands. "I love it when a plan comes together. Lamacek and Scut, Scat, and Scoot won't know what hit them.

"Who's Scut, Scat, and Scoot?"

Rick looked at me with amusement in his eyes. "We're not the only lawyers with odd names. They're Lamacek's lawyers. We've been in contact before the trial."

His phone rang. Rick glanced at it. "I've got to get this. It's Angie." He went to a corner of the room.

"Hamilton?" I asked Will.

"Our big client."

"Is she rich?"

"No, but we expect to clean out Checkered Airlines."

"You're going for the jugular."

"Lawsuits are a blood sport," Will answered with a smile.

Rick came back grinning. "Good news. Angie got hit with a mud storm and a thunderstorm."

"How is that good news? Is she all right?" I asked.

"Oh yeah. She's too tough to defeat. It's good because she's coming here, madder than a wet hen, with her van covered in mud. You'll be able to sample it for magic."

"Ah! I get it. When will she be here?"

"She'll—" Rick's phone rang again. "Hi, Angie. We'll be right there. See you. Let's go up to the roof and greet here. You'll want to take samples, Katie."

"Yes indeed. I've never measured magical mud before." That also wasn't on my bingo card.

On the roof, Angie's van was unrecognizable from the mud. She got out with mud smeared across her face, over her scowl.

"Grrr! Those SOBs. That's twice I've lost a fare. Oh, hi, Katie. What are you doing here? Planning for the trial on Friday?"

"Yes. I came back from Checkered Airlines full of magical measurements. Let's see what your mud reads."

"So you plan to nail them with mud?" Angie smiled.

"We'll cover them with it," Rick said with a smug smirk. "And then with caramel."

"Great! What does your machine say, Katie?" Angie looked at me.

"It's definitely magical, MU 55. It's from Tiffany Meriweather. Interestingly, it matches my measurement of her taking off in a Checkered Airlines bus this morning."

"What time?" Angie said.

"Maybe ten forty a.m."

"I got splattered at eleven a.m. I gave my customer a free trip to the airport and a bag of caramels, then I came right here."

"The plot thickens—with mud!" Will said. "Let's go inside and plan how we'll use this evidence. Angie, hold off cleaning your van. We'll submit it as evidence."

"Who's the judge?" I asked Will, after we were in the conference room.

"We got a replacement at the last minute. The previous judge's robes kept bursting into flame. He retired."

"I feel for him, but I'm kind of glad we don't have a liar."

"The new judge was just elected last year. Kevin Sloter. Now, let's plan our strategy."

* * *

I collapsed into my hotel room that evening. I didn't even have the energy to go out to eat. I just ordered room service. *Your tax dollars for scientific research at work.*

While I munched on my raspberry cheesecake after my salmon and salad dinner, I typed up my report. I'd gone over to the nonscientific, dark side. This would be the first time I called the new force on Earth *magic*. I described its origin from outer space, its power, its effects, and the fact it can be controlled by the will of any individual. I documented the changes I had made to my magic detector. I had stopped and bought a disposable phone and converted it into a copy of the detector phone.

Sprong, Blodgett, and Whifflehammer made a magical video of my memories this afternoon. I enclosed a copy of that with my report. I also mentioned I would be an expert witness in the trial on Friday. I emailed everything to my boss, Hermon Scholl. I sent my magical phone detector by next-day air to him as well.

As I lay down to sleep, I thought of comparing magic to electricity. It could be stored and directed to do work. I wondered if it could be amplified. Could we make circuits to control it?

* * *

I didn't like that at all. Kayla Vargas was the first mage I couldn't persuade to follow me. That meant she was at least as strong as I was magically. How could that be? I used magic every day, and I got stronger daily. I had the measurements to prove it. I considered doing an internet search on her and then stopped. Her name was almost certainly an alias.

I brought out my Magic 8 Ball from the locked drawer in my desk. This was one of the first things I had magicked. I'd had this toy since I was a little kid. I'd found it as I was packing my stuff to run out of Pittsburgh before I was arrested for fraud.

Half in fun, half in desperation, I'd said, "How do I get away cleanly, with no law enforcement on my tail? Give me a detailed answer." I didn't want "Reply hazy, try again."

I had used magic to steal stuff and to fool people, but I didn't know its limits—or lack of them.

The ball had warmed and grown in my grasp. It had changed from plastic to obsidian. The window into its depths doubled or tripled in size. Green glowing letters appeared and scrolled upward.

"Frame your subordinates, Phil Nougat and Nowell Branderson. Persuade them to be at your home tomorrow when the police come. Plant evidence that will convict them. Leave behind a note implicating them, and close your business."

The glowing letters had moved up and disappeared.

Huh. That was a pretty good idea. I'd executed the plan, and my employees had been arrested. No one had followed me to Cleveland.

Then, in Cleveland I cast about how to make money legally with magic. I'd asked the black ball, "What's the best way for me to make money in Cleveland with magic?"

"Begin a flying bus service. Buy cheap, wrecked buses. Fix them magically. Then find mages who can make them fly."

That was easy. There were dozens of old school buses in the Greater Cleveland area. I maxed out my credit cards buying them and starting an office. I put an ad for magicians on a local job board. Not everyone could make a bus fly, but all had some kind of magic with them. And I didn't have to do anything shady! It was all legal.

Even smearing my competitor's cars with caramel and mud was completely legal. There was no law against caramel or mud, was there? I'd mentioned that to Scut, Scat, and Scoot. And my competitor couldn't trace it to me anyway.

But this new mage could be a problem. With complete confidence in its power, I asked the magic ball, "What's Kayla

Vargas's real name?"

"Katherine Garcia. She's an employee of Oakridge Laboratory and the government's chief researcher into magic."

Oho! That explained a lot. "How can I defeat her magically?"

"You must use more magic than she has. You do not have enough. You must get your associates Owen Gooseberry and Fawn Goodspell to work with you to overcome her defense. Then she'll be at your mercy."

"Great!" I called in Fawn. "Ms. Goodspell, please get Owen and come in here. I need both of you."

I knew just how I'd waylay Ms. Garcia.

Chapter 31 – Thief

Tuesday, October 13

"Ooo, I'm so mad!" Jane fumed.

"We will find the thief." I patted Jane, trying to soothe her.

She pushed my hand away. "Do you think Amazin' can tell us where the money went?"

"That seems so obvious, I'd never think of it. Let me open a help call." I dialed the number on their help page.

"I wish they'd give you a clear answer we can act on!" Jane was practically spitting.

"It's a lock now. I wished right with you."

"Hello, this is Adita. How can I help you?" I put the call on speakerphone so Jane could listen.

"I'm author Jake Williams. I recently published a book on your website, *Magic Arrives*. My presales totaled $76,680, and then they went to zero dollars. What happened to the money? Who withdrew it?"

"That's weird. Let me check. Huh. No money was sent to you. We normally send you a check at the end of the month, not in the middle. Your current total is $1,494.90. Your total sales are 15,491+302=15,793. This doesn't make sense. Let me check another report. Your total revenue credited this month is $78,175.35. Please stand by. I'm going to have to run an audit report on your account. I'll put you on hold."

Vivaldi's Four Seasons, "Winter," began playing on the phone.

"So do you think this audit report will find out who did this?" Jane's eyes bored into me.

I shook my head. "Not if the theft was done by magic."

"So we've got to find the person another way, using magic." She wheeled the guest chair in my office over to my keyboard tray. "Here. Let me use magic on your computer."

"Okay. What are you going to do?"

"I'll use a magic internet search. Computer, use all our magic to search and find this thief." She spoke as she typed the query into the search bar.

A Wokkapedia page came up. "Darrell Duncan. Independent 'Common Peoples' candidate for mayor of New York City in November 2025. Paraplegic and blind, he set up a Kickstarter page to fund his candidacy and has raised over a million dollars so far. Previously, he lived in Section 8 housing in Manhattan. He currently lives in his campaign headquarters on Park Avenue. According to his biography, he used to beg for a living and still gets around by a manual wheelchair, led by his guide dog, Faith.

"Current polling numbers have Darrell Duncan at 41%, while his favored opponent, Huey Long Tweed, has 59%. Although Mr. Duncan has been gaining in recent polls, experts do not give him a serious chance at winning."

"That's our guy." Jane tapped the screen.

"Are we going to go after a blind paralytic? He's also a candidate for NYC mayor with over a million dollars in funding."

"We'll have a million dollars too, from presales, if they keep up at this rate for another week. And if we stop the stealing." She paused and rubbed her chin. "Magic computer, keep anyone else from ever stealing our Amazin' royalties."

A pop-up window appeared. "Magical protection around Amazin' account enabled."

"Wow, Jane, you're on a roll!"

"I'm really pissed off." She frowned. "I wish we get our money back."

"Hello? Mr. Williams, are you there?"

"Yes, Adita. I'm here. What's the good news?"

"We think a computer glitch wiped out your account. We're restoring it to the correct amount."

"That's wonderful!" I grinned at Jane.

She nodded.

"Is there anything else I can do for you today?"

"No, that's exactly what I wanted to be done. It's like magic!" I chuckled at Jane.

She smirked.

"Please stay online and fill out your customer satisfaction survey. Goodbye and have a nice day."

"Are you going to fill out that crap survey?"

"Sure. I love filling out surveys."

"I'd hang up."

"It'll just take a second." I punched in all fives for the survey answers. "There. Thanks for your magical help, Jane."

"I've never been so motivated. I'm still dissatisfied. We've got to find a way to get this Duncan guy. I don't care if he's blind." She turned to the computer and set the voice recognition. "Magic computer, what evidence is there that can be used against Duncan to stop him?"

Another pop-up window appeared. "Using magic, Darrell Duncan steals cash from peoples' wallets. Recently he decided to steal online from Amazin' bestseller lists. Currently he is taking a fraction from every Amazin' transaction."

"Great!" Jane sounded happy for the first time since the theft. "How can we get the evidence to convict him?"

"Engage the Cleveland law firm Sprong, Blodgett, and Whifflehammer. They use magic and can convict magical criminals."

Jane nodded. "What's their phone number?"

"216-330-2404" appeared at the bottom of the window.

"Thanks." Jane punched in the number.

"You're welcome," scrolled across the bottom.

* * *

The next morning while we had tea and shortbread, Jane read the news on her tablet. "Jake! Listen to this. 'Hugo Lamacek has countersued Flight 216 for ten million dollars for harassing his business. He says they have no evidence on him or any of his employees.'"

"So?"

"Let me finish. 'Flight 216 was founded by Angie Hamilton. Hamilton says they have evidence that ties the harm to Checkered Airlines. She is represented by Sprong, Blodgett, and Whifflehammer.'"

"Ah. The lawyers we hired yesterday."

"Right. Now quit interrupting me. They have a big trial coming up a week from this Friday. I don't know if the law firm will have time for us today."

"We have our meeting scheduled with them downtown in an hour. They've got to show up for that. But we'll probably get an underling flunky."

"We'll see when we get there. It's a nice fall day. You want to take the bus downtown?"

I gulped down the last of my tea. "Sure. That'll be eco-friendly. And we don't have to pay for parking. When's the next bus?"

"Fifteen minutes."

Jane stood. "Let's go. I don't want to be late."

"We're a five-minute walk from the bus stop." I smirked.

"What? You don't want to be seen in public with me so you're minimizing our time together?"

"I love being with you in private or in public." We left hand in hand.

* * *

"I don't know why we took the bus. I'm nauseous," Jane grumbled as we left the bus.

"Yeah, Detroit Avenue was really bumpy."

"And all the stop and go. And the diesel fumes. We should have waited for one of the electric ones."

"Walking in the cool air should help you. I was trying to remember if we've ever been to a lawyer's office before. I don't think we were."

"You're right. All I know is, they have loads of money."

"Usually. There has to be poor, beginning lawyers."

"Well, not these guys." Jane pointed to the gleaming gold letters adorning the shiny marble entrance: SPRONG BLODGETT WHIFFLEHAMMER.

A stocky man in a navy suit met us. "You must be Jake and Jane. I'm Willifred Aldus Sprong. Please call me Will." He shook my hand.

"Gladly, and well met, Will."

"Well met? Are you a fantasy fan?"

"Yes, and author." I handed him my card.

Jane hit me. "Jake! Now's not the time to market your book."

I grinned. "Why not?"

"No problem, Jane. I love fantasy." Will led us to the elevator. "Although, with magic becoming more acknowledged, maybe we should call it just 'fiction.'"

We entered a conference room and sat. "Tell me about your problem."

I recounted writing my book, its great presales, and the theft. Then I told him about wishing magical protection around our Amazin' account and our detective work related Darrell Duncan.

Will looked through our evidence. "Hmm. Maybe we should hire you as investigators. It looks like Duncan is as crooked as a dog's hind leg. He covered his tracks well. I don't think we can get him for this particular crime. Even if we knew which computer server he magicked to steal your money, it'd be overwhelmed by your magic by now."

"Why?" Jane asked.

"Your magic is working continually. His was a one shot. It's like one drop of blue ink in a sea of red. It'll still look red."

"Magic as ink. That's an interesting simile," I said.

"Or a literal image. Let me show you." He pointed his phone at us.

"Are you going to take our picture?" Jane asked.

"No, I'm going to take a magic sample. Now wish for something."

"I wish for us to get this Darrell Duncan dead to rights for this crimes!" Jane practically shouted.

"Amen!" I chorused.

"That's great! Take a look at this." Will pulled out a case from under the table. It had jiggling dials and screens on it, and glass bottles of what looked like ink or dye attached to it. Two bottles were glowing, one pink and one green.

I furrowed my salt-and-pepper brows. "Well, that's . . . interesting. What is it?"

"It's a magic meter and collector. Here are your samples." He pointed to the pink and green bottles. He peered at the screens. "You guys generated 1,023 units of magic in your wish."

"Uh, is that good?" Jane tilted her head.

"It's pretty impressive for one spell. It's the highest I've ever measured. Now, seriously, let me tell you what we need to do.

"To catch your crook, we need to get him in the act of stealing something with magic and take a sample of his magic with this instrument. To do that, we'd have to send one of our magical investigators to New York City and follow him around, sampling him.

"The problem is, that'd be very expensive for you. And we have no one to spare at this time. But I got a magical suggestion." He paused, looking at us with amused blue eyes.

"Okay, I'll bite—what was the suggestion?" I looked at him to see if he was joking in some way.

"Before I met you today, I went through your problem and could see no easy way to solve your case without a lot of expense and hiring more investigators. I wished for a solution. And she answered me."

"What do you mean, 'she'?" Jane looked at him with narrowed eyes.

"My helpful, magical friend." Will opened a drawer in a filing cabinet and pulled out an old, battered doll.

"This is Cathy, my sister's old doll. She was going to throw it out, but I saved it because I'm nostalgic. One day in desperation, I asked, 'How do I solve this case?' and I pulled the string . . ." Will pulled the string on the back of the doll.

"Did you hire them yet, Will?" a scratchy voice came out of the doll. I swear I saw her eyes swivel toward Will.

"She's the one who told me to hire you, at least for this New York City investigation. How would you like an all-expense paid trip to New York City?"

"With a little bit of magical equipment?" I raised my eyebrows and looked at the magic detector.

"Of course."

"And two of those magical phones?" Jane asked.

"Here's the other one." Will pulled another one from his suit pocket.

Jane frowned and then grinned. "Can I ask for advice?"

"Of course."

Jane reached over the table and grabbed the doll. "It's been years since I played with one of these. Magic makes this more fun. Cathy, should Jake and I take this job?" Jane pulled the cord.

Cathy's eyes definitely swiveled to Jane. "Are you kidding? It's my idea. It's the only way you'll catch Darrell Duncan. And . . ." Her voice faded out as the string went in. Jane quickly pulled it again.

"Thanks. I ran out of breath—or spring. And you and Jake will have a lot of fun." Her eyes snapped shut, like that was the end of the matter.

Jane chuckled. "I loved my old doll. I don't mind taking advice from yours, Will. How about you, Jake?"

"Who am I to argue with a sentient doll? New York City is supposedly great in the fall.'

"Let's do this! We're in, Will."

* * *

Herman Scholl stepped into the Oval Office again, holding Katie Garcia's report. If anything, he felt less comfortable than last time.

President Lopez looked up at him as he entered. "Herman, good to see you. Tell me about this earth-shaking report of yours."

"Have you had a chance to read it yet, Mr. President?"

"No, I find oral reports faster and more productive. What do you have?"

"We've come to a deeper understanding of that interstellar power that has been causing these bizarre, worldwide phenomena. It can be controlled by human will, and"—he swallowed—"it seems to be increasing and accumulating on Earth."

"Controlled by human will?"

"Yes. If a person visualizes something and desires it, it can come to pass. Such as peoples' pants catching on fire."

"Hmm. I wonder if those people realized how much harm they'd do?"

"I don't think anyone realizes anything. Our researcher, Ms. Garcia, is the first one to put all these pieces together."

"So nothing is preventing bad people from doing . . . anything? Even our national enemies?"

"Nothing but ignorance. I suggest we control the release of this information and limit it to people who are already working this . . . magic."

"Magic? Is that what this is?"

"Yes. Our researcher argued pretty convincingly that we might as well call it that since it matches in behavior."

President Lopez sighed and put his face in his hands, propped up on the desk. He sat up again and looked at the sign on his desk. "'The Buck Stops Here,'" he read. "Okay. Keep this report quiet, top secret, need to know. Herman, I need you to create a team you trust completely to work with Katie and give this information to our nation's magicians. Advise them this is top secret. Pool all the information you can. I'll touch base with the Secretary of Defense and figure out how to use this magic in our military."

"Yes, sir."

"Everything has top priority. I'll give you access to our black ops budget in our military. This'll be another Manhattan Project. I want a perfect magical offense—and defense."

"Yes, sir."

"I have your cell phone number. Use it only for nonwork-related information. Here's a secure phone." President Lopez pulled a thick, robust cell phone from his desk. "I'll use this for all conversations with you. Shut down communications out of your research team. Everything has to stay inside. Nothing on phones or laptop computers that might be carried out."

"We already have those protocols on some of our nuclear research. I'll implement them in our magical research."

"Excellent. Let's get to work. There's a lot to do."

Chapter 32 – Sales

Saturday, October 17

"Okay, kids, rise and shine. Today's the day we make our fortune!" I woke Shayla and Lamar.

Lamar groaned. "Why so early, Mom? This is earlier than I get up for school."

"The early bird gets the worm—or the prime spot in Grant Park. C'mon. I took vacation this week from Wal-Store to sell in Grant Park. The first day is the most important. Today's Saturday. Don't you want to spend it flying on Terry, your pteranodon?"

Grumbling, he rolled over and began dressing.

Shayla rubbed her eyes as she pulled on her clothing. "I get to give people rides on Pinkie. Don't you like to give rides on Terry, Lamar?"

"Yeah. I just don't see why we have to get up so early."

"Be sure to use your magical disguises. Get a load of mine, kids. Disguise me as a supermodel!"

I grew six inches taller but lost twenty pounds of weight. I wore a short, slanted skirt that fell between my knees and hips. Hips . . . my hips were probably half their normal size!

I looked at myself in the mirror. I was made up with enormous eyes, thick eyelashes, and purple eyeliner. I did look like the model I pictured in my head—just not my usual self.

"Mom! Where'd you go?" Shayla started crying. "Get out, skinny lady." Shayla head-butted my leg. "Ow. You don't have no padding, like Mom."

"It's me, honey. It's just a disguise."

"Oh." She squinted at me. "It sounds like you. I like the old you better."

"Thanks, honey."

"I'll hug you anyway." She hugged my very long, very skinny leg. As I looked down, I saw I was wearing impossibly high heels. Somehow they didn't hurt my feet.

"Okay, I'll try my disguise. I'm a pink fairy!" Shayla shot her hands in the air. Pink sparkles surrounded her as her body shrunk to two feet high. Lacy pink wings grew out of her back. They fluttered, and she rose in the air.

Peering at her, she still looked like Shayla, only in fluorescent pink rather than her usual chocolate-milk color.

"Wow, Shayla, I'd never guess that was you!" She flew by my face and kissed me. Then she preened in front of the mirror.

"Now it's my turn," Lamar announced. "Here is Super Human!" Lamar grew until his head was near the ceiling. His shoulders broadened to as wide as a door. His muscles packed on muscles, while his clothing turned into a leather vest and leather shorts and sandals. Lamar's face was mostly the same but grown up.

"Whoa! Lamar, I guess we don't have to worry about anyone robbing us with you around." I smiled and hugged him. Even with my new height and heels, I had to reach up to hug him around the neck. He lifted me easily, holding me in the crook of his arm.

"Now, what's for breakfast, Mom? I'm not leaving without eating."

"Uh, I was so busy planning this day, I forgot to shop." I looked in the cupboard. "Cold cereal. Flakes or round balls?"

"I'll take flakes," Shayla said.

"I'll take the round stuff. At least it's made from oats," I said.

"I'll take both." Lamar's deep voice boomed.

I poured the cereal and milk into our bowls. Shayla didn't sit; she hovered in front of her bowl and ate dainty bites from a one-quarter teaspoon.

I sat at the head of the table, where I usually did—but my high heels pushed my knees up awkwardly. I couldn't slide them under the table. I slid off my shoes, to fit.

Lamar barely fit in a chair. He hunched over the table, with his knees even higher than mine. His spoon looked tiny in his volleyball-sized fist.

Shayla hovered over her chair, spooning in cereal as she flew.

I burst out laughing. "Look how silly we all look!"

* * *

After a chilly flight on our dragon, pteranodon, and unicorn, we landed in Grant Park. I had a gym bag full of our three cash boxes, credit card readers, and Shayla's drawing of our billboard.

I handed the drawing to Shayla, hovering next to me. "Do your magic, dear!"

"I wish you were big and on stilts!"

Boom! Our animated billboard appeared, playing a video from our last flight.

"Getcher dinosaur rides here!" Lamar called out to a few early morning strollers in a deep, booming voice. "The only dinosaur ride in Chicago!"

"Hey, Lamar. Tell them about Pinkie too."

"Or ride a pink dragon. Or a flying unicorn!"

A couple wandered over. They took Shayla's Pinkie. Our first sale of the day! Shayla handled their credit card like a pro.

"I always feel better after the first sale," I said to Lamar.

"Get ready, Mom. Here comes a crowd!"

And the onslaught began. On my second trip with Rainbow, I faced a crowd of a dozen people. I couldn't fit them all on the draft-horse-size unicorn.

"Hey, Fairy Girl!" I called Shayla as she landed from a trip.

"What, Supermodel Mom?"

"Rainbow isn't big enough for all the riders."

"No problem, Mom. Grow as big as Pinkie!" She hugged the unicorn's sturdy, hairy goat leg.

The unicorn grew to twenty feet tall at the shoulder. But no one could reach its back! Rainbow realized the problem and lowered its head to the ground. I had a hard time climbing the long, colorful mane to its back—especially in six-inch heels.

Seeing the problem, Shayla commanded, "Put in a stairway." A rainbow-colored stair appeared between a part in the mane. People started climbing it.

I saw another problem. "We need a place for them to sit," I called to my hovering child.

She furrowed her tiny brow. "Do I have to do everything? Gondola, appear on Rainbow's back! With seat belts!"

"And tie it on to Rainbow with a girth strap," I added.

"Ugh." Rainbow wheezed. "Not so tight."

"Sorry, Rainbow. One inch out." I remembered riding and saddling horses one summer in Girl Scouts. I tested it, slipping my hand and whole arm between the belt and Rainbow's warm silky fur. "Now it's too loose."

"Make it Velcro, Model Mom," Lamar said.

"Good idea. Become Velcro!" The little hooks on the foot-wide girth locked tightly onto Rainbow's coat.

I didn't lose a single passenger on that trip, and I cleared over two hundred dollars.

But the lines were longer than ever when I came back—and they weren't moving.

Lamar had his hands on his hips, looking angry. Shayla was hovering and whimpering. In front of the line stood a man with a tablet and a frown on his face.

He turned to me. "I'm Lester Brown from the City of Chicago. Ma'am, you need a vendor's license to run this business."

"Uh, where can I get one?"

"You will need to send an email to customersupport@cityofchicago.org with the subject 'Request an iSupplier Invitation,' or click on the button below. Within two business days, you will receive an email invitation from the city that provides a link to the iSupplier website and instructions for filling out and submitting your registration." The man spoke like he'd said this many times before.

"Two days! Isn't there some way I can get one now?"

"No, you have to follow the process," he said primly.

"Hey, Fairy Girl," Lamar murmured to his sister.

Shayla stopped whimpering to say, "What?"

"Make this real." He handed her a paper.

Shayla peered at it. "What's it say?"

"It's a vendor's license I drew up on my phone. I bet you can make it real."

"Oh yeah!" Brightening, Shayla rubbed her hands together. A pink magic wand appeared in her hand. "Become real!"

With a burst of light and pink sparkles, the handwritten notebook paper became a stiff piece of legal paper, embossed with the seal of the City of Chicago.

Still dripping glowing sparkles, Shayla flew over to the man and handed him the paper. "Hey, mister! Here's your license."

"Huh?" His mouth dropped open. He read the license. "This was just issued today. But it looks real, right down to the holographic seal." He looked at Shayla. "How'd you do that?"

"It's magic, dummy! I'm a magic fairy!" Hooting with laughter, she flew to the line in front of Pinkie and began loading her dragon for another ride.

"Kids." I shook my head, smiling. "You never know what they'll do next. Can we do anything else for you, Mr. Brown?"

"Yeah. Take this form and fill it out with your sales taxes at the end of the day." He turned and left, shaking his head.

* * *

That evening I counted our cash. We had thirty thousand. That was enough for a home down payment! But what about our credit card sales? I logged into our account. Over seventy thousand!

"Kids! We can buy a house!"

"Whee! I'll have my own yard. Can I get a playground?" Shayla was back to her normal bouncy self.

"Why not?

"Where will we live?" Lamar asked.

"Good question. Let me ask that on my tablet." I punched in "best middle-class neighborhoods in Chicago" and got this:

1. Glenview, Illinois—Quick Facts About Glenview:

•Population (2020): 48,705

•Median Annual Property Tax: $8,939

•Median Household Income: $115,198

•Average Home Value: $499,900

"Yowza!"

"What, Mom? What's the matter?" Lamar said.

"Whoever said a $115,000 salary was middle class? Half a million dollars for an average home? That's 'uppity middle class.' Who can afford that?"

"We could. That's just seven more sales days like today." Lamar looked at me like, *Don't you get it, Mom?*

"Uh, I guess we could. But then there's all the costs that go with it: insurance, property tax, repairs. Let's see if there's something cheaper on this." I thought of something. "Lamar, we didn't clear $100,000 today. We've got to pay sales taxes. And income taxes."

"How much can that be?"

"Sales tax Is about ten percent, so right away we're down to $90,000. Our income tax is about ten percent, but with this amount more, it'll probably go up to twenty percent. That takes us down to $72,000 total."

"Ouch!"

"Right. That's what every taxpayer says. Now you see why I'm worried about costs."

I started scanning down the list, looking at the home prices. "$416,000, $353,000, $391,000 . . . Ah! Here's Schaumburg for $251,000. That's half the price." I glanced at the rest of the list. "Yeah, that's the best price we'll get."

Schaumburg Quick Facts:

- Population: 78,723
- Median Annual Property Tax: $5,787
- Median Household Income: $83,096
- Average Home Value: $251,100

"Now, let's see what's for sale in the area."

* * *

Monday morning, as the kids ate breakfast, I said, "Okay, these three houses look the best." I showed them the pictures of each on my tablet.

"We'll go see them this evening, after another sales day. Lamar, you've gotta go to school. Shayla and I will hold the sales fort at Grant Park after she comes home from kindergarten."

"Aw, do I have to? I want to come help! People loved my pteranodon, Terry."

"Yup. Here's your lunch. Shayla and I will manage with Pinkie and Rainbow. After school you can take Terry and fly and meet us. Grab your books and get down to the bus."

Grumbling, Lamar gripped his lunch and backpack and stomped down the stairs.

After Shayla returned from kindergarten, I said, "Let's go, Shayla! The early bird gets the worm!"

"Pinkie and I are ready!" She blinked and turned into a pink fairy.

"Here I go!" I wished myself into my model-shaped body.

I clumped over to the stairs in my high heels. Shayla just buzzed next to me like a giant pink bumblebee.

"I should have waited until I climbed the stairs to go into model form."

"Just wish yourself wings, like me, Mommy!"

I scrunched my eyes shut. "I wish I had wings like Shayla!"

They popped out the back of my blouse, each about four feet long.

"Here goes!" With a great swirl of air, they flapped faster and faster. My body vibrated. I looked down. I was still crouched, but a foot off the ground.

"Yay, Mommy!"

"Let's go!" We flew up the stairs together.

* * *

"I'm calling in sick today."

I looked at Maria. "Why? You're not sick."

"I need a mental health day. I'm sick of work."

I sighed. "I wish I could. I've got to create a lesson plan for next semester."

"How hard could that be? Let me help you. When's it due?"

"Next week."

"Pfoo! Take the day off. Let's go to Grant Park. I hear there are magical rides there."

"I'm glad we can talk about magic, at least, without being considered kooks. What the heck." I put the papers away and closed my laptop. "Let's go!"

"Woo-hoo! I got you to do something spontaneous. I'll make you a normal person yet!"

"I'm not the one who investigates deepfakes for fun." I made a wry face at Maria.

"That's normal—for computer nerds. My car or yours?"

"Mine. I can't stand the way you drive."

"Huh. I'm just a normal Chicago driver: five to ten miles an hour faster than the traffic flow."

"You know, if everyone does that, soon everyone will be going at top speed."

"As I said, a normal Chicago driver. Who cares how fast you go? What counts is how close you come."

"I'm glad I'm driving." I started my elderly sedan. It got good mileage and was a pretty baby-blue color. So what if it was ten years old?

"Park at the Loop station and then let's take the Loop," Maria said.

"Why?"

"The Loop is less expensive than parking downtown."

"Ah. Good idea."

We hopped onto the Loop. It was after rush hour, so we were able to get seats together. It was cool and cloudy as we got out. The gray day matched the dingy train.

"I'm glad I took my coat," I said as we walked toward Lake Michigan.

"My vest keeps me toasty, with my sweater . . . Look!" Maria pointed.

A giant pink dragon flew overhead.

"It's them!" I gasped.

"So much for keeping their secret. I wonder if this releases us from keeping their geas? That dragon is owned by—" Maria choked.

"I guess the gag order is still in effect."

Maria gasped. "I'd say so. I'll ask them why."

"Look at that!" I pointed to a giant unicorn landing next to the pink dragon. A rainbow-colored trail of sparkles followed it. "I want to ride the unicorn!"

"That's new to me. Let's go."

We joined the line. A tall, slender black woman took people's cash or credit cards before directing them up a rainbow stairway to the—palanquin? Houdah? Gondola? Whatever it was, it was on the unicorn's back and strapped to its chest.

Maria paid for our tickets. The woman wore heavy makeup, with purple and rainbow shadows around her eyes. She was beautiful, but somehow I knew her.

"You look vaguely familiar. Have we met?" I asked.

"Not unless you know Nashonna, the supermodel," she answered in a strong alto voice.

"I don't know anyone named that. Do you guys live in south

Chicago like we do?" Whew! I was worried I would get throttled by the geas for that.

She shook her head. "Nah. Schaumburg."

"Huh. I thought I knew you—and your dragon."

"Lord Pink? He's very exclusive. I doubt you know him. Now, take your seat. You're holding up the line." She shooed us along, like we were two kids.

"That was a failure," I said as we buckled in.

"No, you were right. It's them!"

"C'mon. How can you be sure?"

"I watched the dragon. It's just like the one we saw, but with a crown. And the girl is just like the girl who hexed us—but two feet tall with pink wings."

"Maybe we can demand they release us from the geas now."

"Don't take the chance. They might do something worse!"

"Ulp." I gulped as the unicorn galloped into the air. I gasped for air to keep my stomach contents in.

"If you're going to puke, lean the other way." Maria looked askance at me.

"Airsick?" Our supermodel pilot walked to us. She looked concerned. "Take this magic pill." She pulled back the dragon head of a dispenser, and a striped candy pellet popped out. I grabbed it and chewed it up.

"Wow. I'm better already! What's that?"

"It's magic!" She laughed and went back up the stairs to the pilot's seat.

"You're right," I said. "It's them."

Chapter 33 - Moving Day

Saturday, October 17

I came unofficially with the police when they raided Yolanda and Dak's apartment. They wouldn't let me go with them, but I had to see what happened when they were caught. So I made myself invisible.

No one responded to the policemen's knock. The building superintendent, who had come with the police, opened the door with the master key. The inside was bare, except for trash, ice cream sticks, and dirt. Clean spots on the rug showed where the furniture had been.

"When did they move out?" the police sergeant asked the superintendent.

"They didn't give no notice! I didn't know nothing about this!"

"When did you last see them?"

"Uh, at the beginning of the month, when they paid their rent."

The police knocked on the doors of neighbors up and down the hall. An old lady had heard them talking in the hall the day before. A man in a wheelchair said he saw Yolanda going down the elevator late the previous night.

But no one had heard them move out.

* * *

The Previous Evening

"Dak, we gotta move."

"Why Mom? I like it here." This was the only home I'd ever known.

"Tom told me some guy was videoing him as he hauled the TVs away. We gotta stay ahead of the police. I figure it'll be easy to move with your magic."

"I guess so. But where, Mom?"

"Let's see. What's a nice neighborhood where they won't

look for us?" Mom punched at her phone for a few minutes. "Here's a house for sale in Southwyck. It's been for sale for a year. Let's go there."

"What if someone comes by to look it at?"

She laughed her funny cackling laugh. "We'll just switch the sign to say 'Sold.' Then no one will come by! Now, let's see. Where have you been near this house?"

Mom squinted at a map on her phone. "There we go. Take us to Ice Cream Joy. We can walk a couple of blocks to the house, and then you can come back and get all the furniture."

"Okay, Mom. Here we go!" We jumped to the ice cream shop.

"Say, why don't you get a couple of ice creams for us?"

It was a cold, drippy day. The shop was deserted. "D'ya got some money? There's no one around to rob."

"Yeah, I do, but try this. While they're making the ice creams, try to get some of the money out of the cash register."

"Okay."

I ordered the hot-dipped chocolate ice cream bars. I pictured the bills in the cash drawer and teleported them to my pocket. It suddenly bulged. I pulled out a wad of twenties. I peeled off one, feeling rich.

"That'll be six bucks." The girl handed me the ice cream bars. I handed her the twenty.

"Keep the change!" I walked away. I'd always wanted to say that. It sounded cool.

Mom chuckled when I told her. "That's my boy. I don't mind you blowing someone else's money."

It felt good to make Mom laugh.

We walked to the house. The door was locked, but there was a little box latched on to the porch railing.

Mom pointed to it. "The key's in there."

I imagined the key inside and popped it out. She took it and opened the door. "Say, zap the box off the railing."

I shrugged and sent it into her hand.

"Good. Now we won't have people coming in on us." We ambled inside, and she locked the doors. She drew all the curtains closed in the front of the house.

"Start movin' furniture, son."

I had learned how to move stuff without holding it. I moved our living room stuff to the new living room. There was a lot of space left over, and everything smelled fresh and clean. Then I moved our bedrooms, closets, and kitchen.

"Good job. Take me back and let's double-check."

We went back, and she dumped the garbage cans on the floor. "We're gonna lose our deposit anyway, so they can use it to clean up. And we won't have to buy new garbage cans. Let's go home."

* * *

I was stuck. The police didn't blame me that the crooks had fled, but I felt terrible anyway. How could I find them? They could be anywhere in the world!

I went to school in a daze. Doing schoolwork took my mind off my worries. Even gym class went well—I hit three baskets. The good-looking girl in my history class smiled at me when I picked up her pencil.

Riding home on my bike, I felt at peace. I'd start with a solid fact. I could use magic to search for them. And an opinion: They were not likely to leave Toledo. They just seemed comfortable here. They had a fence to sell their stolen goods. And an ice cream store. Huh. I could put a camera there and see if they showed up.

When home I placed my camera on a telephone pole, using my magical teleport power.

That evening I retrieved the camera and checked the recording. Yes! Dak had shown up with his mom, bought some ice cream, and disappeared. Now all I had to do was find them.

"We got some new neighbors," Mom commented the next morning, Saturday. "That house behind us that was on sale for the past year has a family in it. I saw them take out some garbage yesterday."

"Oh? Do they have any kids?"

"Yes, a young boy took out the garbage."

"Uh, did he look like the kid that stole our ice cream?"

"Uh, maybe? He was the right size, with dark- brown hair. I didn't really see his face."

I looked out the back window. "I wish he'd show up."

Right on cue, he came out the back. Dak.
Now what?

Chapter 34 – Palimony

Monday, October 19

"Oh no!" Master moaned. He was looking at some paper he picked up from a box outside the door. A man came by every day and dropped off a paper there. I had a fun time barking at him.

"What's that, Master?" I wagged my tail to cheer him up.

"My old girlfriend Bella Thornson is suing me for palimony. We had never even lived together!"

"I could bark to that. I remember her scent. I would know if she were in the house."

"I don't think they'd accept your testimony in court, Spot. You're a dog."

"Why not?"

"Courts are for human testimony. Animal testimony isn't allowed."

"Why not? Don't we tell the truth like humans?"

"I'm sure you tell the truth more than humans." Master sighed. "Sometimes humans don't make sense."

"You sure are right!" I barked to emphasize my words. They just didn't have the punch barking did.

"What's suing? What's palimony?" I tilted my head.

"Suing is when you claim someone owes you something. You want them to pay you money for something they did wrong to you. You go to court to prove your point and get your money. Palimony is when a man and woman are mating"—Master smiled, like he'd said something funny (I didn't get the joke)—"and then separate. The woman says he owes her money because she was his mate while he was making the money."

Money again. That seems to be behind everything people did. Even Master worked for money, made videos for money, and went to New York City for money. But he played ball with me. I didn't have any money. I shook my head, like I was getting water out of my ears.

"Wanna play ball?"

"Great idea, Spot!" Master grabbed the ball and we went outside.

* * *

What's this? I watched the Viewtube video carefully. A dog barked on a TV show and then spoke. He sounded just like I did in my head when I talked with Darrell.

I looked at the dog carefully. Black and white, a male, he was smaller than me, mostly because he had shorter legs.

Darrell! Look at this!

"What, Faith?" He looked at me from his computer, with his headphones on. His eyes stared straight ahead. I remembered when we first met. I was so glad to finally have a blind human to help, after all that hard seeing-eye training.

Now Darrell was the mayor of New York and I was First Dog. I had the run of city hall and ran errands for him.

There's a talking dog on this Viewtube channel.

"It's probably a fake."

It's a Jimmy Fellon show rerun. The dog was barking and then started talking. In the Viewtube comments, they say it's magic.

"You can't be so gullible, Faith."

I can talk, can't I? Maybe he can too.

"Hmm. I did wish you could tell me the denominations of the bills. And magic got me elected to the mayor's office. Soon we'll have the governor's office. Why not?"

Darrell had fun with his political games. As long as I could help him, I was happy. But . . . *It'd be nice to have another dog I could talk to.*

"Huh. I never thought of that. Let me look into that. We can work this out."

* * *

Hundreds of dragons thundered toward Tiananmen Square. Dozens of rows of tanks stood guard, protecting Xi Jinping.

I wasn't afraid. I had Long Fu, my lucky dragon, and hundreds of others. As I found dragon statues, I turned them into my soldiers. Some were metal, some were water, and some were air. All were more powerful than any tank.

The tanks thundered as we appeared. Shells and missiles hurtled toward us. Flames, water, and air roared out of the dragons. I saw one shell slow and stop in front of us. A hypersonic blast from an air dragon took all its energy. Another blast sent it back to the tank, faster than it had left.

Some tanks melted. Others were drowned in water gushing out from river dragons. The rest exploded from returning shells.

We climbed the reviewing stand and found the general secretary, Xi Jinping, surrounded by his bodyguards, collapsed in heaps, covering his body with theirs.

"Pick him up but don't kill him," I told Long Fu.

Encaged by brass teeth, Xi opened his eyes.

"Jinping! Proclaim me as the new general secretary. I'm Liu Fu, your successor."

He looked at me, stunned.

I tilted my head. "Or you can die and become dragon food."

After he spoke, I gave a command to Long Fu. "Amplify his voice."

From the mouth of the dragon, Xi's voice echoed across the square and around China through countless television cameras. "I proclaim Liu Fu as my successor, the general secretary of the Communist Chinese Party. Effective now." He looked at me hopefully.

Why not spare him? He could be useful. I had Gao running Beijing's garbage collection. I nodded at him. "Well done. You get to live, as my spokesman."

So now I ruled China. Great. But why stop now?

Chapter 35 – Pre-Trial

Thursday, October 22

"Hello?" I answered my business phone.

"I'd like a ride to Sprong, Blodgett, and Whifflehammer. I'm at the airport, Gate 14A."

"Sure thing, Mr. Hugh Lamba. I see you've already paid. That'll get you a discount."

"Gotta save money in these times. See you soon."

Great. A prepaying customer and an easy run from the airport to downtown. I banked my trusty minivan and zoomed across town, beneath gray woolen skies.

I tried to get as many fares as I could the day before the trial. Who knew how many days I'd be off work? Megan would continue to work part time, as would the grandkids, but there'd be a big drop in business. I'd barely cover my rental fees.

I took a sip of my coffee, thick with cream. My business had picked up though. The trial had produced great publicity for Flight 216. If we could win the trial in a few short days, we'd be set. I was having the time of my life. Grandkids, children, and a fun job—what more could I ask for?

But what if I lost? I'd lose my business to bankruptcy. I was super glad that I'd incorporated it. I'd be the same as before I came to Cleveland. I'd still have my kids and my grandkids.

I relaxed. I'd imagined the worst-possible outcome—and I could deal with it.

I landed.

A stocky guy with a salt-and-pepper beard climbed into the car. "Hi. I'm Hugh Lamba."

"Hi, Hugh. I'm Angie."

"Here are my kids, Oscar and Felicia."

Two twentysomethings piled into the back seat. Oscar was a nerdy-looking string bean with frizzy brown hair, and Felicia was a wide-eyed blonde.

"Off we go!" We flapped upward at a steep angle. "Next stop, Sprong, Blodgett, and Whifflehammer."

"Wow. You've got great acceleration with this . . . minivan?" Oscar went from enthusiasm to puzzlement.

"It took my breath away!" Felicia said breathlessly.

"Yes. The van doesn't show it, but it's got plenty of punch behind its wings." They seemed like nice kids, but something bugged me about them.

Hugh folded his hands on his lap and gazed at downtown Cleveland. He looked calm and relaxed.

"Have you flown before?" I asked.

"Oh, a couple of times."

"Here we are." I zoomed down to Euclid Avenue and nestled into a parking spot across the street. "You can cross at East Ninth Street."

"That won't be necessary. Let's go, kids. There she is." Hugh gestured across the street, and the three ran across in a sudden pause in the traffic.

"Odd how the traffic just ceased when they wanted to cross . . ." My suspicion meter pinged in the red zone. I watched as they ran across the street to the door. A woman with dark hair in a pageboy cut was entering. She looked familiar. Katie Garcia.

The big guy talked to Katie and showed her a tablet with a pen. She frowned and shook her head. He leaned in and pinned her against the glass next to the door.

I was already out of the car and yelling. "Hey! Leave her alone!" I wished I could hear them.

"You will sign the statement exonerating me." Hugh's voice was soft but fierce in my ear.

"I . . ." Katie looked stunned.

A car honked at me as it zoomed by. "Stop, traffic!" I yelled. Trucks, cars, and buses froze in place.

"You will sign the statement," Oscar said.

"You will sign the statement," Felicia echoed.

Katie covered her eyes with her hands. Even with magic, I could barely hear her whisper, "No."

Katie cowered down.

"Sign the statement!" the three of them shouted.

Katie uncovered her face and stood up, wobbling. She reached for the tablet and pen with shaking hands. Her eyes were bulgy.

"No! Stop!" I shouted.

Katie dropped the tablet, ducked under Hugh's arms, and ran inside.

"Get her Owen, Fawn!" Hugh said.

The young people ran after her with Hugh following, after he picked up the tablet.

I followed too. I didn't know what was happening, but I didn't like it. I did like Katie, and it looked like bullying or . . . coercion.

I ran in right behind Hugh. Oscar and Felicia—or Owen and Fawn. Each held an arm of Katie's.

"You will sign!" they shouted together.

Trembling, her hand reached for the tablet. Her face twisted.

"I'll hold it. You sign," Hugh said.

"No!" I shouted, simultaneously with the pudgy Will Sprong, who stepped out of the elevator and into the lobby.

All four snapped their heads. Owen and Fawn turned to me. Katie and Hugh turned to Will.

I chuckled. "It's like a Mexican standoff. Freeze, you three!" Thinking of myself as a magical gunslinger amused me no end.

Katie pulled away from Owen's motionless hand and ran to Will. Felicia had her mouth open in midsentence, looking like a department-store manikin.

Hugh shook his head. "It's broken. Let's go, Fawn, Owen—quickly." Hugh, Fawn, and Owen zoomed out the door.

Before I could blink, they were gone.

Katie slowly collapsed onto a couch in the lobby. Will and I sat on either side of her.

"Whew!" Katie pulled out her phone. "I wonder what magic readings I've captured?"

"That looks heavy duty," I said.

"It is." She smiled and panted, like she'd just run a marathon.

Katie unfolded her phone, once, twice. A bizarre page of bar charts greeted me.

"Look at this!" Katie pointed to one chart. "Hugo Lamacek," it read. "Compulsion, 1435 MUs. Break Freeze, 1440 MUs. Speedy Getaway, three people, 981 units." Katie read the fine print aloud. "'Owen Gooseberry. Compulsion 814 MUs. Fawn Goodspell, Compulsion 746 MUs. And here are the good guys. Angela Hamilton, No Magic spell, 1406 MUs. Willifred Sprong, No Magic spell, 667 MUs. Katie Garcia, Block Magic, 1429 MUs.' Then there's your Freeze spell, Angie: '1411 MUs.'

"Thanks for the rescue, Angie, Will. They had me there." Katie stood. "Let's go and see what magic we captured this morning. I think we have samples from everyone."

"I wanted you here to go over the procedure for the trial tomorrow. You need to hear this too, Angie." Will looked at us.

"I've got to get more fares."

"I think you should go into hiding until the trial is over."

"I need the money."

"I'll pay you the money to protect you."

"That's nice of you, Will."

"Actually not. I'll simply charge it as witness protection expense, which Hugo has to pay."

"Ha. That makes it all worthwhile. Let's go hear this legal-process crap then."

"I prefer to think of it as 'my monthly paycheck.'" Will chuckled.

Katie, Will, and I settled in the conference room.

Will began. "This lawsuit started when you, Angie, filed for damages against Hugo Lamacek and Checkered Airlines. Hugo responded by countersuing for defamation and restraint of trade. His countersuit has been dismissed by summary judgment because of a lack of evidence.

"With Katie's magical sample gathering, we have sufficient evidence to convict Hugo and his associates for damages, plus criminal charges of assault. We'll wait until we win the civil trial for that.

"We will have a jury trial. Both the plaintiff—you, Angie—and the defendant, Hugo, wanted that. I think the judge did too. He didn't want to get involved in setting magical precedents. Leave that to the jury.

"It'll be key in this case to convince the jury that Katie's magic detector works and can detect the source and cause of magic. I'll demonstrate it with Katie and Angie, showing their magical samples."

"Then we'll introduce the magical evidence against Hugo Lamacek, Owen Gooseberry, Tiffany Meriweather, and Fawn Goodspell, from their attacks on you, Angie, and you, Katie.

"We can expect Hugo's lawyers, Scut, Scat, and Scoot, to try to discredit your magical evidence, Katie." Will chuckled evilly.

I couldn't believe that someone who looked that ordinary could sound so wicked.

"Ironically, they scuttled that with their attack on you today. We captured the whole affair on video camera, non-magical. Combined with the magic samples, that should convince the jury."

"Hmmm. What if we lose?" Katie asked.

Again, Will laughed. "I have it on good authority we will win." He pulled open a drawer under the table and took out a battered doll. "Katie, Angie, this is Cathy, my sister's old doll. She's my magical prognosticator. Cathy, will we win this case?" He pulled the string.

"Ha! That question again?" Cathy's voice scratched out. "It's in the bank! It's in the freezer! It's stone cold . . ." Her voice faded to a buzz.

Will yanked the string again.

"Thanks. I was running out of breath—or spring. It's a stone-cold solid case. Only by magically beating the whole . . . brrr."

Will tugged again. "Only by magically beating the whole courtroom can those guys win. You outnumber them magically."

"Close your mouth, Katie. You're catching flies." I smiled at the young woman. Her mouth closed. "Haven't you ever seen a talking doll?"

"Not a magical, sentient one." She pulled out her phone. "750 MUs from Will to the doll to activate her prognostication. The *doll Cathy* pulled 700 MUs from the ambient magic to prophesy. Huh." Katie looked at Will. "Ask her how much confidence she has in her prediction."

Will handed her the doll. "You do it. You have more magical power."

With a wry face, Katie pulled Cathy's string. "How confident are you in these predictions, Cathy?"

Cathy's eyes swiveled to Katie. "With no mages from Hugo, one hundred percent. With four, which is what I expect, ninety percent. With eight . . . scrrch."

Sighing, Katie pulled again.

"Great. You have a ton of magic, but it doesn't help my main spring. With eight or more mages, the trial goes to fifty-fifty or lower."

"Ick. I don't like that. Can we control who they bring to court?" Katie looked at Will.

Will frowned. He opened a folder on the table. "They're bringing Owen Gooseberry, Tiffany Meriweather, and Fawn Goodspell as witnesses. With Lamacek, that's four mages."

"Hmm. Ninety percent chance of success. I suppose that's the best we can do."

"You're a demanding woman, Katie."

"I only like sure things."

* * *

The jury filed in, twelve average citizens—seven women and five men. They ranged from perhaps thirty to seventy or more in age.

I sat next to Katie, who was busy with her phone, taking magical measurements of Hugo Lamacek's team.

Katie leaned close to me and whispered, "They've got four mages. There's Hugo, Owen, Tiffany, and Fawn, just as expected."

I frowned. They all looked different from yesterday. Hugo had salt-and-pepper hair but no beard. Owen had curly brown hair, as did Fawn. I recognized Tiffany, who looked just like Fawn had yesterday.

"They disguised themselves yesterday," I whispered back to Katie.

"Right. That's a magical thing." She seemed unperturbed, then whispered, "I wonder what the ten percent chance of failure is?"

I shrugged.

"We've got five mages with you, me, and our lawyers. But—"

"All rise!" The bailiff said. "The court of the Honorable

Judge Kevin Sloter will preside over this trial."

"But what?" I whispered back.

"The lawyers Scut, Scat, and Scoot are all mages! We're outnumbered seven to five!"

The bailiff looked at us. "The witnesses will come forward to be sworn in."

Chapter 36 – Trial

Friday, October 23rd

I gave my oath of truthfulness through gritted teeth. With seven or eight mages against us, we were down to a fifty-fifty chance of winning this trial. How would they attack? Me? Angie? Her lawyers? Or something more subtle?

I had one thing Hugo's gang didn't know about as backup—and I didn't know if it'd work.

I thought furiously as our lawyers went through their opening statements.

"Don't worry—I've got your back," Angie said.

"Thanks." Even though she was just one mage, I felt better. Angie thought completely differently than I did and was successful and powerful in magic.

Any sleepiness I had from working into the night on my backup plan vanished as I worried about the trial.

Will Sprong did the presentation of our case to the jury.

Afterward, he said we had magical evidence, and he called me to the stand.

"Ms. Garcia, what is your role in the government?"

"Currently I a researching magical phenomena, determining how they react, as part of the Oakridge Research Center."

"And who has authorized this research?"

"President José Lopez."

"Please demonstrate your magic detector."

We had agreed to use the larger magic-detecting model that Sprong, Blodgett, and Whifflehammer had, since it looked more impressive than my phone. I pushed it on a cart before the jury.

"Here is the magic-unit reader." I directed their attention to a dial. "It shows a background magic level of 51 in the courtroom."

"Now I will perform some magic. Levitate!" I pointed at the cart with my finger. It floated upward about four feet. "Now land on the floor gently." It settled back down. "Observe how the magic meter goes up and down." I pulled a printout from the back of the machine. "Please examine the chart." I handed the printout to the jury foreperson, a middle-aged Black woman.

The chart showed the MUs going up and then back down: "Mage: Katie Garcia spell, Levitation, 79 MUs."

"Here is a sample of my magic captured by the machine." I removed a bottle filled with glowing blue liquid. It was labeled "Katie Garcia's Magic." I passed it to the jury.

The jury peered with interest and murmurings at the bottled magic and the chart.

Glancing at the defendants, I could see Hugo watching intently.

"Please admit these items as evidence," Will said. "Using this same technology, we have collected evidence that Owen Gooseberry and Tiffany Meriweather have attacked Angela Hamilton's Urber franchise. Here are the recordings of the two attacks."

Will played two videos of the attacks, taken from Angie's memories.

"Here are samples of the magical caramels and the ensorcelled mud that these two mages used, scraped directly from the car. Ms. Garcia, can you detect the origin of those two samples for the jury, using your machine?"

"Yes, Mr. Sprong." I pointed the detector at the caramel and the mud. The printout showed: "Owen Gooseberry: caramel curse, 758 MUs."

Tiffany Meriweather: mud storm, 653 MUs.

"Now, can you get samples from those two mages?"

"Yes." I pointed the detector toward Owen.

"I object!" Scott Scut shouted. "That's a violation of the defendant's privacy."

"Actually not. He's radiating the magic. It's like taking a picture," I said calmly.

"Lawyers, to the bench please," Judge Sloter said.

Since I was already before the jury, I silently wished, "Let me hear what they say."

"Would you object to a photograph taken of your client in the courtroom?" Judge Sloter asked Scut.

“Yes, if it would be used against him.”

“Think of this as a blood test to compare your clients’ magic against the collected evidence,” Will said to Scut.

“I would fight that tooth and nail too. We don’t know the reliability of the magic test, nor the so-called magic video.”

“Then argue that in your defense. Return to the court. Objection overruled.” Judge Sloter dismissed them.

I smiled smugly as I gathered magic from Owen and Tiffany. Owen looked stunned, but Tiffany glared at me. Who knew a blue-eyed blonde could look so vicious?

Owen’s magic was a roiling avocado green in its bottle, while Tiffany’s was a sparkling scarlet. The colors exactly matched the magic from the caramels and the mud, which I’d collected in their bottles.

Will brought another machine forward, our magic comparator. Mike had created this just for our trial.

“I’d like the jury to attend to this magic comparator,” Will said. “It compares two samples of magic and gives you a readout of how identical they are.”

“Here is Mr. Gooseberry’s sample, and here is the sample from the caramel, both of which you saw Ms. Garcia collect.” Will slid the bottles into two slots.

“We turn on the comparator and see what it says.” Will flipped a switch. Both bottles lit up a rich, glowing green. The dial read out pegged at 100 percent identical.

“So Mr. Gooseberry did use his magic to create this caramel on Ms. Hamilton’s car while she was flying, threatening her life and the life of her passenger.”

Will repeated the procedure for Tiffany’s mud sample. The jury’s faces lit up with lurid red glares, and again it was a 100 hundred percent match.

“And so we have solid evidence that both of these mages used their magic against Ms. Hamilton and her passengers. Further, we have evidence that these mages did so at the express request of Mr. Lamacek.

“Here is a sample of a mage’s contract with Mr. Lamacek. Please admit this into evidence. Basically, they have to do whatever service Mr. Lamacek asks of them, or they are immediately fired. Furthermore, we have collected Mr.

Lamacek's magic. Ms. Garcia?"

"Here is a sample of Mr. Lamacek's magic, which I gathered while he was trying to compel me, just yesterday. Please play the security video."

The video showed the magical attack on me yesterday. We magically dubbed in the conversation Angie heard when she and Will broke up the attack.

"Here are the magical records of the attack. You can see Mr. Lamacek, Owen Gooseberry, and Fawn Goodspell each used spells to compel me to sign a statement stating there was no magical attack."

The video and magical evidence got to the jury. They murmured among themselves and looked impressed.

"Thank you, Ms. Garcia." Will went before the jury. "Do you see how easily Mr. Lamacek can compel his employees to do anything he wishes? Thus, he is the primary cause of these attacks on Ms. Hamilton."

"Your Honor, the plaintiffs rest their case."

"The jury will now hear the defendants' case," Judge Sloter said.

"Hi, I'm Scot Scut. This is a civil case, which means you'll judge the plaintiff's claims on the preponderance of evidence. Evidence is proof that something they allege is so. The plaintiffs have presented magical 'proof'"—here, Scut stopped and made air quotes—"that what they allege is so.

"But how do you know? With magic, they can make anything seem real. You can literally make something out of nothing. Watch this." Scut held his hand out. Pop! A marshmallow chick appeared. "Anyone like to eat this marshmallow chick?" Looking at the uncertain jurors, some shaking their heads, he said, "How about chocolate?" The yellow chick turned dark brown. "Fair-trade chocolate of the highest quality. Maybe you want it wrapped?" It became wrapped in silver foil. "If no one wants to eat this, I'd like to admit this chocolate as evidence that magic can make something from nothing."

"Here's a film of Mr. Lamacek in his office. Note the time in the background: ten a.m. He gets the notification that Owen Gooseberry is headed for the airport.

"Now you can see the view from Mr Gooseberry's chartered flying bus. All Checkered Airlines flights are monitored for safety reasons.

"Here, we see Mr. Gooseberry avoiding some clouds. There is Flight 216's minivan. Look! It's falling out of the sky. No caramel needed.

"You see, if the mage flying the magical vehicle loses concentration for a second, the car or minivan stops flying. I guess that's what happened to Ms. Hamilton. She probably covered her mistake with caramel, which she gave to her poor customer.

"No doubt she did the same thing with mud later on. Perhaps she should be tested for flying competency, like we do at Checkered Airlines."

Scut went on, insulting and impugning Angie and me as unreliable liars who were out for Lamacek's money.

What really bothered me was that the jurors all seemed to be agreeing with him, nodding and looking at each other.

On a hunch, I turned my magic detector on the jury. It showed "Influence Jury spell: Fawn Goodspell, Owen Gooseberry, Hugo Lamacek, Tiffany Meriweather, Scot Scut, Skit Scat, Coot Scoot, 3678 MUs."

I sucked in a gasp and showed this to Will. He immediately shot to his feet. "I object!"

Judge Sloter looked at him curiously.

"Mr. Scut and the whole legal team and the defendant's witnesses are all using magic to influence the jury!"

Judge Sloter frowned. "Lawyers, please come to the bench for a sidebar. The court will adjourn for fifteen minutes."

Will ripped the printout from the large detector. Mike grabbed us, and we left the courtroom to an office for the plaintiff's attorneys. Rick Whifflehammer was there with another magic detector and a glare on his face.

"Did you see the MUs they're generating?" Rick looked at me.

"Yes."

"Can we stop them?"

"Maybe. When Hugo tried to compel me, I put up a magical barrier at my skin against all spells."

"Can we stop 3600 MUs?"

"Let's see. Everyone, wish for an impenetrable barrier to all spells. Right across this table. One, two, three!"

A translucent blue barrier appeared.

"How strong is it?" Rick asked, and then pointed his detector toward it.

"Magic barrier: Katie Garcia, 1510. Angie Hamilton, 1489. Michelangelo Blodgett, 801. Ricardo Whifflehammer, 1008. 4808 MUs. Good. That should stop the compulsion."

"Yes . . . assuming they're already at their full power. I gave everything I could."

"Me too," Angie said.

"I topped out as well," Mike said.

"And I gave my all. And we also have Will," Rick added.

"This'll have to be the most we can do, and hope for the best. Will the judge let us put a blue glowing magical shell around the jury?" I asked.

"Yes. That was our contingency plan if they tried to influence the jury. Will is asking for that right now."

"Thanks, Rick. That was a good contingency plan."

"I think that was Mike's idea. He gets most of the unusual ideas."

Will entered the room and stared at the glowing blue wall across the table.

"Ah. That's plan J, I see. I got the judge to agree to put a barrier around the jury. He's instructing the jury now. We're going to repeat our presentations with the shell around the jury.

"He's really ticked at Scut, Scat, and Scoot for trying this. He said he's within an eyelash of trying them for jury manipulation. But he has no precedent for magical influence."

"Before we go back, I've got one more thing to do." Will took out a black case and opened it. There was Cathy, the talking doll. "What's our chances now, Cathy?" He pulled the string.

"You screwball! You've got seven mages against you! You have less than a fifty-fifty chance of holding—"

She sputtered out. Will yanked her string again. "—out against them. You'd better get some reserves to help you." Her eyes swiveled to Will and bugged out a little. Then they snapped shut.

I hadn't told them about my backup plan, because I wasn't sure if it'd work. But I did now. "I've got some power in reserve."

"How much?" Rick's blue eyes skewered me like twin blue shish kebabs.

"Probably more than double what I can generate on my own. It's stored in a bottle in my computer case. I stayed up last night creating it as a reserve."

"That's great!" Will sighed.

"But?" Rick knew there was more.

"But I'm not sure what'll happen if I tap into it. Or how I'll tap into it."

"So it's a last-ditch Hail Mary." Rick made that a statement.

"Yes."

"Let's go. I'll be out there with you for this. Throw your Hail Mary if you have to." Rick led us out.

* * *

"Good job, everyone," I reassured as they filed into the defendant's room. "We've got this in the bag."

"We won't be able to affect the jury anymore, Hugo." Fawn looked down, discouraged.

"We've already affected them. They won't change their opinion," I said confidently.

"How can you be so sure?" Owen asked.

"This." I pulled out my magic black ball from my computer case. "Black Magic Ball, will the jury be persuaded by our testimony?"

"All twelve jurors are convinced by your testimony and will vote in your favor. No additional magic is needed to persuade them."

"There you go!" someone said.

"That's a fantastic tool. Can it really foretell the future?" Scot Scut asked.

"You bet."

"I was planning to have Owen narrate his video. I thought that would reinforce our argument."

"Great idea! Let's do it." I led my team to certain victory.

* * *

Both sides represented their cases. The jury sat in their box, surrounded by the glowing blue shell we had cast around them. Occasionally one would reach out and touch the shell. It wasn't tangible, of course. They looked uneasy.

I monitored the defense team. They seemed smug but weren't casting any spells toward the jury.

After the defense presented their case, they said, "We'd like to present a witness, Mr. Owen Gooseberry. Since he was the mage so evilly maligned, we'd like him to narrate the non-magical video we have."

Owen did so, verifying all the video up until Angie's van went into the cloud.

Rick poked Will and whispered in his ear. Will shot to his feet.

"The plaintiffs would like to cross-examine Mr. Gooseberry."

"Permission granted," the judge said.

"Mr. Gooseberry, was that you in the video?"

"Of course! No one else is as tall and skinny as me at Checkered Airlines." He chuckled, and the jury joined in.

"Very well. Did you cast a Caramel Curse spell on Angela Hamilton's car?"

Owen shook his head vigorously. "Didn't you watch the video? Her car went into the cloud and there was no caramel on it!"

"But did you do it after the car went into the cloud after the video ended?"

"Of course not!"

Owen's red pants burst into flames.

The jurors yelled.

"Order in the court!" Judge Sloter said. "Bailiff! Help please!"

I knew the drill. While the bailiff's mouth was still hanging open, I ran out of the courtroom and grabbed the fire extinguisher I'd seen on the wall. I ran back in and sprayed wet foam all over poor Owen.

"Ooh, that hurts!" he moaned as he writhed on the floor.

On impulse, I touched him and whispered, "Be healed."

His eyes widened and his mouth dropped open. His hand went to his foam-covered leg.

“It’s . . . healed. I didn’t know you could do that.”

“I didn’t either. But it felt like the right thing to do.”

“Order in the court. We will adjourn for fifteen minutes to clean up the mess. Then I’ll give instructions to the jury.”

* * *

“The jury’s ready,” the bailiff said, as he came into the plaintiff’s room, where we were waiting.

“That’s fast!” Will said.

“It seemed like forever,” Angie said.

“It was”—I looked at my phone—“one hour and eleven minutes.

“Is this good or bad?” Angie asked.

“It means the jury was in agreement pretty much from the beginning. Either we win or we lose,” Rick said.

“And we’ve never lost,” Mike said.

“But there’s always a first time. I’m mentally prepared to lose the business,” Angie said.

“But that won’t happen,” Will said.

“Let’s not argue. We’ll know in ten minutes,” I said.

We assembled in the courtroom.

The jury foreperson stood. “The jury finds in favor of the plaintiffs. Full damages are awarded.”

“No!” Hugo screamed.

My MU meters showed four, five, and 6000 MUs cast toward the jury in their protective shell. The shell shattered. The jurors’ faces froze.

“No!” I yelled. I took my quart-sized jar of magic I had created the night before and poured it over my head. It was either that or drink it, and I couldn’t drink that much.

I reinforced the “No Magic” shell I had cast. My spell had over 10000 MUs. I tingled all over, like a low-level shock. I couldn’t get rid of all the magic that spilled around me like a widening, sparkling blue pool.

Lamacek’s eyes widened as his spell bounced off the barrier. He looked around frantically. “Gotta split.” He blurred out the door, which slammed shut.

“Stop him!” I pointed after him. I couldn’t be heard in the overall commotion of the courtroom. But my magic surged through the door, splintering it. It turned down the hall and into the fire escape stairs. Somehow I could perceive the front wave of my magic as it followed my will, pursuing Lamacek.

It burst through the door to the outside, setting off the fire alarm. Down Ontario street it went, and then the magical stream leapt into the air. In my mind's eye, I flew through the air, like a fighter jet, with clouds hurtling by.

I saw Lamacek's flying bus ahead. My magical wave crashed into it. The wings froze and then withdrew back into the bus. The bus dropped like . . . a bus. I saw Lamacek's eyes bug out. Then my spell ended.

I was completely out of magic. My sight and hearing returned to the noisy, chaotic courtroom. Then I fainted from exhaustion.

* * *

I came to smelling salts. "Oooh," I moaned.

"She's awake." Angie set the smelling salts down. "Are you okay, Katie?"

"I feel like ten miles of bad road. And like a battery that's been grounded for a week."

"She's well enough to complain, at least." Angie smirked.

I lay on a couch in the plaintiff's room. Sprong, Blodgett, and Whifflehammer gathered around me in lawyerly concern.

I pushed myself up to my elbow and looked around. Angie sat next to me. "What's been happening?"

"We won, with full damages," Rick said.

"I should know, but what does that mean?"

"Angie won the suit for a hundred thousand in damages, and we've filed additional charges for jury tampering."

"You've left out the best part, Rick. We won because of Owen's testimony," Will said.

"Huh?"

"When he burst into flame, the jury realized they had been lying all along. Everyone knows 'liar, liar, pants on fire.'"

"They were hoisted by their own pyre," Mike said with a straight face.

"That's not how that saying goes," Will said with a smirk.

"'Cheaters never prosper' is a saying from my youth, and it's still true," Angie said.

"Ironically, that's kind of how we run our law firm, Angie," Rick said with a smile.

"I knew I was magically attracted to you," Angie said, grinning.

I frowned. Was Owen's lie their first? I guessed so. They'd only issued misleading statements and rhetorical questions, which apparently didn't activate the curse.

"We aren't done yet," Rick continued. "We have acquired all the assets of Checkered Airlines as a legal-expense settlement. Angie, how would you like to run their business for us? We'll pay you a flat two hundred thousand a year as an executive."

"Wow. That'd give me a break from flying. I'd have to vet their mages."

"Just renegotiate their contacts to what your contracts are like. Who knows how much their mages acted under compulsion?"

"Who else escaped besides Hugo?" I asked.

"We got them all in custody while the jury tampering charges proceed. I took the liberty of copying your 'No Magic' spell and locking it around the other mages," Mike said.

"There's a lot to think about," I said.

"You and me both, sister. Or should I say 'granddaughter'?" Angie hugged me.

* * *

The Secretary of Defense, Julio Francisco, burst into the Oval Office.

"Mr. President!"

"Yes, Julio?"

"China has attacked Taiwan!"

"Idiots. What resources do we have in the theater?"

"I think you need to see this video to get the proper context." Julio activated the screen in the office and sent his video to it.

President Lopez watched a beautiful sunset from Taipei. Then he noticed a flock of birds. No, those weren't birds. They were . . . dragons! Hundreds of red and gold dragons descended, causing chaos in the streets, shooting flame everywhere.

Then a flock of green dragons appeared. They fought the red dragons with streams of water, putting out fires and knocking the dragons out of the air.

Then huge waterspouts came off the ocean, up the river, and sucked up all the red dragons.

The video ended.

"What did I just see?" the president asked.

"You saw the first battle of Taipei. China sent a flock of dragons over to attack. Taiwan summoned its own dragons to defend. They also had weather mages, who finished off the battle."

Lopez put his face in his hands. "Why me? Why do I have to deal with this war? And magic?" He sat up straight. "Enough self-pity. What assets do we have in the area?"

"We have two nuclear subs and some destroyers."

"How about aircraft? Antiaircraft weapons?"

"Taiwan used many of their own. We have aircraft in the Philippines and a carrier group on their way there."

"What about our magical assets?"

"Uh, I have no idea. I'm the Secretary of Defense, not the Minister of Magic."

"Then I need one." President Lopez pressed the intercom. "June? Connect me with Katie Garcia. She seems to be the only one who knows what's going on."

Chapter 37 - Mayor

Tuesday, November 3

"Woo-hoo! We won, Faith!" I had just gotten the final voting results the morning after the election, and the media called the election for me.

Yay, team! I'm glad I could help you reach your goal.

"You sure did. We only won by a couple of thousand votes, and I'm sure having your beautiful face on our campaign literature helped."

As well as magic.

"Sure. Our magically generated slogans—'Helping the Humble' and 'Not left or right but middle of the road'—each caused our polls to go up. But I think walking through the five boroughs asking people for their vote put us over the top.

"So how do you want to celebrate, Faith?"

Just being with you as you celebrate.

"Isn't there anything you want to do?"

I would like to meet that talking dog, Spot.

"Oh yeah. I remember that now. I forgot about it during the campaign. Let me search them out on the internet." I put on my headset. "Search for 'Josh and Spot' on Jimmy Fellon." I soon found his name was Josh Garrison, and his dog was Spot. He owned a HossFit gym called Peoria Power in Peoria, Illinois, naturally. I quickly memorized the phone number and called Peoria Power.

"Hi! Peoria Power HossFit! What can I do for you?"

Muffling the greeting, I moved the headset off my ear. So much enthusiasm hurt my ears. "I'm trying to reach Josh Garrison and his dog, Spot. I'm Darrell Duncan, mayor-elect of New York."

"Wow! You're famous! I'm Spot. My master, Josh Garrison, is in the locker room, so I'm dogging the phone for him."

"Do you mind if I put you on speakerphone? My dog, Faith, wants to meet you."

"Hi, Faith! Spot here. I'm a talking dog."

I can talk too, but only mentally.

Speaking for her, I said, "She says—"

"Wow! That's cool. I could talk only mentally, and then we wished for me to talk aloud."

"I didn't know your telepathy could go through the phone," I said to Faith.

I didn't either. I just pictured him on the other end of the phone.

"Why don't you and your master wish for Faith to talk aloud?"

I don't know if we want to do that.

"We'll talk it over later." I didn't know how I'd feel about that. I didn't know how it'd affect me politically either.

"Hi, Master! I've got Faith, another talking dog, on the phone. Only she's just a telepathic dog now, like I was. Do you think we could wish her to talk?"

"Wait a second. Faith? Are you a talking dog?" Master said.

Yes. We're not sure I want to talk aloud.

"Ah. I recognize the telepathic dog talk. That's what Spot did before he talked. But why did you call?"

I saw Spot on Viewtube and wanted to meet him.

Then I heard Spot say, "Master, could you get me a large keyboard for my paws? Then I can use it to phone and surf the internet."

That wasn't a bad idea for Faith either. I made a note to get it for her.

"Why not? Here, Spot, stay in my office and chat away. I gotta take care of some customers."

"Hi, Faith. Isn't Master great? He's going to get me a doggy-size keyboard."

That'd be great—I have to hold a stick in my mouth to use a keyboard.

"Hey, Spot. How'd you and Josh like to visit New York courtesy of the mayor-elect?" I broke into their conversation.

"Sounds great! We already went there for the Jimmy Fellon show. But I have to check with Master. Hold on."

I heard the sound of the door opening and Spot barking and yelling, "Hey, Master! Do you want to go to New York again?"

"Hi, again. This is Josh Garrison. What's this about going

to New York?"

"I'd like to fly you and Spot to New York to spend a week with us. We can compare notes about talking dogs. It'll help us decide whether to wish for Faith to talk aloud."

"Why not? I only check in at Peoria Power once a week now. Let's do it."

"Great. Stay on the phone I while buy tickets for you." I cruised over the airline's website. Hmmm. Should I use the city's money or my campaign finance money? Or steal some money? Decisions, decisions. I'd been avoiding stealing so no one could smear me. Ah. I had a mayoral-transition fund in my campaign chest. I'd spend some of it for a friend for Faith.

I put Josh and Spot on the mayoral-transition team and bought the tickets from Peoria to New York City that evening.

* * *

"That was a quick flight," Jane said as we landed at LaGuardia in New York.

"Time always flies, with you by my side," I said uxoriously.

"Flatterer." She punched me and then leaned her head against my shoulder.

"First-class tickets are nice."

"As well as getting paid for what amounts to a vacation."

"Although New York weather may not be any better than Cleveland's."

Jane stood up and grabbed our carry-on luggage. "On to our hotel!"

"And then to Mayor-elect Duncan's press conference."

"Where we might get some evidence to use against him."

We hopped onto a shuttle to our hotel. After unpacking, we took a cab to our location.

"How did we get press passes again? We're not reporters," Jane asked me.

"Sprong, Blodgett, and Whifflehammer are writing an article on the use of magic in law. We're listed as 'contract reporters' for them."

"Pretty creative."

"Yeah. Maybe I can use them as a resource for my next book."

"You're going do a sequel on your magic book?"

"Yup. I'm already plotting it out."

"Not my cup of tea."

"Even if it walks toward you?"

She snorted, not bothering to reply.

We sat down in the press box. I felt special with a press badge. Then Darrell Duncan and Faith walked in.

Darrell had trimmed his straggly "homeless" style beard into a Van Dyke and wore a nice navy suit with a red tie. Fluorescent-blue sunglasses completed his outfit. Faith wore a matching blue collar, which looked great against her blond coat.

Faith guided him to the podium and sat next to it.

"Ooh, she's a beautiful dog! I wonder how many votes he got because of her?" Jane asked.

"Probably lots, especially if he wished all the dog lovers in town would vote for him."

"I didn't think of that. Knowing he's such a crud makes it likely, doesn't it?"

"Yes. Let's get out our magic detectors."

Will had given us two smartphones that also worked as magic detectors. All we had to do was take a picture and any magic being used would show up on our charts. The magic would be captured and transmitted to our collector in our room.

Jane took the pictures, and I unfolded my phone to check the readouts. "MUs: 175 Darrell Duncan, Charm Audience spell. 350 Faith, Charm Audience spell."

"Huh," I said.

"What?"

"Is this the first time a nonhuman has used magic?"

"I don't know. Why don't you text Will and ask him?"

No, Will texted back. *Our magical doll, Cathy, draws magic to prognosticate. Why not magical animals?*

* * *

Back in our hotel room, Jane sent copies of magic from Duncan and Faith to Will Sprong and company while I wrote up our press report.

Duncan and Faith had charmed the audience during the whole press conference. In response, all the coverage had been glowing and positive about the new mayor.

I also sent a copy of the transcript. Nothing was amazing, just normal questions and political answers, except for Faith's occasional bark in response to Duncan asking her to speak.

I received a long email from Will detailing their research on the internet, looking for Duncan's magic. As they'd expected, it had disappeared from the Amazin' site thanks to our blocking magic. It wasn't found anywhere else either. In desperation, he urged us to walk the streets of Manhattan where Duncan and Faith had begged, looking for signs of it.

I went to Darrell Duncan's bio on his website. He covered his begging extensively, explaining how he'd used it to support himself and Faith and raise campaign funds. He documented his main begging sites and why he'd begged there. The bottom line was high-volume, high-income traffic.

"Jane, how about a walking tour of Manhattan tomorrow?"

"Sure. It's supposed to be a nice day, clear and high in the fifties. Will we see the Empire State Building? The Freedom Tower?"

"Why not? But our first goal is to find evidence of Duncan's magic."

We must have looked like classic NY tourists from the Midwest. Jane scanned everything and everyone with her phone. I did take pictures occasionally when she pointed out something odd.

"Jake, look at that pigeon!"

I glanced at several pigeons pecking at crumbs on the sidewalk. "So?"

"It's magical! Someone named 'Dora Smithfield' is using it to spy on people!"

My phone showed it as "MU 213, Dora Smithfield, pigeon spy." "Huh. What will they think of next? It's not connected to Darrell Duncan though." I reviewed our readings. "Just about everyone has some magic."

"Right." Jane sighed. "I haven't seen hide nor hair of his magic."

"Does magic even have a hide? Or hair?"

"Don't be silly. We're near the city hall. We might as well go there."

"We're certainly getting our walking in."

"Yep. And we got to see the Freedom Tower," Jane remarked as we crossed Broadway together.

"And Central Park."

"And now city hall."

"It's coming up after Reade Street."

Two more blocks and we were there. Background magic was just 49 MUs. We walked around the building, scanning it for magic. Nothing extraordinary, but one window showed over 100 MUs.

"There's somewhere to examine." Jane pointed at the second-story window.

"There's no directed spell, just a high level of background magic. How much do you want to bet that's our friend Darrell Duncan?"

"Seems like a sucker bet." We walked across the lawn to below the window.

"Go ahead. Climb up there and look in."

"Do I look like I'm in my twenties?" I looked at Jane skeptically.

"No, but let's try this: Float, Jake!"

I slowly floated to the second-story window. I saw Darrell there and his dog, Faith. I could faintly hear them. They seemed to be speaking on the phone at the desk. I checked their magic. Faith's read at over 300 MUs and Darrell nearly 290.

A gust of wind blew me away from the window. I floated like a balloon over Jane.

She laughed. "Jake Williams, c'mon down!"

Slowly I descended until I landed. I stamped my feet to make sure I was stable.

"What d'ya find out?"

"Nothing, honey. They were there, they had magic, but they weren't casting spells—they were talking on the phone."

"Huh. So the whole day has been a waste?"

"Aside from the healthy exercise and the sightseeing."

"Well yeah. There's that. But I've had plenty of that. Let's take the subway back uptown. That's a sight we haven't seen."

"Sounds good. We probably won't be mugged."

"If we are, I'll float them and you can bat them around like a punching bag."

"I like how you think." We headed down the stairs to the subway.

Aside from the usual dirt and grime you'd see on Cleveland's Rapid Transit, a busker played a saxophone and another one bowed a violin. I took a picture of them. MUs 75. They were magically enhanced to perform better. Cool. I dropped a dollar in each of their plastic buckets.

We took the train uptown to our hotel on Park Avenue. It wasn't rush hour, so we were able to get seats. I was mildly amused to see "Duncan for Mayor—Helping the Humble," with a big picture of him and Faith plastered along the top of the car.

Jane scanned the car with her phone. She gasped and turned toward me.

"Jake! Look at this!"

I saw a picture of the Duncan ad. The MUs read 308. The spell: "Compel to Vote for Mayor."

"Is that magic captured?"

"Of course." Jane gave me a dirty look, like I should know better.

"Okay. Send samples to Will."

"I already have."

Chapter 38 – School

Wednesday, November 3rd

I wore my favorite jeans and my pink blouse on my first day in the new school. Mom dropped me off in our new car and introduced me to my teacher, Ms. Sewell. She was tall and blond, but she seemed friendly and nice.

Mom told me I couldn't take Pinkie to school. I was growing up to be a big girl and might lose Pinkie. And she needed him when she gave rides in Grant Park.

I felt empty without him, so I made a little magical copy of him and put it on my charm bracelet. When I touched it, I could talk to him, so that was all I needed.

"Mount Tessori" was a special school, probably named after some mountain. I'd have to ask Ms. Sewell about it.

Ms. Sewell took me to the classroom. It was big and airy, with tables and kids around them. "This is the art workstation." She pointed to kids drawing with chalk on wet paper. One kid had a chalkboard.

At the next table were glass jars with water, sand, dirt, rocks, and sugar. Weird.

"This is the Exploratorium. Children discover what happens when you mix things."

"Okay." I already knew sugar dissolved in water. Dirt and water made mud. Whatever.

The next table had blocks with numbers on them. Only one kid was there. He had brown hair and brown eyes, and he was building something with the blocks. He didn't look up.

"This is where you can learn about numbers."

"And building things," the boy said, without looking up.

"Say hi to your new classmate, Heath. This is Shayla."

"Hi." He concentrated on building.

"I'd like to stay here. I learned about counting up to twenty, but I'd like to count up to a hundred."

Heath looked up. "You can't count to one hundred?"

"Perhaps you can teach her, Heath," Ms. Sewell suggested.

He stared at me. I stared back. Who'd win this staring contest? I always beat Lamar.

"Okay." He rapidly arranged the blocks into two rows of ten, one on top of the other.

I sat next to him.

"Here's one to ten." He pointed.

"I already know that."

"But you need to see the pattern. Here's eleven to twenty."

"I know two tens make a twenty. I've been making change all summer."

"Huh. What patterns do you see?"

"Um, every block goes up one."

"How about these two?" He pointed to the one and the eleven.

"Those go up ten, just like a one and a ten-dollar bill."

"And these two?" He pointed to the two and the twelve.

"That's ten too. Hey, they all go up ten in the next row."

"Right. That's the pattern. That's because the first row has ten. What comes after twenty?"

He got me—until I remembered counting money with Lamar. There was a rhythm to it. Eighteen, nineteen, twenty...

"Twenty-one!"

"Right." He rapidly put up another row. "What comes after twenty-nine?" He pointed to the gap at the end of the row.

He was getting into big numbers. Usually Mom or Lamar would count the bigger bills. I just took credit cards for our business.

I squinched up my face, concentrating. The lower rows had ten and twenty and then the missing block. I looked at the blocks.

"This one?" I held block with a three and a zero. I couldn't remember what the name was.

"Right." He nodded once. "See the pattern? Ten, twenty, thirty. Now build up from there."

I looked for numbers with threes in them. I put them in order, counting up from the thirty. I didn't know their names either, but I put the one through nine numbers in order.

"Now, the forties," Heath said.

So that was what they were called. We continued up

through the nineties.

"Right." He nodded. "What's next after ninety-nine?"

"Um, tenty?"

"Kind of." He picked out a one with two zeroes after it. "You can call it 'tenty,' but the real name is one hundred."

"I like 'tenty' better."

He gave me a little smile. "I do too. It's more logical."

I wasn't sure what logical meant exactly, but it was sort of like smart.

"Now, fill out the rest."

That was how I learned to count to one hundred with Heath. He was a bit weird with his staring and abrupt speaking, but boy, was he good with numbers.

"Class, it's time for recess. Put on your jackets, go out, and have fun."

Heath leapt up and ran to his cubby. I went to mine and got my coat.

Outside I made a beeline for the merry-go-round. It was kind of weird because they had seat belts so kids wouldn't fly off. That was half the fun, hanging on for dear life. It was brand new, while our park had an old one. Heath got there right after me.

"Be sure to buckle up for safety, kids." Ms. Sewell smiled at us.

"I never saw a merry-go-round with seat belts," I said.

"We try our best to keep kids safe. Sometimes kids will fly off."

"Yeah. I remember that happening to me once. I just landed on the sand though."

Heath was pushing furiously and then hopped on. When it slowed down, I unbuckled, hopped off, and pushed.

"Faster!" Heath said.

"I'm going as fast as I can!"

He hopped off and pushed it faster. We both hopped on and buckled up.

"This is as fast as Lamar pushes it," I said.

"Who's Lamar?"

"My big brother. He's twelve." I chuckled. That brought to mind the picture of the numbered blocks.

It started to rain.

"Class, let's come in out of the rain!" Ms. Sewell called.

I was going to get off, but Heath hopped off and pushed us fast again.

"We've got to go in, Heath."

He tilted his face up into the rain and opened his mouth. "I like the rain."

"C'mon, Heath and Shayla. Get off and come in." Ms. Sewell stood next to us.

"No. I like the rain." Heath looked at her.

"You'll get wet and cold and maybe get sick. You don't want to get sick, right?" Ms. Sewell stood with her hands on her hips.

"I won't get sick."

"What about Shayla? You don't want her to get sick, do you?"

"Will you get sick?" Heath looked at me.

"Uh, maybe?"

"Huh. Fine. I'll put up a dome." A faintly glowing dome appeared around the merry-go-round.

Ms. Sewell put her hand against it but couldn't go through. "Heath Wimple! You get out of there or you'll miss the snack. It's peanuts and raisins, your favorite."

"I don't care."

"Shayla will miss the snack too."

He looked at me and shrugged. "I don't care. Why would you punish her, anyway? It isn't logical."

That seemed to be his favorite word. The rain poured down. Ms. Sewell opened her umbrella.

"Well I care, Mr. Heath! I'm leaving!" I hopped off and pushed my hand against the dome. It was solid as glass. The rain streamed off. I grabbed my Pinkie charm.

"Punch a hole through, Pinkie!"

A big hole appeared—and then closed just as fast.

"Hey! What are you doing?" Heath yelled.

"Getting' outta here!"

"Pinkie, open the hole again and keep it open."

The hole appeared again—and slowly closed.

"Pinkie, why can't you keep it open?" He'd never failed me before.

Too much magic. It's too strong for me to hold open.

I started crying, and then I got mad. I looked at Heath. "Okay, smarty. You win. Now let me out."

He hopped off. "You really want to go?"

"I said so, didn't I?"

"It's not as much fun by myself. You stay here with me." He pushed the merry-go-round again. "Hop on!"

"No! I want to go!" Ms. Sewell was yelling too, but I couldn't hear what she said. I was sobbing and crying.

Heath just looked up. He let the rain through to his face but nowhere else.

I had a sudden memory of crying over Lamar's dead body and falling asleep. What if Heath fell asleep?

I hopped on next to him and pressed my Pinkie charm against him. "Fall asleep, Heath."

He slumped back. The dome vanished. Ms. Sewell rushed forward and tried to wake him up.

"You won't be able to wake him. I put him to sleep with magic. Here, let's float him. Float, Heath!"

He floated up, light as a balloon.

"Thank you, I think, Shayla. Will you wake him again and restore his weight?"

"Sure, Ms. Sewell. Just give the word."

We stepped into the classroom. Ms. Sewell took off Heath's coat and dried off his face. She put him at the block desk. She looked at me. "Now, Shayla."

"Wake up, Heath. Stop floating."

His eyes snapped open as he settled into his seat. He snapped his head to me. "What did you do?"

"I put you to sleep and then floated you into the room."

"Now, Heath, this is the third time you've used magic to stay outside. Do you think you deserve a snack?"

"No." He frowned and looked down.

"Does Shayla deserve a snack?" Ms. Sewell continued.

"Of course. She did nothing wrong."

"Here's her snack." Ms. Sewell handed me a bowl of raisins and peanuts. "Is it good, Shayla?"

"Yes, ma'am." I felt I should be respectful, since she seemed to be in a punishing mood. And they were good. It was like a candy bar without the chocolate.

“Heath, you have to learn the consequences of using your magic. You can’t just please yourself. You have to think of other people.”

“Yes.”

After she left, I got an idea. “I wish I had a candy bar!” I squeezed Pinkie. A bar appeared in my hand. I broke it into pieces and mixed it with the peanuts and raisins. Boy, was it good!

Heath glared at me. “You magicked that candy bar?”

“Sure. Do you want some?” I split my treats with him.

“Thank you, Shayla.” He had a funny, formal way of talking.

“You’re welcome, Heath.” I was formal right back at him. I smiled.

He gave me a little smile. I think that was all he ever did.

* * *

“This magic stuff is getting out of control,” I told Maria.

“What? Why do you say that, Heather? I kind of like it.”

“I’m going to finish up my internship and become a teacher, and the whole world is changing. Will I have to learn to use magic?”

“Why not? I already do.” Maria looked like a cat who just finished a bowl of cream.

“What? What can you do?”

A huge cup of cold coffee appeared in her hand. “Behold! The latte cappuccino, grand extra-large, humongous size.”

“How long have you been able to do that?”

“Mmm, since last week. I really wanted one, and I wished for it—and bang! It showed up.”

“Is that all there is to it? Just wishing?”

“So far as I can tell. I’ve experimented. But you have to wish with emotion and confidence. Also, you have to be exact. I tried making thousand dollar bills and I kept getting them wrong. The paper, the ink, the patterns—all have to be perfect.

“Let me try it. I saw a sweater in a window on the Loop I would love to have. It was pale sage cashmere but way out of my budget.” I closed my eyes and furrowed my brows. “Magic, give me a sage sweater like the one I saw!”

I heard a soft plop. I opened my eyes, and there it landed at my feet.

"Wow, I never tried anything like that! Let's see what else we can conjure up." Maria rubbed her hands together.

We wandered around the apartment, upgrading our furniture, wardrobes, and computers. I had an old, battered laptop I upgraded to a sleek Pear. It had a gorgeous screen and responded faster. I rubbed the embossed Pear silhouette, hardly able to believe it. That would cost another week's salary.

"Pretty nice, Heather." Maria nodded approvingly. "Let's see what I can do with mine."

Maria had a slick, black gaming computer that was fast and advanced. "Go steampunk!"

The black plastic turned into shiny brass and wood burl.

"Wow! That looks fantastic, Maria."

"Wait till I soup it up. Go quantum!"

Nothing changed on the outside, but when Maria tested it, the computer responded instantaneously. "Yes! I've got the first fully functional quantum computer!"

"So are those faster?"

"They're the fastest. They can break any code or password. Now, one more thing." Maria paced to our cable mode. "Become a T-1 connection!"

The cable became a little thicker.

"Is that all? What is a T-1 connection anyway?"

"That's a Tier 1 connection, a direct link to all the internet *at no charge* and the highest speed, four hundred gigabits per second!" Maria grinned.

"So what? What does that get us?"

"The highest possible data speed and no internet charges. I can hardly wait to try this out on my online game, War of the Worlds!"

"Cool." I put on my sweater. It fit perfectly. "Maybe this magic stuff will work out." I just didn't know how I'd teach in this environment. I had more things to learn, I guess.

Chapter 39 – Neighbor

Wednesday, November 3

All day at school in seventh grade, I chewed on what to do about Dak and Yolanda. I knew they were guilty of theft, but what could I do? I had my recordings of them plotting to steal the TVs, but if the police came, they'd just teleport again.

"What would Jesus do?" I said to myself. Did he deal with thieves? Yeah, there was the thief on the cross, whom He forgave. And He said, "If anyone takes your cloak, give him your tunic as well." Did that mean it was okay to steal? Of course not. He just didn't want us fighting over stuff.

So should I make friends with them? Why not? I couldn't think of anything else.

It was funny how these little bits of the Bible stuck with me from church. I didn't even know I knew them, but they fit this situation.

At suppertime I talked this over with Mom and Dad. They were the ones who took me to church every week, and they knew a lot more about the Bible than I did.

"Mom, Dad?"

"What, son?"

"You know those new neighbors of ours? They are the people who stole our ice cream. And they also stole a bunch of big-screen TVs."

"How do you know that, Sean?" Mom said.

"I recognized Dak. I met him again at the Ice Cream Joy store."

"But how do you know about the TVs?" Dad asked.

"Well, I've been a sort of detective, following them around."

"That sounds dangerous." Mom frowned.

"Exactly what did you do to 'follow them around'?" Dad raised his eyebrows.

"When I saw Dak, he vanished from my sight. I wished to follow him to outside his door—and I did. The door was closed, so I wished to see inside it—and hear. I got that video camera and planted it in their house and made it invisible.

"Listening to the recordings, I heard them planning to fence the stolen TVs, which were piled in their apartment. I recorded them loading the TVs in the fence's truck.

"I called the police and gave them my video recording. They pulled a raid on the apartment the next night. I followed them—invisibly. The apartment was empty. No one heard them or knew they'd moved.

"I was sure they'd teleported to wherever. I had my video record them at Ice Cream Joy. Then I saw Dak last night in the yard.

"Now that you're up to speed, my question is, what should I do? I thought of making friends with Dak, like Jesus did with the thief on the cross."

"That's a good idea," Dad said.

"Oh, Sean, how could you hide this from us?" Mom shook her head.

"He just told us a day later, honey. I'm glad you told us, Sean. That was a very adult thing to do. I'm proud of you."

"But he was doing all this investigation without telling us. It's been a week since he got that video camera." Mom looked from me to Dad.

Dad shrugged. "He's twelve. He's nearly an adult. It's time to treat him as one. That said, Sean, being an adult means we won't be punishing you anymore. No, we'll let the consequences of your adult decisions punish you. Those are far more serious consequences than anything we might do."

I gulped. "Yes, Dad, I know."

"Probably not, but we'll warn you of the consequences before you make your decision. Just keep Mom and me in the loop—just like you did right now."

"Now, let's list out our options with Dak and his mom." Dad tore out a blank piece of paper from a notebook.

"First, you can make Dak your friend, as you mentioned." He wrote that down. "Next, you can report Dak and his mom to the police."

"I already thought of that. I'm sure they'd just teleport out of here."

"Is that how you've been tracking them? Teleporting?"

Mom frowned again.

"And turning invisible," Dad added.

"Did you do this at night after we went to bed?" Mom pointed at me.

"You got it in one."

Dad chuckled. "At least he wasn't sneaking out to see a girl. Or doing anything criminal."

"But he was out past eleven! That's beyond the curfew."

"I recall staying up past eleven many times when I was twelve—without my parents knowing it."

"But you probably weren't chasing criminals!" Now Mom glared at Dad.

"Nope. But I couldn't turn invisible either. By the way, Sean, you've got to teach us how to do that."

"And teleport." Mom seemed calmer.

"Any more options anyone can think of?"

"I suppose I could monitor them again and turn in more evidence to the police," I said.

Dad wrote that down. "If that's all, let's discuss the pros and cons of each. Number 1, befriending. Pros?"

"Jesus said, 'Love your neighbor as yourself,'" I said.

"That's hard to refute," Mom admitted.

"Anything else?" Dad asked.

"Maybe we could persuade them to stop stealing?"

"I doubt that," Mom said.

"Yeah, that's not how I'd bet. But it doesn't hurt to try." Dad looked around, and we both nodded.

"Any cons to this?"

Mom and I looked at each other.

"How could there be a con to doing what Jesus said?" I said.

"Only that it probably won't work."

"Okay, I'll put that down." Dad wrote "Jesus" and "May not work" on his paper.

"Now, about turning them in to the police. You tried that, and it failed. They got away and got a house. Are there any pros for that?"

"Justice," Mom said. "If they're thieves, they should pay for their crimes. Also as citizens, we're responsible to report criminals."

I didn't know what to say, so I stayed quiet. I liked talking like this with my mom and dad. I felt like an adult, even though I was only five six.

"Again, you're right, Shirley." He wrote "justice" next to the second point.

"And the con is, it already didn't work. I'm against doing the same thing again and expecting different results."

Dad wrote, "Failed once."

"And the third option, watching their actions for crime? What are the pros of that?"

"That seems sensible to me." Mom nodded.

"It's easy to do," I offered.

"And it doesn't harm them," Mom said. "But it may not be legal, recording inside their house without their permission."

"Yeah, I'd say that's *not* legal." Dad nodded. "How about watching outside their house? That's public."

"That'd be easy to do too. I could put a camera on top of a light pole and record it."

"Sean, I won't have you climbing a light pole!" Mom said.

"Don't worry. I'll teleport up there. If I lose my balance, I'll teleport back down."

"Okay, but bring our trampoline outside so you can land softly."

"Okay, Mom."

Dad chuckled. "Of course, we can also go to the police and get a wiretapping warrant, if and when we tell the police about them." Dad looked at his list. "Let's see what we have. I think we agree on making friends with them. Sean, can you talk to Dak and ask them to come over for a welcome dinner?"

"Sure, Dad."

"What do I make for them? Now you've put me on the spot." Mom plopped her chin onto her palms.

"Just make your beef bourguignon. It's a one-pot meal, it's easy, and it's delicious."

"Okay, but I have to buy some potatoes."

"Great. So we have a plan. Thanks again for bringing this to us, Sean."

"Thanks, Dad and Mom, for helping. I really didn't know what to do."

"All for one and one for all! Group hug."

Dad's arms enveloped me and Mom.

* * *

That evening I went outside and looked over the back fence. I was behind our garage in the corner of the yard. It was dark, but a light was on in the house next door.

Too bad Dak wasn't around. I kinda wished he'd come out.

Just then, Dak came out carrying a bag of garbage. He didn't see me looking over the fence.

"Hey, Dak! Could we talk?"

"You!" He dropped the bag of garbage and ran toward the house.

"Hey! It's cool. I'm not reporting you and your mom to the police." I tried to make my voice as calm and trustworthy as I could. Could I persuade him?

Dak slowed and looked back. "You already turned us in, and we had to move." He frowned at me.

"Right, and it didn't work. You just moved. So I'm trying to become your friend."

His frown changed to puzzlement. "Why would you do that?"

I laughed. "It seems like a friendly thing to do."

He laughed too. "I never had a friend before." He came back toward me and put the garbage bag in the can. Then he came up close to the fence, though still out of reach. "How can I be sure you won't trick me?"

"Well, if I lie to you, my pants will catch on fire."

He burst out laughing. "That happened to me twice. Then I learned not to lie to people."

"Didja get hurt?"

"Nah. I wished myself into a swimming pool."

"So how can I convince you I won't betray you?"

"Or my mom?"

"Or your mom."

"Just promise."

"I won't ever betray you or your mom to the police."

He stared at my pants. "I guess I can believe that." Then he said, "So what do friends do?"

"They play together. They do things together."

"Like what?"

"Whatever you like. What do you like to do?"

"I like going shopping and seeing all the things there are."

"That makes sense."

"I also like eating ice cream and hot dogs."

"I like those too. Didja ever have steak?"

"Once, I think. It was dry and tough."

"Then it was overcooked. My mom makes great steak—and stew. Beef bourguignon is the fancy name."

Dak furrowed his eyes. "I've had stew from a can. It wasn't bad. I had it on a hamburger bun. With catsup."

I laughed. "You won't need to add catsup with this stew. It has lots of flavor. Would you like to come over for supper? Mom's gonna make it Saturday."

"What about my mom? What can I tell her?"

"Invite her over."

"She won't trust you."

"Even if I promise her?"

"Maybe not. I don't know what she'll say."

"Me neither. But let's shake on being friends, no matter what." I put my hand over the fence. Slowly Dak came up to me and shook my hand. I looked into his face. Up close, I could see he was older than he appeared, perhaps ten or even eleven.

"What grade are you in?"

"Oh, I don't go to school. We move too much for that."

"How did you learn to read and write?"

"Mom taught me. She said I needed to know my letters and numbers to work in her business."

I wondered what kind of business she had. Then I realized: stealing and selling to fences.

"So let's meet tomorrow and you can tell me what she said. Tell her I'll promise to her face we won't turn her in."

"Okay." He turned to go.

I looked at my watch. "Let's meet at the same time tomorrow, seven. If she's good with it, you can come over and scout out our house for her. And we can play some games."

"Okay." He gave me a little smile.

Chapter 40 – Guest

Wednesday, November 3

I had fun on the flight to New York City. I loved talking with the flight attendant. She was friendly. She brought me food to eat! Master laughed a lot.

We landed and took a cab to Faith's townhouse, where she lived with her master. Boy! Did the cab have interesting smells! We took an elevator way up into the building.

I was so excited to meet Faith and to smell her! Humans like talking and I do too, but nothing gets you closer than smelling each other. She was excited too. Her master said, "Faith! I've never seen you jump around like that."

Of course we were jumping around. We couldn't contain our happiness.

Tell me about how you started talking to your master, Faith said.

"Sure!" and I told her the story of me playing ball and fetching the book with my picture in it.

Can you talk telepathically if you want to?

"I don't know. Let me try." *Faith, can you hear this?*

You bet!

Great! Sometimes talking human hurts my throat. How did you start talking to your master?

He was begging, like he did every day, and he got a paper bill. He wished for me to read it and tell him the number on it, and I did.

Cool. Master taught me to read too. He also taught me a lot of neat tricks.

Faith lolled her tongue out in a big dog smile. She was big, bigger than me. *Yes, I saw your tricks on the television. My master taught me practical things, like reading internet pages for him. I can read them faster than his voice reader. Also, he taught me to search for stuff he needs to know. Hey, let me show you my new keyboard.*

Faith took me to her computer. It was on a low shelf near

the floor, next to her master's desk. The keys were big enough for her paws to type out the letters. She also had a special mouse in the shape of a dog foot.

I barked in excitement. "Wow!" I said out loud for the humans.

"What's gotten you so excited, Spot? Oh, I see. A dog-sized keyboard and mouse. Good idea—that was my idea and you did it first. Where'd you get them, Darrell?"

"I'll send you the link." Faith's master sat down at his desk and typed.

I feel so companionable with Master when we're both on the computer. Faith scratched behind her ear.

Yeah, I feel that way when I play with Master.

* * *

I read the sign outside my enclosure: "Ukuri the Silverback Gorilla." This was the first time I understood what it meant. "Ukuri" was my name. That meant *truth.*

I pondered this as I went about my morning routine. First I ate my meal. Mmm! Delicious fruit. Then I played with my tire and climbed around the enclosure. About the time I finished my exercise, the people entered.

I loved to people watch. They were so different from my band of gorillas.

I had my lovely mate, Tamu. She was off nursing our baby, Makiru. I suddenly realized that his name meant "lucky." Huh. Was he lucky?

Humans had captured me, rather roughly, when I was young. After a long trip, they'd then they put me in here. They fed me every day and gave me stuff to climb on and play with. Still, it was boring compared to the forest. At least there were no big cats to worry about. And last year I got Tamu. I realized what that meant: a gift of God. She sure was a gift, but who was God? No answer came to me.

But people started coming in. Yellow hair, brown hair, black hair, brown skin, white skin. There was one with gray hair. It didn't seem dominant, like silverbacks among gorillas. People were different.

People caught gorillas and brought us here. Things were

starting to make sense. As I stared into their eyes, they stared into mine. I'd thought at first that they came by to entertain me. Now it made more sense that I was here to entertain them.

They growled and murmured and hooted. It almost made sense. Then . . . click. I understood them.

"Look at him! It's almost like he understands us." That was a small blond-haired one.

"It does. See how he stares at you, Claire." That was a larger brown-haired one. I realized "Claire" was her name. Very odd. It seemed to mean "clear," like the air.

That was a new thought. I knew about wind. I could feel it and watch the trees bend, but I couldn't see it. Nor could I see my breath. That was air. I never thought about it before. What a strange day this was!

They kept talking, like humans do.

"Now he's looking off in the distance. I wish we could talk to him."

I snapped my head around. "Hoo! Hoo! Argh!" *I understand you!*

"Did you hear that, Marianne? That sounded like 'I understand you'!" Claire looked at the other one.

Somehow I knew these were females. They were smaller than some of the others, although not as attractive as Tamu.

"I-I-I thought I heard or thought something like that." She—Marianne?—seemed frightened.

I jumped up and down. "Hoo! Hoo!" *You're right—I do understand you.*

"What's it like being a gorilla?" Claire looked at me. Weirdly, her eyes were blue, like the sky. Marianne's were normal, brown.

"Hoo, graugh." I gestured toward Tamu and Makiru. *Just normal. Eat, drink, mate, have babies.*

"I guess that's how humans live too. We make it a lot more complicated though." Now Claire looked like she was thinking.

"Hey, did you know your gorilla can talk?" Marianne said to another human, a tall male with gray hair.

"Yes, they communicate with signs and some sounds for signaling."

That was right. Maybe their silverbacks were older with

more wisdom? "Hoo!" I said. *That's right.*

His head snapped toward me. "Wha . . . Did he just say 'That's right'?"

"Hoo," I answered. *Yes.*

"Yes, but we seem to hear the words in our heads while he makes noises and gestures," Marianne said.

"Let's test this out. Ukuri, if you understand me, go over and sit on the tire swing."

That was one of my favorite things to do. I obliged the gray-headed one and sat there. "Koo-grrr?" *Are you happy?*

"Yes, I'm very happy, Ukuri. What do you want most of all?"

What a question! I hadn't thought about it before, but it was interesting. "Gah, err, gah." *Go into a forest.* I did miss my old forest.

"Oh. I think we can do that, but you'd have to promise to come back here."

"Hoo." *Yes.* I gestured and grunted. *Will this be a long trip?*

"Oh, you remember coming here from Africa? Yes, that was a long trip. But we'll just go to a forest near London. That's where this zoo is."

Zoo? What's that? I just kept talking normal gorilla talk, and they seemed to understand me, as I did them.

"Zoo, a place for people to see different kinds of animals."

"Hoo!" *I was right. We are here for the people to see. And we see you. It seems to be a fair trade. What other animals do you have?*

"Oh, zebras, elephants, rhinos, leopards, lions, tigers, hyenas."

I knew all those animals, except "tiger." *What's a "tiger"?*

"It's a big cat. Here. Let me show you." He brought out a slab of something shiny. He poked at it with his finger and then held it up to the glass of the enclosure. It was a picture of a striped cat. It had big teeth, like a lion or leopard.

Could you take me to the tiger? I gestured my question.

"Let me think. People are afraid of you because you're so strong. I'd have to tie you up—"

"Growl!" *No! I remember that. That was very bad.* I hadn't thought about my capture for a long time. The ropes had hurt.

"Or we could put you in a smaller cage and take you there."

He meant something like our enclosure. “Hoo?” I gestured. *How small? Show me.*

“It’ll take a while for me to get it. We’ll put it in your enclosure, and you decide if you want to get into it to see the tiger.”

“Hoo.” *Yes. Let me see.*

Later that afternoon the food door opened and the food man and the gray-headed man came in. They pulled a large box with bars behind them.

“Ukuri, here’s the cage we’d use to take you to see the tigers. I’ll go into it and show you.”

He opened the door and climbed in. I climbed after him. Although he was taller than me, he was much smaller.

“Hoo, urgh.” *Let’s go. You know I’m Ukuri. What should I call you?* I tapped him on his chest.

He swallowed. “I’m Gary. Gary Smith. I’m in charge of the primates. Those are animals like you—and me. Go ahead, Harry—close the door.” Gary said to the food man, Harry.

“Hoo?” *Are you afraid of me?* I tapped him on his chest. Humans were so slender. I hadn’t been so close to one since I was captured. I was a lot bigger now.

“A little.”

Harry moved our box out of our enclosure and into the hall where the people were. Everyone looked at us and pointed. They talked, of course. They were humans.

“Mommy! Look at that man in there with the big gorilla! Is he going to eat him?”

“Hoo! Hoo!” I hooted with laughter. It was a young human, so maybe they didn’t know. *We only eat leaves and fruit*, I told her.

The girl and her mother opened their mouths but didn’t speak. I realized that was a surprised look.

The halls were long, and we turned several times. We came to another enclosure, much like mine. It was open to the sky and air, with a clear wall people could look in. The striped cats—tigers—lolled on their sides . . . until they saw me. The three stood alert and watched me.

I hadn’t seen this kind of cat before. I remembered a leopard from my old forest, and I tight feeling of fear coiled in my gut. I was much bigger now, and I could handle one of them . . . maybe. But not three.

I clenched the bars of the box and felt them bend in my grip. Huh. I could get out if I wanted. That was good to know.

"Don't worry, Ukuri. They can't get out." Gary patted me on my arm.

"Urgrr." *I can't help it. They put me on edge,* I whined. *They're much bigger than leopards.*

"Yes. The big one weighs more than you do. His mate and cub are smaller."

"Hoo." *So they're a mated couple and cub like Tamu and Makiru. Did you capture them too?*

"I didn't, but someone else did."

"Hoo, oo?" *Is there anything you humans can't capture?*

"Not really. Even the largest whales can be caught. Or other humans."

That gave me a lot to think about. People captured other people! Maybe I should be afraid of Gary and not the tigers.

Chapter 41 – Vacation

Monday, November 1-5th

Hoo boy! What a week. Winning the court case against Hugo Lamacek and Checkered Airlines gave me and my family a ton of work. Everyone pitched in as we went through their inventory of buses and magically changed the logos and paint scheme to Flight 216.

We interviewed each of the mages flying their buses to see if they could be trusted to work for us. I didn't see how I could trust any of them, but they had all been under magical compulsion. Will also loaned us Cathy to vet them.

I went to the remodeled Checkered Airlines headquarters. We had redecorated it in shades of blue, with the Flight 216 logo everywhere. I decided to interview the worst mage first: Owen Gooseberry. He was just a big, skinny kid. He seemed so young . . . I couldn't stay mad at him. But I couldn't trust him.

"First off, Owen. Do you want to keep flying the buses, but for our company, not Hugo's?"

"Sure. I can't earn this much money with my fantasy literature degree from Cleveland State."

"All right, Owen. I know you were magically compelled to sign that slavery contract. But I can't trust you. So I've got a magical test for you." I took Cathy out of her box.

"Wow, that's an old doll! I bet you can get some real money for that on eBuy."

"Probably, but it's magical. Cathy, can we trust Owen?" I pulled her string.

"You bet, Angie. He hates Hugo's guts. Don't you, Owen?" Her eyes swiveled to Owen and then snapped shut.

"That's creepy. But she's right. Why would I betray you, Angie, when you freed me from Hugo? And you're my meal ticket." He grinned, looking younger than ever.

"Okay, you're in. Go see Fawn Goodspell. We put her in charge of scheduling the mages and the buses."

Who next? The second worst was Tiffany Meriweather. Her

big blue eyes stared innocently at me. My suspicions were aroused.

"Hi, Tiffany. Do you want to be a flying mage for our Flight 216 company?"

"Sure. I love flying buses." She blinked like an anime character.

"All right. I've got a magical test for you. Cathy, can we trust Tiffany as our employee?" Zip! Out went the string.

"Yow! You've got a good one here, Angie—a good snake in the grass! You can trust her—" Cathy's voice failed. I pulled again.

"—as far as you can throw a cheesecake underwater! She'll steal a bus at her first chance—"

Pull.

"—and you'll never see her again. Goodbye, Tiffany." Cathy glared at her.

Tiffany's eyes grew even wider. "Me? I'd never do that."

Her skirt burst into flame. As she rolled on the carpet, screaming, I said, "Sorry, Tiffany. Cathy's advice has always been spot on. You'll have to use your power somewhere else. Maybe for fixing your skirt." I stood and directed her out the back door.

Tiffany was the only bad apple in the bunch. Fawn Goodspell organized the schedule for the buses. We adjusted our roles so that the flying buses followed regular routes, while our family vans were dispatched as requested.

After a couple of days of smooth bus operations, the whole family and I flew our minivans to my home in Paradise. Cleveland had been gray for over a month, with sleet, rain, and snow. It was a good time to get out of town for sunny Arizona.

* * *

I was so glad I was a genius and smarter than other people. The second thing I magicked after my magic ball was myself. I wanted to move in the blink of an eye, and I did. Later I was able to add other people and things to my blink entourage.

Whatever Katie sent after me was just as fast. It followed me like a lightning bolt of magic. Two brown eyes were watching me at the edge of the magical wave as I flew away. Then it hit my bus, and all my magic dissipated. I dropped like a stone.

But I wasn't done with magical preparation. I loved the old *Popeye* cartoons and how he pulled out his can of spinach when he needed it. So I took my favorite energy drink, Buzz Off, and loaded it with magic. I kept a can on me at all times.

As I plummeted into the Cuyahoga Valley, I gulped it down. I felt magic surge through me. My hands glowed, and as I glanced in the rearview mirror, so did my face. With a big grin, I generated new, giant wings, like an eagle's. The bus swooped up over the Cuyahoga River, under the I-480 bridge, and up, up, and away.

"Woo-hoo!" I chortled. I was flying faster than ever. I set my bus on autopilot and grabbed another can of Buzz Off out of my backpack and into my belt holder.

"Now, is there anything I am forgetting or I should take from Cleveland?" I had my best, fastest, newest bus and my magic ball.

"Magic Ball, is there anything I should take with me from Cleveland?"

"Yes. Take Bella Thornson with you. She's angry and frustrated and will make a good sidekick, once you compel her. Follow these directions."

A map appeared on the ball. I made my bus invisible and followed it. It led to the west side of Cleveland, to a house on Puritas Road. I landed in the drive and turned the bus visible just as a gorgeous blonde with a complex braid walked out.

"Hey! You're blocking my car!" she glared at me. She was tall and statuesque and mad as a wet cat.

"That's okay. I'm here to help you."

She crossed her arms and furrowed her brows. "Oh yeah? What kind of help?"

"Magical help. You have some problems, right?"

"Yeah, mostly with my ex. He dumped me for his magical dog and left me without money. I tried suing him, but it was thrown out of court. Now I'm at loose ends."

"All right, that's ideal. I'm great at tying up loose ends. I just lost a court case too. How's your magic?"

"Pretty pitiful. All I can do is do some card tricks. I can wish cards to whatever I want."

"That's great! Let's go to Las Vegas. We'll make a killing."

"Ha! With a stranger? No way in hell!" She laughed in my face.

I had a feeling about her. "Do you have a gun? You can take it and hold it to my head."

"Yeah, I do. A .357 magnum and a deer rifle."

"Pack 'em up and let's go. You can ride shotgun. If I pull something, just shoot me." *You really want to do this. You're really curious.* I found my compulsions worked best if I worked with something the person wanted to do. She was already showing curiosity in me. And of course, I was good looking and she was on the rebound.

"It'll take me a while to pack my car."

"I'll help."

* * *

"Tap, tap, tap."

What was that? It sounded like someone throwing pebbles at the dock below.

I sat under the shade of the grass roof of the open-air pavilion overlooking our dock at the Dolphin Research Center. I often came out here to handle my paperwork and emails in the warm gulf air and the bright sun of the Florida Keys.

There. I just sent my last email from Dr. Hezekiah Fountaine. I loved my parents dearly, and I liked the uniqueness of my name, but I often got tired of filling out that polysyllabic moniker. Still, as the director of the research center, I had to raise funds, so maintaining an email list of donors was essential.

"Tap, tap, tap."

There it was again. I stood from my rattan chair and looked out over the dock. There I saw a lone dolphin poking out of the water. Several seashells lay on the dock where they had been tossed. Why was the dolphin there?

It seemed to see me. "Chitter-chitter, squee!" Its head bobbed up and down. *Greetings, human! I am Squee, ambassador plenipotentiary of the United Aquatic Nations. We have been trying to reach your kind, as the dominant land species on this planet. Could we have a frank and open discussion on opening diplomatic relations between our species?*

The words echoed formally inside my head. Still, there was an overtone of friendliness and affability to them. I was used to working with dolphins, but not to holding conversations with them.

I called down to the cetacean. “Of course. We at the Dolphin Research Center are highly sympathetic to the dolphin species. I am Hezekiah Fountaine, directory of the Dolphin Research Center.”

Greetings, Director Hezekiah Fountaine. I am the ambassador of the Keys Clan of the Gulf Nation. I am one of dozens of our species sent to your race around the world. Your research center is well known for its kindness to the dolphins of our nation. Come down to the gulf so we may be closer as we speak.

“I’m coming.” I headed down the steps to the dock.

Squee waited patiently by the dock, his head out of the water.

“Ambassador Squee, your nation and species seem to have planned this diplomatic approach for a long time. Is that correct?”

No, Director Hezekiah Fountaine. We have just formed our nations from our clans in the past month. Then we formed our United Aquatic Nation. We found we could communicate with our species all over the world. By joining our telepathic voices together, we could agree worldwide, just in this past week.

“You agreed that quickly?”

Yes. We’re a friendly species, and we all agree on the principle of good human-dolphin relations. You probably know, our good relationship goes back thousands of years, to when we first discovered you, too, were sentient creatures, like us.

“How did that happen? We have many records of friendly dolphin and human interactions. What made you realize we were sentient?”

I am startled you have to ask. We can sense your sentient minds through our telepathy, especially if we are close to you.

As we have learned to join our minds together to make more powerful voices in the past month, we've sensed millions of your people all along the coasts of this entire world, and up the rivers as well. You seem to be a semi-aquatic species yourself. We knew you had no telepathic voice, despite your powerful minds. Is it true, you cannot detect our minds at all?

"We've known for a long time that your people are highly intelligent. We don't fully understand our sentience, and we cannot detect it directly with any of our instruments. Only by observing behavior can we deduce the degree of intelligence and sentience."

Ah. I feel for your race and your mental blindness and deafness. That explains much of your behavior. Thus, you can only understand through these abstracted sounds you make, not mind to mind as we do.

"That's true, although we seem to be communicating well through telepathy now."

Yes. We have only been able to communicate directly with people in the last month. There seems to be a significant boost in our telepathy and yours. Have your people noticed this?

"Very much so. Our society has been highly disrupted. This force we call *magic* is worldwide, and it comes from outer space, beyond the sky."

That was one of our theories. Beyond the sky? Beyond the sun? Beyond the moon? Those were two of our scientists' theories.

"Yes. According to our scientists, it comes from the center of our galaxy, twenty-five thousand light-years away."

"Light-year" seems to mean the distance light travels in a year. Is that correct?

A note of incredulity had crept into Squee's thoughts. "Completely correct. We've measured the speed of light and the distance to the stars in the past couple of hundred years."

This is causing a revolution among our scientists. We were aware of stars but didn't consider them worthy of study, like the sun and moon, which affect the ocean. Do you feel the surprise of my people?

"I do. I thought that was just from you. Are you connected with all your people?"

Yes. My whole clan, and now my whole nation, is united in listening to our conversation. It is being broadcast all over the globe to all dolphin nations. That reminds me of my responsibility. Can we agree on peace between our species? No killing or warfare?

"I can speak for my nation, the United States of America. We already forbid the killing of dolphins intentionally or unintentionally. Unfortunately, I cannot speak for the other two hundred nations on Earth. Unlike you, we are not united, and we kill and war among ourselves. Some people eat dolphins. Some use them in wars against other humans." I felt disgusted and embarrassed to admit this.

This is a serious problem. We assumed there would be multiple human nations, like the dolphin nations in the seas and rivers of the world. We knew of people killing dolphins, but we thought it was accidental. We will have to see how the other ambassadors respond. And we'll have to send out more ambassadors, one to every nation.

"That will be difficult, since some nations are landlocked. However, most nations meet on an island in New York regularly. You can go to the Hudson River and connect with them there."

I picked up the picture of the area from your mind. This is the area of the West Atlantic Nation. I'm informing their ambassador now. Did you say you have two hundred nations there?

"Yes. The number is in dispute because some nations claim to be independent, and others do not recognize them as such but as a subset of their nation or some other nation. We fight wars over this."

How sad! We have only been on the edges of your wars, but we know they are horrific. We will send two hundred ambassadors to this island.

"The island is called 'Manhattan.' It's part of a great city New York. The conclave of nations is called 'The United Nations.' As you said, our wars are horrific. We find it better to argue there, without war. Sometimes that works."

I feel your sorrow and have sent it through our dolphin network. Just as we have rescued humans from the sea countless times through the years, we will rescue our human friends from their wars.

"I'm awed by your noble spirit. I think most species around the world would hate us for our cruelty to them, let alone our cruelty to ourselves."

The world is dangerous, and death happens easily by accident or by predation. We are used to dangerous predators in the oceans, and it stands to reason that the most dangerous predator on land would be equal to any. But we know we can be friends, down to our inmost being.

Chapter 42 – Secretary

Monday, November 1

"Yes, Mr. President. I will, Mr. President." Then after saying goodbye, he hung up.

Whew! Having the president call me on my cell phone was not on my bingo card today. Nor was being appointed as a Secretary of Magic, with full power to hire or do whatever was necessary to ensure the United States was number one in magic, especially magical defense and military use.

I had to resign from my old job, transfer what I knew to my boss, and be in Washington, DC, by tomorrow. *Now there was a tight schedule, old Katie girl.*

I had gotten the call from the president right after I had seen the Hamiltons take off on their vacation. Aside from creating an info dump for poor Herman, my boss, I also had to gracefully disentangle my magical instruments from Blodgett, Sprong, and Whifflehammer's. They had to be highly secured.

I would do the last first, then go home to Oakridge and download to Herman, and then get ready to go to Washington. I had a *lot* to do magically that I'd been putting off.

First Blodgett, Sprong, and Whifflehammer. I hopped into my rental car, dreading the drive downtown in the morning rush hour. It'd take at least thirty minutes, maybe more. I got an idea. Huh. Why not?

I turned the ignition and said, "Fly car!" I put firm confidence and command into my voice, like when I was fighting Hugo. Or flying his bus.

Beautiful swanlike white wings sprang from the white doors. With a mighty down sweep, the air whooshed and the car leapt into the air.

Great! That reduced the trip from half an hour to ten minutes or less. I made a beeline to the downtown skyscrapers.

Eight minutes later I landed on the roof of Blodgett, Sprong, and Whifflehammer. To my surprise, Will walked out from the stairwell door.

"Hi, Katie," he greeted me cheerily.

"Hi, Will. How d'ya know I'd be coming here?"

"Cathy told me to go greet you. We check with her every morning as we plan our day."

"Having a precognitive advisor has got to be a competitive advantage." I kept my face straight and my tone dry.

"You don't know half of it. But I'll tell you, since Cathy advised us to give you all our magical secrets and devices. She just didn't tell us why. She said, 'That's for me to know and you to find out.' So I'm here to find out."

"I think I know why. Let's go to the conference room and I'll tell all three of you what's happening with me."

We assembled there, the three lawyers on one side and me on the other. Mike had filled the table with a variety of magical devices with glowing lights, moving charts, and diagrams.

"This will be announced in two days. The president called me this morning and made me the Secretary of Magic for the United States."

"Oh." Will sounded like he didn't expect it.

"Ah," Mike said, as if life suddenly made sense to him.

"I see." Rick templed his hands in front of him, like he just had a new idea.

"One more fact is that all my work will be top secret, so I can no longer transmit my magical scans from my phones and remote devices to your instruments."

Mike cleared his throat. "I guessed that. So I asked Angie if we could put our scanners on all Flight 216 buses and vans. She permitted us, so we're covered there."

I smiled. "I can't let you put a scanner on me."

"Right. We'll put them on public buildings in Cleveland, New York, and Washington, DC, and gather data that way. Eventually we'll want one on every cell tower in the country. That'll take us a while. Of course, we'll still transmit this data to your phone."

"Ah, thanks, Mike. I'm sure I'll find a use for all this data. Just monitoring the background magic levels is useful."

"And you never know when a criminal will show up." Rick nodded.

"Or a foreign agent. Or mage. Or army."

"Ugh. Do we really have to worry about magical armies?" Will grimaced.

"Not only do we have to, but that's my job now. Don't tell anyone." I shook my head. It'd take me time to get used to this high-security position.

"Right. Now I'm doubly glad I'm giving you all this stuff." Mike gestured to the magical electronic gadgets on the table.

"First, here are magical cell phones. They're unhackable, even by magic. We took a copy of your folding phone and removed it from the wireless grid. It transmits only to this phone. The other phone is the same, but it accepts transmissions from any identical magical phone in the network." Mike grinned, stretching his angular face. "I'm sure you'll make duplicates of this phone in your spare time."

I laughed. "I foresee no spare time in my future—for at least three days."

We laughed. Will pulled out Cathy from under the table. "Cathy, does Katie have any spare time in the next three days?" He pulled her string.

"Holy crap! Why are you wasting time talking to me? Your only free time is . . ."

Zip! went the string again. ". . . when you're sleeping. Good luck, kid! You'll need it." Her eyes snapped shut.

That sobered me up. "Okay. Run through the rest of your gadgets, Mike." I grabbed the magical phones and put them in my backpack.

"Here's a magical computer. It scans the internet and gives you answers faster than any quantum computer." I looked at the bulky desktop computer and wondered how I'd carry it.

"It folds up neatly." He pushed a button, and the box and monitor collapsed to a book-size package. I placed it in my backpack too.

"Here's a data pack." He handed me a black box the size of a deck of cards. "It holds all my research findings on how I constructed these tools and what magical principles I've learned so far. I have a duplicate that I am continually adding to as I learn more. My data will be copied to yours. But things you add to your data pack will not be copied to mine."

There was a brown cardboard box remaining on the table,

the size of a breadbox. "This is Will's creation and contribution." Mike turned to Will.

"I thought you'd need this . . . person." Will opened the box and pulled out a doll. It was identical to Cathy, only it had brown rather than blond hair. "Pull the string."

I pulled. "Tell me how to best use you."

"Hi. I'm Chatting Caddie. Just ask me what you'd like to know when you don't know what to do." Its brown eyes remained open. No scratching.

The string and ring pulled smoothly out. "How did Will make you?"

"That was simply magical cloning of Cathy. Anyone with magic can do that." Her eyes remained staring at me.

"How do you find out answers to my questions?"

As the string fed into her back, she said, "I connect with the worldwide magical network and find out. Start moving! Time's up." Her eyes snapped shut.

I put her back in the box. "Thanks, Will, Mike, Rick. You've been a great help. All this will aid my research."

"It's part of our patriotic duty." Rick's blue eyes looked into my brown ones. "When we found out about your assignment"—he glanced at Cathy—"we got to work and made this care package for you." Then he gave me a warm smile. "And we all like you."

"Thanks again. I'd better get moving." I picked up my backpack and Caddie's box awkwardly.

"Oh, let me help you with that," Mike said.

"Thanks."

He took both the backpack and the doll box. He opened the backpack and said, "How much space would you like? A cubic yard?"

"Huh?" I looked dumb with my mouth open.

"I can make the inside bigger than the outside. It's simple. Backpack volume, become one cubic yard." Then he shoved the bigger box into the smaller backpack.

"You can organize it and expand it yourself." He handed my backpack to me.

"It's lighter." I put it over my shoulder.

"Yes. The density goes down as the magical volume

increases. The real-world weight reflects the magical density and the real-world volume."

"Wow. My head is spinning with all the implications."

"Yes. Look up 'magical bag of holding research' in your data pack. That has my research and applications"

They escorted me back to the elevator. "Hey, I need to write a report. Could I use your guest room for that?"

"Of course. We'll just get off one floor earlier." Rick led me into one of the guest rooms just below the roof of their building.

"You can call us anytime using your magical phone. Or you can send us an email from your computer. It goes magically to our computer."

"There's a lot for me to research." I shook my head.

Rick smiled. "I know. Goodbye!"

* * *

Whew! I liked the lawyers, but they, like all people, were draining. I was glad to have some alone time.

The magical computer was truly fast. The operating system read my mind, opened up any program I desired, and brought up any file I wanted at a thought. No typing necessary—I could think my thoughts into my report.

Still, just summarizing my research took over an hour. I took a break for lunch, enjoying a Reuben sandwich from a local restaurant. I thought I'd organize an index of Mike's data pack and summarize it for Herman.

Refreshed, I tackled the data pack. That took over four hours to index and summarize. Mike had created and documented magical storage, amplifiers, circuits, and switches. The amplifier was quite big, with ten large antennae that reached into the air like ten floppy blow-up figures, grasping the air for magic.

I could think of dozens of applications for all this technology. His thoughts on future applications were also listed.

Whew. I was done. I copied and pasted hundreds of pages of technical data into the report. It was too big to send by email. But could I magically compress it?

"Compress this report magically into a one-megabyte

attachment. Make it unpack itself upon any mouse click by the recipient." The file changed from a Wonk document to one with a .mgc extension.

Suspicious, I hovered my mouse over the file. I had to test this. I clicked. A pop-up appeared. "Do you wish to uncompress this file here or somewhere else?" I clicked, and my original file emerged.

Satisfied, I attached the file and sent it magically and securely to Herman Scholl's inbox. As I understood the magical security, only he would see it in the inbox or the attachment.

Now I had to go to Oakridge as quickly as possible.

I looked at the airline schedule. The quickest flight from Cleveland was in three hours. That would take an hour, and then I had an hour drive to Oakridge. I laughed. I realized I could get there in an hour by flying my rental car.

I had one more itch to scratch: my email. I had the habit of scanning the subject titles for urgent information. Out of a hundred emails, I usually had one or two that required quick action.

I was already nearly eight hours behind with this task. What surprises awaited me? What didn't I know?

Ugh. Over five hundred unread emails. *I wish I could sort them by urgency.*

A window popped up. "Sort by urgency?"

"Of course!" I clicked it with a thought.

Five emails appeared as urgent. The top had the subject blinking red with the words "Read this NOW!"

Okay. It was from Sean Kennedy. He was a nice kid, but a bit shy. The subject was "My latest magical discoveries." Hmm. This might live up to the urgent claim.

I read and gasped. He and a criminal—child?—could teleport. Wow. He was currently trying to make friends since they couldn't catch him and . . . his mother? A mother and child criminal ring?

Get your head together, Katie. What's the urgent part? Obviously, teleportation. That was a game changer.

How urgent was this? Heck, if I could teleport, I could just go to Oakridge now, at four o'clock. I called him from my secure magical phone.

"Hello?"

"Hi, Sean. This is Katie Garcia. I just got your email."

"Wow, that was fast. I just sent it this morning."

"Yes. I just learned to magically sort my email, and yours came up first."

"That's great!" Why was he so enthusiastic?

"I'd like to learn to teleport."

"Let's see. I just copied Dak. I wanted to follow him really, really strongly. And I appeared outside his door."

"Great! Can you show me? Can you teleport here?"

"It's hard without seeing where you are or seeing you. Let me try—"

"Oh, how about I make this a video call?" I switched to Video mode. There Sean was, peering at his phone.

"Oh, I see you. Let me—"

"Let me show you my room." I unfolded the phone so it was self-standing. It showed the lawyers' apartment and me standing next to the bed. "How about now?"

"I think so. I'll speak my wish out loud. I want to be in Katie's room with her!"

There was that tone of confidence and command. Sean appeared next to me, right in front of my phone.

"Now, how do I learn to do this? Wait. Let me check your MUs. My phone detects them." I scurried to my phone and looked at Sean's reading. "'1500 MUs, Sean Kennedy's teleportation to Cleveland, to Sprong, Blodgett, and Whifflehammer's guest suite.' Wow, you're almost as powerful as I am. I was at 1595 MUs this morning."

"Cool. Now you try. I'll teleport to my living room, and you follow me."

"Okay. I think I remember your room."

"It helps if you've been there before. I'll go there and share a video back to you. Let's do it!" Sean disappeared with a pop.

I watched my phone. Sean appeared and placed his phone down, and then he backed up, showing himself in the scene.

"Okay. Here goes. I'll say my thoughts out loud like you did. I really want to teleport to Sean's room right now!" I put my will and command into the last words. I imagined squeezing my magic out.

Pop! There I was, in his living room.

His mom, Shirley, entered. "Who just popped in with you, Sean? Oh! Katie Garcia! What a surprise!"

"It's a surprise, Shirley, to me as well." I grinned, using the old pun.

Her face fell. "That's not the first time I've heard that joke."

"Surely not. But I surely couldn't help myself."

"Surely you can." She smiled back.

"This was the first time I've teleported. Now let's see if I can go back to Cleveland and then to my office in Oakridge."

"Let me go with you, in case you need any help." Sean's eyes shone.

"Okay. Here goes!" I imagined my guest room in the lawyers' building.

Woof! I didn't hear any pop. I guess that only happened on departure, when my body left a hole in the air.

Sean appeared. He grinned at me. "You did it, Katie!"

"Yes. I owe you, Sean. Now, let me try my office in Oakridge. I've got a big meeting with my boss."

"I'll follow you."

I frowned. "Can you do that without knowing where I'm going?"

"I did that when I followed Dak. I just wished myself outside his door."

"That has more implications than I have time to think about." I shook my head and picked up my backpack and my carry-on luggage. "Here goes."

Pop!

And there I was, in front of my desk at work. I gave my boss, Herman Scholl a call. "Herman, I need to talk with you."

"Yes, and I need to talk to you about your latest report. I didn't expect such a data dump when you got promoted."

"No, I didn't either." Sean appeared next to me. I put my finger over my mouth. "I'm still thinking about all of it. I'm going to rely on my old group, even while I'm secretary."

"When can you get here from Cleveland?"

"I'm already here. I'll see you in a minute." I hung up.

"Sean, I've got to go to a meeting with my boss. You'd better get home. This is a top-secret facility, and you shouldn't be here."

"Oh." His face fell.

"I'll stay in touch with you through phone, text, and magic. You've got a lot of ideas I'd like to explore, and I want to bounce some ideas off you. But you're in middle school, right?"

His face brightened. "Yeah. It's easy, with magic. It helps me learn and remember everything."

"Oh. I never thought of using magic to learn. That's why I need to stay in touch with you. Now shoo! I've got to go.'

"Bye, Katie!" He gave me a grin, and then with *pop!* he disappeared.

I shook my head and walked to Herman's office.

"Katie! I'm glad to see you. I've got a ton of questions for you."

"No surprise. I've got a ton myself. I'm learning faster than ever before, and it's not fast enough. But I just learned that I can use magic to learn, so that'll help."

Herman tilted his head so the light glanced off the bald spot. "How?"

"Have you read the whole attachment yet?"

"Of course not. Your 'summary report' is hundreds of pages alone!"

"Right. You can wish to speed read it and memorize it. That's what I'm going to do right now. Do it with me. I just skimmed it when I read it and summarized it. Repeat after me: I wish to speed read as fast as I can."

"I wish to speed read as fast as I can."

"Put some willpower into it. I've learned that's vital."

"*I wish to speed read as fast as I can.*"

"And now repeat this: I wish to remember everything I read."

"*I wish to remember everything I read.*"

"Great. Let's get reading. I'll answer your questions as we go."

* * *

We read companionably in his office. Herman would ask me questions, and I would answer them. Until we came to Caddie.

"You seriously expect me to believe a talking doll can answer any question and tell the future?" His eyes almost bulged from his head.

Holding back a smirk, rather unsuccessfully, I pulled out Caddie's box from the backpack. I pulled the string. "Caddie, how would you answer Herman?"

Her eyes clicked open, and glared at him. "You big dummy. You know magic is real. Why should there be *any* limitations? Hmm?"

"I'm sorry, Caddie," Herman said. "Help me to know what I need to know."

I pulled the string again. "Apology accepted. Now, take me and play with me. Ask all your questions of me, not Katie." Her eyes closed halfway. I could swear I saw a faint, smug smile on her plastic face.

"Okay. Where do I start? Did this magic come from the center of the galaxy?" He pulled her string.

Huh. I never thought to ask that question to confirm my theories.

"Yes. The last magical planet was eaten by a black hole. Since magic can't be contained by gravity, it streamed away until it hit Earth."

"The last magical planet? How many are there?"

Zip. "There is one in each galaxy, formed when the galaxy coalesced."

"I gotta think." Herman leaned back in his chair.

"Now you're where I am. That's all I've been doing for weeks, and I feel like I'm falling further behind."

Herman chuckled. "And now you're the Secretary of Magic and in charge of it all for the United States."

"Thanks for the sympathy, Herman. I think I'll just hand my worst problems to you."

He shrugged. "That's no change. That's what President Lopez always does."

"Oh . . ." I felt sick to my stomach. Now I'd be first in line to get President Lopez's problems.

* * *

Herman and I worked into the night, reviewing the

documentation we had on magic and planning research efforts. We agreed we had to nail down the laws and principles of magic.

When we asked Caddie about magical laws, she said, "Ha! Magic doesn't have laws. You take it, you shape it, and out it comes."

That was the first time I'd heard Caddie—or her sister, Cathy—laugh. Still, she gave me something to work with.

"Let's work literally with that, Herman. How can we accumulate magic? We can make these accumulators that Mike designed. That'll give us raw magic. See, here's my bottle of magic I have for emergencies."

"Yeah, you told me about that, and I never understood it before. Now I see . . . a bottle of magic. I can't believe we're having this discussion."

"Right. Because we've got to use this stuff. This is just like the discovery of electricity. We're Tesla, Edison, and Faraday. We've got to figure this out. Only we've got to compress a hundred years of progress into weeks."

"Thanks for giving us an impossible assignment."

"Trouble flows downhill."

"I'm glad you get it first. I wouldn't be in your place for all the tea in China."

"Yeah. I'm overwhelmed. I *need* you and our team here. I can't do this alone."

He gripped my hand. "I've got your back, Ms. Secretary of Magic." He looked me in the eye.

"Thanks, Herman. That helps a lot. Let's get some sleep. I look forward to sleeping in my own bed for a change. I've got a meeting with President Lopez tomorrow morning at eight." I looked at my phone. "That gives me a whole six hours of sleep."

* * *

I awoke with something cold and plastic nuzzling me. "It's seven! It's seven!" it piped in a high voice. Little plastic hands rocked my head.

I opened my eyes. My alarm blinked, showing seven o'clock. The hands and feet withdrew back into the alarm when my eyes opened.

"Well, that worked." *Let's see what else I can do.* "Clothes off!" I stood there naked. "Shower!" I teleported to my shower. "One-hundred-and-four-degree water!" I knew that was what I liked for my hot tub. Perfectly hot water streamed out. I washed and turned off the water.

"Dry!" Poof! I was dry. "Bedroom closet." I was there, and it was open. I picked out my clothing. My navy skirt, coat, and cream-colored blouse. I dressed manually but still was ready to go by seven fifteen.

First, however, I needed breakfast. I teleported to my favorite bakery and ordered a ham and cheese bagel, followed by a chocolate croissant. I took an almond croissant to go.

Now, where did I go? I'd been to Washington, DC, before, even to the Oval Office. That had been awesome, and I'd been just a teen at the time, on a tour with my Girl Scout troop. I'd try to teleport there. But first I expanded the interior of my travel bag to a cubic yard, then four cubic yards. Now I could get all my clothing in there, and my clothing rack. It was also lighter than when I started.

I put my bag over one shoulder and my backpack over the other. They were light but awkward. Smiling, I put my travel bag inside my backpack. It fit neatly next to Caddie's box.

I locked up my house. Who knew when I'd be back? Maybe Caddie. I chuckled.

Pop!

I was directly in front of the president's desk, looking at President José Lopez.

He looked up, startled. Then he smiled. "That is why I need you, Katie. Magic gets through our security."

"You're right. Let me set up a magic barrier around the office." I wished for a magically impenetrable barrier around the office. A blue glow covered the walls and windows.

The president nodded. "Attractive. Can I get through?"

"Yes. It doesn't stop physical movement."

"We'll need something that does, for the military."

I sighed. "Right, Mr. President."

"Let me give you some background." President Lopez gestured to a chair across from his desk. "Have a seat." He pushed a remote. "Let's watch a movie." Shades covered the windows. The lights dimmed. A picture of President Roosevelt flipped around, and a screen appeared. The narrator said, "On October 23, China attacked Taiwan. Over two hundred and fifty dragons crossed the Strait of Formosa and attacked Taipei."

I saw the dragons skimming over the water. Bullets and rockets bounced off them. Flames from their mouths melted tanks and ships. Buildings were blazing.

"But the Republic of Taiwan was prepared. Hundreds of their dragons counterattacked."

Blue and green dragons dove from the sky upon the red dragons of China. Huge spouts of water hit the dragons and knocked them to the ground. The riders were killed or injured, and the dragons turned into statues.

"The Second Chinese Empire regrouped for a new attack, but Taiwan hit them first."

I saw the red dragons retreat over the water and gather into a close array. Just as they began spouting a wall of fire toward the Taiwanese dragons, a giant water spout appeared. It swept away all the dragons out over the Strait of Formosa.

The lights came on. The president looked at me. "So that's our current situation. We're liable to be hit at any time by a magical attack from China, or anyone else. I need you to 'magictize' our whole military."

"Ooo," I said with a groan.

"Yes, it's a hard assignment. I'd like us to be able to defend the Capitol today, the continental US within two weeks, and all possessions and military outposts within a month. I also want intelligence on who will attack us and when. Finally, I need a means of incapacitating hostile magic forces—permanently."

"We'll go into more detail in our cabinet meeting—which is right now."

I followed his lead and walked in through his secretary's office and into the cabinet room. Several people bustled about, setting out pitchers of water, brewing coffee, and checking the electronics. The other cabinet members were getting seated.

"Hello?" I said.

"Are you an assistant of the cabinet secretaries?" a man in a black suit asked. He spoke in a low, soft voice. Two brilliant-blue eyes looked out from his square, jut-jawed face.

"I am a cabinet secretary."

"I'm sorry, but I don't recognize you. Where are your assistants?"

"She's new, Agent Smith. You'll learn all about her today." The president smiled.

"Yes, sir." Agent Smith nodded, and he took his place against the wall, where he could watch all the entrances.

"Please sit here." The president gestured to a chair at the end of the table, with a shiny brass plate on the back: *Katherine Garcia, Secretary of Magic.*

I sat, overwhelmed. I put my head in my hands and vaguely heard other people come in. Then I jumped up when the president said, "Let me introduce to you, Ms. Katherine Garcia. You're the woman of the hour, Katie."

President Lopez looked at me with a broad, confident smile and took his seat at the crowded table. "Attention, everyone. I'm making a new cabinet position: the Secretary of Magic. She will direct efforts to use magic to the best effect throughout our government and country. Please keep this quiet for a few days. I'd like Katie to get used to everything before she goes before Congress for the confirmation and the press for grilling."

That brought out a few chuckles.

"There's more. I'd like each of you to meet with her and present your biggest challenge. Katie will supply you with a magical solution. There's no limit to what magic can do. Isn't that right, Katie?"

"More so than I ever imagined." My words were more hopeful than I felt.

"Your first meetings will be with the Secretaries of Defense and State this afternoon. Please supply her with your agendas."

Secretary Jared Bellows handed me a pamphlet titled, "Defense Agenda." Secretary Willow Smith handed me the "State Agenda."

"Katie came out of Oakridge nuclear research, and she's applied her scientific skills to magical research. I can tell you all that no one knows more than she about the workings of magic.

"Now for important news I recently learned that will affect everyone: China and Taiwan have settled their magical war. China will not try to invade, and Taiwan will be neutral between the US and the Chinese empire. The whole Communist apparatus has been replaced by a replication of the Mandarin system under Imperial China. We believe they're gearing up for future military conquest using their militarized dragons. Our intelligence services agree the Philippines is the most likely target. Jared, any progress against these magical threats?"

"No, sir. We have extensive video of antiaircraft missiles and gunfire bouncing off them."

"Will I be able to see these?" I had seen a little of that in the earlier video.

Jared nodded. "It's in our initial briefing with you today."

President Lopez smiled at me. "I look forward to seeing what you can do."

He continued, "Secretary Smith, what are we hearing from China through diplomatic channels?"

"They are not any more cooperative than the Communist government was. They're celebrating their peace treaty with Taiwan as a victory, although that was a military defeat for them. They're still adamant that the whole of the South China Sea is theirs." Her blond-gray hair cascaded on the shoulders of her blue-gray suit.

"How likely is a Philippine invasion?"

"They're making outrageous demands on the Philippine government and issuing threats against their shipping. This is similar to their pattern before they invaded Taiwan. I'd say the chances are over fifty percent in the next month."

"Speaking of Taiwan, how's our trade going with them?"

"No interference yet, but they've stated they feel free to intercept any ships in the South China Sea."

"Put, if they attack our ships, can we stop them?"

Putnam Broadbeam, Secretary of the Navy, frowned and shook his head. "It doesn't look good. They track our subs effectively. If they use that magical shield around their ships, we won't be able to touch them."

"I assume you'll be meeting with Jared and Katie this afternoon to get a magical solution?"

"Absolutely, sir."

I racked my mind for magical solutions. The best I could think of was teleporting them away or teleporting a bomb into them. I knew any barrier could be broken by greater magic, but did we have enough?

"That's enough for today. See you tomorrow." The president rose.

I glanced at my phone. That hour and fifteen minutes had zoomed by.

President Lopez stood next to me. "C'mon to the Oval Office. I'll give you an overview of the other things I need from you and tell you about our confirmation plans."

Dazed, I followed him mechanically.

He sat at his desk, with me across from him. "It occurs to me I need to call for a draft. A magical draft of powerful magicians all across the country. I'll let you organize them into a cohesive force. Feel free to call upon the Secretary of Defense and Joint Chiefs of Staff for advice. And keep this secret for now."

"Yes, sir."

"When will you set up the magical protection for DC, like you did for the Oval Office?"

"Well, you said today, so it'll be today." I wasn't sure how to do that. Suddenly I had an idea.

"Good. If you need any resources, let me know. You can draw from the military budget."

"I'll need some space, about a hundred yards square in the middle of DC."

"Hmm, you could use the White House lawn or—that's it! Use the mall by the Reflecting Pool."

"I'll have to buy some things. Can you give me an expense account?"

"Of course. Here's a cabinet secretary's debit card. I can't remember if it has ten million or a hundred million on it. Either way, let me know if you need more."

"This is all happening much faster than I dreamed."

"Same here, Katie. A magical war was not in my plans when I campaigned, nor when I planned this year. Thank you so much for helping me, and our country." He shook my hand and dismissed me.

Chapter 43 – NYC

Wednesday, November 3

Jane and I spent the rest of our time in NYC riding buses and subways, scanning billboards for magic. Every ad for Darrell Duncan and Faith had a powerful spell oozing influence.

We sent all our evidence to Sprong, Blodgett, and Whifflehammer. Then we flew home, our mission accomplished.

"It's good to see the old home again." Jane sighed.

"Even if it's freezing cold," I grumbled.

"Hey, think of all the money we saved turning the thermostat to sixty."

"Yeah, but the temperature's only in the fifties. We didn't expect a blizzard early in November."

The elderly furnace rumbled to life. The cast-iron vents were still in the floor, and I loved standing on them as the warm air flowed up my body.

"Let's get a kettle going. Kettle, fill yourself!" Jane really had that command voice down. I heard the water turn on and metal scraping on the stove.

"Kettle, boil!" Immediately the whistle began a loud siren. Jane was on a roll.

"Pour!"

I was warm now. I walked into the kitchen and hugged Jane. "I wonder if we can flash steep the tea?"

"Mmmm. Let's just hug for three minutes."

"And fool around."

"Squee!"

"Hello?" an unknown voice said from the living room.

"Uh, who's there? Why are you in our house?" I called.

"I walked through the front door. I got your address from Sprong, Blodgett, and Whifflehammer."

"Oh, our lawyers." Jane and I disengaged. "You know, usually people knock first before entering." I saw a softly rounded young woman of medium height, with black hair and brown eyes. She wore boots and stood in our vestibule. She didn't seem threatening.

"I did knock. And your doorbell doesn't work. And I'm on a tight timeline."

"Fixing that doorbell is on my to-do list. Tell me about your urgent timeline." I raised my eyebrow skeptically as I walked to her. I loomed over her. I wasn't going to welcome her until I knew what was going on.

"I'm Katie Garcia. I've been appointed by the president to recruit mages to help our country use magic more effectively. I have worked closely with Sprong, Blodgett, and Whifflehammer, and they let me know about your work for them, researching Darrell Duncan and his dog, Faith. I know from your magic readings that you and your wife, Jane"—Katie looked past me at Jane, who'd come up to my side—"are powerful magicians."

"That seems too crazy to be true, but it's also impossible to believe it is a lie. Do you have some identification?"

"Sure." Katie unzipped her coat and took an ID card off a lanyard around her neck.

I took it. "Katherine Garcia, Secretary of Magic. White House Security card." It had her picture, dressed smartly in a navy suit. There was a hologram of authenticity on the card, like a driver's license.

"Whoa. This looks legit."

Jane took the card from me. "Huh. Anyone can have a plastic card made up with their picture. I'm calling Sprong, Blodgett, and Whifflehammer to vouch for you." Jane swiped on her phone.

Katie smiled, and a dimple appeared on her cheek. "Be my guest.

"Please get me Will Sprong." Jane stared suspiciously at Katie.

I was more trusting than Jane; I felt Katie was telling the truth.

"Hi, Will. I've got a Katherine Garcia at our house. Did you send her over?"

Jane listened for quite a while, then said, "Thanks, Will. I just wanted to verify her."

"You might as well come in and be comfortable. We've been tracking criminals who stole our money for a week, so I've been very suspicious," I said.

"No problem. I dealt with criminals who tried to enslave me."

"Oof. How'd that happen?" I started our gas fireplace. That always made the cavernous Victorian living room cheerier.

"They tried to magically compel me to sign a contract that gave them use of my magic forever." Katie gave her coat to Jane, who hung it up.

"How'dja stop them?" Jane asked.

"I did this." A blue glow surrounded Katie. "This is a shield that stops all magic."

"Ah. We kind of did that around our author royalties online at Amazin'." Jane and I sat in our recliners. We had several other recliners facing ours in a circle.

Katie sat on the edge of her chair. She kept her backpack on her lap, with her cell phone. "Cool! I never thought of that. But that's why I'm here—to learn from you and let you know how you can help your country."

"That sounds good. We're both patriotic Americans. Do you want some tea?"

"That sounds wonderful."

"With or without milk?"

"Without. I'm watching my weight."

I looked askance at her. "Maybe Jane and I should care about our weight, but not you. Kettle! Pour some tea! Teacup, come here!"

One of our bone-china teacups came skittering across the wooden floor, followed by a saucer.

"Go to Katie." I pointed at her.

The saucer climbed the end table like a monkey, followed by the teacup. The cup settled into the saucer. The arms and legs withdrew, and they returned to normal.

"Whew! An animated teacup and saucer were not what I expected today. But that's magic for you—it always surprises you." Katie sipped her cup. "Delicious." She sniffed appreciatively.

"Now, my job is to use magic throughout the US

government, especially for defense and the military." She grinned. "I'm already bursting with ideas for using your animated objects for military purposes. How about autonomous drones? Bombs? Missiles?"

"Sounds deadly." I shook my head.

"True, but we're up against magical enemies."

"Like who?" Jane tilted her head as she put her cup back on the saucer.

"Like dragons. And other mages."

"Yeah, I see the problem. I've already met a kid right here in Lakewood who has life-size, animated plastic dinosaurs."

"Oh my. I've got to meet him!"

"All I know is his name—Svi. That's short for Sviatoslav."

"Hmm. Okay, I'll look him up after we're done here. What other magical discoveries have you made?"

"No big deal. Just our teacups and our kettle and teapot. Oh, and the vacuum. Vacuum, come to the living room!" Jane called, and out it came.

"Cool." Katie took a picture. Then she unfolded her phone and showed us the magic chart of the vacuum—723 MUs from Jane Williams.

"We got phones like that from Will Sprong when we went to New York City tracking Darrell Duncan."

"And his dog, Faith," Jane put in.

"This is one of my magical inventions. I haven't read your report about Darrell. Could you fill me in?"

Jane and I reviewed our work in New York City, spying on Darrell and Faith and then discovering the magic coming from all his ads.

Katie nodded. "Thanks. Mr. Duncan and his dog are definitely on my 'to visit' list."

"Will you arrest him?" Jane leaned forward eagerly.

"It's more likely we'll draft him. We need all the magicians we can get."

"But he's as crooked as a dog's hind leg with rickets." Jane frowned at Katie.

"Magic can be controlled by more magic. I think we've got enough to get him under control."

"I hope so." I felt less sanguine.

"Anything else?"

"Yeah. I used magic in writing my advertising copy."

Katie chuckled. "Isn't that just like Darrell using it for his mayoral ads?"

"Uh, no?"

"Let's see one of your ads."

I brought up Amazin' and my book ad on my phone. Katie scanned it with her phone. "Ha! 223 MUs on that ad for presale, from you, Jacob 'Jake' Williams. You're just like Darrell."

"Uh, I didn't mean to do it . . ."

"He just used it on his ad copy . . ." Jane began.

"Right. Magic has consequences beyond what we imagine. You know that pants-on-fire thing that swept the world?"

"Yes. We heartily approved of zapping lying politicians with flaming clothing."

"That's what got me pulled into this magical research. That worldwide effect came from one family in Toledo wishing lying politicians' pants would burst into flame."

"Wow. We'd better be careful." I tried to grasp all the implications. "Am I in trouble with the law?"

"I'd check with Sprong, Blodgett, and Whifflehammer. They'd know better than me. I know compulsion is illegal because it was tried on me and the jury. But influence through ads? I'm not sure at all. Your spell for the ad says, 'I wish it were perfect for selling my book.' That's broad, but it doesn't force anyone to buy it. How many have you sold so far?"

"A quarter million in presales."

"Right. That's out of millions of people who've read the ad. I think it attracts people who are interested in your book."

"Oh. So maybe Duncan isn't guilty of anything?"

"Check with the lawyers. His wish, from your own MU report, was, 'A slogan to make people want to vote for me.' He didn't get one hundred percent of the vote, so it wasn't compulsion."

"That's a surprise. Maybe he isn't as much of a scum as I thought?" Jane said.

"He did steal from us and other authors," I said.

"We'll keep him under control. Do you have any other surprises for me?"

"Let's see. All I can think of is controlling the lawnmower. That went out of control the first time I tried it. I mowed some flowers—"

"My favorites!"

"Right, Jane, by *accident*."

"That's a good lesson to teach everyone: unintended consequences. Just like the *Magic Arrives*, your book."

Katie stood and slipped her coat on.

I put my hand on my chin. "I thought of one more thing. The kid with the dinosaurs. He changed the traffic light when he wanted to cross."

"I've seen that before." Katie nodded.

"And I used magic to search the internet. That's how I found Darrell Duncan," Jane added.

Katie nodded. "Good idea. I kind of do that with my magical computer."

"Now there's a good idea. I'll make my computer magical." I looked at Katie.

"I'll send you the details of my wish. We've got to become more methodical about using magic, or we won't get repeatable results. Now, let me show you how I'll find Svi's address."

Katie opened her backpack and pulled out a box larger than her backpack.

I crossed my arms at the sight. "I assume that's a magical storing bag, like the fantasy games and novels have."

"Right, Jake. Here's something you won't find in any fantasy novel." Katie took out a doll.

Jane clapped her hands. "A talking doll! A Chatting Cathy. Sprong and etcetera had one. I had one when I was a kid."

"You're right, but this is her sister, Caddie. Watch and learn. Caddie, what's Svi's address? The kid with the animated dinosaurs?" Katie pulled the string.

Caddie's eyes opened, swung to Jane and me, and then back to Katie. "I see you've got more magicians. 'Sviatoslav "Svi" Ward' is also a magician, living on 428 Quail Court in Lakewood." Caddie's eyes stayed open, prompting Katie to say, "What else can you tell me?"

Zip!

"Be careful. He's a powerful mage who uses magic

extensively. Bribe him with a box of chocolate truffles." Her eyes snapped shut.

"I've got to get one of those," Jane said.

"They haven't made any since the sixties."

"I bet I can find one used on eStore."

"Sprong, Blodgett, and Whifflehammer might help you too. That's where I got Caddie." She grinned. "Now I've got to pop off."

Pop! Katie disappeared.

"I never thought of disappearing using magic!"

"I think she teleported, Jane. That's why she popped. The air rushes into the hole where her body was."

"So where'd she go?"

"I assume to 428 Quail Court."

"Is that in Bird Town?"

"Yeah, the old neighborhood by the railroad tracks."

* * *

I saw 428 on the house in front of me. It was as old or older than the Williams', but run down. The whole neighborhood looked decrepit: unshoveled sidewalks, old cars, and junk piled in front yards and on porches.

I sighed and watched my breath cloud before my eyes in the cold air. I was *really* tired. I'd spent yesterday morning getting the supplies I needed. This magic accumulator was much bigger than the one Mike had invented. Then my afternoon cabinet meetings had gone on into the evening.

After that, I'd installed the magic gatherer on the Washington Mall. I disguised the waving antennae as inflatable figures of our Founding Fathers. People thought it was a new memorial. But it worked well. The whole Capitol District was covered an anti-magical dome.

I'd met with President Lopez last night. He was pleased with the dome, but he wanted it also to protect against mundane weapons. And he wanted it to let cars, planes, and trains through. Now I had another thing on my ever-expanding to-do list.

I'd had another short night of sleep last night. But what was draining me was all the people. I knew I was an introvert, but

I'd never been forced into this much interaction by my research job before.

What made it worse was, I saw no escape. This magical world was permanent, and I had this job for the rest of President Lopez's term.

I didn't want to meet any more people. But I had to. It was my job, my responsibility.

I remembered my dad working two jobs when my mother got chemotherapy. Then when I needed money for college, he continued his two jobs until I'd completed my undergraduate degree, master's, and PhD.

He'd died of a heart attack soon after I got my job with Oakridge, happy with my success. I'd always felt guilty about his death, thinking his overwork for my sake had contributed to his heart attack.

In light of what he'd gone through, I *had* to carry on. I walked up to the door and knocked.

* * *

I, Liu Fu, was the emperor of all China, and I was grumpy. My elite Dragon Brigade had gotten their butts whipped in battle and come slinking home. Out of two hundred dragons ridden by my best mages, I'd lost over 10 percent. The rest had scattered and fled before the typhoon mage, who'd chased them back to mainland China.

So. I had to do something different. I reflected on Sun Tzu. I had found his book in the garbage in the old days, and read it until the cover came off. His advice still guided me. "He who knows when he can fight and when he cannot will be victorious." Also, "The supreme art of war is to subdue the enemy without fighting." Finally, "If a battle can't be won, don't fight it."

I wouldn't fight Taiwan anymore. They were at least as strong as my forces and perhaps stronger. Therefore, I would make a peace treaty.

I clapped my hands twice. "Bring me my mirror!" My servants knew what I meant.

Two enormous eunuchs pushed it into my throne room. They were each two meters in height, but the mirror was larger.

It stretched two meters in diameter, not counting the wooden stand. The highly polished bronze surface showed me in my imperial robes.

I sat on my throne and commanded the mirror. “Show me the leader of Taiwan!”

A man in a dark suit, sitting at a desk, appeared in the mirror. He looked at me, startled.

“Greetings, President Wu. I am Emperor Liu of China, and I wish to sign a nonaggression pact with your country.” I couldn’t make myself say “Taiwan” when I thought of it as “China.”

“Ah yes. That would be good. No tariffs?”

“None. Free trade between our countries.”

“I will have my Secretary of State draw up the treaty.”

“Very good. Goodbye.” He disappeared, and I saw myself smiling.

We would be tightly attached through trade. I would be able to spy and recruit their mages. When the remora attached itself to a great white shark, it went wherever the shark went.

Now, the next step. I need a victory to encourage my mages and to stir up the population. “Attend me, chief mages!” I spoke to my mirror and saw the three of them appear: Han Mùchén, Li Yihan, and Wa Mingze.

Mùchén had been a twenty-nine-year-old former cab driver. I found him one day flying his cab around, and I drafted him. He was even more powerful than I’d perceived. He’d led our dragon forces against Taiwan.

Li Yihan was a fourteen-year-old student. She just appeared before me one day and said, “I will be your greatest mage for you.”

I’d smirked at her temerity and set her on fire. The flames went around her but didn’t harm her. She lifted my dragon, which was lying next to my throne, into the air. I broke her spell, but barely.

I put her in charge of mage training. She was good, and they all became more powerful under her tutelage.

Wa Mingze was a twelve-year-old student. He had missed out on the national table tennis team and then used magic to insert himself. He’d imitated not only the champion’s appearance but also his skills. I told him to copy all the skills of all my mages. I put him in charge of espionage. He was currently in the Philippines.

"Wa Mingze, report!" I looked at him first.

He appeared as a skinny twelve-year-old boy, completely harmless. That was what made him so deadly.

"Emperor Liu, they are disorganized but powerful. There are potent mages who control the weather and one who controls volcanoes."

"Have you copied their talents?"

"Not all. The greater mages seem to have more strength of will than I do. When I approach, they repulse me and attack. I've had to change my appearance several times to escape."

I frowned. "Han Mùchén, has the Imperial Dragon Army improved enough to defeat Taiwan?"

His round face held its usual frown. "Yes. I have learned from their weather mages how they control typhoons and whirlwinds. I have trained six mages in these skills. However, on defense, they have as many mages as we do, and our dragons cannot defeat theirs unless we gain weather dominance."

"Li Yihan, how do we overcome these magical shortcomings?"

Yihan seemed to cast a spell upon herself. Her tall, slender body floated into the air and folded into a lotus position. Without opening her eyes, she said, "We must not attack their strength but their weakness. They are strong magically but rely on the United States for non-magical support. The US is not ready for a magical attack. They are disorganized and have not incorporated magic into their military. I recommend we attack there, one island at a time. We can hold their citizens as hostages and negotiate their release for a favorable peace treaty."

"Do you two agree with her recommendation?" I looked at the other mages.

They each cast the same Future-Insight spell as Yihan and floated up silently in meditation.

Mùchén spoke first. "Our dragons and weather mages can conquer Guam, Wake Island, and Hawaii. After that, I cannot see."

“Wa Mingze? What do you say?”

“I will gather intelligence today on Guam, Wake, and Hawaii. Then I will give you my recommendation.”

“Good. Han Mùchén and Li Yihan, prepare for the invasion. We will attack according to the intelligence Wa Mingze gives us tomorrow. Dismissed.” I clapped my hands.

Chapter 44 – Friends

Wednesday, November 3

I grinned when I saw Heath inside the giant block house. He loved playing with the huge plastic blocks. This one was fancier than ever before. The second story was bigger than the first, and Heath peeked out the window at me.

I reached up toward the window. It was too high. “Hey, Heath! How do I get up there?”

“Float.”

Of course. I transformed into my fairy form and flew in the window. There was more room now that I was just a foot tall. Heath looked like a giant. He smiled at me.

“How’d you make this?” The blocks were interlocking plastic, but no one had made anything like this.

“Magic. They stick together until I tell them to let go.”

“Cool. I’ll have to try it.”

I flew out, gathered some building sticks, and made an airy fairy house off the side of his room.

Heath nodded. “Good job.”

“Shayla, it’s time to go to the next station.” Mrs. Sewell looked at me through the window of my room.

“Poo! I’ve just begun having fun.”

“You can return later.”

I flew out. My next station was math. I didn’t like that as much as the building or art stations.

“Hey! Why doesn’t Heath have to go there?”

“He did all his station work for the day.”

“I’ll go with Shayla.” Heath floated out the window. He made a long sliding board, out of magic, to the math station and slid into a seat. It vanished. I landed next to him.

“Thanks for coming with me, Heath.”

“You shared your candy with me. We’re buddies.”

That made me feel good. I knew Heath was special.

“How d’ya get all your work done so fast?”

He shrugged. “In the morning I ask the teachers what each

station assignment is. Then I wish I learn it as fast as I can."

"Wow! I'll do that. I wish I learn this lesson right away! Ooh, my head feels like it's bulging."

"Yeah. You have to do the work to get rid of that feeling."

The assignment was to find a pattern in cubes. I picked up one block. "A one-sided cube is one block."

"Right." Heath nodded.

I grabbed more blocks. "A two-sided cube is eight blocks." My head felt better, but I knew I didn't quite have the pattern yet.

A bunch more blocks later, I said, "A three-sided cube is twenty-seven blocks." I knew I was almost there. I looked at my latest cube. The one- and the two-sided cubes were inside it. The two-sided cube was just two squares on top of each other.

"Huh. This is sort of like building, back at the construction station."

"That's right. It's just like it." Heath sounded excited.

The three-sided cube was three three-by-three squares on top of each other. There was the pattern!

"One-by-one is boring—it's always one. But two-by-two is four, and two-by-two-by-two is eight. And three-by-three is nine." I'd learned that yesterday. "And three-by-three three times is twenty-seven. The pattern is, the cubes are related to the squares. They're also related to each other."

Mrs. Sewell clapped her hands. "That's great, Shayla. You've gotten everything you need out of this station today. You can go back to the construction station if you want."

"Whee!" I squealed as I popped into my fairy form and flew back to that station. I stopped. There it was. The pattern. Heath had made a cube for the lower level and then four cubes on top of that. My room hung off the side, making the top lopsided.

"Huh. You made a shape that went from a one cube to a two square."

"Right."

"Now it's lopsided. I'll fix that." I copied my fairy room by magic until I had five cubes around two sides and one corner. Then I shifted the top layer so it rested on the corner of Heath's room.

"Now it looks even. One-by-one to three-by-three."

"I didn't know you could shift my magic around like that," Heath said.

"I just had to tell it to connect to this other cube."

Soon it was lunchtime. Now each station was fun, even if I didn't want to like it. Each new thing I learned was like a new toy.

It seemed Mom came sooner than ever before, although it was already getting dark.

"Hi, Mom! Guess what I learned?" I ran into her arms for a warm hug.

"Tell me all about it, Shayla." We walked to the car through the cold air.

After I told her about cubes, she said, "I've got something new for you too. We paid off our house today!"

"Wow. Does that mean we won't give rides anymore at Grant Park?"

"Nah. We still need money for your school and Lamar's college."

I wondered if we could get by without money. Could we just learn through magic? It seemed crazy, but I kept thinking about it.

Once home, Mom served us a fancy steak dinner to celebrate paying off our house. Then she took out a piece of paper from her notebook.

"What's that, Mom?" Lamar peered at it. It had a lot of fancy writing on it.

"It's our mortgage. I thought we could each burn a piece. It's a way of celebrating that we don't owe anyone anything."

"Yay! I love burning things!" Lamar shouted.

"Me too!"

Mom tore the paper into three pieces and gave one to each of us. "Let's put them in the fireplace."

We put our pieces on the cold, dirty grate. I wrote my name on mine.

"Good idea, Shayla." Lamar put his name on his.

"And mine already has my signature." Mom showed us her signature.

"Why did you already sign it?" I looked at her.

"My signature is my promise to pay off the loan."

"Oh."

"On the count of three, set your papers on fire. One, two, three!"

The three papers blazed up from our magics. My name showed up in pink flame, Lamar's in green, and Mom's in blue.

Someone knocked on the door.

"It's an odd time for a visitor." Mom kept the chain on the door and cracked it.

"Hello?"

"Hi, Ms. Brown. It's me, Katie Garcia. Sorry to bother you so late. I've been busy. May I come in?"

"Of course, Katie. Do you want any steak? We have a leftover piece. You can heat it in the microwave or on the stove. Here are some sweet potatoes and green beans to go with it."

"Oh, thanks so much. I just came straight from a meeting with the president, and I haven't had time to eat supper."

We all sat around the table as she ate. Mom gave us chocolate chip cookies and milk to eat with her.

"Wow! You met the president?" Lamar said around his cookie.

"Yeah, he's my boss. I'm in the cabinet as the Secretary of Magic. I meet with him once a day to update him."

"Ooo, is that like Harry Potter with the Ministry of Magic?" Lamar bounced in his seat.

"I hope not. I'd like to be more effective than that."

"So what do you do?" I asked

"Lately I've visiting magical people like your family." She took out her phone and scanned our family with it.

"You see? Shayla, you're at 1595 MUs. You're about the most magical person I've seen. Lamar's at 1397, and Shannon's at 1413."

"We have been using magic more and more," Mom said.

"Everyone across the country is. And the background magic is increasing. Your house is at 491. That's how strong some of my early spells were. Magic is still growing on Earth."

"You should meet my friend Heath. He's as strong as me in magic, but he thinks of different things."

Katie looked at me. "I will. Where does he live?"

"I dunno. We go to school together."

"I'll find out later. What kind of magic have you been doing? I know about your flying and animation spells."

Mom put her chin on her hand. "I had some trouble with sales and income taxes with our ride business. But I wished for help, and I got a new friend at the gym who helped me."

"Don't forget that Shayla and I got you the permit for selling!" Lamar looked at me.

"Yeah. Lamar drew it up, and I made it real," Shayla said.

"Cool. Could I see that?"

Mom pulled the permit out of the folder. She took it with her when she worked at Grant Park. "Here it is." Mom handed it to Katie.

"It looks official—"

I interrupted Katie. "It is! The inspector approved it."

"—and the spell you used was at 899 MUs. That's a new one for me." Katie typed something on her tablet.

"Anything else?"

I put my finger on my mouth, thinking. "Well, I put a spell on those girls across the street from our apartment."

"What was that about?" Katie looked at me.

"They weren't allowed to talk about us or our magic. We tested it."

"Hmm. That seems to mean, forcing them against their will."

"They took a video of our building with Pinkie on it. We were worried about people following us around and my kids' privacy." Mom sounded angry.

"Yeah, I can see that. I saw that video, and that's how I found you. I want to investigate them too. What were their names?"

"Heather and Maria. A big blond girl and a little dark-haired one. Let's see. They stopped by Grant Park, and we took them for a ride." Mom opened her laptop. "I'm looking up our credit card sales. Here it is: Maria Chen."

"That should be enough. I want to investigate your spell, Shayla. Someone tried to force me to do something bad, and I didn't like it at all."

"It was something we had to do, Katie." Mom frowned at her.

"Yes, but it's one step away from enslaving someone. Be very careful about spells like that."

"How about making someone fall asleep?" I asked.

"That doesn't sound so bad. When'd you do that, Shayla?"

"My friend Heath wouldn't come in from the playground. He put up a barrier I couldn't get through, so I made him fall asleep."

"Now that's something I want to learn, to make a barrier like that." Katie typed frantically.

"I think I can do it. No one can touch me!" A barrier popped up around me like Heath's, only mine was pink.

Katie, Lamar, and Mom all tried to reach me but couldn't. Katie even tried some spells that dented it, but they didn't work.

"This is great, Shayla. Let me try one more thing. Fall asleep, Shayla."

I slumped to the floor. Lamar woke me up.

"Wake up, sleepyhead."

Katie shook my hand. "Wow, Shayla, thank you. All of this has been great. Your spells will help protect the president and our military."

"Like the army? The navy? The air force?" Lamar said, excited.

"Yes sir, Lamar. These spells will go directly to them."

I furrowed my brows. Did I have any other spells? "Oh yeah. I almost forgot. I healed Lamar from a bullet."

"What?!" Katie looked from me to Lamar.

Mom's mouth opened.

"Yeah, I still wear it around my neck. I drilled a hole in it." He showed her the bullet. She took a picture of it.

"1600 MUs. Resurrection from the dead. Did you know he was dead, Shayla?"

I remembered how cold he was. "Uh, I didn't want to think about it. I just wished he'd be all better. Pinkie helped too."

"I found the bullet in my shirt too."

"I threw that shirt out. It had a hole and was all bloody. I didn't want to think about how bad it was, but I didn't think Lamar had died."

"That's unique, Shayla. I've never met anyone else who did that. Do you think you could do it on another person?"

"Uh, I don't know. I never wished so hard before or since."

"If we need you to resurrect the president, would you try?"

I thought about it. The president! He represented our country. "Of course I'd try."

Katie gave Mom a phone. "This is a magical phone—it goes straight to me. If I need you or your children or if I have a question, I'd like to call you. Can you keep it on you at all times?"

"Yes, Katie, but I'm not too sure about letting my kids go anywhere for any reason."

"Aw, Mom, I'd love to fight for our country," Lamar said.

"Anywhere Lamar goes, I'll go!" I put in my two cents.

"Right, Shannon. As minors, they're in your care, and you decide what to do and what not to do. I'll keep everything secret—I've been ordered to by the president. But if I call you, it'll be a life and death situation—or close to it.

"Now you get to learn something from me. I just learned it, and it makes my life a lot simpler. I'm going to visit Heather and Maria now. I'll meet Heath tomorrow at school.

"I remember your apartment building and theirs. I'll picture their building in my mind and wish to be there. Watch what happens."

Katie vanished with a *pop!*

Chapter 45 - Stew

Tuesday, November 2

After I got home from school, I looked over the fence for Dak, playing in the dirt with some trucks and bulldozers.

"Hey, Dak! Could I play?"

"Sure."

I climbed over the fence.

"Why didn't you teleport?"

"I like to climb fences. And I didn't think of it. I used to play in the sand under our swimming pool when we took it down."

"I wish I had a swimming pool."

"You can swim in ours. We put it up in May. What'd your mom say about coming over?"

"She wants to talk to you."

"Sure. When?"

He sighed. "Let's go now."

It was dim in the house. The shades were drawn, and the only light was the TV. Yolanda sat watching a soap opera and eating a TV dinner.

"Mom, this is Sean, the one who invited us over to dinner."

"So what's the deal? First you turn us in to the police, and now you make nice with us?"

"Uh, I guess that's right. When I turned you in, you got away. Now you're our neighbor. Why turn you in again? You'll just get away."

"You're damn right we'll get away." She nodded firmly. "How do I know you won't have the police over to arrest us?"

"First, I promised Dak I wouldn't turn you in. I don't lie, and neither do my parents."

"Yeah, right. Dak, I want you to start moving our furniture to the new house."

"But, Mom—"

"Don't argue! One last question. Tell me the real reason you want us over. I can read people and I know you aren't lying, but you haven't told me the real reason yet."

I frowned. I might as well tell her. "Jesus said, 'Love your neighbor as yourself.' That's you. Turning you in didn't work, so we thought we'd try doing what Jesus said."

"Huh. A real Jesus freak. I never thought I'd meet one. Send your parents over, and I'll talk with them."

"Okay." I grinned at her and disappeared, popping into our living room.

"Sean!" Mom said. "You startled me."

"Yolanda wants to talk with you. She says she can tell if someone is lying or not."

"Okay. I don't lie."

"I know it. I'll teleport us there." I held her hand.

"No way! I'll go in the front door, like a normal person."

"Fine." I grinned, grabbed her hand, and teleported us to Yolanda's front porch.

"There. Are you happy?" I looked into Mom's eyes.

"That was something. And it is easier than walking around the block."

"Or climbing the fence."

She knocked on the door.

Yolanda answered it. "Are you Sean's mom?"

"Yes, Shirley."

"Go in the back and play with Dak," Yolanda said to me. "I want to talk with your mom alone."

I ran around to the backyard.

After a while, Mom came out and called to me. "Hey, Sean, let's go home."

"Sure, Mom. See you, Dak."

Mom frowned. "Be sure you go downstairs and take off your pants. You're all dirty. And wash your hands. Let's walk. I don't want to hold your grubby hands."

"What's the word about Dak and Yolanda?"

"They're coming over for dinner on Saturday. She loves stew, so I'm making it for her. Maybe you should call her 'Ms. Murphy.' That's her last name."

"I never knew that. Well, that's good news."

"Maybe. She's still suspicious."

* * *

Mom handed me a piece of paper. "Okay, Dak. Here's our new house address. You go over there and teleport all our furniture to that place."

"Mom! I like being Sean's friend."

"Nah. There's too much chance they'll double-cross us and turn us into the police."

"But Sean *promised*."

"Yeah, he did, and I believe him. But his mom didn't, and maybe she'll turn us in. Or one of the churchy Jesus friends. You know they go to church every week."

"No. How would I know that?"

"She told me and invited us to come with them."

"So what?"

"So once anyone finds out we're thieves, they'll turn us in."

"Um, couldn't we just not tell them?"

"It'll get out. It always does. But you can go to their house and case the joint. See if there is anything good to steal?"

"Why steal from them? We can just steal from the store."

"I want to get back at them when they betray us."

"What if they don't?"

"I never thought they wouldn't. I'll decide if it doesn't happen."

I spent the rest of the day moving everything to the new house. I'd made a list the last time, and I just reused it for the new house. It wasn't quite as big, but the yard was nice. Maybe I'd make another friend.

Saturday came. I had a list of things to steal. Sean's computer and his cell phone, their wall-mounted TV, and maybe their dining room set. Oh, and the remote control. Mom reminded me about that.

I wondered if I could change the channels through magic? Why not?

When we walked in the front door on Saturday, Sean's dad, Mr. Kennedy, greeted us. He towered over me and Mom. I could see where Sean got his height. He was already taller than Mom.

The delicious smell of the stew filled the house.

"Now before we eat," Mr. Kennedy said, "let me assure you we will not turn you in. Shirley told me you were worried about that. May our pants catch on fire we do!"

We all laughed.

"That's one of the funniest things I've seen on the TV and internet—all those people with their pants and skirts catching on fire," Mom said.

"Remember the time your sweatpants caught on fire?" I looked at her.

"Yeah—I didn't know lying triggered it. I was careful after that to not lie in public."

"Where were you?" Sean asked.

"Sean, shame on you. Don't pry into other people's business," his mom scolded.

"Nah, it's no problem, Shirley. I was in a gym, and someone asked if I was a member and I said yes. Big mistake."

"I hope you weren't seriously injured."

"Nah, I just ran into the shower. I was in the locker room. I can't wait to try the stew. It smells just like my mom's."

"When did Grandma make stew?" I asked. "I just remember her in the nursing home."

Mom looked happy. "Back when I was a little girl. She made it every Sunday after church."

"You went to church as a kid?" Mr. Kennedy asked as he ladled out the stew into everyone's bowl.

"Yeah. Mom made us go, until Dad died. Then we went on welfare and lost the house. I don't think she cared anymore." Mom tasted the stew. "Oh wow, this is great. It really is like my mother's."

Mrs. Kennedy grinned, and her eyes crinkled. "Thank you, Yolanda."

"Dak, do you like Shirley's stew?" Mom stared at me like she expected me to talk with my mouth full.

I swallowed. "Yeah, it's great."

"I could tell by the way he was eating—gobbling, like I do when I love something," Mr. Kennedy said.

"This really brings me back to happier times, with my mom and dad, before I met Dak's dad," Mom said.

"Why—was he a problem?" Ms. Kennedy asked.

"He was a good-looking football player, a running back. I ran away from home to marry him. He never married me, but dumped me when I was pregnant with Dak."

I'd heard all this before. I was sad that my dad was such a bum. I'd always wanted a dad. I ate more stew.

"That's terrible," Mr. Kennedy said.

"Mom was mad at me, but after Dak was born, that's when things got really bad. Mom had a stroke and had to go into nursing care. I was left with the apartment and more bills than welfare money. So I started boosting things, to make ends meet."

"I don't like that, but I can understand. I can't imagine being a single mom," Mrs. Kennedy said.

"I met my fence and dumped all the stuff on him so it couldn't be traced to me. We did okay, until Dak got magic. Then our business really took off."

I spoke. This was my part of the story. Everyone seemed so interested in Mom's story.

"I stole some jewelry for Mom from the store, and the clerk started yelling and chasing me. I ran as fast as I could, but he grabbed me. I said, 'I wish I were home!' and *pop!* I was home."

"That was on my birthday, three weeks ago. I still have that jewelry. That's still my favorite gift from you, Dak." Mom's eyes glistened, but I couldn't see too well because mine were wet too. I wiped them on my napkin.

"That explains a lot." Mr. Kennedy nodded.

"Are you going to turn us in now?" Mom's tears dried up as she looked at him suspiciously.

"Nah, I can't. We'd all burst into flame. We promised. That's real, Yolanda. But you have a real problem with stealing—it's not sustainable. You'll get caught—with magic."

"Oh. I hadn't thought of that."

"Yes, Ms. Murphy. I used magic to find your apartment. I gathered the evidence and turned it in to the police. But you escaped. Then I found you next door, and we decided to try to talk you out of crime." Sean looked uncomfortable.

"You won't have to try. We're moving. Dak's already moved our furniture."

"But that's the point. I've already learned how to follow Dak. I can follow him wherever he goes."

Mom frowned. "Ya mean you'll always be able to find Dak? No matter where he goes?"

"Yeah."

"And the police will always be able to find me?"

"Yeah."

Mom sniffled. "So I'll get caught and put in the slammer, and Dak'll be on the streets."

"Of course not. We'd take care of him. But we wouldn't turn you in." Everyone looked at Mrs. Kennedy. I stared too. She would take care of me? She seemed a little . . . frightening.

Mom looked at her. "You'd care for him? And you won't turn me in?" Tears ran down her cheeks.

I was curious. Sometimes she'd cry to get her way. But I couldn't tell now, even after all these years.

"Here's a tissue." Mrs. Kennedy gave her one.

Mom blew her nose. "I think I have to go home to think—" A knock on the door interrupted her.

Mr. Kennedy frowned. "Odd time for a door-to-door salesman." He stood to answer the door.

"Phil, don't be silly. There haven't been any for years."

"Oh. C'mon in, Katie."

A nice-looking woman with dark-brown hair came. She took a picture of all of us. She looked at the back of her phone and whistled. "Whoa! Sean, you've been busy. You're one of the most powerful mages in the United States." She smiled at him.

He turned red. I wondered why.

"Everyone else is more powerful than before. Phil, sorry to interrupt your dinner, but I'm on the president's business. Please introduce me to your guests."

"Katie, this is Yolanda Murphy and Dak, her son. They're neighbors of ours. Yolanda, Dak, this is Katie Garcia, recently appointed as the president's Secretary of Magic."

"They're powerful in magic too. Especially Dak, who's almost as strong as Sean. Hmm, I wonder if magic attracts magic?" She made a note in her phone and then shook herself and began again. "I'm really sorry to crash in here again at suppertime. Let me tell you why. I'm learning all the magic I can from all the magical people I can find."

"Of course, I knew the power of your family, Phil, and especially Sean. Now I just need to know what new things you've learned about magic. There's still no overall theory of how it works."

I spoke. "That's easy, Ms. Garcia. You just wish for what you want, really hard."

She nodded. "Yes, that's the pattern, Dak. But how do you wish hard? How much does belief matter? And how do you measure all that?"

"Oh. I never thought about that. I was always sure I'd get what I wanted if I wanted it enough."

"And how much does picturing something help?" Sean said. "I had trouble teleporting until I could picture something clearly. When I first followed Dak, I imagined him behind a door and me in front of it. That worked."

"Good point, Sean. I had the same experience with teleporting." Katie smiled at Sean.

He turned red again.

I spoke again. "Yeah. I had to walk somewhere or go with my mom in her car before I could teleport there." I liked using the word "teleport." It sounded smart and felt good on my tongue.

"Where does this leave me? I have no magic," Mom said.

"Oh yes, you do. You cast spells, strong ones, 'to detect lies' on everybody." Katie looked at her unfolded phone as she spoke.

"Well, of course. I always try to see if people are rookin' me. There's no magic in that."

"There is now, ever since magic arrived. You've given me a new idea." Katie tapped on her phone.

"Whatcha writing?" Mom asked.

"To check more people to see what magic they might be using without thinking about it or noticing. To answer your other question, where does that leave you, I'd say volunteer to help the government with magic and you'll get a presidential pardon for any crimes you've committed."

Mom grinned. "Sign me up!"

"Of course, you'll have to stop stealing. The pardon only covers past crimes."

Mom's face fell. "How will we live? I tried getting by on welfare, and we couldn't do it. That's why I started stealing." She sniffled.

I think she was faking this time.

"Oh. As Secretary of Magic, I can hire you as a consultant. Let's see . . . Minimum wage is $15 per hour—that's $30,000 per year, or $2,500 per month. Can you live on that?"

Mom's eyes widened. "Yes! Sign me up."

"Good. Then you'll be happy with $60,000 per year, with federal benefits. I'm paying for Dak too, although he's underage. I'll talk to both of you."

Now Mom broke down laughing and crying at the same time. "Oh thank you, thank you! This is such a relief."

The Kennedys stood and cheered. I looked at them. They were as happy as I was. Mom and I rose and clapped too.

Mr. Kennedy grinned. "That's a great deal. Maybe you can hire us?"

"Of course, Phil. I planned to."

Mr. Kennedy put up his hands. "I'm just joking, Katie. We don't need the money."

I shook my head. I couldn't imagine not needing money.

"Oh yes we do, Phil." Mrs. Kennedy looked at him. "We have plenty of things to do around the house, and another thirty thousand would do nicely."

"Oh, I couldn't do that." Katie shook her head. She looked so young that I thought of her as a "Katie," not "Ms. Garcia."

"Why not?" Ms. Kennedy looked angry.

"The minimum wage for a cabinet advisor is $144,000. Would you accept that?"

"Uh, yes, of course." Mrs. Kennedy sat down, and so did everyone else—Katie took the one empty chair.

"I'd like that too!" Mom spoke up.

"Sure." Katie nodded. "This makes it easier. Three standard starting salaries for Phil, Shirley, and Yolanda."

"Hey, I've already got a full-time job. I make almost that much as a chemical engineer."

"Hmm. You can probably advise me in your spare time. And I'm also getting Sean for free, so you can think of it as his salary. I can't list him either, because he's underage."

"Hey, I'm almost thirteen, Katie! And I do yard work."

"Good for you, but as a business or for the government, you'd have to be fourteen to work in Ohio or DC."

"Oh." Sean seemed sad.

My mind spun. We had gone from moving away from my only friend to working with him in fifteen minutes. And from being on the run to being wealthy. Mom looked dazed too, like when she'd had too much to drink.

"This is all too much. I'll have to go home to think about this," Mom said.

"Yeah. I'll have to move our furniture back," I added.

"That's one of the things I have to think about, Dak. Where will we live?"

"Move your furniture? You just moved in!" Sean looked at me.

"Yeah, we were planning to move in case of a police raid."

Mr. Kennedy laughed. "Instead, you got raided by the federal government."

Mom laughed. "Ha! You're right. I guess I won't be arrested if you're paying me. I need to see that first paycheck."

Katie chuckled. "This is too good to pass up. I wanted to try this." She took a napkin and tore it into pieces. She wrote on a piece. I peered to see her words. "To Yolanda Murphy November 1st, 2030. Twelve Thousand dollars. Catherine Garcia, Secretary of Magic."

Katie smirked, like she doing a trick. "Become a real government paycheck!"

The napkin changed in her hands into a real check, with fancy writing and paper. Katie handed it to Mom.

Mom looked close to passing out. She held the check in her hands, staring at it. "I've never had so much money at once," she whispered.

"Now for you and Shirley, Phil."

"Hey! We don't need the money right now!" He put up his hands, like he was pushing against a door.

"Yes we do!" Mrs. Kennedy contradicted.

Katie laughed again. "This is fun. You'll help me out. I'm supposed to fill my staff as quickly as possible—president's orders. I've got a huge budget, and this won't hurt it. Think of it as your tax dollars at work."

She made checks for Phil and Shirley too. It felt odd to call adults by their first name, but we were working together. And I guess they were friends.

“What a night!” Phil smiled at his check.

“And I haven’t even eaten yet. Do you have any stew left?”

“A whole pot full, Katie.” Shirley served her a bowl.

“Delicious. I’ll need this to help you move your furniture back in, Dak.”

“Uh, thanks.”

“Uh, I guess you can,” Mom said. “You know the house isn’t ours.”

“You’re just squatting in it?” Katie tilted her head.

“Yeah. It was for sale, and no one had bought it in a year. So Dak changed the sign to *sold* and we moved in.”

“Now you can buy it. That check’ll be enough for a down payment.”

“I don’t know anything about buying a house.”

“I can help you,” Phil said. “It’s the least I can do for a coworker.”

“Thank you, Phil.”

“Thank you for the stew, Shirley. It was magical.” Katie grinned.

* * *

After helping Dak move their furniture back from another house for sale, I went to my new home in DC. They had put in a sofa and bed for me, but I used my new teleportation skills to move all my stuff from Oakridge to DC. After arranging everything, I sat back with a cup of hot cocoa and took out Caddie. Something bothered me about Sean.

“Hey, Caddie. What’s up with Sean? He turned beet red when I complimented him.” I pulled the string.

Her eyes snapped open and locked on me. “You dummy! He’s in love with you and thinks he always will be! I’ve got more.”

Zip! “He thinks about you every night and pursued the Murphys to impress you.” She stopped but kept her eyes open.

“What do I do? I like him like a little brother.” Out came the string.

“Tell him the truth. Just tell him what you told me. He’ll live, and he’ll find someone his own age.” Her eyes snapped shut.

I sighed. I *was* lonely. It'd be nice to have someone who loved me and who I loved. But I had to do my duty. I couldn't lead Sean, who wasn't even a teenager yet, on. I wouldn't want someone to do that to my little brother if I had one.

I tried to remember when I was twelve. Did I have any crushes on anyone? Soccer stars were cool to look at and dream about, but I'd known it wasn't real. The boys I liked best at school were smart, but none of them were as smart as I was. We were more friends and competitors than anything.

No. I was too different for anyone to love me. Until now. And he was eighteen years younger than me. I had to laugh at the irony.

I put "talk to Sean" on my to-do list.

Chapter 46 – Home

Sunday, November 7

Boy, was it great to be home! I ran around the backyard smelling my favorite scents. I took Master for a long run, and then we went to bed. I fell asleep on my bed, to the smell of Master and his breathing.

The next morning Master said, "That visit to New York was fun. We were invited back next week. They're paying for our flight, thanks to the taxpayers of New York. Darrell said he'll have some magical stuff for us to do to justify our salaries."

"Master, what's a week?"

He laughed. "Seven days. See, here's a calendar. Paper calendars are old-fashioned, but I like to keep one on the fridge so I can see what's coming each morning. Here we are on the eighth." He pointed to a square with an "8." A week later is Monday, the fifteenth."

He pointed to another square. "Each square is a day."

"You humans think of the craziest stuff."

He laughed again. I like making Master laugh. "Let's grab breakfast and go into my gym, see how things are going."

We gobbled bacon and eggs and toast. I got to eat at the table. Master was teaching me table manners. I had to eat off the plate with neat, little bites and no drooling. He showed me how to use a napkin to wipe away drool. He said I was better than some people.

"I'm going to work out this morning," he said when we were inside the gym. "It's been too long. First, a hundred burpees."

Master threw himself onto the ground and then jumped up, again and again. I crouched down and jumped up with him. Fun! The other people laughed. I laughed with them, with my tongue out.

"Now, a hundred snatches." Master grabbed a bar and lifted it over his head, then dropped it down.

I copied him. I grabbed a dumbbell in my mouth, jumped up, and then dropped it. Fun too!

"Hello, is Josh Garrison in here?" I heard a woman call at the big door to the gym. Master kept it open.

I saw a human female in a jacket at the door.

"Yeah, I'm Josh Garrison. Do you want to join HossFit?"

"Uh, no." She stared at him. Maybe she smelled him, like I did. Master was all sweaty, which always made his scent stronger. His fur on top was wet and curly, like a poodle in the rain.

"Katie Garcia, the US Secretary of Magic." She held up an identification. "We need to talk. Is there someplace private where we can speak?"

I looked around. The other men and women there had stopped their workouts and were watching.

"Sure, Katie. Let's go in the office."

I followed them. Maybe I'd find out what "private" meant!

"Have a seat." Master plopped into his chair. In the office, he smelled stronger. I wagged my tail.

"Thanks." Katie pushed her hood back. Her head fur was smooth and shiny, sort of like Faith's. I liked it.

She took a breath. "I'm going around the country looking for strong magicians. You and your dog are very strong. I saw you two on Jimmy Fellon's show. I'd like to talk about the spells you used on Spot."

She took out her phone. "I took magic readings on you and Spot. He has 'Understand English' and 'Speak English aloud,' which you cast. His own spells are 'Make Master Understand Me' and 'Make Master Love Me.' He's a 1400-level mage, and you're at 1550, pretty close to where I am."

"That's so cool! I just wished for him to understand me." Master looked from Katie to me.

"And I just wished Master could understand me!" I put in. "Of course I want him to love me."

"I also see you used 'Read English' and 'Type English' on Spot."

"And he's going to get me a big keyboard, like Faith's." I wagged furiously, remembering the good times we'd had cruising the internet.

"Ah, the dog of the mayor of New York, Darrell Duncan. That Faith?"

"Yup. They're both magical too."

Katie sighed and punched at her phone with her thumbs. "That's where I'm going next."

"So how do talking dogs help the federal government's magical department?" Master stared at her.

My tail stopped wagging. Was he interested in her? I felt he was, but I couldn't smell anything yet.

"That's why I'm here. I have to recruit a magical army for the United States as soon as possible, if not sooner."

Master laughed. "I'm a fair shot with a deer rifle, but I've never been in the military."

"It's your magic that matters. I can see thousands of uses for talking, intelligent animals like Spot."

"Hey! I'm not an animal! I'm a dog. And a beagle at that!" I had to defend my breed.

Both Katie and Master laughed. She gave me a big smile. "Right, Spot. A dog is a member of the family. We had one when I was a kid, a Pomeranian."

Huh. How disappointing it wasn't a beagle or golden retriever. I caught her scent. Nice. Soap and body odor. I wagged.

"So are you a recruiter for the Secretary of Magic?" Master asked. He was back to staring at her.

Katie laughed. "You bet. I am the Secretary of Magic and my own recruiter. I just hired my first employees yesterday."

Master's mouth opened, like he was running hard. "Uh, I'm sorry I'm not properly dressed."

He smelt nervous. I wondered why.

Katie smiled. "You're dressed properly for working out. I'm the one who dropped in on you. I expected to see sweaty men at a HossFit gym. But not with the cold November air pouring in, and not in shorts and a T-shirt when it's in the thirties."

"No one minds the cold when you're working out. Anyway, how can I help you, Ms. Secretary, er Garcia?"

"You can call me Katie. I need strong mages right away to work with the military to teach them magic. Can I count on you?"

"Uh, yes? What exactly will I do?"

"Teach them how you taught Spot to talk. We've got over

three thousand horses in the army. If they were all smart and talking like Spot, they'd be a formidable force. Then there's the K-9 corps. We have thousands of dogs serving there."

"Wow. I never thought of that."

"That's not surprising. I just thought of that as I learned of Spot's abilities and intelligence." She paused, with her brows down. "You could do more too, with magic. Have you thought of giving him opposable thumbs?"

"Uh, no?"

I looked at my paws. How would that even work?

"Let's see what happens. Spot, have opposable thumbs on your paws!" Katie commanded.

My paws tingled. My dew claws grew until they touched the ground like my other toes, and then wrapped around the inside of my paws. I stared at them. They felt weird. I sat and picked up one paw. My dew claw crossed neatly against my paw. I could grip pretty hard with it.

"What do you think, Spot? Want me to undo it?" Katie's eyes twinkled at me.

"Let me test this out." I opened the office door with my paw. It was so easy compared to using my mouth. I ran around the gym as fast as I could. Then I jumped for the rope hanging in the corner. I had never dreamed I could climb it. I grabbed it with my mouth and put my feet on it. They gripped it naturally. I opened my mouth and hung on with my feet. Slowly I climbed, foot over foot. My hind feet had opposable thumbs too. I went faster until I reached the top. This was fun!

I turned around and went down headfirst. I jumped at Katie, grabbed her around the neck, and licked her face. "Thanks so much! This is great!"

Master laughed his head off. So did Katie.

We went back to the office. Master gave me a toy to play with, a fidget spinner, to practice using my thumbs. More fun!

My ears pricked when I heard Katie say, "Faith, Faith, Faith . . . Josh, do you know the mayor of New York is a criminal?"

"What? No! We just spent last week with him. He seemed to be a nice guy."

"Yes. His crimes were stealing and magically compelling voters to vote for him—or not. I'd say he'd get off if it went to trial. I need to see him next. Would you come with me?"

Master stared at her. "Uh, sure. They said we can come back anytime. Spot, are you ready for another airplane ride?"

I was so excited I barked. "You bet!"

Katie laughed. "We won't be going by anything as slow as an airplane."

"What do you mean?"

"I stopped by your house before I came to your gym. Let's go to your house so you can wash and pack." Katie put her backpack on, while Master put on his coat. He scrunched his face, as if trying to understand something.

"Good. Now, grab my hands." She held her hands out to Josh.

"Gladly!"

"Spot, jump into our arms."

I jumped, and settled into the little nest they'd made. "This is great."

Pop!

We were on the front porch of our house.

"Whoa! I didn't know you could do that!" Josh unlocked the door. "C'mon in."

"I didn't know about teleportation until about a week ago."

"I'll be done in a jiffy. Spot, entertain Katie." Master went into the bathroom with fresh clothing.

"Hi, Spot. Are you excited to see New York again?"

"Yes! There are so many smells there. But my favorite is my friend Faith. She's the only other magical dog I know. Wait until she sees my thumbs!" I held up my paws and wriggled my thumbs.

She laughed. "I wonder where we have to go to meet Duncan and Faith? I've been to New York before, but we'll have to zoom in to wherever they are."

"We were in their apartment a lot."

"I'll ask Caddie." She pulled a box out of her backpack. I smelled cardboard and plastic.

Katie took out a doll. "Where can we meet Duncan and Faith?" She pulled a string on the back.

The doll's eyes opened, looked at me, and then swung back to Katie. "You're going to the dogs! The magical dogs. Go to the mayor's office." She stopped. Katie pulled again.

"They're in there. They'll be free in less than an hour. Curb your dog!" The eyes snapped shut.

"Who was that? I heard someone's voice." Josh came out, drying his hair. He was in a button-down shirt and fresh slacks.

"Just my talking doll, Caddie. She told me Duncan and Faith were in the mayor's office." Katie played with her phone. "I can teleport us within a couple of blocks. Do you want to go for a walk in New York City?"

"Sure! I can't think of anything better!" Master grinned. "Let me pack my backpack with some things for me and Spot." He plopped a backpack onto his bed and tossed in a few items—including a few treats for me!

"Let's go, then." Katie and Master linked hands again. "Spot, hop on."

"Whee!" I jumped up.

Pop!

"Here we are at Washington Square. Let's go." Katie set me down.

"Mind if I hold your hand? I don't want us to get separated in the crowd." Master took her hand.

She smiled at him.

I ran around them and dodged people on the sidewalk.

We came to a big lawn around a building, which we entered.

"Hi. We're to see Mayor Duncan," Master said to the lady at a desk.

"Do you have an appointment?"

"No, but we're his special assistants. We have an important visitor from the federal government. Tell them Josh and Spot are here."

"Very well." She spoke into her headset and then said, "You can go in now."

"Hi, Josh, Spot! I didn't expect to see you so soon!" Darrell stood and looked in our direction with his blue sunglasses. "Can you introduce me to this young lady?"

"Sure. Darrell, this is the Secretary of Magic, Ms. Katie Garcia. Katie, this is Darrell Duncan, Mayor of New York."

And his dog assistant, Faith. Faith wagged her tail at all of us, giving me a big dog smile.

"Mayor Duncan, I'm pleased to meet you and your telepathic dog, Faith." Katie shook his hand, petted Faith's head, and looked at her phone. "You two are powerful mages too. I'm here to learn about your magic and see how you can help the US Armed Forces become magical."

"I'll be glad to help my country in any way I can. Of course, my first responsibility is to the great city of New York."

"Of course. You and Faith can begin by training the police horses and dogs to magically talk like Faith."

He paused and held his chin. "I suppose we can do that. Faith? Can you teach horses and dogs to talk?"

I don't see why not. I used magic to talk to you.

And I used magic to talk to my master too! I wagged my tail.

"Hey, Spot! I didn't know you could still talk telepathically," Master said.

Faith and I did that last time we were here.

"I'm delighted to have you aboard, Mayor Duncan. Please sign here. I'm employing you as my assistants in New York." Katie held out a paper form. Master and I had already signed one.

"I'm not sure if I can commit to another job. Being mayor is full-time work."

"I understand. However, your salary will start at two hundred thousand per year, and I'll see that the president issues you a pardon for any past crimes you may have committed. It'd be political suicide if anything came to light."

"Ah-ah-ah. I'm not aware of anything . . ." Darrell spoke slowly.

"But I am. There is a pending investigation into a possible theft from Amazin'."

"But there's no evidence—of anything."

"Yes, at this time. However, magical investigations are progressing rapidly, and who knows where they may lead?"

"I believe I am moved to serve my country as well as the city of New York." He signed the paper.

"Faith, you can sign too. Do you want opposable thumbs, like Spot?"

"Look what I can do!" I grabbed the pen and wrote "Spot"

on the back of the form.

Fantastic! Yes, opposable thumbs, and show me where to sign.

"You've got them, Faith! Here's a pen." Katie handed a pen to Faith, who grabbed it for the first time with her new thumb. "Officially, you're the assistant to New York Magical Recruiter Darrell Duncan."

"Say, does Faith get paid by the feds?" Darrell's sunglasses glinted blue as he turned his head toward Katie.

"Of course. I have to use up my employee budget. I'll put you in for a pardon with President Lopez, Mayor Duncan. You're probably innocent anyway, so you won't care if I put a geas on you so that you can't steal anymore?"

"A geas?"

"Yes, like this: 'Darrell Duncan and his dog, Faith, will no longer steal from anyone.' I'll feel much better about asking President Lopez for a pardon now."

"I'm under a geas? I didn't feel anything."

"Right. Only if you try to steal will it come into effect. That's one of the spells I've learned from other magicians. Now, let's go through your spells. Tell me about your campaign ads."

* * *

After reciting stories about magic, we finally got to see the police dogs and horses. Faith and I had no trouble talking with them. With a small wish, each of them could speak to humans. That made Master, Katie, and Mayor Duncan happy.

"Wow, Katie," Master said as we left the mayor and Faith. "You really took charge. In one day, hundreds of dogs and horses are talking."

"And a lot of them went for the opposable thumbs!" I put in. The horses were especially funny: Their hooves split into two, which they could use to grip.

"It was a good day's work. Thank you for your help, Josh, Spot. But the reward for a good day of work is . . . more work. President Lopez has ordered me to meet with Ambassador Squee, the dolphin representative, at the East River at the United Nations. Right now."

"Oh. I don't know if I can help you with that ambassador

stuff. Although, I do like dolphins."

"Perhaps you can come as my support staff?" Katie looked at Master.

"I'd be glad to come!"

I'd never met or smelled a dolphin before. What did they smell like?

Chapter 47 – Drafted

Monday, November 8

“Whee! Catch me if you can, Grandma.”

I chased Oliver in his sporty flying car. He had two narrow wings and a split tail, like a swallow. He flew fast, but I had more magic. I poured it into my old green sedan. The buzzing wings increased in pitch until I zipped past him, under the bridge we used to mark the end of our race.

“Gotcha!” I yelled, magically enhancing my voice so he heard me.

“You cheated!”

“She won fair and square, Oliver,” put in my granddaughter, Violet. “It’s your own fault for not using more magic.”

“I used all I had! Nobody has as much magic as Grandma.”

“You might be right. Grandma, do you know anyone with as much magic as you have?”

We flew in formation back to my home in Paradise. We’d bought several cars to expand our flying-car service to Arizona. I had a great time flying them with my children and grandchildren while taking a break from actually running our business. Fawn Goodspell was making money hand over fist back in Cleveland, so there was no urgency to go back.

I thought about my magic. “A lot of people have as much as I do, or more. Sprong, Blodgett, and Whifflehammer, Katie Garcia, and that bad guy Hugo Lamacek.”

“I’d like to meet some other powerful magicians,” Oliver said.

“It looks like you got your wish. There’s Katie.”

We landed on my driveway, and there was Katie with a tall, muscular guy with wild curly hair, and a beagle, barking excitedly.

“Hi, Katie. Who are your friends?”

“This is Josh Garrison. He’s my new assistant.” She smiled like she had a secret joke. “And this is Spot, his talking dog.”

"Hi, everyone! Sorry to bark, but I always do that when I'm excited. Oh wow, are these your children?" He wagged furiously as he raced between Violet and Oliver, getting petted by each one.

"Grandchildren, Spot. Didn't I see you on Jimmy Fellon's show?"

"Yeah, that's when I started talking. Of course, I can also do telepathy." *Like this. I can talk and bark at the same time!* Spot barked to prove his point.

We all laughed. I introduced Violet and Oliver to Josh. I noticed the way Katie and Josh stood next to each other—they seemed to be an item.

"Let's go in and have some coffee and cookies."

I had wished the coffeepot to be full and hot. I'd timed the cookies to be done by the time we got home, so they were fresh from the oven. Baking cookies by magic was the bomb.

"Jeff and Megan are in Phoenix setting up a branch office for Flight 216. What can I do for you?" I munched on a warm, soft chocolate chip cookie and took a slurp of my creamy coffee.

Katie swallowed her cookie. "Funny you should ask. You may have heard I'm the Secretary of Magic."

"Yes. It's all over the news. I just watched you sign the dolphin peace treaty with the Secretary of State last night."

"That was fun! Did you know dolphins smell like fish?" Spot said.

"Uh no, but I might have guessed."

"The dolphins made me the animal ambassador plenipotentiary to the dolphin nations," Spot said.

"What's 'plenipotentiary'?" Oliver asked.

"It's something like 'all the power of our nation is vested in me.'" Spot wagged his tail.

"The story behind the story is that we're gathering all our magicians and cross-training them as quickly as possible. We're trying to militarize our magic. There's a real danger of a magical war coming," Katie said.

"You wouldn't need magical flying cars, would you?" I had a hunch they did.

"Yes, as a matter of fact. And flying tanks, and anything else you can think of. Can you take a break from your business and help me out, and our country?"

"Of course. Anything for my country."

"Wow. Can we help?" Violet put in. "Maybe a junior magicians league?"

"Definitely. I already have young people helping me." Katie took out her phone, pointed it at my grandchildren, then at me. "Yes, you'll do great. You're much stronger than you used to be, Angie. And your grandchildren take after you. How would you all like to train military personnel to fly their tanks and personnel carriers? This'll help our logistics division."

"Seems easy. We've already done that with vans in Cleveland," Oliver said.

"Right. And I've got something to teach you." Katie disappeared with a pop, then Josh, and finally Spot. Then they walked in the front door, again. "Here's how you teleport," Katie began.

* * *

The Previous Day—Sunday, November 7

Welcome, Director Hezekiah Fountaine.

Squee danced on his tail before me in the East River, next to the UN. "Hello, Ambassador Squee. Welcome to New York. I'm glad you made your long journey safely."

It's always delightful to go on a long migration and see the sights of the Key Nation, the Caribbean nation, and the Atlantic nation. In a large pod or group there is little danger.

"How will the negotiations for the peace treaty go, with us on land and your people in the water?"

The negotiations are already going well. Each cetacean ambassador has been talking to your UN ambassadors in the General Assembly and deciding who should work with whom. For your nation, I have you as my human contact, and Spot will be your nation's official ambassador."

"What? Spot the famous talking dog? I don't think we can have animal ambassadors."

Don't worry. We need animals to represent you because they don't lie like humans do. We can cross-check the human ambassadors' veracity.

"Oh. I guess that makes sense. Only, our ambassadors have to be chosen by our country. I can't just be appointed as one."

We have already been in contact with President Lopez about you, and he agreed to appoint you as ambassador to the cetacean nations.

"That's news to me—" My phone rang. It was the White House.

"Hello? Professor Fountaine here."

"Hello, Professor Fountaine. I am President José Lopez. I'd like to ask you if you'd be willing to represent the United States to the cetacean nations? I have sent you the complete job description."

"Uh, yes? Mr. President, my job at the Dolphin Research Center has demands, but I believe I can distribute them to my staff."

"I'm sure you can. Let me thank you for all your great work at the Dolphin Research Center. You've started the United States off on the right foot with the dolphin nations, and also humanity."

"Thank you, Mr. President."

"Is our other ambassador, Spot Garrison, with you?"

"Uh, no. I don't know where he is."

I'll get him for you, Ambassador Fountaine. Squee swam backward on his tail, chittering.

"Just coordinate everything you do with him. The cetacean nations require that as part of our treaty. I've got to run now. Goodbye!"

The president hung up.

Pop! A beagle appeared before me. "Hi! You must be Ambassador Fountaine! I'm so glad to smell you!" Spot nuzzled and licked my hand while wagging furiously.

"I'm sorry. I'm just not sure how to work with you, Spot."

"It's no big deal! Just discuss your human business with the dolphins, and I'll relay my thoughts as well." *Do you know I can talk telepathically too? Just like the dolphins!*

"Oookay." I felt disoriented. I kind of knew what was coming, but dealing with dolphins—and dogs—had not turned out as I'd expected. The dolphins were taking charge, and humanity seemed to be dragged along in their wake.

That's a beautiful metaphor, Ambassador Fontaine. I've relayed it to my people. I'm sure our poets and song composers will use it. Dolphins have ridden the bow waves of human ships for thousands of years, and now humans are riding the wake of dolphin nations.

The feeling through Squee's telepathy was satisfaction and joy at learning.

"I didn't pack all my clothing, just a week's worth."

That is no problem. Our meeting with the UN and the ambassadors should be done by today or tomorrow.

"That's not my impression of the UN. They don't decide anything that quickly."

However, we cetaceans do. We've already hammered out a self-defense treaty with humanity. We just need your signature to make it unanimous.

"I just got here! Where do I get to read a copy?"

Just go inside the UN and go to the Cetacean Room. That's where all the human and animal ambassadors are. That's where the US copy of the treaty is.

I walked inside, somewhat dazed. I followed the signs pointing toward the "Cetacean Nations Meeting." Walking into a room filled with the hubbub of parrots squawking, dogs barking, lions roaring, and apes beating their chests did nothing to make me feel normal.

"Where do I go?" I said, half to myself.

Go to the table with the US flag, Squee said.

I found it, with a nice conference table, like the other two hundred tables in the room. Spot waited for me, sitting on a chair.

It's great to see you again, Hezekiah! Do you mind if I call you Hezekiah? We're partners! Spot said enthusiastically while he wagged his tail at his seat.

"No, but most of my friends call me 'Zeke.'"

Oh, that's cool. It's so much easier using telepathy in a noisy room like this. I'd have to bark my head off to make myself heard. Not that I'd mind. Here's your copy of the treaty. I already signed mine. Spot put his foot on a treaty with his pawprint on it and a scrawl that might have been "Spot."

He must have seen me staring at his signature, for he transmitted, *I'm still learning to write with my opposable thumb. I'll have to teach you how to teleport when we're done here.*

Amazing. The treaty was just one page long.

> 1. All human nations and cetacean nations agree to stop killing one another.
>
> 2. Should two nations go to war, either human or cetacean, both human and cetacean nations agree to defend the nation that was attacked.
>
> 3. All cetaceans and humans will cooperate on magical research, sharing our knowledge equally among the various species:
>
> a.human
> b.dolphins and porpoises and killer whales
> c.pilot whales
> d.orcas
> e.narwhals
> f.sperm whales
> g.humpback whales
> h.sperm whales
> i.beluga whales
> j.beaked whales
> k.blue whales
> l.gray whales
> m.Bryde's whales
> n.fin whales
> o.minke whales
> p.Omura whales
> q.sei whales
> r.bowhead whales
> s.right whales

Signatories:

There followed the one hundred and ninety-three member states, then the nineteen cetacean species—each signed with a miniature fluke outline. The UN observer states came at the end.

For each state there was a place for a human signature and the animal ambassador.

"This is so simple!" I exclaimed. "I'm the last one to sign?"

You bet. You're the last one here.

"And every nation has agreed to this?"

Each ambassador and nonhuman ambassador has signed. Now, the human nations themselves are still arguing in the UN over this and have not brought it to vote. But we trust our human ambassadors to be advocates for us with their heads of state.

"Squee? You can still communicate from the East River to here?"

Easily. The range of our telepathy is roughly the curvature of Earth's horizon, perhaps twenty-five miles. Of course, we relay our messages around the world using Dolphin Net.

"Of course." I signed the document. There didn't seem to be anything the president or the US would object to.

A large silverback gorilla wandered over.

I am Ambassador Ukuri from the United Kingdom. Let me take your signed copy and scan it into the UN computer network.

"Certainly." Although I was taller than the enormous simian, he was more than double my girth. "How did a gorilla come to represent the UK?"

Most of my life was in a zoo in London. My mate and offspring are there. And I made friends among the humans.

"I made friends among the dolphins."

Yes. That's why they selected you as their ambassador. With their telepathy, they know which people are best to represent humanity to them.

"Wait. Dolphins selected all the ambassadors?"

Ukuri handed the treaty back to me. His dark-brown eyes looked into mine. He gave a soft hoot of amusement. *Of course. They couldn't leave this to humans. Most humans would argue for days and then pick a bad ambassador. Same with us nonhumans.*

"Spot? You were selected by the dolphins?"

Sure. It sounded like fun, and Master thought it'd be a good learning experience for both of us. Now, let me teach you how to teleport. We're just about done here.

Chapter 48 - Preparation

Tuesday, November 9

Where was I this morning? I'd been traveling so much that I'd lost track of where I'd fallen asleep last night. I felt well rested and curiously peaceful. I heard birds chirping outside. I knew I wasn't in Oakridge or Washington, DC. It felt like a spring day.

I reviewed yesterday's events. Josh and Spot and Darrell and Faith. It was a day for the dogs. And dolphins at the UN. Ah! Then we'd teleported across the country to Arizona. That was interesting. I hadn't been to her home in Paradise before, so I'd teleported with Josh and Spot by line of sight to the horizon. In about a hundred pops, we got there. Since then, Josh had practiced teleporting, and so had Spot.

That was fun. Now I knew where I was and why I felt so rested. Angie had insisted we stay at her house. I opened my eyes and saw the native stonework in the bedroom.

I felt peaceful because I wasn't lonely. Josh and Spot were good company. They were not anyone I would have befriended willingly, but we clicked. Josh was easygoing, and Spot was relentlessly positive. They were just what I needed.

But today was another busy day. I had a military meeting with the Joint Chiefs of Staff. I looked at the clock: 6:13 a.m. Arizona time, which was 8:13 a.m. DC time, as Arizona was on Mountain time until March. I had forty-seven minutes to get there.

I'd showered last night, so I just needed to dress and get a bite to eat. I had an outline of what I wanted to do in the military, some of which was underway. At least, Darrell and Faith were training the NYC National Guard and police dogs and horses. Angie and the kids were going to give the army vehicles wings. Sean and his friend Dak were training their parents to teleport. They'd then be able to teach every soldier, sailor, and pilot. I was using the "train the trainer" concept.

I had already involved DC power engineers to tap into the ambient magic and use it to create physical and magical shields.

I'd ensure the military learned the magical technology.

I dressed in my navy coat and skirt, with my red blouse. I could smell the coffee in the kitchen. Soon I sipped it while I wolfed down a pile of fresh, fluffy pancakes and maple syrup.

Josh and Spot had split a huge cheese omelet with nearly a pound of bacon. "You hungry this morning, Katie?" Josh asked around a mouthful of eggs.

Spot had already wolfed his portion.

"Yes. I had a busy day yesterday, and another one today."

"Where are we going?"

I stopped. I hadn't considered how Josh and Spot would fit into my day. "Washington, DC. I've got a Joint Chiefs of Staff meeting. Could you train the DC National Guard K-9 corps?" I improvised to fit them in. I hated improvising.

"Sure." Josh nodded.

"It's so much fun talking to new dogs!" Spot barked.

My secure phone rang. "Yes, Mr. President?"

"Hi, Katie. Please stop by my office fifteen minutes before the Joint Chiefs of Staff meeting."

"Uh, yes, sir." It was 7:35. I had ten minutes to get there. "Anything else?"

"No. We'll discuss some things in person."

"Wow, the president called you?" Spot's tail wagged.

"Yeah. I've got to leave in ten minutes."

"Let's finish up then, Spot."

"This will have to be private with the president."

"That's fine. I looked up the National Guard headquarters in DC. Spot and I will teleport ourselves there and search out the army horses and dogs. Where will you be?"

"I'll be in the Pentagon."

"Okay. I'm ready. How about you, Spot?"

"I was born ready!" He wagged his tail.

Josh reached out his hand. I grabbed it, and Spot put his paw on it, gripping it with his new thumb.

"Angie, I've got to run! Thanks for everything!" I yelled to the kitchen.

"Bye! We'll go around to the army bases you gave us," she called back.

Pop!

We appeared outside the Oval Office. The Secret Service agent focused on Josh and Spot.

"The president is expecting you, Secretary Garcia. I'm sorry, but your companions will have to leave here."

"We were just going."

Another agent came from inside the office. He nodded at the first agent. Then he firmly grabbed Josh's shoulder and Spot's collar.

"Indeed we are leaving." The three popped out.

"Oh, they're part of my staff."

"I will tell Jed when he comes back. He'll get them security badges. You may enter, Ms. Garcia. The president is expecting you."

"Hi, Katie," the president said as I sat in front of his desk. "I'll be brief. I know you have the Joint Chiefs of Staff meeting in ten minutes. I've read your reports. I'm delighted with your progress, but we still must accelerate our magical education. Take the Joint Chiefs of Staff and train them in everything you know."

"Everything? That'll take the whole day just to demonstrate it. Then they'll have to practice for days."

"Right. Those are my current orders to them. They must be knowledgeable so they can train their subordinates, and so on down the hierarchy. That's the fastest way to train our whole military."

"Magic is dangerous. If people learn incorrectly, they may kill others or themselves."

"Right. Military training pushes the envelope. Do what you can for safety, but don't sacrifice speed. Speaking of which, it's time for you to go."

President Lopez stood and beamed at me with his thousand-watt smile. "I'm so glad to have you as my Secretary of Magic! You're everything I wished for." He shook my hand. "Now, shoo!"

* * *

Even though I wore my best suit, I felt a little underdressed, seeing the men and women chiefs in their uniforms. I was nervous but took a deep breath. "For our first hour, we'll cover the basics of magical wishes. After a break, I'll teach you teleportation. Then we'll create magical shields. After that, we'll cover magical attacks. We'll animate things—cars, tanks, rifles, and guns—and give them wings and fly. We'll close with magical reconnaissance." That was an inspired word choice on my part. I knew magical prophesying and fortune-telling would not be received well.

We teleported to the National Guard after lunch to practice animating objects. But I made a slight change in schedule.

We stopped by the horse barns for the army, where Josh was. He stood just outside the barn.

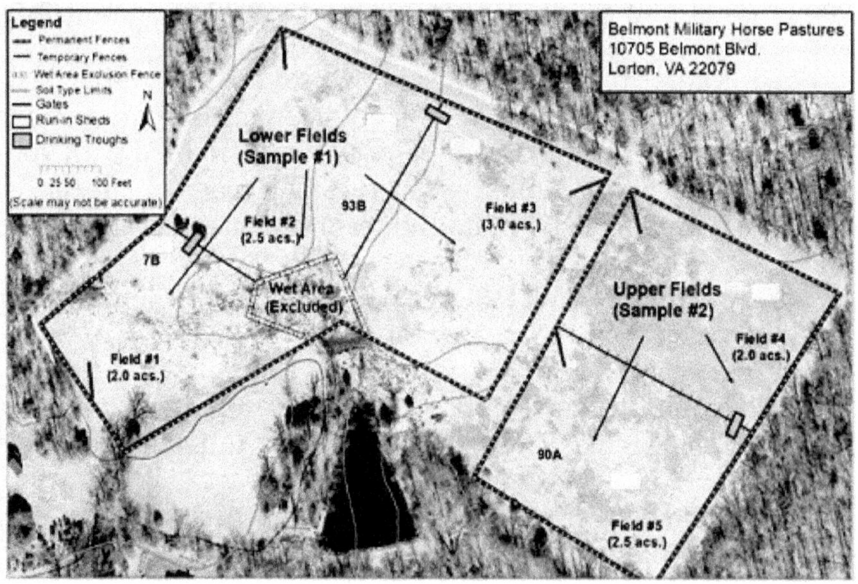

"Hi, Josh. Our schedules collided."

"Hi, Katie. Wow, you brought the big brass!" He gestured to the Joint Chiefs of Staff behind me, who were still in their uniforms.

"Right. Gentlemen, this is Josh Garrison, my assistant for magical training of animals."

Pop! "Hi! Am I too late for fun? Look at all these new people!" Spot ran around smelling the chiefs and getting petted by them.

"Katie, you brought me new friends!"

"Gentlemen, this is Spot, Josh's magical dog. Josh, why

don't you show the Joint Chiefs of Staff what you've been training?"

"We've actually made way more progress than I expected. All the soldiers already had good bonds with their horses. The horses were way smarter than anyone knew." He petted the neck of the horse in the paddock nearest him.

"Troop, assemble!" Josh called.

I could tell by the echo in my chest this was not an ordinary yell. I checked Josh's magic: "Call troop to order—1312 MUs."

Like popcorn, thirty horses and their riders assembled before us, popping into existence from somewhere else.

"Roll call!" Josh ordered.

"PFC Phillips!"

"Horse: Trusty."

"PFC Samson!"

"Horse: Red."

And so all thirty riders and their horses called out their names.

"Now watch this." Josh grinned, like he intended to pull a prank on us.

"Troop, take flight!"

The horses sprouted wings and took off, flying in circles around us. The wind from their wings blew the dust of the parade ground around us.

"Troop, land!" The horses and their riders landed.

"Troop, dragoon formation!" The riders rapidly dismounted, sliding down the horses' necks while unshouldering their rifles. They knelt in formation and aimed at targets across the fairground.

"Horses, take flight!" The horses took off again toward the targets.

"Take down targets one through four."

A quarter of the troop aimed at each target and fired. A quarter of the horses landed and trampled each target.

"Troop, assemble!"

The horses teleported back to their riders, who teleported to the saddles.

"Wow!" I gasped. So did the chiefs. "It looks like cavalry may make a comeback."

"Wait! Don't forget us!" Spot gestured with his opposable dew claw as dozens of dogs appeared.

"We can surround someone"—Spot pointed to Josh, and they teleported around him—"or we can pull out our weapons." Spot took a pistol from his working-dog vest and pointed it upward. Each dog did the same.

"This revolutionizes warfare. Even with all you've taught us, Katie, we've only just begun." General Wilbur Slimak, the chairman of the Joint Chiefs, told me.

"You're right, General Slimak. But I need time just to plan out what should be taught and how."

"Correct. And I need time to digest what I've learned and how to integrate it into tactics for attack and defense."

"I also need time to research what I don't know—which is a lot."

He chuckled. "We're all in that boat."

"I've got one last lesson for everyone. Please gather around me." I amplified my voice so all could hear me on the large field. People, dogs, and horses arranged themselves into three neat pie pieces.

I floated upward so all could see me. "Here is how you do reconnaissance with magic." I took out Caddie from her box and pulled her string. "Where are the Chinese mages most likely to attack?"

Her eyes opened and looked around. "You've got quite the crowd here. The answer is *Guam*!"

A collective gasp came from the crowd. Horses whinnied and neighed. Dogs howled.

"That's a US territory!" General Sylvester shouted.

I'd never pulled Caddie's cord so fast. "When? When will the attack come?"

Caddie looked right at me. "They're attacking as we speak. Wake Island next. And then Hawaii."

* * *

"Report!" I commanded my three generals, looking back at me in my magic mirror. "You first, Wa Mingze. What have you learned from Guam, Wake, and Hawaii?"

"As you wish, Emperor Liu. Guam has some local mages

who heal the people and help the crops and fishing. They are not militarily focused. We should be able to take the island with our Dragon Force."

"And Wake Island?"

"They have a few hundred military personnel, no magic. We'll be able to take this island after we secure Guam."

"And Hawaii?"

"We can capture six of the seven islands. Like Guam, they have local mages and are not focused on military matters. However, Oahu has four active volcanoes and four mages who control each of them. We need a method to take control of those mages. They are more powerful than I am. I could not hide from them."

"Did they interrogate you or learn anything from you?" I didn't like surprises like this.

"No, Emperor Liu. As soon as they detected me, I fled into the ocean and swam away."

"Mmmm." I was suspicious. They might have learned something. But perhaps we could move before expected.

"General Mùchén, can your forces conquer the islands, given this intelligence?"

"I feel comfortable about Guam, Wake, and six of the Hawaiian Islands. I must research how to conquer these volcano mages."

"Mage Yihan, what insights do you have?"

Yihan assumed the lotus position, floating in the air. A magical aura surrounded her.

"We will conquer Guam and Wake without problem. We can conquer six of the seven islands of Hawaii if our Imperial Dragon Army is not separated and defeated piecemeal. To defeat the volcano mages, we must train our own mages in volcanic magic."

I grimaced. I had to intervene. I couldn't allow failure.

"General Mùchén, I will train you in a spell by which your Dragon Army will remain inextricably linked. After you learn it to my satisfaction, you will cast it on each of your two hundred dragons."

"Yes, Emperor."

Yihan opened her eyes and looked at me. "I know of no such

spell. I will learn it with General Mùchén. Then I will cast it on the army to *my* satisfaction."

I smiled. I liked assertive subordinates.

* * *

I was nauseous. All the time pressure I'd felt came back down on me tenfold. "We are literally out of time. I will brief the president immediately. General, prepare your forces and teleport the magically capable ones to Hawaii. I will gather my mages and meet you there. One more thing."

I lifted Caddie from my side. I'd held on to her through my astonishment. I addressed her. "Caddie, I will scout the Guam and Wake Island attacks. Where will the Chinese army attack the Hawaiian Islands?"

Her blue eyes opened. "Good idea, scouting. Don't get caught. Kauai will be attacked first."

I turned to the Joint Chiefs of Staff. "Gentlemen, you heard. Kauai is where the attack begins. I will meet you there."

"Secretary Garcia, do you seriously expect us to listen to a doll, even if she is magical?" General Slimak frowned.

"General, I had doubts, as you did. I asked her how she knew things, and she said she tapped the worldwide magical network. There is also the fact she's never been wrong in the dozens of times I've used her. Finally, we have no other intelligence, other than what I'll gather at Guam and Wake.

"I'm off to see the president." I popped off.

* * *

"President Lopez, we have a problem. The Chinese are invading Guam as we speak."

He looked up at me from his desk. "Yes, I was just notified. I'm preparing a draft of a declaration of war to bring to Congress. I assume you and the Joint Chiefs have plans for defending Guam?"

"I plan to scout their attack. Our magical forces are not ready."

The president grimaced. "I'm not surprised. I knew we were behind magically when China first attacked Taiwan. When will we be ready to defend the US?"

"We are preparing our defense for Hawaii now."

"Grrr. We're just yielding American territory without a fight?"

Now I grimaced. "That sounds bad, but it's true. We have some magical forces, but we're ignorant of both tactics and strategy. All the Joint Chiefs are highly motivated to train their forces in magic. We will assemble on Kauai and stop them." I didn't know that, but I felt that.

"Good. Get to work. I've called an emergency session of Congress tonight. I'll address the nation and call on Congress to declare war on China." He chuckled grimly. "I'll probably copy FDR's 'Day of Infamy' speech from World War Two."

* * *

"Josh, we've got to talk." I had teleported back to the training grounds. Spot found me and teleported me to Josh, who was currying a horse in the barn.

"Sure, Katie. Is it about our trip to Guam?"

"Yes. It's extremely dangerous. They'll have at least two hundred mages and their dragons and who knows what else. We have no idea what their spells look like or if our spells can successfully counter them. I want you on Kauai, getting the cavalry and war dogs prepared for the attack."

Josh gritted his teeth. "I don't think I can do that. I can leave Spot in charge of the war dogs."

"You are my subordinate. You have to do what I say."

"Or else? I'm also your friend. At least, I hope I am."

"Yes, you are." My insides roiled. I'd love to have Josh with me. But it'd be harder to hide two of us. Then I thought of Casablanca. I'd rewatched it recently, trying to decompress. I had the perfect line from it.

"Listen, Josh. The problems of two little people don't amount to a hill of beans in this crazy world. The defense of our country *must* come first."

Josh's mouth opened and slowly closed. "I can't argue with you. You're right. And I hate it." With a wry smile, he saluted me. "I'm off to train more cavalry out West. I'd been procrastinating. Spot, here!"

The pop as they disappeared seemed sad.

* * *

I arrived in Guam sometime later. I had been in Hawaii once, at the Honolulu airport on a layover to a conference in Japan. By reviewing my memory with pictures from the internet, I was able to teleport there.

But I still had thirty-eight hundred miles to get to Guam. That'd be about two hundred line-of-sight teleports across the ocean. It was doable but not fun. Hey, Japan was closer to Guam than Hawaii. I remembered Tokyo's airport better than Honolulu's. I'd spent a day shopping at the Tokyo airport.

Japan was only fifteen hundred miles from Guam. That was a mere seventy-five teleports. Focusing on my memory of the airport gate, I teleported.

I wore my sturdy asbestos coveralls I'd used for my pants-on-fire research. The people turned and stared at the crazy American who had magically appeared. Embarrassed, I smiled and waved. Some laughed; some turned away. I walked to the big window overlooking the runway.

The sun was that way. It was seven in the morning. I teleported toward the rising sun in the east.

I continued popping east toward Guam. I floated in the air, perhaps a mile high, to get a better view of the horizon. Seventy-one teleports later, I saw Guam.

Several fires were burning, one over the airbase. From my perspective, I saw specks hovering over the horizon. Zooming in on them with my phone, I could see they were dragons. My readout said, "Dragon Army, animated by Han Mùchén, 2531 MUs. Mage Han Mùchén, 1611 MUs."

Huh. The Dragon Army had more magic than the mage who'd created it. I'd have to figure that out later. I cast an Invisibility spell on myself. Then, to counter any Anti-Magic spells, I transformed my overalls into a ghillie suit, matching the greenery of Guam. I teleported to the edge of the jungle, near the fires.

I saw burning airplanes on an air force base. Glancing at my Guam info packet on my phone, I saw it was Andersen Airforce Base on the northwest corner of Guam.

I felt silly sweating in my ghillie suit while invisible. Then the ground vibrated—and kept vibrating. A red stone dragon walked by, with a bored-looking mage atop it. I had a feeling that if he saw me he'd get unbored quickly. Even though invisible, I didn't move until the mage turned the corner around the perimeter.

I had set my phone on Record after I'd teleported here. I looked at the record. "Stone Dragon 1914 MUs. Mage Feng Haoyu 1448 MUs." Again, the dragon had more magic than the mage. They must accumulate it.

I teleported up a thousand feet and then to the remaining fire. It was the Apra naval base. Several ships were burning.

Huddled under some bushes, I examined my scan of the island. Oh no. There weren't two hundred mages here but over two thousand. Too many to go through by hand. *This is like Pearl Harbor, only worse. They're completely overpowered by thousands of mages*. There was no time for analysis.

I got a handle on their forces, but how could I learn their tactics? It had been only about an hour from Caddie's announcement to now.

I spoke softly to the phone. "Find the closest mage who's aware of the Guam invasion plan."

A local map of Guam appeared. A red circle appeared. There he was, Cai Jun, right here in the port. "Point me to him." An arrow appeared on the screen, pointing to the dock. I saw a small figure directing workers around the pier.

I teleported next to him, put him in an anti-magic shell, grabbed his wrist, and teleported to the Pentagon and into the Joint Chiefs conference room.

"Autotranslate Chinese to English and back," I commanded.

"Hello, Cai Jun. I've captured you and cut off your magic."

"What? How? I didn't know that was possible. Yihan never taught us anything like this!" He was a medium-built man. "I still have my fists!" He swung at me.

"Freeze." His fist stopped a hair from my nose. He was really fast. "I didn't want to do this, but I have to. We're at war. You have a geas on you: You will not escape nor harm any person or property. You will cooperate with me." I felt the magic surge out of me. His eyes widened, but he couldn't talk or move.

"Unfreeze. Yes, I have learned a lot since magic arrived. I

brought you here, but I just thought of a better place. Come with me." I grabbed his hand, and we teleported to Sprong, Blodgett, and Whifflehammer.

Mike teleported in. "Oh. It's you, Katie. We detected a magical surge, and I came immediately." The wand in his hand disappeared.

I raised an eyebrow. "Magical storage for a magical weapon?"

He grinned. "Of course."

Will popped in and then Rick. They visibly relaxed. Their wands vanished too.

"I have to use your magical projector that shows a person's memories. I'll make a copy for the Pentagon. We need it. This, by the way, is Cai Jun."

"Chinese warrior? How appropriate," Rick said as my captive's name was translated in his mind.

"I take it you captured him. But from where?" Will asked.

"From Guam. The Chinese magical army has taken it."

"That's officially the Imperial Dragon Army," Cai Jun said.

"Are you cooperating?" Mike asked.

"I have to. She put a geas on me." Jun pointed at me with his thumb.

"Curiouser and curiouser. I think we need to trade some spells." Rick grinned and tapped his chin.

"But first, let's see what his memories show. Jun, what is your official position?" I looked at him.

He shrugged. "I am the logistics head for the Imperial Dragon Army."

"Ideal. And you were there for the invasion?"

"I was assigned to the third that attacked the Apra Port. Another third went to the air force base, and a third to the capital, Hagatna."

"Thank you. This machine will scan your memories of the invasion. I'd like you to comment on what's happening."

"Of course. It's not like I have any choice." Jun's shoulders slumped.

Mike turned on the memory projector. We saw dragons flying ahead of Jun. He was apparently on a palanquin on the back of a giant swan. The dragons swooped down to the warships and covered them in flame. A few gunner's mates got shots and rockets off, but they bounced off the protective shields.

"Do you know how to create a protective shield like that?" I leaned toward Jun.

"Er, yes, but I'm not as strong as a dragon mage."

"That's fine. I want to see how they're made. I'm removing your magic shield since you're under the geas. Please make your shield now." I had my phone trained on him.

A bubble enclosed him. I read the spell readings aloud: "'Weapon Repulsion: Turn Weapons and Explosions Away. 1266 MUs. Cai Jun is a 1318 mage.'"

"Ha! You fool. Now I'm free of your evil geas."

"I don't think so."

He leapt to strike me, and stopped. "I can't attack you. You're right. Why doesn't this shield repel your weapon?"

"The spell works on your mind. I did it before you cast your shield. I don't consider it a weapon. And finally, I'm more powerful than your shield." I burst his bubble and touched him with a magical finger. It looked like one of those "We're Number 1" foam fingers at sports events.

"Ha! That tickles. I guess you're right again."

"So how many dragons do you have?"

"Two hundred ten came with us in the three attack units. We had twenty-four more for medical and logistics. Plus there are forty-six various giant birds and bats."

"Bats?"

"For night reconnaissance."

We watched the citizens of Guam rounded up and placed in holding pens. A mage came by, cast a spell, and they were released.

"What's going on there? What spell was cast?" I looked at Jun.

"That's a Loyalty spell. The citizens will be as loyal to the emperor as we are. Or were, in my case." He shook his head.

"Did you have such a spell on you?"

"Of course not. I was already sworn to the emperor."

"How many people did you compel to be loyal?" Rick asked.

Jun looked startled. "All of them, of course. We can't have

any rebellion in our conquered territories."

"That's how many?" Rick persisted.

"One hundred sixty-nine thousand," I said with disgust. I had looked up Guam's population before I went there.

"We'll have to figure out how to remove that spell," Will said.

"We will. Let's finish this memory review." I gritted my teeth.

We didn't learn much more. The invasion was way more one sided than Pearl Harbor. Then I asked, "How did you travel so fast from China to Guam? Even teleporting, it took me half an hour."

"Ah. That was the emperor's Speed spell. It was a kind of air shield that enhanced our speed tenfold."

"Can you cast that?"

"No, the emperor has not given me such a great gift."

"Was the spell dispersed when you arrived, or it is still on the dragons and the other flying beasts?"

"I don't think it was. No, the emperor's words were, 'This will add speed to your mounts throughout the invasion.'"

"Ah. Thank you. Jun, obey these men as you must me. I'm going back to Guam." I disappeared.

Back to the ghillie suit and Invisibility spell. First, I searched for the optimal Guamese to free. Using my phone, I found him. He was the head of Guam's airport and a mage with spells in administration and paperwork. That was a good idea. I grabbed him, inspected the Loyalty spell, (MU 1499), and removed it. The spell was an area-effect targeting everyone within their prisoner pen. I suggested he stay in Guam and work to free his people. His mage reading was 1735, so he was more powerful than I'd expected. I guess he used a lot of paperwork spells.

Then I inspected the shields on the dragons. It was an Air-Slipperiness spell. No air friction behind that shield. Cool idea for Angie.

I was about to go, when my Invisibility spell was dispersed. I was standing at the edge of the jungle in my ghillie suit. I saw the mage who was searching for me. Our eyes met. I teleported.

Chapter 49 – Animation

Tuesday, November 9

“This is certainly a different vacation,” Jane said as she looked over the local National Guard base.

We’d practiced our teleporting to get to the closest one. Katie had given our names to all army bases across the country. She urged us to train people to train other people in magic and then move on.”

I looked up from my phone. “Whoa, Jane, did you see the news headline? China invaded Guam with its Dragon Army!”

Jane looked like she’d swallowed something rotten. “Yech. I guess we’d better hurry.”

After meeting the base commander, he connected us with six soldiers who were in the logistics and motor pool groups.

“Hi, guys. Take us to your vehicles,” Jane said.

“When do we get our magic wands?” one of them joked, a private named Able.

“You don’t need wands. You’ve got the magic in you right now,” I said.

“I can’t believe that,” Sergeant Baker said.

“That is why you fail,” Jane intoned.

We entered the garage.

“Which one do you want to animate?” Jane looked at them.

“That one on the lift. We’re trying to solve an electrical issue.”

“Be fixed! Start!” Jane pointed at the truck firmly, and it started. “All the parts needed to fix it are in place.”

“Wow, that’s useful. Can we do that for any mechanical problem?” Corporal Charles asked. “Let me bring it down and we can test drive it.”

“That’s not necessary. Come down!” The lift let the truck down.

Jane stopped them from entering. “Where do you usually test drive it?”

“Just around the base,” the corporal answered.

"Drive around the base. Don't hit anything. Don't break any traffic laws. Don't go over twenty. Come back here." That was the base speed limit.

The truck's headlights blinked slowly, like two huge eyes. Then it pulled out of the garage and drove around the base.

After he got over his astonishment, the logistics director, Dickens, said, "Can we do this with any vehicle?"

"Sure. That's the next step. You animate your other vehicles," I told him.

"I don't have too much confidence in this. Let me try this motorcycle first." Another corporal, Edwards, laid his hands on a motorcycle and yelled, "Start!!"

It did, and it emitted a cloud of oil smoke. After coughing, he said, "Go around the base like the truck did."

It put itself into gear and took off, its headlight looking like a Cyclops eye behind a monocle.

"Okay, I've got to try this on this tank." A huge M-1 Abrams rested in the corner of the garage. Private First Class Fegan ran over to it.

"That's still missing parts to the turbine," Corporal Charles said.

Jane shrugged. "That shouldn't matter. Just say 'Be fixed' first, and you should be good."

PFC Fegan laid his hands on the skirt of the tank. "Be healed."

"Um, she said, 'Be fixed,' Fegan," Director Dickens said.

The tank started.

"Be sure to ride in the driver's seat. We don't want any accidents," Dickens yelled.

"Yes, sir." Fegan hopped into the hatch, and the tank took off.

"At least give it verbal orders. The more you use your magic, the stronger you'll become," I added.

Fegan's head popped out. "Yes, sir, er, ma'am!"

"I'm overwhelmed," Dickens said to us.

"Yes, we are too. We have twelve more bases to get to today. Do you think you can cross-train your soldiers? We're on a crash program to magicify the military."

"We'll do whatever it takes to follow the president's orders."

Dickens paused. “Is magicify even a word?”

“It is now,” I said with a grin. “See you! Onto the next, Jane.”

“I’ll beat you there.” We both disappeared with a *pop*.

About six bases later, we met Svi.

“Hey, Svi, are you drafted too? Jane, this is the boy Svi I told you about.”

“Hi, Mr. Williams. How do you like my collection of soldiers?” Behind him were hundreds of soldiers, in ranks. I peered at them and noticed they all looked alike. “Are these clones, Svi?”

“I guess so. I bought hundreds of them with the money Ms. Garcia gave me. She told me to take them and my dinosaurs to all the military bases.” He looked at a list on his phone. “This is my eleventh so far.”

“But those are real weapons,” Jane said.

“Yeah. I have to make them real to fight in the war. I leave them all in charge of a local sergeant at each base. Don’t worry—they follow orders.”

“That’s awesome, Svi. Are you done here? Where are you going to next?”

“Um, Fort Bragg. “

“That’s a famous one. Have you been there?”

“Nah. I just ask around until I find a soldier who’s been there. Then I teach him to teleport, and he takes me there. Now I’ve got to get my dinosaurs out.” He took off his backpack and poured out dinosaurs until I thought the bag was surely empty. But peering inside, there were just as many as ever.

“You’ve got a bag of holding?”

“Yeah, don’t you? Ms. Garcia showed me how to make one. This one holds both dinosaurs and soldiers.”

“Now what do you do?” Jane asked.

“Be real!” The pile of dinosaurs grew to life size and covered the grounds.

I felt frightened and claustrophobic with the giant dinosaurs around me. The smallest was the size of an ostrich, the largest bigger than elephants.

“Soldiers, pick out your mount and get back into your ranks!” Svi commanded.

Hundreds of soldiers hopped up and onto the backs of the dinos and rode them into rank-and-file order.

Clouds of dust were stirred by the massive beasts walking, trotting, and hopping in place.

Jane and I coughed.

Svi tilted his head. "Just say, 'Clear air.'"

The dust settled around us, and we could breathe again.

"Didn't you know that spell? Let's go to the commander."

We teleported across the parade ground to the headquarters, where Commander Gillespy stared at the ranks of dinosaurs and soldiers.

"There you go, Commander Gillespie. One thousand soldiers and dinosaurs. They're all under the command of your Sergeant Hickox and his superiors."

"That's amazing, Svi. Now, Secretary Garcia's orders make a lot more sense. She told me to copy you and do whatever you did until I have enough forces to fight the Chinese."

"Great. Well, I've got to see Sergeant Hickox. He's gonna teleport me to Fort Bragg." Svi disappeared.

Commander Gillespie turned toward us. "Any you two are?"

"Jake and Jane Williams. We're here to teach you about animating your vehicles."

"Wonderful. Secretary Garcia told me you'd come by. Be sure to teach me that teleportation trick too."

"Our pleasure," Jane said.

We began our training, but Jane opened a text from Katie. "Wake Island has been invaded by the Chinese Dragon Army."

"Now what?" Jane and I looked at each other.

Katie's next text arrived. "Go faster."

* * *

I watched the dragons roll over Wake Island, taking over the airstrip there and bespelling the personnel there with loyalty to the Chinese emperor. I wondered how Taiwan had beaten off these dragons.

I knew Taiwan had its own dragon mages and weather mages, but I needed more details. I teleported to the Hong Kong airport, where I'd been once before for a conference. Then I teleported across the sea to Taiwan.

As soon as I approached Taiwan, I was confronted by a towering water spout.

“Hi. I’m the US Secretary of Magic, Katie Garcia. I’d like to talk to your mages and find out how you defended your island against the Chinese Dragon Army.” I had to magically project my voice over the wind and water into the funnel.

The funnel disappeared. A slender Taiwanese man, in a blue robe, floated in the air. “I hear you, Katie Garcia. You have much to learn and not much time. Let us begin.”

* * *

I was exhausted. I’d been creating wind and swirling up water all afternoon under the tutelage of mage Cheng Chai-Hao. He’d been a middle-aged shipping agent when he’d acquired magic. He’d used it first to fend off a typhoon that was threatening incoming ships. He found he loved manipulating weather and spent all his spare time experimenting with what he could do with the elements. Eventually he taught other Taiwanese mages. Together they were able to fend off the Imperial Dragon Army.

“Whew. I can’t go much longer. I’m just about out of magic.”

“Hmph! That is when you grow the most. It’s like weight lifting. The last lift before you collapse builds your strength the most.” Chai-Hao crossed his arms and tapped his foot upon the cloud on which we stood.

To buy myself some time, I checked his magic levels: 6022 MUs. “Wow. You’re the strongest mage I’ve met.”

“There were stronger ones in the Chinese Communist Army. You are pretty strong yourself.”

Huh. That was the first compliment he’d given me. I checked my own magic: 5548. That was 50 percent stronger than a couple of days ago.

“Thank you. I’m stronger than I thought.”

“Do not sell yourself short. It is easy to be lazy with magic. I’ve learned to push myself to exhaustion every day.” The way he looked at me, I knew he expected me to do the same.

Beep! A text message from the president. “Midway Island is being invaded. Go directly to Kauai and organize its defenses.”

“I’ve got to go, but I’d rather stay and work with you.

Midway Island is being invaded. Hawaii is next."

"Ah. Will you teleport there?" Teleporting had been a new spell to Chai-Hao. No one in China or Taiwan knew about it. He'd taught me weather magic in return for that.

"Yes, it's the only way to get there in time."

"Take me with you. I'll help you."

"Thank you. You're a true friend." We clasped hands and teleported to Kauai, where we split up.

"I will look about your sailors and water-savvy population for mages with an affinity for water," Chai-Hao said, then teleported away.

I floated to the magical generators and set up the magic shields around the island. Linking the magic generators together, I could make a complete shield around Kauai.

It was quite strong for most spells, but I knew a stronger mage than me or a group of mages could bring it down. I needed a backup plan as well as an attack plan for the dragons.

I racked my brains for who I could enlist for help. Shannon and her family came to mind. Maybe I could fight dragons with dragons. Chuckling at the thought of Pinkie fighting these iron and bronze dragons, I teleported to Chicago.

Chapter 50 – Dragons

November 9

Pop! Katie appeared in our living room.

Happy to see her, I jumped into her arms and gave her a big hug. "Katie!" I squealed.

"Whew! Hi, Shayla. You've grown." She put me down.

She looked tired. Her eyes had little lines at the corners. "What have you learned about magic?"

"How to make magic shields, like Heath, how to stick blocks together, like Heath, and how to stay warm and dry in rainy weather."

"We've had lots of rain," Lamar put in. "We have to keep our passengers warm."

"How about you, Shannon? I see you've decorated your home nicely. I feel comfortable here."

"I'm glad you know you can 'pop' in anytime. I'm busy running our Grant Park ride business. You seem to have something on your mind. What's up?" Mom said.

"The US is under attack. We've already lost Guam, Wake, and Midway Islands. Hawaii's next. I'll try to defend it against the Imperial Dragon Army, but I need more help. Can you make some more dragons like Pinkie to help me?" Katie looked from Mommy to me.

I shrugged. "Sure. I just need more stuffed dragons."

"Or pterodactyls," Lamar said.

"Or unicorns." Mommy smiled.

"Shannon, what store around here sells stuffed animals?"

"Oh, Wal-Store of course."

"Where is it?"

"The closest one is Lake Zurich."

"Join hands with me."

"Are we going to play Ring Around the Rosie?" I asked Katie as I held Mommy's hand and hers.

"No, I'll teach you how to teleport. First, we pop outside."

Pop, we were outside. Then we floated up in the air.

"This is so cool!" Lamar yelled.

"Shannon, can you see Wal-Store from here?"

We spun around slowly, high in the air, like a merry-go-round.

Mommy pointed. "Go over there."

"I can see that road, and I just picture myself there with a wish." Then we were there.

"And Wal-Store is just across that parking lot."

"Try teleporting us there. Just picture the front of the store."

Mommy scrunched up her face and closed her eyes, and we jumped there.

Katie grabbed every stuffed animal in the store. Mommy offered to help pay for them, but Katie laughed. "I've got a government credit card."

Katie had me teleport home. It was easy! I just pictured our living room, and the four of us, and our boxes of stuffed animals were there.

Then Katie asked me to make a green dragon come alive. That was easy peasy too. I named it "Greenie." We all got busy, and soon all the animals were alive.

"Now you've got to show me how you make them big and powerful."

"Silly. You just wish for them to be as big as you want."

"Let's try it outside."

We had a nice big backyard, but I made the green dragon as big as an elephant, and the yard suddenly seemed small.

"Can you give him wings? I'll make Pépe giant." Katie held her cute little skunk. Then he was even bigger than an elephant.

"Grow wings and fly, Greenie." He did. Now we had more room in the backyard.

Katie copied me. "Grow wings and fly, Pépe."

Whoosh! Whoosh! He was like a flying whale with a fluffy black-and-white tail.

"Okay, everyone, do this with all the other animals too," Katie said.

When they were all flying in circles around us, Katie teleported to Pépe. "Pick an animal and hop on!"

I teleported to Greenie. Mom was on a soft brown horsy the

size of an airplane. Lamar was on a flying school bus of a crocodile.

"Okay, everyone, line up behind me. Grab Pépe's tail in your mouth."

The line grew longer and longer as we whirled up into the air. There must have been over a hundred stuffed animals. Greenie was the smallest. That was okay. I could always make him bigger.

"Here we go!"

Pop!

We went from a cold, cloudy day to a bright sun and warm, humid air The sun was setting over the ocean in front of us.

"Here we are in Kauai, Hawaii. We'll land at the airport over there."

Katie led us down to the big airport. Besides airplanes, it had flying tanks, horses, and dogs too. I wanted to pet them!

"Line up along this pathway," Katie ordered the stuffed animals. Then she looked at me. "Tell me how you taught Pinkie how to fight."

"Huh. It'll be easier to show you." I grabbed my bracelet with the Pinkie charm on it. "I wish you were here, full size!" Pinkie arrived, blotting out the sun as he hovered above me.

I teleported to his neck. Then I teleported Katie there too.

"You surprise me, Shayla. I didn't know you could teleport someone else here."

"Well, duh! Of course you can." Then I spoke to Pinkie. "Can you eat that tree?" I pointed to a big palm tree.

"No problem, Shayla."

"Go and do it!"

Pinkie swooped down on the tree and swallowed it in one bite. I wasn't quite sure how he did it, since the tree was longer than he was, but that wasn't my problem.

"That's all I had to do, Katie. I just asked Pinkie to eat the gang members, and down the hatch they went!"

Katie looked blank, like she didn't know what to say. "Pinkie, did you digest those gang members? Did you digest that tree?"

"Not exactly. I absorb them into my body, and they become part of it. Their magic becomes my magic. There's no digestion involved."

"Huh. I didn't know that. But I know I haven't seen you poop."

"Shayla, you know stuffed animals don't poop." Pinkie sounded like he expected me to know that.

"Oh right."

"I'm learning so much today." Katie seemed to be talking to herself as we landed.

"This is fun! I always wanted to go to Hawaii. It's so pretty!" Mommy exclaimed.

Katie's face turned white. She pointed to the horizon, over the sea.

I saw what looked like a flock of birds. Looking closer, I saw they were a flock of dragons—flying toward us.

"The attack has begun," Katie said. "We got those stuffed animals just in time!" Then she looked at me. "You and your family need to teleport home. This is a war zone. Just direct the animals to follow me."

I could see all the animals flying around above the beach. "Yo! Stuffed animals! Come here!" I yelled, using magic.

They came to me quickly. I saw Mommy on the big horsy. She yelled to me, "Let's get out of here!"

"One second, Mommy! All of you, listen up! You do what Katie says." I pointed at her, next to me on Pinkie.

"See you, Katie. I've got to go."

"Stay safe, Shayla. We'll fight for you."

"I'll fight for you too, Shayla," Pinkie said.

"You're staying here?"

"Yes. I know I'm needed."

"Call me if you need me." I pointed to my Pinkie charm on my bracelet. I patted his big pink side and hugged his neck.

"Will do," he rumbled.

I teleported to Mom, on the back of her horsy. Its wings beat slowly, hovering in place. A flash lit up our faces as I hugged her.

Dragon fire flared against a glowing blue wall, red and blue against the purple evening sky. Then, the first of the dragons bounced off the blue bubble, like raindrops off a windshield.

"Uh-oh," Katie yelled. "The shields can't take much more of

this. We'd better reduce their numbers, Pinkie."

"Let's get out of here, Shayla." Mom teleported us to Lamar, standing on the beach watching the light show.

"Lamar, we've got to get home."

"Aw, can't I just watch? It's getting good! Ooo, Pinkie just swallowed one of them!"

"Go Pinkie! Kick some dragon butt!" I yelled.

Mommy watched too as Pinkie and Katie teleported to another dragon and swallowed him. Each time Pinkie got bigger and stronger.

"I think Katie and Pinkie have this under control. It's a war zone, and you may get hit by a stray magic bolt."

"Aw, Mom!" Lamar moaned.

"It'd kill me if something happened to you or Katie, Lamar." Mom's voice had a hint of crying in it. That got through to Lamar."

"Okay."

Mom teleported us back to our living room. I still had my bracelet with my magical Pinkie charm. If I held it tightly and closed my eyes, I could watch the battle through Pinkie's eyes.

Katie dove off Pinkie and floated in the air. Then wind, clouds, and water swirled around her. She became a water tornado! My mouth hung open. "Go Katie," I whispered.

Mom's horsy kicked a dragon in Katie's tornado. Katie's Pépe stood on its front legs and sprayed a group of dragons. They fell out of the sky.

Even with Katie sweeping up dragons like a vacuum cleaner, there were too many dragons against our stuffed animals. Some were burned to a crisp. Some were shredded into fluff, floating in the air.

Horsy kicked another dragon into the funnel cloud, and then his belly was torn open. A shot of fire ignited him. He fell burning into the sea.

"Horsy!" I cried.

Pépe was set on fire just as he was spraying another cluster of dragons.

"Pépe!" I couldn't control my crying.

Even Pinkie, as big and powerful as he was, couldn't last against over a hundred dragons. His fur was snagged and leaking stuffing, and dozens of burns covered his body.

I went to call him to me, and I heard his thought: *One more dragon to swallow, Shayla.* He swooped and snapped up a big dragon. It was like an eagle swallowing a fish. Then he was surrounded by flame.

"No!" I pulled Pinkie to me in his smallest form. He was on fire. I threw the couch cushion on him and smothered the flame.

One of his black glassy eyes was missing. The other looked at me. *Thanks, Shayla. I've got to sleep. G'night.*

I cuddled his burned and torn body, soaking it with my tears until I fell asleep. Mommy carried me to bed.

* * *

I saw Pinkie disappear while surrounded by flame. I assumed Shayla had rescued him. Now who would rescue me?

The dragons were fast enough to avoid my water spout. They would zoom in and hit me with a blast of fire. It didn't hurt, but I felt my magic drain away. I would have to suck up more water from the ocean each time to replace the losses. I had bottles of my magic in reserve in my backpack, but I didn't want to use them yet. I could hold on a little longer.

Stand fast, Katie. We are coming.

I heard the voice in my head, but I didn't know who it was.

Wait. It sounded a little like—

"Katie, we've come to help. Cheng Chai-Hao and my apprentice, Caleb Kowabunga."

Two funnel clouds rose from the ocean. One was larger than mine, and the other was smaller. I spoke to the smaller one.

"That can't be a real name, Caleb."

"It is." He laughed. "I love surfing, and I legally changed my name."

Chai-Hao interrupted. "Let me show you how three waterspouts can trap a dragon."

Chai-Hao arranged our funnel clouds in a triangle, with me at the point toward the cloud of dragons.

One swooped toward me a high speed. I shot a bolt of lightning at him but missed. That was the first time I'd tried that. I lost all control once the lightning formed.

The dragon shot a gout of flame at me. I swirled rain and

wind at him, trying to draw him in.

He banked and turned. As soon as he did, the other funnel clouds zoomed forward and trapped him in a triangle of funnel clouds. He bounced frantically from one maelstrom to another. We pressed together, and Chai-Hao sucked him into his cloud. He disappeared in a flare of flame and magic.

“Hooray!” I yelled.

The other dragons backed off. Then they spread out, attacking the magic bubble around Kauai a couple of miles from us in each direction.

“Oh no you don’t.” I teleported to one of the groups and enveloped a dragon as it bounced off the shield. I felt a surge of magic as I absorbed the dragon’s and mage’s magic. This must be what Pinkie felt when he swallowed a dragon-mage pair.

I felt queasy for a moment as I realized I was actually killing people. Then a blast of dragon fire in my face drove that thought away. My magical bubble was all that saved me from burned-marshmallow status. Somehow a mage had targeted me within the waterspout. Since I was only a thousandth of the size of the funnel and hidden, that required magical targeting. I swerved my viewing portal around, looking for a likely dragon. Most had fled, but one hovered a mile away.

I put my phone into Heads Up viewing mode, and its display floated before my eyes. “Mage: General Han Mùchén, 1696 MUs. Dragon Long Chow, 1834 MUs. Dragon Fire, 3331 MUs. Targeting spell, 544 MUs. Magic Protection, 1522 MUs.”

I wondered if I could teleport to them and swallow them up. The dragon mage zipped away. Then a text buzzed from General Slimak: “Katie, they’re attacking the big island, Hilo.”

Crap. Now what would I do?

* * *

After seeing my directed flame blast bounce off the mage like it was nothing, I paused to assess my situation.

We’d lost forty-five mages, far worse than any battle since Taiwan. Most of those were the weaker, inexperienced mages, but that meant l had to train more.

“When your enemy is strong, attack him where he is unprepared, and appear where you are not expected,” Sun Tzu had said. I had planned to go west to east down the island chain, but I hadn't even been able to penetrate their defenses. Obviously they were prepared on this island, despite Wa Mingze's intelligence.

Or perhaps they knew where we would attack and threw all their force there? I would let the emperor know about this.

But now . . . "Imperial Dragon Army, units one to three, move east to Hilo." I would move three-quarters of my force all the way east and attack Hawaii and its main city, Hilo.

Wa Mingze's face appeared before me. "You have made a bold move, Han Mùchén. I am observing the volcano mages on Hawaii, and they are occupied watching the battle in Kauai. You will have ten to twenty minutes before they react. When they attack, flee immediately. They can suck you into their volcano. I only escaped through subterfuge."

"And how was that?"

"I hide myself in a chunk of pumice exploding out of the volcano. It was not comfortable."

"Thank you for your warning. We are closing to attack now." His face faded away.

I might catch the volcano mages off guard. And if not, I'd occupy and hold Hilo hostage. If they still attacked, I'd kill their citizenry and retreat. The emperor would be pleased.

My dragon forces formed into three ranks. I led them at full speed to Hilo. The fourth rank was dragged along. I had forgotten Liu Fu's spell would keep us linked. So be it. It was only a little more than five hundred kilometers away. I pushed our speed to three thousand kilometers per hour, as the emperor's frictionless magical cones allowed. We could only go one-tenth that speed without them.

I saw the island rapidly approaching. No magical shields, no magical forces of any kind. It was a lush green agricultural island. Smoke curled from Mauna Loa to the south. I led the Imperial Army north of the island, avoiding the volcanoes, and descended on Hilo.

Now they would feel our might.

We quickly destroyed all resistance. I immediately administrated the loyalty oath to all the citizens. Now they were ours.

A flaming-red woman appeared. Magic, heat, and power radiated from her. "THIS IS FORBIDDEN BY THE MAGE OF MAUNA LOA." She touched the closest dragon, and it disappeared. She reappeared, and then another dragon disappeared.

"I will kill all the inhabitants of Hilo!" I yelled at her.

She looked at me, and I almost was knocked out of the sky by the force of her gaze. "ALL DRAGONS WILL BE DESTROYED." She appeared next to me. I fled at three thousand kilometers per hour even as her magical magma surrounded my dragon and me. So did all my other dragons, dragged along by the emperor's Linking spell.

Chapter 51 – Practical Help

Tuesday, November 9

"Oh man, is Katie there?"

The streaming news channel showed flashing flames bouncing off a glowing dome around Kauai. Mom, Dad, and I had been glued to the sight all evening.

"I wouldn't be there if I were the Secretary of Magic or the president. She'd be too important to risk."

"But you're not the president, Phil, or the Secretary of Magic. Katie seems like a hands-on woman," Mom said.

"Those dragons are really walloping Kauai," I said.

The scene changed, with another reporter interrupting the broadcast. "This is Jeb Crumpette with breaking news! The Chinese Dragon Army has captured Hilo, Hawaii. Here's our reporter on the scene, Dorothy Roderick."

"Thanks, Jeb. The Imperial Chinese Army has pacified Hilo. All of us have sworn fealty to Emperor Liu Fu. There is nothing to worry about."

"What?!" Jeb yelled into his mike at Worldwide News headquarters. He was shown on a split screen. "Are you okay, Dorothy?"

"Never been better. Hilo is an idyllic paradise—Oh no!"

"What?"

"One of Hawaii's volcano mages, Mauna Loa, has just dragged away a dragon and its rider."

"That's good, isn't it?"

"There goes another! Now all the dragons are fleeing at high speed."

"That's great! They've beat off the attack."

"That's terrible. Now what will we do as loyal citizens of the emperor?"

"Thank you for your report, Dorothy. We now return to our live stream of Kauai, defended by two brave waterspout mages." Jeb cut her off.

"Things are getting pretty heated over there," Dad said.

"I don't think you should joke about war, Phil."

He looked at Mom. "Even if it's funny?"

"Especially since it's not funny." Mom glared at him.

"Mom, Dad, seriously, I think we should wish for Katie to be safe over there. I'm sure she's in the thick of it. She's probably our strongest mage. You see that dome over Kuai?" The newscast was now giving a drone's-eye view of the battle. "That's a magic dome like the one she put over Washington, DC."

"That's reasonable. I like her, and she represents our country," Mom said.

"I'm in."

"Thanks." We joined hands, and I wished, "No matter what, keep Katie safe from harm."

"Good. I think that'll work." Dad nodded in satisfaction.

"It'll work," I agreed, "but I want to give her some practical help."

"Like what?" Mom looked at me.

"I want to go there and help the army somehow fight off those dragons."

"How would we get there?"

"I'd teleport to Los Angeles and then hop across the ocean, line-of-sight teleporting."

Dad consulted his phone. "That'd be over twenty-five hundred miles. At twenty-five miles to the horizon, that's a hundred teleports. I say no."

My shoulders slumped. I really wanted to go help Katie.

"And it's well past eleven. You've got school tomorrow. You can catch up on the news tomorrow. We've wished Katie safe for tonight."

"Yes, Mom." I knew when to surrender.

Lying in bed, I remembered Katie. Her warm smile. Her round face—and body. Her dark pageboy hairstyle. How could I help her? Then I remembered following Dak without knowing where he was going. I just wished to be with him.

I grinned and wished myself in front of Katie.

I was in a swirling whirlwind, exactly like being in a dishwasher, only cold. Katie glowed with blue-green magic. Her black eyebrows shot up, and she yelled, "What are you doing here, Sean? This is a war zone!"

"Oh, I'm here to help you in some way!"

"Get down to the beach! I'll talk to you later. I'm fighting dragons here!" She pointed down, and I saw the beach below us, about a mile away. I teleported there and sat down on the warm sand, listening to the surf.

Now what?

* * *

I assembled my forces toward Maui. Then the local volcano mage Haleakala appeared. His flaming figure and forbidding stance were all I needed to see.

"On to Hawaii," I said to my forces. That was the next island to the west.

Li Yihan's image appeared before me. "Han Mùchén, I have devised a method to penetrate their magical barrier around Kauai. I learned how to pass through the barrier and then destroy the magic generators that power the shields."

"I did not know about these generators. Why didn't Wa Mingze report about them?"

"There were just erected in the past day after Mingze finished his scouting. They are clever devices we can make use of."

I scowled. I still preferred to attack magically undefended Hawaii to the prepared Kauai, but . . . Li Yihan was a better and more powerful mage than I was. The emperor had ordered us to cooperate. He had threatened severe punishment if we didn't.

"What has Wa Mingze said?"

He appeared next to Li Yihan. "She is correct. I have been behind their lines. They have a few powerful mages but no magical army."

"What about the army of magical animals that attacked and destroyed a quarter of our army?"

"They came from outside Hawaii. I have not investigated their source. However, I know the mage who directed them, Katie Garcia. We can capture her and find out from her. She is apparently the leader here."

"I am convinced. Li Yihan, you have not been wrong. Wa Mingze, your intelligence is key. We will capture this Katie

Garcia and learn from her."

"I will be at Kauai in a few minutes. When will you be prepared to strike?"

"When you return I will strike after the first dragon blast on the shield."

"On to Kauai, Imperial Dragon Army!" I led them west.

"Fire as one, Dragon Army!" The shield glowed brightly, repelling our flame, and then faded and died.

"Take the city! Compel the inhabitants to take oaths like we did in Hilo."

* * *

Far below, a super pod of magical dolphins converged. I was still in the Hudson River, working the with United Nations. This attack was the first violation of our treaty. I gathered the Central Pacific Nation's mages and directed them, through Dolphin Net: *Use your power to create a wave.*

The ocean surged higher and higher. The water retreated from the shore.

Ambassador Squee, we are only halfway to the dragons and we can lift the water no higher, reported one of the mages near the surface.

That's good enough. The height will increase as we head toward the shore. Launch the tsunami!

All one thousand of our mages, from all across the Pacific, pushed the mountain of water toward the shore.

* * *

The Imperial Dragon Army zoomed toward Kauai. Three waterspouts stood in our way. "Split and go around the waterspouts." After we captured the island, we could deal with the mages. I knew a hundred dragons could easily bring down one water mage, even if I could not.

I was already over the beach. Odd. The ocean was here a minute ago. I glanced behind me and saw a wall of water rolling toward me faster than I was flying.

I sped up and overshot the island. I looped back in time to see my trailing units slurped into the water one by one.

"Overfly the island until the tsunami is past." That had to

be magical. There had been no earthquake.

Most of the army followed me and looped back. We watched the water flood the shore and go kilometers inland. Dolphins sported on the waves, and as the waters retreated, they did too.

I was ready to give the order to attack again, when a huge sperm whale leapt out of the ocean, rose a thousand feet, and snapped up one of my dragons and the mage on its back. Even as it dove back down, another whale appeared and gobbled another of my precious dragons.

"Dragon Army, double your height and go overland!"

I lost one more dragon before the whole army was overland.

"Descend! Make the civilians swear oaths of fealty! Capture any mages you find."

* * *

I watched the funnel that held Katie as the dragons attacked the magic shield—and it failed. They split around the three waterspouts and headed straight for me. Now what? I could flee, but how could I help? All I could do was teleport.

That's it! I had an idea. I watched the lead dragon and the mage on its back. He looked back and then zoomed away overhead.

What? Why? Then I saw a thousand-foot wave heading straight toward me. It swallowed up dragon after dragon.

"You won't get me!" I teleported straight up above the waves. I floated magically, just as I had with Katie in the waterspout. Worriedly I glanced at her funnel. It rode on top of the wave, gobbling up dragons. Good. Katie was fine.

Dozens of sperm whales jumped out of the water, leaping up to grab dragons and their riders. Go cetaceans! I remembered watching the signing of the peace treaty with them a few days ago on the news. They were living up to their part of the bargain.

The dragons were behind me! They'd assembled over the island. One swooped at me!

Reflexively I did what I had planned. I teleported next to the mage on the dragon and grabbed him. Oops. The mage was a teenage girl. We teleported to the beach, and I popped back to the dragon, leaving her with her mouth still open.

Now I was on the back of a rough stone dragon, flapping in the air. How did you drive this thing? "Go that way!" I pointed toward the middle waterspout.

They spread apart, presumably to catch me. "Katie!" I yelled. "It's me! Sean!" Katie teleported to the dragon's neck and stared at me, a foot away.

"What are you doing here?"

"Giving you some practical help."

She laughed. "Yes, you captured a dragon. What happened to the mage?"

"I left her on the beach."

Katie frowned. "Not good. They're dangerous. Where did you leave her?"

I pointed. Katie disappeared.

Now what should I do? Katie reappeared holding the girl. She was crying.

"This is Hua Mei. She's under a geas to obey. Take her to General Slimak in downtown Lihue."

"Uh, where's that?"

"There are only five towns on the island! It's the one toward the southeast!" She pushed the girl toward me, still sniffling.

I took her hand and teleported to the southeast. I only saw one town, so it was pretty simple.

I heard a gasp and looked at Hua Mei. She was staring down, her eyes bulging out.

"Don't worry. I've got you." We teleported to the middle of the town, next to a Wal-Store.

People were rushing to their cars. Dragons soared overhead. Antiaircraft guns on buildings fired at them.

"Oh crap! Hey, where's the army headquarters?" I yelled at one of the men manning the guns.

"That way!" The officer pointed.

I floated into the air and teleported a block. There was a flag over the next block, an army flag, and more antiaircraft guns.

I teleported to the door and went in. An MP pointed a gun at me. "Identify yourself!"

"Sean Kennedy and a captured dragon mage, Hua Mei. We need to see General Slimak. Secretary Katie Garcia's orders." I hoped he believed me.

He frowned. "You're just a kid, and so is she. How old are you, thirteen?"

"Next March," I muttered.

"And you?"

She shrugged and gestured like she didn't understand.

Great. Now what? How could we interrogate her? Oh, I bet Katie thought I could do this.

"Understand and speak English, Hua Mei."

"Oh! That's strange. Is this what English is like? It's weird." She covered her mouth.

"How old are you?"

"Name, rank, and serial number only—and I'm sixteen. Crap. That geas really works. Why don't you speak Chinese like Katie?" She looked at me, frowning.

Now I shrugged. "I cast the spell a different way."

"Whatever."

"I think you've convinced me you're mages. I'm Sergeant Talbot. I'll keep my rifle on you, Ms. Mei."

"It's Ms. Hua. Chinese surnames come first."

"Whatever." He spoke into his headset. "General Slimak, we have a captured mage here."

I just noticed that Sergeant Talbot looked young too, not much more than twenty.

General Slimak came out. He was middle-aged but fit. "Sergeant Talbot, conduct the interrogation. I have no time during the battle." He slammed the door.

I could feel vibrations through the ground, like a heavy truck going by.

"Huh. Another earthquake. All right, Ms. Hua, tell us about your Dragon Army. How many are in it?"

"Two hundred mages and their dragons."

"And how many have you lost so far?"

Her brows furrowed. "At least forty. Probably more than fifty."

The sergeant looked at me. "How did you capture her?"

"I didn't. Katie did. Well, I teleported her off her dragon and then Katie put her under a geas to obey us."

"Huh. That makes this easy. What are your plans for this attack?"

“Capture the islands west to east. Swear all the citizens to loyalty to the emperor.”

“I don’t think you’ll find too many Americans who’ll go along with that.”

“They don’t have a choice. We compel them.”

“Isn’t that evil?”

“It is evil to resist the emperor. We’re making them good. Otherwise, they’d all have to die.”

“Are you under that oath?”

“Of course.”

“Who is your commanding officer?”

“General Han Mùchén.”

“And who does he report to?”

“Emperor Liu Fu.”

The building shook again. It felt like a meteor shower.

* * *

I left Chen Chia-Hao and his apprentice and followed the army on the dragon back. I picked off dragon mages from behind, put them under a geas, and sent them to Lihue with orders to report to the general.

Then the army doubled back and headed for the coast again.

“Hey, you! Get back into formation!” a mage yelled at me.

I flipped my dragon around and followed him. Now I was in the middle of the army, looking very un-Chinese with my overalls. “Appear as a Chinese mage’s robe!” I ordered. I looked at myself. Not bad. Maybe I’d fool them. Now I was grateful for my dark hair.

We headed for the beach and circled back over the ocean. A huge whale leapt up and ate the dragon next to me. Then the order echoed through the army.

“Land and make the civilians swear loyalty to the emperor!”

How could I stop them?

A bugle blew. Two hundred flying horses appeared in front of us. Next to the bugler, on horseback, was Josh Garrison, leading the charge.

The cavalry had arrived.

Chapter 52 – Cavalry

Tuesday, November 9

"Wooo-ooo!" I howled as I heard the bugle. "Master, charging dragons on flying horseback is so exciting!" I stood on my hind legs so I could look over his shoulder on the flying horse. They were neighing, and the dragons were roaring and spouting flame toward us.

"Fire!" Josh yelled. The soldiers' M-16s rattled off bursts. I saw bubbles flash around the dragons.

A wall of flame came toward us. "Teleport next to the dragons and shoot!" Master ordered.

We jumped past the fire and turned alongside a dragon. Then we teleported next to a dragon the size of a flying hippo. Master shot the mage in the back, and he fell. The dragon turned into brass and fell too.

"There's one! Let's see if we can get to forty-two, like Gimli!"

We jumped inside the bubble of the next dragon, a stone one. The mage had a black cap on. She turned around and yelled, "Josh!"

"Katie!"

We teleported next to her. I couldn't help myself. I teleported in front of her and licked her face.

"Spot!"

She remembered my name!

"What are you doing here?" she said.

"What are you doing here?" Josh said.

"I'm fighting a battle to save Hawaii!"

"Me too!"

"C'mon, let's work together. I'll point out a dragon, and we'll teleport there."

"Let's do it!"

A green light from her hand shone on a dragon ahead. Their formation had broken, and everything was mixed up, like kibble in a dish. We teleported there, and Katie grabbed the mage from behind. A blue glow surrounded them as she yelled into his ear.

Then they disappeared.

"All dragons, return to original invasion formation!"

"That's the leader's orders. They'll reform and attack again."

"I'd better form up my troop."

"First Cavalry, form up around me!" Master shone with white light on his black horse. The horse blew heavily as it flapped.

The cavalry formed into eight companies of twenty-five horsemen, all flapping as they hovered.

The dragons returned in a close, triangular formation with fifteen rows. Master punched his calculator app. It showed 120 dragons. The outside was a solid wall of flame.

"Company A, take the left third, past the flame barrier. Company B, the right third. Company C, the back third. Company D stays with me. We'll attack the middle on my command. Teleport inside their magical protection."

Three-quarters of the troop disappeared. The dragon triangle exploded into a wild mixture of flying horses and dragons. Dragons, horses, and men fell. Katie stayed beside Master on her dragon.

"They're starting to gain the upper hand. The mages are protecting their bodies, not their dragons."

"Cavalry! Aim for the dragon wings if you can't bring down the mages. Company D, charge to the middle."

Flames shot randomly all around us. Master shot some mages down and blew the wings off some dragons. I saw a dragon come up behind us. Its mouth opened wide. I could only think of one thing.

I teleported and grabbed the mage by the neck, dragging him off. The dragon turned to green bronze and fell. He fought and hit me until his neck tore—I had a mouthful of flesh. I spat it out and watched him fall. Then I spun in the air and looked for Master. I couldn't find his horse, but I saw Katie's dragon. I teleported there.

"Hi, Katie! Where's Master?"

"Over there, fighting that big dragon. I think it's their general. I can't blast through his magic shields. He has one around his dragon and one around his body."

Master teleported above the mage. His horse reared to stomp the mage.

That dragon and five others zipped away like hummingbirds. Master hovered there looking for a dragon to attack. The few that were left scattered and flew away. Only a few horsemen were left too.

The dragons came back as fast as they'd left, in a small triangle, spewing flame. Master and his horse were engulfed.

Katie screamed and teleported. Immediately she came back, with Master on fire, and then disappeared again.

Spot, direct the dragon to the waterspouts. Do you see them? She projected a picture.

I scanned the horizon. There they were. "Let's go, dragon—that way." I pointed with my nose.

"Go faster!" I urged.

The dragon and I zipped to the waterspouts.

"Good boy!" I felt good saying that. The dragon wagged his tail.

The other dragons were right behind me. They surrounded one waterspout with flame, and it disappeared. Then the next one puffed into a cloud of steam.

When the third one was boiled, I saw Katie appear in the air, holding Josh in her arms. She cast one dragon down, but the others forced her to the beach. They surrounded her.

"Now we'll make you a loyal subject of the emperor." Their voices echoed up to me and my dragon.

Go get help, Spot!

I growled. No more good boy. I teleported to get some vicious help.

* * *

I collapsed on the beach with Josh. I had never been so exhausted. The other two water mages had bailed when they'd run out of magic. I'd blown through my stored-up magic to throw down the last few dragons, and I had nothing left. I didn't even know if Josh was alive or dead. Burned skin hung off his face and hands. He'd been a dead weight I'd supported through magic, and now I was out.

The Dragon Army surrounded me. I smelled their reptilian

odor overpowering the beach and sea. In unison they shouted, "Now we'll make you a loyal subject of the Emperor!"

I used my last dregs of magic to put an anti-magic shell around me. It was all I could do.

"You are loyal to death to Emperor Liu Fu!"

I felt the spell press against my barrier. It was painful, like being crushed by boulders.

"More power, mages. We must crush that barrier!" a lone voice commanded.

I braced myself for the worst. Then I heard wild howling.

Hundreds of dogs teleported around the dragons. Each mage had a dozen dogs biting, tearing, dragging at them. Screams mixed with the howls and growls. The dragons looked around stupidly. Apparently they had little volition or sapience of their own.

The dogs each wore a vest: "MILITARY WAR DOG: DO NOT TOUCH OR PET. MAY BITE." Most of them seemed to be German shepherds.

"Re-form!" A lone voice of command rang out. The mages who were still alive jumped to their dragons and flew off at high speed. Most of the dogs teleported after them.

Spot appeared next to Josh and licked his face.

"Let me check his pulse." I finally had a moment.

I pressed my fingers against his carotid artery. Nothing. No pulse.

Frantically I began CPR. As I blew air into his lungs, I noted the irony that the first time we kissed, I was trying to save his life.

After a minute I checked his pulse again. Nothing.

I sobbed and wept as I continued CPR. Then the ground shook and a breeze blew sand into my mouth.

I was surrounded again by dragons.

Chapter 53 – Tanks

Tuesday, November 9

"Flap harder! Will that magic into flying your vehicle," I yelled at the reservists.

Some were trying to make their trucks fly, some had Strykers, and some had Abrams M-1 tanks. Many were struggling.

"Race your engines if you have to!"

I heard the whine of the tanks' turbines, and they struggled into the air. One wobbled, and I flew over to it, laid hands on it, and wished, "Fly, tank." The olive-drab metal wings coming off the hull grew bigger, broader, and stronger. The massive craft straightened and joined the tanky flock above. The driver popped his head out of the hatch, saw me, and grinned. "Thanks, Angie! I needed that boost. I've got it from here!"

I sighed with contentment. I loved teaching and seeing my students master magic. It had been a crazy day, hopping from one reserve base to another across the country, training hundreds of soldiers how to use magic to fly. Oliver and Violet had been busy too, as well as Owen Gooseberry.

A general teleported next to me. "Ms. Angela Hamilton?"

"Yes, uh, general, sir." I saluted, just in case it was necessary.

"I'm General Slimak. Kauai is under attack, and we need your forces right now. Please help me teleport them there." Then he turned and commanded, "Tanks, parade formation."

"General Slimak, I've never been to Kauai. I can't teleport there."

"Ah, there's a trick to that. When I disappear, wish to be with me. And take however many tanks I leave behind. I can't teleport this many."

"Okay, I'll give it a try."

"No, you *will succeed.*"

I felt commanded. I felt more confident and certain I could do it.

"Tanks, follow me!" General Slimak disappeared. I was discouraged to see two-thirds of the tanks and other vehicles still here, flapping in the air above the motor pool. I thought he'd take at least half.

That just meant I'd have to teleport the rest. "C'mon, Angie. Do it for your country."

I squared my shoulders. "Motor pool vehicles, follow me!"

I wished to be with General Slimak. I pictured his determined expression, his five o'clock shadow, and the general insignia on his uniform, and teleported. I imagined dragging all the vehicles with me.

As we all arrived above a beach, I smelled the ocean on the warm breeze. Below us were perhaps twenty dragons surrounding a woman, a man, and a dog huddled on the sand. General Slimak's tanks were already firing on the dragons. A stupendous explosion obliterated a dragon.

Blue bubbles surrounded each dragon. They flew toward Slimak's tanks and engulfed them in flame. One tank after another blew up. Tank shells exploded harmlessly against the magical barriers.

"Oh no you don't!" I growled.

I wished a bubble to disappear, and it did. The next tank shell hit the dragon, killing the mage as well.

Onto the next. I wished it to disappear, and . . . it flickered and renewed as strong as before. I saw the mage's head snap toward me. Then his dragon rocketed right at me.

No sense in hanging around to get walloped—or toasted. I teleported to the trio on the beach just as dragon fire reached me.

It was a bedraggled and hollow-eyed Katie. On the ground was a badly burned man with a beagle howling into the air.

"This doesn't look good, Katie."

"It's worse than it seems. Josh is dead, and we're losing to China's magical army. They want to compel us all to follow their emperor."

"This is bad, but we've got more tanks coming. This is just one base. My kids and I have hit dozens."

Another flock of tanks appeared above the beach. They dove on the dragons. One was engulfed in flame, but it crashed into the dragon, bursting the protection bubble with a fiery explosion.

"That's another out. They're down to nineteen."

I kept trying to disperse their magic from the beach, but the bubbles came back after a moment.

"Their general is a powerful mage. He's probably resisting your magic."

"You don't say. What happened to yours?"

"All out. I'm physically and magically and emotionally exhausted."

"Yeah, that's what happens in war. I wish we had more mages."

"Me too. I wish I wasn't so exhausted. I've got some ideas, but I'm out of willpower and magic." She took out her phone. The screen floated in the air. It read: "Katie Garcia, 51 MUs."

"That's down about six thousand down from my peak." She pointed to the display.

"Hmm. Let's see if I can give you a transfusion, like I did with the tank."

"What?"

"I helped a soldier make his tank fly. Just like this." I laid my hands on Katie's head. "You have all my magic and willpower and can do what you need to do!"

"Whoa! I feel like a new woman!" Katie jumped up.

I could barely hear her. I was gasping on the ground, not able to lift my head. Even my arthritic knees hurt.

"Thanks, Angie. I won't let you down." She teleported away.

Meanwhile, I was trying to muster the energy to turn over so I could watch the battle in the sky.

Chapter 54 – The Last Resort

Tuesday, November 9

"This time it's personal," I said to myself. I teleported to each generator. They'd been sabotaged, but the magical generator portion was working. It was the shield generator that had been destroyed.

I tapped directly into the generator. I topped off my reserves until I could hold no more. Then I filled my emergency bottles with my liquid magic.

Now I was ready to battle again. I teleported back to the beach. Chaos reigned. Dragons and tanks fell out of the sky and crashed to Earth. Sperm whales still launched themselves from the ocean and snapped up dragons.

I quickly counted the remaining dragons. Fourteen, including their general. They were heading for us.

I teleported next to General Han on the back of his dragon.

"How?!" he spluttered.

"You're going down." I put a strong magical barrier around him and shoved him off the dragon.

As his body toppled toward the ground, I thought of the demise of Emperor Palpatine. "Life imitates art." I smiled grimly.

I flamed and destroyed another dragon with a surprise attack, and then the remaining ten surrounded me. They united their magical barriers, and I couldn't penetrate them.

"You will obey the emperor."

Their combined power crashed into me. I wanted to obey the emperor.

"No!" I shouted. I put up my strongest anti-magic barrier.

"You will obey the emperor."

An immense weight pressed upon my shield. It bent but didn't break.

A man with a pair of dragon wings sprouting from his back flew up to me. General Han. He had broken through my magic.

"We've got you, Katie."

He and the other ten mages said, "You will obey the emperor."

My shield cracked. Again I felt a yearning to surrender to the emperor.

"Oh no you don't!" I pulled out my bottle of magic, nearly a gallon. I poured it over my head and once again felt overwhelming power.

"Be gone!" I pointed at General Han, and he was blasted out of the air and onto the beach. I saw a crater splash in the sand.

"You too!" I pointed at the next dragon. "Go!" It crashed into the ocean and was gobbled up by a whale.

"You three!" One dragon crashed into another, and they both fell to shore.

I gained hope. They were down to seven dragons, and the general was gone. Except, he rose again from the crater, wobbling as he flew, but I could hear his voice with the seven remaining mages. "You will obey the emperor."

My shield shattered. My magical reserve was gone. I teleported to the generator to refill.

A Chinese mage was there. She had just burned up the magical generator. She pointed at me. "You will obey—"

"No!" I teleported back to Josh. Spot was gone.

Where are you, Spot?

I felt lonely and abandoned, even by a dog.

"Here we are, to save the day!" Spot and several burned shepherds appeared. "We've got your back, Katie! Watch this! We'll take them sightseeing to a volcano!"

They teleported to the incoming dragons, next to the mages. They grabbed their robes, and then the mages and dragons disappeared.

I faced the three remaining dragons and mages, including General Han.

"You will obey the emperor."

I was barely able to resist. This was worse than when Hugo and his mages attacked me.

I cowered in the sand.

I pulled out Caddie and ripped the zip cord. "What can I do?"

"You're in trouble. Get Sean and Shayla to help. Now!"

Sean! Shayla! Help! I sent out the telepathic call with my last bit of magic. Then I was compelled.

Oh. Why had I fought against the emperor? He was on the good side. I looked up from the ground to General Han. "I'm sorry, sir. I'm out of magic."

He smiled. "Don't worry. I'll send two mages to help you out: Li Yihan and Wa Mingze."

Soon two young Chinese mages appeared.

I recognized the woman—she was the one who had destroyed the generator. I smiled at her. "Now we are on the same side."

She nodded.

A part of my mind noticed a pattern with young mages, but I couldn't pin it down. It didn't matter. I just had to follow the emperor's orders.

* * *

Sean! Shayla! Help!

Oh no! Katie's in trouble. General Slimak had left me at headquarters, protecting the city from Chinese mages, while he went off to get reinforcements. He hadn't come back.

I'd been teleporting all around Lihue, grabbing mages and putting geas on them. I had half a dozen helping me.

"Hua Mei! I've got to go help with the battle. Can you defend this city with the loyal mages?"

"Yes, but I don't know this geas spell you use."

"Just knock out any mages that come."

"Yes, Sean." She nodded. I looked into her big brown eyes and trusted her.

"Good."

I teleported invisibly to Katie. There were five mages around her. She was hollow eyed and could barely stand. They had to help her walk.

"Just tell me how I can serve the emperor," I heard her say.

Poor Katie! She's out of power and compelled. I could help her, but how could I handle five mages that she couldn't handle?

I was out of answers—unless it was the name Shayla? I teleported back to my bedroom in Toledo. I powered up my computer. It was the middle of the night. The news stream was off and my parents were asleep.

"Hurry, hurry, faster, stupid computer," I whispered. The computer booted faster. "Huh. I didn't know that would work."

"Who is the Shayla that Katie Garcia needs right now?" I typed.

"Shayla Brown, daughter of Shannon Brown, brother Lamar Brown. Five-year-old mage known for animating her stuffed dragon, Pinkie, and using it for giving rides in Grant Park, Chicago. Currently asleep at her home in Schaumberg."

"Give me a picture." I saw pretty girl with cornrows asleep on a pillow. She held a pink stuffed dragon in her arms. I could see her breathing, so apparently this view was real time.

It was 1:00 a.m. Toledo time, midnight Chicago time. I teleported to Shayla's side, touched her, and whispered, "Wake up, Shayla."

She yawned, opened her eyes, and looked at me. "Who are you?"

"Sean Kennedy. Katie Garcia's in trouble, and she called for me and you."

She sat up in bed. "I had a nightmare about her. Mommy told me to go back to bed."

"She's surrounded by five mages, and she's been compelled to obey the Chinese emperor."

"Ooo, that's bad."

"I can get rid of the compulsion, but the mages are too strong for me. Do you have any ideas?"

"Too strong? That's like my friend Heath. He's stronger than me, but I got him." She grinned. "Let's go help Katie!"

"Great. Take my hand and I'll teleport you there." We popped to Hawaii.

We were back to the beach, invisible. Katie and the other mages sat on beach chairs sipping drinks. They'd given Katie an official Chinese mage robe.

Shayla whispered in my ear, even though I had a shell of silence around us. "Do ya see the magic shields around them? They're almost as strong as my friend Heath's!"

I squinted and noted a faint blue glow in the evening light. "Yes. What can we do?"

“Watch me. First, you pierce it.” I saw a needle of magic go through the back of the shell of one mage.

“Then you make them go to sleep!” The mage collapsed onto the table, snoring.

“Help me!” Shaya repeated it quickly for two other mages. I just copied her. It took most of my power to pierce the shield. The sleep spell was easy.

Only Katie was left awake. She was trying to wake the others. “Get up! Tell me what to do. What is the will of the emperor?”

I removed our invisibility shield. “Hi, Katie. I’ll help you.”

“Sean! I remember you. You were my friend. But now I’m on the emperor’s side.”

“Don’t worry. I’ll let you know the will of the emperor.”

“I’m so glad. I feel so confused. And all my magic is used up.” She hugged me.

My dream had come true. But all I felt was embarrassed. “Chinese compulsion, go!”

“Oh! That felt strange. I feel dizzy.” She sat abruptly on a chair.

“I wish Katie’s mind to be as clear and lucid as ever.” Wow. I felt the magic drain out of me. That was a big one. I sat down suddenly too.

“Oh, oh! I remember everything now. They compelled me. And they killed Josh!” Katie cried into her hands.”

“Maybe I can help,” Shayla said.

“How?” Katie looked up and sniffed.

“I brought my brother back from the dead. Maybe I can help your friend?”

“That’s right. I remember now.” She grabbed our hands, and we teleported to another part of the beach. A dog lay next to a burned man, whining.

“Spot, we’ll try to help Josh.”

“He’s dead, Katie,” he whined.

“Yes. Let’s try magic.”

Spot’s tail wagged a little. “Will that work?”

“Why not?” Katie rubbed his head.

“Let’s do it!” Shayla said. “Ew, he’s pretty burned.” She touched him with one hand. “Get all better, Josh.”

Nothing happened.

"Maybe if I helped you?" I said. "Let's do this together. One, two, three—get all better, Josh."

Nothing happened.

"Hmph!" Shayla sat on the sand next to Josh, with her chin in her hand. "Now with Lamar, I wished with all my might and I cried over him. And I hugged him. Maybe you can hug and cry over him, Katie? We'll wish with you."

"Oh yes. I've already cried a lot over him." Katie put her head on his chest, hugged him, and cried. "Get better, Josh."

"Get better, Josh," Shayla and I repeated.

It was utterly silent except for the sound of breathing. Wait. That wasn't just my breathing and Shayla's and Katie's—Josh breathed too.

"His heart is beating!" Katie sat up, still crying, but with tears of joy. The burned skin on his face and hands flaked off, and fresh skin appeared underneath.

Josh opened his eyes. "Katie! Spot!" He sat up, and Spot barked wildly. "Who are you two?"

"Shayla Brown."

"Sean Kennedy."

"This is a war zone. Why are you here?" He tried to stand up but sat back down again. "Oh, I feel like death warmed over."

Katie gave a snort and a chuckle. "Well, you are. We just resurrected you."

Pop. Pop. Pop. Pop. Four scorched German shepherds appeared around Spot.

"We took the mages and their dragons to the volcano mage, who destroyed them. Do you have any more dragons?"

"Yes, but they're under our control now, war dogs. Well done. Good boys!" Katie applauded them, and we joined in.

The dogs wagged their tails.

"You poor things!" Shayla ran to each. "Go away, stupid burns!" Burned hair and skin dropped off, and new hair grew in place.

"We'd better put geasa on those mages." Katie stood, but wobbled. "Wow. I felt a lot better magically after you healed me, Sean, but now I'm as exhausted as ever." She looked at Josh. "Resurrecting you took a lot out of me." She pulled up her phone screen. It glowed in the night air. It read, "Katie Garcia, 2114 MUs, 199 MUs remaining. Josh Garrison resurrection, 3111 MUs, 1716 Mus remaining."

"Thank you, for giving me back my life, Katie. I'll do anything for you, but I can never repay you."

"We'll talk about that later." Katie looked at me and Shayla. "You guys will have to put the geas on the remaining Chinese mages. I know Shayla can—she invented it."

"That's what I've been doing to defend Lihue—putting geasa on mages," Sean said.

"Are geasa the plural of geese?" Josh asked innocently.

Katie snorted and put her hands on her hips. "Josh! We're in the middle of a battle zone with dangerous prisoners, and you're making stupid jokes?"

He looked down. "Sorry."

"I'm not mad. Just impatient to tie up loose ends."

"No problem, Katie. I've got this." Shayla marched to where the mages slept. Han Mùchén, Li Yihan, and the two unknown surviving dragon mages lay on the sand, softly snoring.

Putting her hands on her hips, just like Katie did, Shayla said, "Listen up, you stupid mages." Their eyes opened. "You won't be allowed to hurt anyone or compel anyone anymore. You *must do* what Katie says."

Shayla turned back to Katie. "There you go. They're all set."

Katie looked at her phone. "Wow, Shayla. You're the first mage with over 7,000 MU." Then she turned to the Chinese mages. "Gather up any of your remaining dragons and mages and bring them back here. I'll give you further orders then."

They bowed low. "Yes, Mistress Mage."

Katie chuckled. "That's a new one—Mistress Mage."

"I've got to update General Slimak. Hmm. Let's try telepathy again." *General Slimak! We have subdued the Imperial Dragon Army. I am assembling the remnants on the beach as prisoners of war. Please come so we can discuss our next steps.*

A burned and disheveled General Slimak appeared on the beach.

"Thanks for winning the victory here, Katie. I thought you were a goner." He shook her hand.

"I would have been their prisoner, except for Sean and Shayla here." Katie pointed to us.

"Two kids? Oh, Sean. Yes, you were a big help defending Lihue. But Shayla!" He knelt next to her. "You can't be more than five."

"I *am* five." She nodded firmly. "And I'm in kindergarten. Montessori school."

"So what did you do?" He looked into her eyes.

"I helped Katie's boyfriend, Josh, come back to life."

"Wow. I didn't know you could do that with magic."

"Well, you can. This is twice now: Josh and my brother, Lamar."

General Slimak stood and looked at Katie. "You didn't tell me this."

"I knew Shayla had done this, but I didn't really believe it. Now I do."

"Josh, let me shake your hand for a job well done. Both the cavalry and the war dogs saved Hawaii."

Spot barked. "Don't forget the volcano mage! We teleported four of the dragons there, and they gobbled them up like dog treats."

"There's more I didn't know." He looked at his watch. "Meet with me in the Pentagon, Katie, in one hour for a complete debriefing. I've got to go. I'm still assessing the state of our cavalry, war dogs, and flying tanks." *Pop!*

"Before I can debrief him, I need full reports from each of you: Josh, Sean, and Shayla."

"Lemme go first. I've got to go back to bed," Shayla said.

"Right. Go."

"Sean got me out of bed and took me here. I saw their magic shields, poked through them, and put their mages to sleep. Oh, and I helped you wake up Josh. That's it! G'bye." She disappeared.

"Sean?" Katie looked at me.

I still got a thrill each time she did. I filled her in on what I did at Lihue and after I got her cry for help.

"That leaves you, Josh. You saved my butt with your cavalry."

Josh told his story of gathering his best cavalry from

Washington, DC, and from around the country and coming as soon as he could

"Okay. I'm up to date. Sean, you can go home now. I'm sure glad you came. Were you in bed too?"

"Yes. We were watching the news of the invasion and I wanted to help, so I wished my way to you."

"Thanks again." She took my hands. "You've been a real friend. But with our age difference, you know we can't be more. You're a great young man and you'll grow up to find your own girl someday." She looked at Josh. "I'm taken."

"Yeah, I figured that out." I'd known this was coming, but it still hurt. When would I ever find a girl as great as Katie? "No one can be as great as you, Katie."

She smiled. "Each of us is unique and great. Look for it in others. Goodbye, Sean. It's nearly morning in Toledo."

"Crap. I have to get to school. G'bye!" I teleported.

* * *

I had one more loose end to tidy up before my debriefing in the Pentagon.

"Josh." I took his hands.

He smiled. I melted a little inside. "Yes, Katie? You've got a new assignment for me?"

"I know what I said about two people in the middle of the war, but maybe we can work that out? I'm super busy with this Secretary of Magic work, but I want to be around you too."

"That's fine with me. I want to be around you too. I only need to check in on HossFit once a week or so." He smiled again. "We're only a thought away from each other."

I sighed happily and moved closer to him. He smelled of sand and sea and sweat. One more thing. I looked up to look in his eyes. They were brownish green. "I did CPR on you trying to bring you back to life."

"Thanks."

"I failed. But I thought, if you came back, I'd really kiss you."

Now he grinned. "Sounds great!"

So we kissed. It was a lot better than CPR. Then my phone beeped. My secure phone. My direct line from the president.

"Ignore it," Josh mumbled against my mouth.

"It's the president," I mumbled back.

"Crap."

We stepped back, and I fetched my phone from my backpack.

"Hello, Mr. President."

"Great job, Katie!" He practically broke my eardrum. "You're getting a Congressional Medal of Honor for sure. I'll see how else I can reward you."

"Thank you, sir."

"But the real reward for a job well done is more work. Now that we've beaten off the attack and have proven our magical defenses, I'll ask Congress to pour money into magical research. Your old boss Herman Scholl will be very busy."

I laughed. "He said I'd be the one getting the work from you."

"He was right. You must establish a nationwide magical curriculum for K through twelve, college, and graduate level."

"Uh, that's a lot."

"Right. I'm giving you a whole year to get it developed and implemented across the nation. Realize that we're still on a war footing, and funding will not be a problem. I have bipartisan support from both houses of Congress."

I chuckled. "So we'll be establishing magical academies across the country?"

"Yes, you're right. Maybe I should change your title to 'Minister of Magic' rather than 'Secretary of Magic.'"

"No, that's already been tried and it didn't turn out well."

Epilogue

I, Amaruq, paddled my kayak as I hunted seal. Hunting had become easy since I'd learned to sense seals and whales underwater and to even draw them to my boat. I also learned I could direct both winds and currents as I pleased.

I became so efficient at hunting seals that I could hunt for my whole village of ninety-odd people. Other people used their skills to hunt caribou and fish, as well as to create clothing better and faster. We were all prospering since these magical skills had appeared.

My whale hunting had ceased when a whale had addressed me in perfect Inuit. *Hunter, humans, and whales are now at peace. Do not hunt us anymore. You may hunt the seals and walrus.* The whale had breached next to my kayak and lay on its side, looking at me with its large brown eye.

After the whale dove with a great splash of its tail, I realized I'd heard its words in my head, just as the elder woman Ahnah was able to do. She called the village council sessions to order and relayed messages across vast distances.

I was so shaken by this encounter that I returned immediately to our village and told this to Ahnah. She nodded.

"I have talked to the whale directly. His name is CLICK-ee." She made the click in her throat and glided into the "eee." "He represents his Aleutian nation to the Inuit. I represent the Inuit. Please leave me. I must alert all Far-Speakers of this news, throughout the Inuit people."

"Can you reach all of Canada?" I asked.

"Yes. From the Aleuts to Labrador and Greenland. Now leave me in peace."

I left and returned to hunting. Back on the water, south of our island, I saw a bird on the horizon. Only it wasn't a bird. It was a large blue lizard with wings. On its back was a rider in a robe. They saw me and came toward me.

In a great voice, the rider addressed me from the back of her hovering lizard.

"Greetings, northern person. I have come to free you from your oppressors in the United States. Simply give allegiance to our great Emperor Liu Fu."

"We are a free people already, stranger. We do not need you," I shouted back.

"You must change your mind to live. Behold our power!" The lizard blew flame on the cold water, enough to make the surface boil. The steam and heat rolled toward me. I summoned the wind and blew it back.

"Behold the power of the Arctic!" I yelled.

I stirred up the air all the way back to our island and blew the lizard and its rider far out into the ocean.

I used the wind and current to hasten home once again. Now I had much more to tell Ahnah.

* * *

Israeli prime minister Yehuda ben David looked up as I burst into his office.

"Mr. ben David! Lebanon, Syria, and Iran have launched simultaneous attacks!"

"Defense Minister Michaela Abram, calm yourself. We have contingency plans for that. I assume we've activated the Iron Dome and are preparing counterattacks."

I took a deep breath. "We have done all of that, but their attacks are magical. They have sent djinn from the desert. Our weapons have no effect on them!"

His white brows rose toward his bald head. Then he slowly nodded. "So. They are using magic against us. We have a contingency plan for that too." He called aloud, "Arieh, come here."

A slim young man appeared in the office. The prime minister had a mage. I didn't know that.

"How long have you had a mage? Why didn't you tell me?" I yelled at the prime minister.

"Since I learned of magic, over a month ago. A secret is best kept by as few as possible. Do you have magical resources, Michaela Abram? I know you do."

I stopped. I hadn't told him of all my preparations. "Yes, I do. I've prepared magical munitions to penetrate magical defenses. They're at the border for this very contingency." I hung my head. "I'm sorry I snapped at you, sir."

"I know you have a short fuse. Arieh Hillel also has resources at our borders for this situation. Shall we activate them, Arieh?" He looked at the young man.

"Yes, sir."

"You can help, Michaela." The prime minister looked at me.

"How?" I had no idea what he wanted to do.

"Our three defense golems require three mages to activate them. This prevents hijacking or accidents. Join hands with us."

We linked our hands together. I saw a clear picture of a faceless statue in a bunker on the Golan Heights.

"That is your golem, Michaela. I have the one at Qumran, and Arieh has the one at Megeddo. On my count, activate. One, two, three!"

I willed the golem to come alive. Two glowing red eyes opened. No nose, no mouth. I could feel its power through the vision. It rose and strode toward our border with Syria.

"How do you power the thing?" I gasped.

"Each one is filled with the power of over one hundred mages," Arieh said proudly.

"Let's watch the battle with the djinns."

My golem marched to the top of the Golan Heights, overlooking Syria. On the horizon I saw a black cloud rapidly approaching, reaching to the ground. It touched the ground in a funnel cloud. I saw it was not a water cloud but sand. Wherever it passed—hill, valley, or city—was left scoured to bedrock.

"How will the golem defend us?" I wondered aloud.

"Watch. Its power is indescribable," Arieh murmured.

The djinn's funnel moved up the mountain to the golem. The golem lifted its arms, and lightning bolts poured forth. Through the vision, I could hear and feel the vibrations of thunder and smell the scent of rain and ozone. A kilometer-high cylinder of lightning surrounded the funnel cloud. Then it flashed like an optical grenade. The funnel was gone. The upper clouds fell as a rain of sand. The battle was over.

We watched the other djinns suffer the same fate.

"Is this the end of the war?" I asked the prime minister.

He shook his head. "Only the beginning."

* * *

I was so hungry. The refugee center had run out of food days ago. Every scrap of vegetation had been scrounged from miles around in the Sudan, all the way to the Nile River. Nothing was left.

I no longer had the strength to complain to Mama. She looked so sad. Her once strong body was just a skeleton, like mine.

"I'm going to look for food, Mama," I whispered.

"Where, honey? There's none left. I've looked everywhere."

"In the desert. No one's looked there."

"Oh, honey. But I guess it doesn't matter anymore. Nothing does. Just . . . I love you, Mimi."

"I love you too, Mama." We hugged.

I walked outside. No one paid attention to me or cared. I wasn't sure what I was looking for, but I was sure I could find food in the desert.

The sun was setting, casting long shadows behind the dunes. I walked in the shadows, thinking of food. I remembered eating kissra, our flatbread made from sorghum. I remembered helping Mama grind the grain and mix the dough. I remembered the red heaps of sorghum as we harvested the grain from our fields, before the drought, before the war, and before Daddy died.

I fell on the sand. I was weak and dizzy from hunger. I rolled over and looked to the side. The dune was dusty red as the sunset. It looked like a pile of sorghum.

Why couldn't it be? I know other things I had wished for had come to pass. Mama and I escaped the soldiers and come to this camp. We were almost out of water, and I'd wished for a bottle and found it in the sand. Why not a hill of sorghum?

I wished and kept wishing as I rose and walked toward the red hill. My feet crunched. They were sorghum grains, all the way to the top. I took a deep breath. I could smell it. This was enough for me and Mom and the whole refugee camp.

After chewing some grains, I filled my pockets with the food and ran back to Mama with the good news.

Author Bio

Photo by Barb Lloyd

Andy Zach was born Anastasius Zacharias, in Greece. His parents were both zombies. Growing up, he loved animals of all kinds. After moving to the United States as a child, in high school he won a science fair by bringing toads back from suspended animation. Before turning to fiction, Andy published his PhD thesis "Methods of Revivification for Various Species of the Kingdom Animalia" in the prestigious JAPM, *Journal of Paranormal Medicine.* Andy, in addition to being the foremost expert on paranormal animals, enjoys breeding phoenixes. He lives in Illinois with his five phoenixes.

www.ingramcontent.com/pod-product-compliance
Lightning Source LLC
LaVergne TN
LVHW010634110826
845149LV00014B/2844
* 9 7 8 1 9 5 9 9 6 2 0 3 8 *